The Mirage

The Mirage

Naguib Mahfouz

Translated by
Nancy Roberts

The American University in Cairo Press
Cairo   New York

The American University in Cairo Press
113 Sharia Kasr el Aini, Cairo, Egypt
420 Fifth Avenue, New York 10018
www.aucpress.com

English translation copyright © 2009 by Nancy Roberts

Dar el Kutub No. 16952/08
ISBN 978 977 416 265 7

Dar el Kutub Cataloging-in-Publication Data

Mahfouz, Naguib
        The Mirage / Naguib Mahfouz; translated by Nancy Roberts.—Cairo: The American
    University in Cairo Press, 2008
            p.   cm.
        ISBN 977 416 265 X
        1. Arabic fiction   I. Roberts, Nancy (trans.)   II. Title
        892.73

1 2 3 4 5 6 7 8 9 10   14 13 12 11 10 09

Designed by Andrea El-Akshar
Printed in Egypt

1

I'm amazed at the fact that I feel called to take up the pen. Writing is an art I have no experience with, either as a hobby or as a profession. In fact, it might be said that with the exception of school assignments in my boyhood and the clerical tasks relating to my job, I've never written anything at all. Even more amazing is the fact that I don't recall ever having composed a note or a letter in the entire time I've lived on earth, which comes to more than a quarter of a century. The truth is that letters—like speech—are a symbol of social life and an expression of the ties that bind people in this world, and these are all things of which I know nothing. Don't we prune trees, cutting off the branches that have grown crooked? Why is it, then, that we keep people who aren't fit for life? Why do we show such tolerance—nay, neglect—by imposing such individuals on life, or by imposing life on them against their will? As a result, they roam the earth as frightened strangers, and sometimes they're gripped with such panic that they go wandering about like someone gone mad with fever, trampling innocent victims beneath their stumbling feet.

I say once again that I don't recall having written anything that deserves to be called 'writing.' In fact, for as long as I can remember,

I've found it an exhausting, nearly impossible enterprise even to converse. If I've had no choice but to speak, I've stammered helplessly, not knowing how to express myself. However, this helplessness goes beyond the matter of speaking or writing. It's more serious and dangerous indeed, for the inability to express myself and the attendant sense of constriction and impotence are, without a doubt, the most trifling of its consequences. Hence, it's only fitting that I should wonder what it is that now impels me to write. After all, it isn't just a letter to be penned. Rather, it's a vast distance to be covered, so vast it will leave me breathless. I'm astonished at the energy and fervor that compel me to write, feelings I'm not accustomed to. I imagine myself continuing to write, without hesitation and without growing weary, day and night, with a determination that knows no lassitude. But why subject myself to such torment? Haven't I spent my entire life seeking refuge in silence and suppression? Haven't the secrets in my heart been unable to find themselves a closed grave in which to rest and die? How to explain this passionate urgency? How is it that I've unsheathed the pen to unearth a grave over which the dust of concealment has accumulated? Life has been lost, and the pen is the refuge of the lost. That's the fact. People who write are, generally speaking, people who aren't alive. This doesn't mean, of course, that I was alive before. However, I never ceased looking for a joyful hope by whose light I could find my way, and now that light has been extinguished.

I'm not writing to someone else. After all, it isn't in the nature of those afflicted with timidity and shame to bare their souls to another human being. Rather, I'm writing to myself, and to myself alone. I went on concealing my soul's whispers until I lost sight of its reality, and now I need desperately to reveal its hidden face honestly, frankly, and without mercy in the hope that this might lead, even in defiance of destiny, to healing. As for the attempt to forget, it offers no such healing. Truth be told, forgetting is nothing but a cleverly devised fairy tale, and of such fairy tales I've endured enough. Perhaps my beginning to write is a sign that I've given up the notion of suicide once and for all. Not that suicide wouldn't be a fitting penalty for a man who's taken two other lives. On

2

the contrary, it's far less than what such a man deserves. Yet what can I do in the face of life's insistence on finding a way to defend itself? If the past were a piece of the physical place in which I find myself, I'd turn on my heels and flee. However, it follows me wherever I go like my shadow. I have no choice but to meet it face to face with a steady heart, and without blinking an eye. Be that as it may, death is easier to face than the fear of death, and the act of facing death has a magic to it that may turn these pages into a pristine, transparent soul.

I make no claim to knowledge. In fact, there's nothing to which I've been more hostile than knowledge, and I confess to being a stupid, lazy man. However, I've endured bitter experiences that have shaken me to the core, and there's nothing like experience to unearth what lies buried in people's souls. I long to lift the veil and penetrate my secrets, to put my finger on the site of my malady, the seat of my memories, the wellspring of my pain. Perhaps in this way I can avoid a lamentable end and escape this pain that is more than I can bear. I'm feeling my way in the darkness.

In reality, I'm nothing but a victim. I don't say this in order to mitigate my own guilt or shirk my responsibility. Nevertheless, it's the honest truth. The truth is that I'm a victim. However, I'm a victim with two victims of my own. And what pains me beyond words is that one of these two victims was my own mother! As unbelievable as it is, it's the dreadful reality. How could I have allowed myself to forget that she was the secret of my life and happiness, and that I couldn't bear to live without her? But I was living on the brink of madness, and thus I lost everything and found myself in a terrifying, lightless void. I'm a man of deep faith, and I know for a certainty that I'll be raised to life on the Appointed Day. I don't fear the sufferings and horrors of that day— when I'm stripped bare in the presence of God, with nothing to show but my good deeds and my bad—half as much as I fear being raised in a state like the one I've endured in this world. I truly desire resurrection to a new life, and when that happens, my sufferings will become as nothing, to be annihilated for all eternity, and I'll be able to meet my loved ones with a tranquil heart and a pure, untainted soul.

My mother and my life were one and the same. My mother's life in this world has ended, but it still lies hidden in the depths of my own. Hardly can I think of any aspect of my life without her beautiful, loving face appearing before me. She stands ever and always behind both my hopes and my sufferings, behind both my love and my hatred. She gave me more happiness than I could ever have hoped for, and more misery than I could ever have imagined. It's as though she herself was everything I've ever loved or hated, since she herself is my whole life. Is there anything beyond love and hate in a person's life? So let me confess that I'm writing in order to remember *her* and in order to recover *her* life, since with the recovery of her life, all life will be restored. In this way, I may be able to repair the thread of my life that's been broken. Perhaps hope will be renewed through such a recovery. At this time, everything seems vague and obscure, as though Satan had cast sand into my eyes. Even so, I feel my way patiently and deliberately, led forward by the hope of rescue to which a drowning man clings.

What moves me is a genuine intention to renew my life and resurrect it as a new creation. So, if the path is too arduous, if despair overwhelms me, or if shame and diffidence get the better of me, nothing will remain for me but death.

2

What reward do the dead receive from the living once they've disappeared under the ground? We flee from their memory the way we flee from death itself. Perhaps this fact conceals a precious wisdom. However, our selfishness insists on concealing it beneath a veneer of bitter, laughable sorrow. I fled in terror from our house, leaving everything behind. Then I began to come to my senses and regain some degree of composure. I realized the terrible momentousness of what had befallen me, and my hands sought refuge in the closet of memories. As I brought out everything that remained there, what should I find but a photograph.

It was a large photograph that showed my grandfather decked out in his medal-festooned military uniform. He was sitting in a large chair with his voluminous body, his big potbelly, and the white mustache that looked like a crescent moon over his mouth. I was standing next to him, the top of my head hardly rising above his knees. I was looking into the photographer's lens with smiling eyes, my lips pursed like someone who's trying to suppress a laugh. My mother was standing to my grandfather's right, resting her left hand on the back of the large chair. Clad in a long dress that enveloped her from neck to feet, its long sleeves revealing nothing but her hands, she stood there with her slender frame, her rectangular face, her delicate, straight nose, and wide green eyes that radiated tenderness, though her glance lacked that luster that bespeaks vigor and sharpness of temper. It was a face that the Merciful One chose to replicate so completely in my own that it used to be said that the only way you could tell us apart was by our clothes!

The picture peered out at me from the world of memories. I fixed my burning eyes on the beloved face for such a long time that I no longer saw anything else. Its features grew larger as I looked at them until I imagined myself a little boy again, living under her protective wing. The silence around me grew so thick, it seemed her closed mouth would open into a smile and allow me to hear the sweet conversation that I'd known until just a short while before. Photographs are an amazing thing. How could I have failed to notice this fact? This was my mother, with her body and her spirit. This was my mother, with her eyes, her nose, and her mouth, and this was the tender bosom that I'd clung to all my life. Lord! How can I convince myself that she's truly departed from this world? Indeed, photographs are wondrous things, and it now seems to me that everything in this world is wondrous. Curses on habit that kills our spirit of wonderment and awe! This picture used to be hung in such a way that it was visible at all times. However, I was seeing it now as something new. In it I perceived a profound vitality, as though a breath from her liberated spirit were hidden within it. In her eyes I saw a distracted look that stirred up a sense of pain. This photograph was alive without a doubt, and I refused to withdraw my eyes from it even if it drove me mad not to do so.

I pored over it at length. Then I was gripped by a powerful desire to imagine the life of the woman depicted there in all its phases, from the cradle to the grave. I imagined her as a baby crawling, then as a little girl playing with her dolls. If only she'd left me pictures that could help me recapture the happy dreams of her childhood! Then I imagined the period of her tender youth, when she was a lovely young woman looking upon life through those tranquil eyes of hers with hope and delight and enjoying her impassioned adolescence. I'd witnessed a part of that sweet era, and was a fruit of its fertility and freshness. However, its signposts had now been lost sight of and its effects obliterated, enveloped in darkness as though I'd never nestled in her bosom or nursed at her breast. When I brought that era to mind later in life, the thought of it would bring confusion and anxiety, and I would wonder, dismayed and indignant: Didn't the untamable desires that so preoccupy young people rage in her blood too? Perhaps it was these unexpressed emotions of mine that drove me in my boyhood to tear to pieces the only remaining trace of that early youth.

One day I came suddenly into our bedroom and found my mother leaning over an open drawer in the wardrobe and looking intently at something in front of her. I approached her gingerly, prompted by the mischievousness for which spoiled little boys are known. As I slipped my head under her outstretched arm, I saw her clutching a picture of her wedding. She tried to return it to its hiding place, but as she stared at me in astonishment, I stubbornly grabbed hold of it. I saw a young man seated and my mother standing and leaning against his chair like a succulent rose. My eyes clung to the man's image, and I realized that he was my father even though I was seeing him for the first time. Indeed, I was seeing him after my heart had been filled with fear and loathing toward him. My hands trembled and my eyes grew wide with dismay. Then before I knew it, my hands were tearing it to shreds. She reached out in an attempt to rescue it, but I thwarted her in a furious rage. She didn't utter a word, but in her limpid eyes there was a look of grief and disappointment. Then, as though I weren't satisfied with what I'd already done, I turned to her angrily and asked her in a censorious tone, "What are you upset about?!"

With some effort she put on a happier face and said, "What a contrary child you are! Can't you see that I'm sorry over the picture of my youth? You've torn up your mother's picture without knowing it."

Every now and then the memory of that incident would come back and pain me, filling me with consternation and angst. I would wonder what had really led her to keep that picture, and why it saddened her to see me tear it up. Then I would try to penetrate with my imagination to what I'd missed of her life, but the attempt would just leave me preoccupied and distressed.

This was how I lost the picture of her early youth, and I'm truly sorry now to have lost it—very sorry, indeed. But isn't this a laughable sort of sorrow now that I've reached out and destroyed the picture's very subject?

3

I took no notice of the one affliction that had been visited on her life. One day she told me the story of her marriage. She did so with great caution and care, especially in view of the fact that she was narrating the happy memories, rare though they were. She would mention them hurriedly, tersely and with restraint, as though deep down she feared me, or as though she feared that the pleasantness of the memory might mitigate the intenseness of my loathing for my father.

It was on the Ismail Bridge that my father had seen her for the first time. Some days in the late afternoon, my mother and grandfather would take an excursion in the Victoria. One day they were passed by another Victoria, in whose front seat there sat a young man with one leg crossed over the other. He appeared to take pride in his youth and his wealth—or, more properly speaking, in the wealth he anticipated. His glance fell upon her face, and before long he had steered his carriage behind theirs and begun following them to our house in Manyal. Whenever the two of them left the house, they would happen upon him in the road as though he'd been waiting. I didn't allow this chapter of the story to go by without comment. I asked her about how flirtation took place in those days. She received my question warily. However, I kept after her until she gave in to me, surrendering to the geniality of the recollections. She told me that he would cast her furtive glances that subtly concealed a smile. Or he would turn toward her with interest as he twisted his luxuriant black mustache. At the same time, he never overstepped the limits of propriety. I mused for some time, lost in the wilderness of dreamy imagination and feeling astonished, bewildered, and distressed. Then I looked up at her—our sole comfort during those days being that of endless conversation—and I asked her with a smile how she used to receive these flirtatious overtures. Not missing the mischievousness in my question, she giggled. Her body shaking from head to toe as it did whenever she laughed, she told me that she would ignore them, of course, and look straight ahead. She would register no response at all, as though she were a statue clad in a white veil. Unconvinced of what she was telling me, I said I was asking about the inward, not the outward; about the heart, not the face. I was tempted to tell her frankly what was going on in my head. However, my courage failed me and shyness tied my tongue. Yet if I'd consulted my heart, I would have known the answer. After all, my own heart was part of hers, and the same blood flowed through both. Indeed, the two of them beat as one. And could I possibly have forgotten the many times when I myself had remained unmoved as a statue even though my heart was ablaze?

The young man came forward and asked for her hand. He had neither a job nor an education. In fact, he had no money, at least not at that point. However, he was one of two sons of a man who was both well known and well-to-do. When my grandfather learned that the young man's father had agreed to the proposed marriage and was prepared to support his son and his family, he was thrilled with the engagement and delighted with this old, respectable family's wealth and prestige. He was told that the suitor was as ignorant as a plebeian. "What does he need with an education?" he replied. He was told that he had no job. "And what does he need with a job?" he asked. In fact, he was told frankly that he was a young man with untamable passions and that he was a riotous drunkard. And to this his reply was that he knew that he was just a young man, and not a monk. My grandfather wasn't greedy or covetous. However, in addition to his being somewhat dazzled by the name of the family that wanted to become related to him by marriage and his confidence in their fine reputation, he wanted happiness for his daughter, and he believed that money would be sufficient to achieve it. Besides, my grandfather himself hadn't finished primary school, and had a penchant for drinking and gambling.

Thus it was that his daughter became the wife of Ru'ba Laz, or Ru'ba Bey Laz, as he was generally known. My grandfather supposed that by marrying off the younger of his two daughters, he'd relieved himself of his duties toward her. However, barely two weeks after their wedding night, my mother returned to my grandfather's house, tearful and broken-hearted. Hardly able to believe his eyes, my grandfather was exceedingly upset. Then he learned that less than a week after his wedding, the young man had resumed his former way of life in pubs, that he wouldn't come home before sunrise, and that he'd beat her violently on the day she left his mansion.

My grandfather was appalled. Despite his strict military upbringing, he was tenderhearted and was ever so solicitous toward his two daughters. Consequently, he was enraged over what had happened and took off straightaway for the Laz mansion, where he loosed the full force of his force on both the young man and his father. My mother stayed in my grandfather's house until she gave birth to my older sister. After this, a group friendly with both sides went to work to patch things up and bring the couple back together. Their efforts were crowned with success, and my mother and her baby girl returned to the Laz mansion once again. Her stay there lasted for two months, after which her patience ran out and she left once more, broken-winged, for my grandfather's house. The fact is that she hadn't known more than a few days of comfort. She had persevered, however, resigning herself patiently to the situation in the hope that the passing of the days would reform what was corrupt. But he only grew worse, and no longer could she see anything in him but a rowdy drunkard who held nothing sacred. So, despairing, she sought refuge in her father's house. The man tried to get her back, admitting his addiction to drink and trying to convince my grandfather that married life would be possible even with his addiction. However, my grandfather took a hard stance with him and insisted that he divorce her. Some months passed and my mother gave birth to my older brother. She went on living under her father's wing, enjoying his affection and tender, loving care.

During those days she heard bizarre reports concerning Ru'ba Laz according to which, in a moment of impetuosity and greed, the reckless young man had tried to poison his father in the hope of hastening his portion of the inheritance. However, the father had discovered the crime through the cook and banished his son from the mansion. He then decided to set half his bequest aside as a religious endowment and bequeath the other half to his elder son. It appears that he may not have been willing to bequeath all of it to the elder brother for fear of endangering him by stirring up his younger, wicked son's rancor against him. Be that as it may, it thus happened that after having dreamed for so long of a vast fortune, Ru'ba Laz woke up to find himself in relative poverty. All he possessed now of this world's vanities was a quarter of a family endowment that he had inherited from his mother (who wasn't his brother's mother), which came to around forty pounds a month, and a two-story house in Hilmiya into which he had moved after being evicted from his father's home. The news brought anxiety and distress to my grandfather's household, troubling the hearts of those who feared for the future of the man's two young children. As a result of the disinheritance, the support they received was reduced to a mere pittance, and their future looked bleak. My grandparents and my mother consulted together concerning the matter, and it was decided that my grandfather would meet with Laz senior and attempt to win his sympathy on behalf of his two innocent grandchildren in the hope that he might change his will for their benefit. My grandfather went to Laz's mansion and spoke with the man. But he was met with a hard heart and deaf ears. In fact, the man cursed both his son and his son's progeny in my grandfather's presence, whereupon he returned home, saddened and enraged.

One of the ironies of fate was that Laz's father died the very year in which his son had tried to do away with him. Seven years then passed. My sister Radiya was eight years old and my brother Medhat was seven or thereabouts. Those days witnessed an event that changed the tranquil course of our family's life. As fate would have it, the change took place as a result of a trivial incident of the sort that happens when one is walking down the street. As my grandfather was leaving a gambling establishment on Imad al-Din Street a little before dawn one day, he saw a bunch of hooligans gathered around a gentleman and beating him as he stumbled about in their midst, fuming and reeling. My grandfather shouted at them to leave the man alone, then approached them in a rage. He was joined shortly thereafter by a policeman. The mob scattered, and who should my grandfather see but Ru'ba Laz with a bloodied nose and in an obviously drunken state. Despite being startled and disconcerted, my grandfather came up to the man without hesitation and supported him with his arm, seeing that he on the verge of falling. By this time all that had transpired between them in the past had been forgotten, or nearly so. At the same time, and in spite of the man's unpredictability and riotousness, he'd been consistent in sending financial support to his two children. Consequently, there was no enmity between the two men. My grandfather summoned him over to his Victoria and he obeyed. Then my grandfather instructed the driver to go to Hilmiya. A peculiar silence fell over the two men along the way, and neither uttered a word. When the carriage reached the house, my grandfather cleared a space for Ru'ba Laz to get out, but he grabbed hold of my grandfather's arm and invited him inside. My grandfather declined apologetically given the lateness of the hour. Still inebriated, the man wouldn't take no for an answer and insisted that my grandfather come in with him. Against his will, he surrendered to the younger man's wishes, and as dawn's blue threads began mingling with the darkness, the two of them made their way together to the reception room.

Ru'ba Laz threw himself down on a chair, then drew my grandfather toward him and sat him down on a seat near him. Before long his silence had left him and he was overcome with agitation and emotion. With a heavy tongue loosed by a combination of alcohol and anguish, he said, "Did you see how those rascals punched and slapped me? Do you see what an insult this is to my dignity? After all, I'm Ru'ba the son of Laz, denizen of this old, venerable residence! That's the world for you, Uncle. But why should I call you my uncle? I'm over forty years old now, and you're barely over fifty, so it would be more fitting for me to call you my brother. But I call you my uncle out of admiration and respect, since you're like a father to me. May God forgive me—you're greater and more venerable even than that! Pardon me for the things I'm saying. After all, words are trivial things. As for being kicked by a gang of thugs, it's a serious matter, wouldn't you agree? My father died angry with me, and they say that no one who's been deprived of his parents' approval will ever achieve happiness. Is that really true, Uncle? Even if one of those two parents was my father? Lord, I'm fed up with this world. It's nothing but fever, delirium, and madness without end. Oh, what I'd give for calm and peace of mind. Isn't this what they call regret? Give me your hand, Uncle, and let's swear by this new morning to make a new start, without wrongdoing or debauchery. Send me my wife and children and let my family live with me. Please!"

His eyes grew redder and redder until my grandfather thought he was weeping, and he felt he had no choice but to comply with his request. By the time the Victoria took off with him in the direction of Manyal, the streets had begun filling little by little with people coming out in pursuit of their daily bread. As the carriage moved along, he closed his eyes with satisfaction and thought at length about the matter. He wanted to see his daughter become the mistress of a household of her own. That very month, my mother was sent back to her former husband and the family was reunited. However, this new life only lasted for two weeks. In fact, it may not have lasted for more than a single day. As for the remainder, my mother endured it patiently until, fearful that the wild drunkard might do harm to her two young children, she picked them up and fled back to my poor grandfather. In a violent rage, he betook himself forthwith to the phony repentant and raked him derisively over the coals. Ru'ba Laz listened to him in silence. Then he told him that his wife was to blame for not wanting to live with him, and that his only fault was that he got drunk. My grandfather took leave of him in a miserable state, divorce certificate in hand.

It was then that their married life ended once and for all, and I was the fruit of that bogus repentance. My grandfather once said to me jokingly, "You came into this world on account of my stupidity and no one else's!" Many indeed are those who have come into this world on account of stupidities.

I grew up in my grandfather's house, which was the only home I ever knew. In fact, the only family I knew was my grandfather and my mother. By the time I was old enough to be aware of what was happening around me, my father had reclaimed my brother and my sister and my grandmother had died. I only learned that I had a father based on the things my mother said about him in bitterness and sorrow, and my hatred for him grew with the passing of the days. Then, as if he hadn't been cruel enough to my mother already by taking back his son and daughter, he prevented them from seeing her. Year after year passed without her catching even so much as a glimpse of them. At the same time, we heard it said that the man virtually imprisoned himself at home, fleeing from the world and those in it by keeping himself in a state of perpetual inebriation.

4

My grandfather's house in Manyal was my birthplace, my playground, and my world. It consisted of two spacious stories, of which the upper one was where we lived, and a small courtyard. I don't want to talk about the house. At the same time, I long to recapture the past, and what past is there but that it has a house around which its memories hover? My life is inseparable from that house, and will remain so for as long as I live. Of course, a house isn't just a building. Rather, it's a tower fixed in time to which the doves of memory repair for refuge, cooing with nostalgic longing for what's passed of our lifetimes. So let me delve into the depths of the past for whatever waves of memories my head can receive. I close my eyes, disappearing from the world of things tangible, hoping to provide my spirit with the stillness it needs to take off into the eternal past. Let me confess that I long intensely for the past, and that of late this longing of mine has become a veritable ache. Perhaps this is nothing but a yearning for childhood. I realize what a serious thing such nostalgia and longing can be, since herein lies the secret of this regrettable malady of mine. Yet, although I've lived my life looking to this past, whether happily or otherwise, and despite my awareness of the powerful bond that draws me back to it, I still stand helpless before its impenetrable veils, and my memory retreats wearily from even its most critical and important eras.

I close my eyes full of anticipation and questions. Out of the darkness my eyes glimpse a faint light. I see my small hand as it reaches for the moon from atop my mother's shoulder. What a memory! How often have we reached for moons that are no less unattainable? I recall the tremendous effort I once expended trying to take hold of my mother's nipple, only to be thwarted by something with a bitter taste; tugging with delight on my grandfather's crescent-shaped mustache; and shattering the flower pots, one of which landed on and nearly broke the Nubian gatekeeper's arm when it plummeted off the edge of the balcony. Most days I would refuse to go to sleep until I'd climbed onto my mother's shoulder and had her carry me the length and breadth of the house, and whenever she slowed her pace, I'd spur her on with my feet. I used to strut about constantly in girls' dresses, my hair hanging down to my shoulders. One day my mother had the idea of making me a military uniform complete with stars and medals, so I put it on gleefully and proceeded to traverse the length of the house with a haughty, self-satisfied gait: the distinguished officer with a braid dangling down his back. My grandfather didn't approve of such gratuitous pampering. However, he had no time to oversee my upbringing, since he generally didn't get up till noon and wouldn't return from the casino until nearly dawn. Besides, he feared upsetting my mother in view of the ill-fortune life had dealt her, and because she was all he had left in his old age. Thus the three of us lived: the father who had no one but his daughter, and the daughter who had no one but her son.

My mother would snatch at memories of my sister and brother with a tearful eye and a broken heart, and she yearned passionately to see them if only for an hour. And since, in her sorrow, she found no solace but me, she would set me in her lap and not want me to leave it. Indeed, she would have liked me to make it my entire world.

Life's breezes blew gently. Thus, I didn't realize until after it was too late that it was an unwholesome affection which had exceeded its proper limits, and that there's a kind of affection that destroys. She had been cut to the quick in that place where her motherly instincts lay, and in me she found solace, comfort, and healing. She devoted her entire life to me. I would sleep in her lap and spend my day on her shoulder or elsewhere in her presence. Even during those brief times when she was busy with household affairs, I wouldn't leave her, or rather, she wouldn't allow me to leave her. In the kitchen I'd ride on her shoulder, resting my cheek on her head as I amused myself watching the cook light the fire, cut up the meat, and chop the onions. We would even take baths together. She would place me naked in a washtub, then sit before me nude as I sprinkled her with water. Then I'd take a handful of suds off her body and massage myself with it.

We rarely left the house, since relations with my father's side of the family had been severed and my maternal aunt lived in Mansoura with her husband at that time. When my mother did go out, however infrequently, to visit one of the neighbor ladies, she would take me with her. The one place we visited regularly was the shrine of Sayyida Zaynab. This may well have been the only visit that we truly looked forward to. There was nothing she disliked so much as having some lady she knew say complimentary things about me, as people tend to do with children. She saw such praise as a bad omen and, with fear and trembling, would recite incantations over me to protect me from the evil eye. Yet strangely, I don't remember such incantations and amulets with derision or contempt. Instead, I believe in them. In fact, I believe in everything my mother believed in. I acquired a certain degree of culture and finished secondary school. Even so, my faith remained intact. After all, how could my faith in God, His messengers, and His saints, or in the power of supplications, protective amulets, and shrines ever be shaken?

At the same time, I can't say I took completely to our sheltered life. In fact, there were many times when I may have wearied of it and wished I had more freedom. Perhaps my impatience with the life we lived began to increase as I grew older. One sign of this was that my mother began keeping me constantly in her lap and frightening me with all manner of things in order to set me against the freedom and autonomy I'd begun to want. She so filled my ears with stories of goblins, ghosts, spirits, djinns, murderers, and thieves that I imagined myself living in a world filled with demons and terror. Everything in this world was something to be wary and fearful of.

That era is long gone now, but it still lives in my heart and flows in my blood. It was this that placed fear at the center of my soul, turning it into the hub around which my entire life revolved. In so doing, it destroyed my peace of mind and cast me into a state of unrelenting misery. I was nothing but a frightened spirit that, if it weren't confined to a body, would flee in terror. I was afraid of people. I was afraid of animals and insects. I was afraid of the dark and the chimeras that stalked me there. I would have done anything to avoid being alone with a cat, and never in a million years would I have slept in a room by myself. Even so, fear ran deeper in my life than the things through which it manifested itself to me. Its long, thick shadow loomed over the past, the present, and the future, wakefulness and sleep, my way of life and its philosophy, sickness and health, love and hatred. It left nothing untouched. I lived most of my past life heedless and ignorant, not knowing the reason for my misery. Ordeals and afflictions later clarified certain aspects of my life to me, rending with their harshness the veils that had kept my distressing secrets concealed. Still, my sense of helplessness hasn't left me. It's a sense that rests, in truth, on my inadequate education and sophistication and a lack of confidence in my mental powers. My mother was the source of these torments. Yet, she was also my sole refuge from them, and I repaired to the shelter she offered without hesitation.

Among the memories I carry from that unforgettable era are the times when we—my mother and I—would stand beside my grandmother's grave during certain seasons, crowning it with basil and reciting the Fatiha as we called down divine mercy upon her. We would talk often about the grave and those in the grave. How do they sleep? How are they received? What do they face by way of affliction and divine judgment? How do verses from the Holy Qur'an descend upon them as light that drives away their forlornness and gloom and alleviates their sense of isolation? Since it was my grandmother's grave, I loved it intensely. When my mother wasn't looking, I would rush over to one side of it and plunge my fingernails into its soil, then dig with a fury in the hope of catching a glimpse of the unknown that lay buried under the ground. It would distress me no end to hear her repeating, "To God do we belong, and to Him shall we return," or, "To dust shall we return," or, "Death is the final end of everything that lives."

Once I asked her in astonishment, "Are we all going to die?"

Vexed by my question, she tried to distract me from it, but I refused to let it go.

"After a long life, God willing," she said.

Eyeing her fearfully, I asked again, "And you, Mama?"

"Of course," she replied, concealing a smile. "I'll die some day."

Pained by her words, I cried, "No! No! You'll never die!"

She patted me affectionately on the head and said soothingly, "Pray for me to have a long life, and I'll pray for the Most Merciful and Compassionate One to answer your prayer."

So, holding my two little palms heavenward, I prayed to God from the depths of my heart, my eyes filled with tears.

5

as I going to stay in her lap forever, as though I were part
of her body?

I was all of four years old, and the time had come for
me to want to play and have friends. I had nowhere to escape to in the
house except the balcony, which overlooked the courtyard and the street
beyond. The children of the family that occupied the first floor would
play in the courtyard, and I would look wistfully down at them. Sometimes they'd look back up at me with an unspoken invitation in their
eyes that shook me from head to toe, and one day I asked my mother's
permission to join them.

"What's happened to your mind?" she asked me in alarm. "Don't
you see that they fight all the time? What would I do if they hit you or hurt
you? Or if they took you out to the street where cars are passing by all the
time? What will you learn from them but mischief and bad manners?
As for me, I tell you stories, and if you want to, we go out together to visit
Sayyida Zaynab. If you really love me, don't leave me."

Seeing the look of exasperation and resentment on my face, she
continued, "I've been deprived of seeing your sister and brother, so
you're all I have left in the world. And now you want to leave me. May
God forgive you!"

"I love you more than anything in the world," I said, "but I want to play!"

However, she wasn't about to give in to this desire of mine. When I found myself at my wits' end over her unrelenting stance, I would cry or throw temper tantrums, pulling my hair and ripping my clothes. But there was nothing in the world that would have caused her to yield to my desire to distance myself from her. Apart from this one thing, however, she spared no effort to please me. She would buy me toys of all shapes and kinds, and when she sensed that I was cross or bored, she would invite one of the neighbor children to play with me under her watchful eye. But none of this was sufficient to satisfy my thirst for freedom. One day, taking advantage of a moment of inattentiveness on her part, I managed to slip out of the flat. As I fled, I was beside myself with joy, and I was received by the children in the courtyard with an incredulous welcome. Although we were somewhat acquainted with one another, I still didn't know how to approach them. I stood glued to my place, flustered and shy. It wasn't long before my mother looked down from the balcony and called to me in a sharp, angry voice. But the oldest of the children came up to me and invited me to play, saying, "Don't pay any attention to her!" And for the first time in my life, I ignored what she was saying. I rushed forward into the circle of players and took my place with delight beyond measure. However, hardly had a few minutes passed before an argument broke out between me and one of the other children, and he slapped me in the face. I was stupefied, as it may have been the first time I'd ever been slapped in my life. I threw myself on his arm and plunged my teeth into it, whereupon, without hesitation, his friends fell upon me with blows and kicks. My mother shouted at them with angry threats, but they didn't leave me alone until she'd threatened to throw a pitcher at them. By the time they'd finished with me, I was in a pitiful state indeed, panting and teary-eyed. She called me to come up to her but I was overcome with shame and embarrassment, so I stood there with downcast eyes as if I were pinned to the ground and made no move to answer her call. In fact, I didn't budge until the gatekeeper came and carried me up to her, whereupon she washed my face and legs for me.

"It serves you right! It serves you right!" she said in an agitated tone. "This is what happens to people who disobey their mothers. God will forgive us for anything except defying our mothers. This is what it's like to play with other children. So, how was it?"

I wasn't pained by the beating half as much as I was by my defeat before her. Lying, I assured her that I'd been the one at fault, and that I was the one who had attacked the other boy first.

I found it strange that my mother herself didn't mix with people very much, and that we rarely received visitors in our house. Vexed by her isolation, my grandfather would urge her constantly to spend more time with people as a way of cheering herself up. Then God Himself decided to send her some company: my mother's sister and her family came to stay as guests at our house. My aunt lived with her husband, who worked as an Arabic teacher in Mansoura, and they'd come to Cairo to spend a month of their summer vacation at our house. Suddenly I found myself in the midst of six boys and a girl, and despite my mother's best efforts, things slipped out of her control. The eldest of the boys was ten while the youngest was still crawling. The quiet house was transformed into a circus hopping with monkeys and other wild creatures. I frisked and frolicked till I was nearly delirious with joy. We played al-gadeed, hopscotch, choo-choo train, and hide-and-go-seek.

When we got tired of being in the house, we'd take off for the street, and I could hardly believe my good fortune. My mother wanted to prevent me from going out with them, but my aunt would object, saying, "Let him play with the other children, Sister! Even if he were a girl, it wouldn't be right for you to confine her too soon!"

The two sisters had distinctive temperaments despite the many ways in which they were similar. My aunt was exceedingly plump and was the cheerful sort that likes to joke and laugh. She didn't cause herself misery by worrying unduly about her children, and when my grandfather left the house, she would sing with a lovely voice in imitation of Munira al-Mahdiya. As for my mother, she seemed to be the very opposite of her sister. She was thin, reclusive, full of fears and worries, and almost abnormally attentive and affectionate. The circumstances of her life had frayed her nerves, and the minute she found herself alone, she'd be engulfed by a cloud of melancholy. She may not have been entirely pleased that her sister stayed with us that month, not due to any lack of affection toward her but, rather, because her sister's children had monopolized my time and attention, thereby spoiling my undivided allegiance to her. Once she complained to my aunt of her fear that I might be hurt while playing in the street. My aunt just laughed nonchalantly and, in a slightly reproachful tone, said to her, "So is your son flesh and blood while mine are made of steel? Be strong and have more trust in God!"

As for me, so overwhelming was my bliss that I forgot all my mother's instructions. I gave myself over to fun and enjoyment for that entire month, which had broken in on my monotonous life like a happy dream. I flung myself into the arms of diversion the way a starving man falls upon a long-awaited meal, and not for a single moment did I feel bored or tired. When we came back to the house at night, I would put my uncle's turban on my head, mimic the way he talked, and burp the way he burped. Following the burp I would mutter, "Oh, pardon me, please!" to the delighted laughter of everyone around me.

That month was like a dream. But dreams don't last, and like a dream, it came to an end. I found myself looking on dolefully as bags were packed and piled up near the door in preparation for their departure. Then the time came for the inevitable parting with its embraces and goodbyes. The carriage picked them up and bore them away as I bade them farewell from the balcony, tearful and disconsolate.

My mother said to me, "That's enough playing and running around in the street for you. Settle down now and go back to the way you were before, when you didn't leave me and I didn't leave you."

I listened to her in silence. I loved her with all my heart, but I also had a yen to play and have fun. Some time after this my mother brought us a young servant girl whom she allowed to play with me under her supervision. She was better than no playmate at all, at least. She was a homely girl, but she was better for me than the aging chef and old Umm Zaynab.

My mother performed her prayers regularly. I began imitating her when she prayed, and it seems she saw in this a fitting opportunity to teach me the principles of our religion as she understood it. She started out by teaching me about heaven and hell, thereby adding new words to my vocabulary of fear. This time, however, they were accompanied by sincere emotion, love, and faith.

6

This state of affairs between my mother and me led to a delay in my school enrollment. I got to be nearly seven years old without having received the least bit of education. Finally, though, my grandfather intervened. He called me one day as he sat on the porch on that long seat of his that rocked back and forth. He tweaked my ear playfully, then said to me, "For a long time you've wanted to be able to join other boys your age. Well, now God has set you free, and we're going to let you share their life for a long, long time. You're going to school!"

I listened to him in bewilderment at first, since I didn't know a thing about school. Then, realizing that he was granting me my freedom, I looked at my mother questioningly, not knowing whether to believe him or not. And great was my amazement when I saw her smile at me encouragingly with a look of acquiescence on her face.

Nearly bursting with joy, I asked my grandfather excitedly, "Will I play at school like the other children?"

"Of course, of course," replied the old man with a nod of his hoary head. "You'll play a lot and learn a lot. Then later you'll become an officer like me."

"When will I go?" I asked impatiently.

"Very soon," he said with a smile. "I'll register you tomorrow."

Autumn was upon us, and the next morning they dressed me up in a suit, a fez, and new shoes, which brought back happy memories of the holiday. My grandfather took me to Atfat Qasim, which wasn't far from our house. We went into the second building we came to on the left, which was Roda National Primary School. The school, which had been chosen due to its proximity to our house, consisted of a medium-sized courtyard and a one-story building with three rooms: two classrooms and the principal's office. The principal—who was also the owner of the school—received my grandfather respectfully and even reverently, and in his presence he treated me with kindness, complimenting me on my cleanliness my new clothes. Consequently, I felt friendly toward him and expected good things from him in the future. Within minutes, I'd been enrolled along with the other students in the school. My grandfather paid the fees, and we headed home.

As we left the school my grandfather said to me, "Now you'll be an excellent pupil! School will start next Saturday."

My mother announced her satisfaction with the new development. However, she wasn't able to conceal the melancholy she felt. Seeing this, my grandfather was annoyed with her and said to her somewhat sharply, "What will you do if, once he's seven years old, his father reclaims him?"

"Over my dead body!" she cried, gaping at my grandfather at horror and anguish.

On the appointed Saturday, my grandfather took me to school, then returned home. As he was about to take leave of me I clung to his hand, feeling a sudden pang of fear that caused me to forget how I'd longed for this very moment. I even suggested that he take me back home with him, but he simply laughed that resounding laugh of his and, pointing to the other pupils, said, "Meet your new family!"

I stood near the door feeling more flustered than I'd ever felt in my life, and a feeling of regret came over me. Looking timidly and apprehensively at the pupils scattered about the courtyard, I hoped no one would notice me. But my smart new clothes caught people's attention, and I lowered my gaze feeling agonizingly shy. How long will this torture go on? I wondered.

However, a boy came up and greeted me, then stood with me as though we were friends. Then he asked me for no apparent reason, "Did your father bring you?"

Since I considered my grandfather both a grandfather and a father, I nodded in the affirmative.

"What does he do?" he asked, "and what's his name?"

Even though conversation was a cause of distress for me, I still welcomed this question in particular, and replied proudly, "Colonel Abdulla Bey Hasan."

The boy told me that his father was So-and-so Bey too, though I've forgotten his name now. Then, as though he'd grown weary of my quiet, stuffy manner, he left me and went to join some other buddies. Feeling lonelier than ever, I wondered: Will I be able to fit in with these boys? Will I really be able to play with them, or will the disaster that befell me in our courtyard at home be repeated here too? My heart was gripped with fear, and if I'd had the courage to retreat and go home on the spot, I would have. Then the bell rang, delivering me from my thoughts, whereupon they stood us in a line and brought us into the classroom. It hadn't occurred to me up to that point that school was anything but a huge playground. However, when I sat down at one of the school desks and the elderly teacher began the new school year with the traditional instructions having to do with maintaining order and not moving around or talking in class, I was certain that what I'd entered was nothing less than a prison. Perplexed and disturbed, I thought: Did my grandfather make a mistake, or did they deceive him? My imagination went soaring home, where I pictured my mother sitting alone. Do you suppose she's forgotten me? I wondered. At around this time she'll be overseeing Umm Zaynab as she sweeps the rooms and dusts the furniture. Hasn't she thought about me? Can she bear to part with me for the entire day?

When the first lesson ended, I hadn't heard a word the teacher said. And it was no wonder, since I'd decided that this first day would also be my last. During recess I saw the principal passing by the classroom door, and I breathed a sigh of relief. Not having forgotten the kindness he'd shown me when I came to enroll with my grandfather, I approached him without hesitation. As I came up to him timidly, he turned toward me with an uncomprehending look on his face. Then he cast me a harsh, quizzical gaze, and I thought he'd forgotten who I was.

In a voice that was barely audible I said, "I'm Colonel Abdulla Bey Hasan's son."

"And what do you want?" he asked in astonishment.

Gathering up my courage, I said, "I want to go home."

"Get back to your desk, damn you!" he thundered in my face.

Stunned by his shouting, I returned to my place, nearly swooning from fright and anguish. From that moment onward, I stayed put, terrorized and distraught. As the day dragged on I started to feel I needed to go to the bathroom, but I was so afraid, I held it in. Not once did I think of asking the teacher for permission to leave the class. Even during recess, I was so apprehensive, I couldn't bring myself to ask someone to show me where the toilet was. I started fidgeting and writhing like someone who's been stung, pressing my knees together in torment and anguish. The time passed heavily and miserably until, when the bell rang at last, I took off as fast as my legs would carry me. I reached the house in a matter of seconds and ascended the stairs in leaps and bounds. In the flat I found my mother waiting for me, and when she saw me she exclaimed, "Welcome, light of my eyes!"

But when she happened to glance at my trousers, a look of distress came over her and she murmured softly, "My Lord, you've wet yourself!"

As for me, I burst into sobs, saying, "I'll never go back to school! Grandpa doesn't know anything about the place. I hate the principal, the teachers, and the pupils. Tell me I don't have to go back, and I'll never leave you as long as I live!"

Drying my tears and undressing me, she said gently, "Don't say things like that. You'll get used to it and like it. After all, how can you stay at home when all the other boys are in school? And how will you become an officer like your grandpa if you leave school?"

I kept up my crying and my importunate complaints as she spoke soothing words to me in an attempt to alleviate my distress. However, she warned me not to let my grandfather hear me complain lest he be angry with me and look down on me. So, for the first time in my life, she turned a deaf ear to my laments.

As a way of encouraging me to persevere in my new life, my mother decided to escort me to school every morning. We would arrive there together, after which I would go into the schoolyard while she stood on the opposite sidewalk. Once inside, I would stay glued to the fence, exchanging glances and smiles with her through its iron bars as melancholy descended over my heart and angst gripped me about the neck. I loathed school and everything about it. Nevertheless, I was forced to go, and neither defiance nor tears got me anywhere. Hence, I knew for a certainty that I'd been doomed to a long imprisonment. For the first time I found myself envying adults their freedom, and housewives the luxury of staying at home.

My love for Thursdays dates back to that time. Of all days of the week, Thursdays were my favorite. As for the other days of the week, I shrank from them, finding them heavy and tedious. Late on Friday afternoon I'd feel a depression coming on. Saturday, Sunday, Monday, and Tuesday would pass in weariness and boredom until, when Wednesday morning arrived, I'd start breathing more easily. Then I'd waken at dawn on Thursday and turn over under the covers in blissful delight, hardly able to contain my excitement. Consequently I excelled in Thursday's lessons, which included nothing but memorizing passages and religion classes.

Even so, that era wasn't without its happy memories, though at the time they appeared to me against a background of severity and harshness. One of those memories is of the way we used to buy donut-shaped loaves of bread with sesame seeds on top during recess and, if we had no salt to put on them, we would use in its place the lime that came leaching out of the courtyard walls. Our aged teacher used to like to drink a glass of licorice tea during the first period. As he drank it, he would command us to stand up and turn our backs to him for fear that some harm might come to him from our voracious eyes. He came to class one day with a sour look on his face. He said that he'd had a stomachache the night before and that he had no doubt but that one of us had stolen a glance at him as he drank his licorice. He warned us that unless we revealed the culprit's identity, we'd all get a smack on the hand. And since we were ignorant of who the culprit was, we all got the promised smack. Our other teacher was also an elderly man. However, being a gentle soul, he never struck any of us unless he was at his wits' end. His favorite method of getting us to be quiet and maintaining order was to frighten us with talk of the goblin that had lived since ancient times under the room's floorboards. He would tell us that the goblin didn't like loud ruckuses, and if things got out of control, he would crouch down and tap on the floor. Then, in a tone of meekness and dread, he would say, "Pardon them, master! They don't realize what they're doing! Don't ride their backs, please, and forgive them this time!"

On the academic plane, I learned nothing whatsoever. I suppose the only thing I mastered at Roda National Primary School was the art of measuring time by watching the sunlight move down the classroom walls as I counted the seconds before the bell rang. If the teacher addressed a question to me, all it meant was that I would get so many smacks with a ruler on the back of my hand, and in the course of an entire academic year, all I memorized were a few short suras from the Qur'an that I used to hear my mother recite during her prayers. When it came time for the final exam, I earned a set of zeros that, if if had come in some context other than that scandalous report card, would have sufficed to make me a millionaire.

When my grandfather saw the report card he was furious.

"This is the result of your pampering," he told my mother sharply. "You've spoiled him, Madame!"

Then, threatening to make the school principal pay the consequences, he went to meet him at the school. An hour later he returned, saying with satisfaction, "Well, sir, you've passed by force! And don't you dare fail next year!"

I'd entertained the hope that in view of my failure, they might decide not to send me back to school again. So when my grandfather announced the glad tidings of this 'success' of mine that he'd wrested by force from the powers that be, I felt disappointed. When the second year rolled around, it was no better than the first. In fact, my misery was intensified by a slip of the tongue that made the remainder of my days at the Roda National Primary School even more loathsome than the ones that had preceded them. One day I raised my hand to request the teacher's permission to leave the classroom. However, instead of saying, 'sir,' I called him, 'Mama' by mistake!

The whole class roared with laughter. The teacher himself laughed, replying sarcastically, "Yes, mama's boy?"

And with that, the class broke into loud guffaws all over again. Speechless and mortified, I sat there in a stupor while my eyes filled with tears. I didn't have a single friend or companion among them, and in fact, it was during that time so long ago that I began suffering the inability to make friends. Not one of them had the least compassion for me. From that time onward they called me 'Mama' until they even stopped calling me by my real name. Defeated and helpless, I avoided them, though a fury raged within me.

At the end of the year, I got another report card filled with zeroes, and this time my mother accused the school of negligence. My grandfather decided to enroll me in a public primary school, but because I'd graduated from a private school, the principal stipulated that I'd have to take an entrance examination. Shortly before the academic year was to start, my grandfather took me to the school, then waited for the results to be announced. In fact, there was nothing to wait for. My grandfather pleaded with the principal to accept me in spite of the test result, and the man wanted to oblige him in view of his advanced age and his eminent standing. Hence, he asked simply that I write my name, 'Kamil Ru'ba.' However, I wrote Ru'ba incorrectly, so the man apologized, explaining that it wouldn't be possible to accept me after all. My grandfather mocked me all the way home. Then, heaving a sigh of disgust, he said to my mother, "It's no use sending him back to kindergarten. I'll get him a tutor this year."

I could hardly believe my ears. Trying to conceal my delight, I asked, "Will I stay home this year, then?"

Glowering at me with his green eyes, he said heatedly, "Yes. *That* ought to make your mother happy!"

7

For the first time in my life I had a fruitful year of study, sitting safely and placidly before my venerable teacher and being taught the principles of Arabic and arithmetic. Despite the fact that, as usual, the hours dragged on heavily and miserably, I was at last taking my first steps along the path of learning. In order to ensure that the teacher treated me well, I had my mother sit near the door to the teacher's room so that I could summon her to the rescue if need be. And it's no wonder that I felt as I did, since the memory of the two years I'd spent in Roda School—from the teachers' blows to the pupils' assaults—were still fresh in my mind. Up to that point, I had yet to comprehend the fact that education was an unavoidable duty that I'd spend a good part of my life fulfilling. Instead, I viewed it as a punishment that had been inflicted on me for some unknown reason, and I still held out the hope that some day my grandfather would relent and exempt me from it altogether.

As for my mother, she was no happier than I was. She was enduring torment of another, more brutal sort. She'd grown more dejected during those days, and the minute she found herself alone, she would break into bitter tears. Whenever she was with my grandfather, she would speak to him about the matter that was robbing her of sleep. In just a few months I would be nine years old, and once I reached that age, my father would have the right to reclaim me. In fact, he was certain to do so, just as he had my sister and brother before me. The same danger had loomed over us when I turned seven. However, my grandfather had written a letter to my paternal uncle, who was an influential farmer in Fayoum, asking him to intercede with my father and persuade him to leave me in my grandfather's care until I was nine years old. By a miracle from heaven, the intercession yielded the hoped-for result. Now, however, I was approaching my ninth birthday, and I was sure to be wrested from my mother's arms this time unless my father waived his right to take me back.

One day my mother began weeping in my grandfather's presence. She said, "I lost Radiya and Medhat, and I haven't set eyes on them for nine years now. Kamil is all I have left. He's my only consolation in this life, and I don't know what I'll do if the man takes him away from me!"

My grandfather shook his gray head crossly, as this topic never failed to distress him.

"And what can I do about it?" he asked. "This is the ruling of Islamic law, and we have no choice in the matter. Besides, the man to whom you're referring is his father, at least, and not some stranger."

"His father!" she cried indignantly. "Do you call that monster a father? Poor Radiya and Medhat, living in the house that drunkard's turned into a tavern! He doesn't have a fatherly bone in his body. Kamil has grown up in my care and received my love and affection, and he doesn't have any experience with perverse creatures like his father. If the man takes him, Kamil will perish there with him, and I'll perish here alone!"

Choked with tears, she fell silent. After she'd caught her breath, she continued, "Baba, can you imagine Kamil being able to live away from his mother? It's these two hands of mine that feed him, dress him, and put him to bed. He's afraid of his own shadow. He's scared out of his wits by the chirping of a cricket! How can Islamic law allow such a child to be taken out of his mother's care?"

My grandfather knit his brow wearily, seemingly annoyed at her objection. However, his face wasn't an accurate reflection of what he felt inside. There were many times when he would seem angry or displeased even though his heart was full of tender compassion. All he said at the time was, "That's enough complaining and crying. If he's meant to stay with us, he will, and if God wills for him to go to his father, there's nothing we can do to resist His decree."

This is what he said. However, what he did was something else altogether. One day, taking matters firmly in hand, he went to my father to negotiate with him over the matter of leaving me in his care. If the truth be told, my grandfather loved me deeply. He loved me because I was a companion to him in his old age, and because childhood has a way of stirring something deep in the heart of the elderly. He also loved me because he loved my mother, who had stayed by his side after her mother's death, nurturing him with her affection, compassion, and tender, loving care. He went to my father and we stayed behind waiting, our hands on our hearts. Never as long as I live will I forget the agony my mother endured during that wait. Unable to sit still or concentrate on a thing, sometimes she would talk to me and sometimes she would talk to herself. At other times she would invite me to join her in making earnest entreaties to God, asking Him to crown my grandfather's efforts with success. I observed her forlornly until, infected with her anxiety, I broke down and cried. We waited for a long time—or so it seemed to us—shrouded in a mantle of sorrow and worry, our eyes swimming with tears and our tongues uttering prayers of urgent supplication. Then at last we heard the ringing of carriage bells. We went rushing to the balcony and saw my grandfather crossing the courtyard with his usual heavy steps. Then we hurried back to open the door for him. He entered without saying a word, eyeing us with a look whose meaning we couldn't divine.

He proceeded to his room, so we followed him, but my mother didn't have the courage to ask him what news he brought.

"O Lord! O Lord!" she whispered in a trembling voice.

He took off his fez slowly and deliberately, all the while avoiding my mother's eyes. He sat down on a large chair near his bed, gave us a long look, then said in that gruff voice of his as though he were talking to himself, "The man's a criminal! And what do you expect from a criminal?"

My mother's faced turned white as a sheet, her lips began to tremble, and there was a look of despair in her eyes. I began looking back and forth anxiously and fearfully between my grandfather and my mother. My grandfather left us in our misery for a little while. Then, taking pity on us, he removed his mask of gloom. Breaking into a raucous laugh, he said triumphantly, "Don't kill yourself with grief, Umm Radiya. The old devil hardly put up a fight!"

We were speechless at first. Then our faces lit up with the glad tidings, and my mother's eyes sparkled with joy. Kneeling before my grandfather and bathing his hand in kisses, she asked fervently, "Really? Really? Has God taken pity on my broken heart?"

My grandfather began twisting his mustache with satisfaction as my mother asked again with the same fervor, "Did you see Radiya and Medhat?"

He shook his head regretfully, saying, "They were at school."

She uttered an impassioned prayer for them, her eyes filled with tears. My grandfather hadn't been in the custom of visiting them, since he disliked my father and didn't expect to be well received in his house. He then related to us how, when he met with my father on the veranda, the latter had had a bottle of liquor and a full glass in front of him. He told us that my father had received him with bewilderment and surprise, and that the only work he had left to do in life was to drink. Perhaps, my grandfather said, this deterioration on his part was what had caused him to go along with the proposal rather than clinging to his old stubborn ways.

A first he seemed skeptical, my grandfather said. However, when things became clearer to him, he laughed derisively, yet without obstinacy or anger, and said simply, "I'm in no mood to raise anybody or be a wet nurse all over again. Keep him if you want, but don't ask me for a red cent. That's an explicit condition! If I'm asked for a single penny in the coming days, I'll take him away from you, and you won't lay eyes on him as long as I live."

My grandfather agreed to my father's condition. In fact, he'd had a feeling even before going to see him that he would make this sort of demand. Even so, it came as a shock to him that the man expressed no interest in seeing his son, and that he didn't even ask about me once.

Then my grandfather said, "Ru'ba Laz isn't a human being anymore. The man's finished."

"Poor dear Radiya and Medhat!" muttered my mother glumly.

However, my grandfather said reassuringly, "Radiya is seventeen years old now and Medhat is sixteen. They aren't children anymore."

Thus, having been rescued from the fear that had loomed so large on our path, we went back to our usual peace and quiet. I carried on with my studies at home, plodding my way laboriously through them. Another year passed, autumn rolled around, and there was frequent talk of school, so I knew for a certainty that my return to prison drew nigh.

One day I said to my mother, "If you love me so much that you won't agree to let my father take me back, why do you let school separate us?"

Laughing that delicate laugh of hers, she said, "For shame! How can you say that when you're the perfect man? Don't you want to be a high-ranking officer some day like your grandfather? If you leave school, what can you do but work as a fuul vendor or a tram conductor!"

My grandfather took me to the Aqqadin School in Heliopolis, and this time I passed the entrance examination. The academic year began and I began reluctantly attending school. The carriage would take me there in the morning and bring me home in the afternoon. Given this new arrangement, my grandfather forbade my mother to escort me herself as she'd done during my days at the Roda School. Hence, I returned once more to school and suffered anew the lessons, the regime, the teachers' cruelty, and the other students' derision. My entire school life was misery from start to finish. Moreover, my misery was reinforced by the fact that at home I was an undisputed sovereign, and at school a dutiful slave. Year after year I lived the confused, schizophrenic life of someone who at home is showered with affection, and at school is the target of his classmates' ridicule and blows from the teachers' rod.

I earned the teachers' hostility thanks to my stupidity and dullness of mind. Some of them even dubbed me "the first-rate dunce." Whenever my mathematics teacher finished explaining a lesson, he would ask me about it and keep after me until I'd given him a satisfactory answer. Then, with a sigh of relief, he would turn to the other students and say, "If Mr. Kamil has figured it out, then you must have, too!" And the class would roar with laughter.

As for the pupils, they made fun of me whenever they got the chance. My inability to make friends is a bitter reality of which there can be no doubt, since it's something at which I've never succeeded in my entire life. The fact is that I'm no worse than a lot of people who enjoy happy friendships. However, I'm painfully shy, I love solitude and isolation, and I'm wary of strangers. What makes my disposition even more unhappy is the fact that by nature I'm withdrawn, unable to express myself without faltering and searching in vain for the right word. Never in my life have I been good even at talking, much less joking or playfulness. For all these reasons the other students accused me of being disagreeable. It so pained me to be described in this way that I asked my mother one day, "Mama, am I disagreeable?"

She stared at me in horror.

"Who said that about you?" she asked me tartly.

"All the other students," I said hesitantly.

"Well, their tongues ought to be cut out!" she cried, furious. "They just envy you for your perfect manners and the carriage that takes you to school while they dawdle along on foot! Don't you dare make friends with any of them."

As if I were in need of such advice! Thus, I endured life at school alone, with hostility and hatred peering at me from all sides. If I'd taken part in the pleasures school afforded, it might not have been all that bad. However, my inordinate shyness forced me to boycott the various activities others were involved in, from scouting, to ball, to physical education. My mother wouldn't even agree to let me go on field trips for fear that some harm might come to me. The other students would talk about the pyramids, the Sphinx, the Museum of Antiquities, and Fustat while I listened in on their conversations feeling bewildered and disheartened, as though I were listening to tourists relating stories about distant lands. I can hardly describe the embarrassment that came over me when I realized that all I'd seen of vast, far-flung Cairo—the only city I'd ever inhabited—were a few streets within walking distance of our house. My sole consolation during those days was to sit alone with my mother on the balcony or in our room, where we would talk for hours on end. Thinking of the teacher's rod would remind me that there was a homework assignment I needed to do before going to bed. So I'd take to the book in loathing and disgust, studying wearily and without enthusiasm until, before long, I'd begin nodding off and sleep would dim my eyes.

One day in religion class the following verse from the Qur'an was recited to us: "At length, when there comes the Deafening Noise, that day shall a man flee from his own brother, and from his mother and his father." I can't recall ever being as upset by anything as I was by those words. I couldn't bear the thought of fleeing from my mother on any day, no matter how horrible it happened to be, or of abandoning her to such a day's horrors with her delicate, willowy frame and her gentle green eyes. Not realizing what I was doing, I interrupted the teacher, crying, "No! No!"

My interruption caused an astonished silence to fall over the classroom, since I usually didn't utter a word, and no one understood what I'd meant. However, it wasn't long before they broke into raucous laughter. Furious, the teacher held me responsible for disturbing the peace. Coming up to me in a rage, he gave me a forceful, exasperated slap in the face. I welcomed the slap as an excuse to cry, since I'd been fighting back the tears valiantly, but to no avail.

These words from the Holy Qur'an shook me to the core. They were the first portent to me of life's tragedy.

8

It was a monotonous life, but I endured it despite my aversion to it. Even so, it wasn't without its earth-shaking tremors. One evening my grandfather came home early. This worried my mother, since he generally didn't come home before dawn. He burst into the room, his face full of foreboding. My mother rose, anxious to discover what the matter was, and I looked up from my book. But before she could ask him what was wrong, he struck the edge of his shoe with his cane and said brusquely, "Zaynab, there's been a disaster in the family. It's a scandal that will make us the talk of the town."

"Lord have mercy, what's happened, Baba?" cried my mother, her voice trembling and panic in her eyes.

His green eyes grew hard and he said crustily, "Your daughter . . . Radiya . . . has run away."

Her face went pale and her eyes darted nervously about the room. Then she cast my grandfather a look of incredulity as though she couldn't believe her ears.

"Ran away . . . ," she murmured in what sounded like a moan. "Radiya! That's impossible!"

He stomped his foot on the floor until the corners of the room shook.

"Impossible?" he bellowed. "Well, that's exactly what's happened! It's the naked, appalling truth, and it will deal the death blow to our honor!"

My mother made no reply, as though she'd lost the ability to speak.

His breathing slightly labored, my grandfather said as if to himself, "What sort of madness has robbed her of her senses? This corrupt, infernal blood doesn't belong to us! Yet its rotten fruit points to its source. After all, her grandfather died calling down curses on her father's head, and the curse has fallen on his children."

"God, what a catastrophe!" murmured my mother in horror, swallowing with difficulty. "That drunken good-for-nothing has ruined her life! How miserable she must be!"

"Don't make excuses for her," my grandfather said indignantly. "There's nothing in the world that could justify her doing something so disgraceful."

"I'm not making excuses for her," my mother murmured in a feeble, pathetic voice. "But she *is* miserable. There's no doubt about it."

A gloomy silence fell, and they sat there exchanging looks of grief, worry, and desperation. I listened to their conversation with rapt attention, understanding its more trivial parts while missing its true significance. It had to do with a sister of mine whom I'd never laid eyes on. But why had she run away? And where had she gone?

"Why didn't she come to us?" I wondered aloud.

"Shush!" shouted my grandfather in exasperation.

Then he flung himself onto a chair and continued, "Her paternal uncle came to see me at the casino and told me the news. He said he didn't know the details, but that Medhat had wired him, asking him to come immediately, and he'd come without delay. Then the young man had told him of his sister's disappearance. As for that degenerate carouser, all he had to say was, 'To hell with her.' Then the uncle and I went to see a friend of his who works for the governorate. We informed him of the shocking situation and asked for his help."

My grandfather paused for a minute, then went on, saying, "Damn that old sot! He's the one who's to blame for this tragedy, and I swear to God, I'll go and bash his head in!"

My mother's eyes flickered with distress.

"No, no!" she said fearfully. "That would only make our situation worse!"

"He should be repaid evil for evil," insisted my grandfather.

"He's no concern of ours," said my mother imploringly. "Let's just focus our attention on finding the girl in the hopes that we might be able to straighten her out."

Eyeing her skeptically, my grandfather asked, "Why do you insist on preventing me from going to see him?"

"I'm afraid of things getting worse," she murmured with a flustered look on her face.

Exasperated, my grandfather retorted, "Rather, what you're afraid of is that if we have an argument, he might take Kamil away from you. You don't care about anything but yourself. Damn the whole lot of you!"

Such a pall descended on the household after that, you would have thought it was in mourning. Black days came upon us and life turned cheerless. I nearly suffocated in that dismal atmosphere. Meanwhile, my grandfather changed his lifestyle. He abandoned his usual evenings at the casino and would stay out all day long without our knowing a thing about his whereabouts. As for my mother, she spent her days grave-faced or in tears.

Then one evening my grandfather came to us, and when he saw my mother he hailed her with the words, "We've finally found what we were looking for!"

"Really?" she cried as she came running up to him. "O Lord, have mercy on us!"

In a tone of joy and satisfaction he said, "The crazy girl sent a letter to Medhat informing him that she was living with her husband in Banha. She asked him to forgive her for the way she'd acted, saying that she'd had no other choice.

Her eyes welling up with tears, my mother heaved a deep sigh and said, "Didn't I tell you? Radiya is an upstanding girl, but she's had miserable luck. Lord! Where is she now? Tell me everything you know!"

"Her uncle, Medhat, and I went to Banha," my grandfather said calmly, "and we found her living with a kind, respectable family. We met her husband, a young man by the name of Sabir Amin who works at the Ministry of Justice. He told us he'd rented a flat on Hidayet Street in Shubra and that he'd be moving into it this week. Radiya said that her husband had asked for her hand, but that her father had turned him rudely away. She said that he'd also turned away another young man who had asked for her hand before this. Perhaps on account of the liquor, he seemed to have lost the last vestiges of his humanity, as a result of which he'd forgotten his duties and frittered away his income. So, overcome by despair, she'd eloped with the young man. They'd gone straightaway to his family, where the justice of the peace was waiting for them."

As she listened to him, my mother wept hot tears, but they were tears of both sadness and joy.

Then she said, "I'll go see her tomorrow."

"You'll find her at home whether you go tomorrow or the day after," replied my grandfather reassuringly.

Then she wondered aloud, "Why didn't she come to me?"

As if to apologize for the girl, my grandfather said, "Maybe she would have been embarrassed to bring her fiancé to us when she was running away from her father. In any case, let's praise God for this happy ending, an ending happier than any we could have dreamed of."

9

We all got in the Victoria together for the first time ever. My grandfather and my mother rode in front and I sat in the back. My mother was in a state of utter elation. After all the worry and grief she'd suffered in the days that had passed, she looked as though she'd regained her early youth. Her eyes sparkled with joy, and her tongue was uttering praise and thanks to God. Her joy was infectious, and I too rejoiced in the happy journey we were embarking on. I began thinking in amazement and delight about this sister of mine whom I'd be seeing for the first time in just a few minutes. At the same time, my thoughts were accompanied by a sense of anxiety that I couldn't explain. What do you suppose she looks like? I wondered. And how will she receive us? Will she like us?

My train of thought was interrupted when my mother asked my grandfather eagerly, "Will Medhat be there?"

Resting his hands on the grip of his cane, my grandfather replied, "Most likely he will. We'd agreed that he would be."

A look of warmth and anticipation glimmered in her eyes.

As the carriage made its way to Shubra, I entertained myself by watching the pedestrians, other carriages, and the tram. At last the

45

Victoria reached its destination and turned down Hidayet Street, then stopped in front of a medium-sized, three-story house. We got out of the carriage and went up to the second floor as my mother said in a near-whisper, "My heart is pounding so hard!" My grandfather rang the bell and opened the door. As we entered, I saw a girl and two young men, but before I'd had a chance to get a good look at them, two of the three came running up to my mother. Then all I could see was heart-felt embraces, and all I could hear were tearful sighs. I gaped at the three of them in perplexed, timid silence. The hugging went on for a long time, as did the crying.

At last my grandfather intervened with a laugh, saying to my mother, "Meet your daughter's husband, Sabir Effendi Amin!"

The young man approached my mother and kissed her hand, and she kissed his forehead.

Before long, however, I found everyone looking at me.

Smiling through her tears, my mother said, "Your brother, Kamil."

My sister rushed over to me and pressed me to her bosom. Then she proceeded to kiss me warmly while I stood there in resignation, not moving a muscle and not uttering a word.

"My Lord!" she cried joyfully. "You're a young man! He looks just like you, Mama!"

Then my brother gave me a squeeze and a kiss, saying happily, "What a shy young man he is!"

Up till that moment I hadn't taken a good look at any of their faces. Instead, I'd kept my head bowed, my forehead and my cheeks burning with self-consciousness. Then they took us to the sitting room. My mother sat between Radiya and Medhat, my grandfather sat next to my brother-in-law, and my sister had me sit beside her.

Drying her tears, my mother said, "Mercy! You were children when you were taken away from me, and here you are, all grown up! Praise and thanks be to God!"

Moved by the occasion, my brother-in-law said, "What a tragic life it's been for you! I thank God for letting me be the occasion for this reunion!"

Long-felt yearnings came pouring out in animated conversation that seemed to know no end as memories and thoughts came over them in waves. Every one of them spoke of his worries and heartfelt concerns, and tears mingled with smiles. Every now and then there would be a glimmer of amazement in my mother's eyes, as though she couldn't believe that God had brought the family back together again after it had been scattered for so long. When they got so busy with each other that they forgot about me, I began to get over my shyness and regain my composure. Feeling myself now to be more or less alone, I breathed a sigh of relief. However, it wasn't long before a sense of anxiety and distress came over me, and I began stealing glances at Radiya and Medhat. I was dazzled by my sister's beauty. She was slightly shorter than my mother, with a whitish complexion and a figure that was full and voluptuous. Her face was an exact replica of my mother's, and of my own as well, with her limpid green eyes and her delicate, straight nose. As for Medhat, he represented another type: stocky but not obese, with a round face and head, a fair but rosy complexion, and black eyes. Even though he was just eighteen, he exuded an air of masculinity and strength. He would break into loud laughter for the slightest reason, and he seemed happy and in robust health.

After stealing a number of curious, interested glances in their direction, I felt drawn to them by a feeling of love and affection, and I was reassured by their buoyant spirit and conviviality. My sense of aloneness didn't last long, as glances began coming my direction and efforts were made to draw me into the conversation and encourage me to share with them in their happiness. However, I went on not saying a word, content to do nothing but smile back at them. Everything around me was a cause for delight. Even so, I couldn't seem to rid myself of a vague apprehension that more than once gave me the urge to leave.

Radiya said to me warmly, "Yours was a difficult delivery. God knows how Mama suffered having you. Medhat and I were in the other room crying. Then finally they let us come in and we saw you all wrapped up, this tiny little thing that was hardly bigger than a fist, and we started kissing you all over!"

47

"I wanted to feed you a piece of chocolate," Medhat added with a laugh, "so they carried me out!"

"When we were alone at our father's house we would try to picture how you were. We'd say, 'Maybe he's crawling by now,' or 'Maybe he's walking and playing,' or, 'It's time for him to start school.' By the way, what year are you in school now?"

I could feel the warmth of a blush in my cheeks and my tongue was tied. Answering for me, my grandfather said in a tone not lacking in scorn, "He's repeating first grade at the age of ten."

"Like me!" replied Medhat with a chuckle. "I enrolled in agricultural school after failing two years of secondary school!"

"Your grandfather wants to make him into an officer," said my mother.

"He'll have to finish the baccalaureate, then," Medhat replied with a nod.

My grandfather, who'd enrolled in military school when he was primary school age, said derisively, "Today's baccalaureate isn't worth yesterday's grade-school diploma!"

Then the conversation turned to life in my father's house.

Radiya said, "Actually, we lived by ourselves. We'd only see Baba once a day in the early morning. The rest of the day we'd spend together, studying, playing, or talking. And we praised God for that isolation."

Taking special note of the last part of what Radiya had said, my mother heaved a sigh of pity.

"If your father really did exempt you from his company, then he did a good thing for which he deserves to be thanked!" declared my grandfather.

The whole day passed in an atmosphere overflowing with love and nostalgia, and we went back to Manyal consoled and comforted. After this we were in regular communication with my sister, and Medhat would come to see us whenever he had the chance.

It was an exciting year that brought with it a mix of confusion, curiosity, and harsh experience. The year had opened with the shock of my sister's elopement and the subsequent news of her marriage, then her pregnancy, then her giving birth to a baby girl. I asked myself, and my mother as well, what all this meant. Why had she run away from my father to a strange man? Why hadn't she come to us? Why had she married him? How had she gotten pregnant? And how had little Zaynab come into the world? Ill at ease in the face of my insistence and intrusiveness, sometimes my mother would concoct evasive answers, and at other times she would tell me I needed to wait till I was older. If I was too importunate, she would put on an unaccustomed air of firmness, and my efforts yielded nothing to satisfy my curiosity. At the same time, I felt that some sort of secret was being kept from me.

It was then that help came whence I'd least expected it. The servant girl volunteered to reveal that which had so perplexed me and fired my imagination. She was years older than I was and quite unattractive, but she devoted all her free time to serving me and every now and then, on those rare occasions when my mother was too busy to oversee us due to some task or necessity, she would be alone with me. It seems that one day she'd overheard the conversation between me and my mother concerning the mysteries that had awakened me from my slumber. Thus, she declared to me that she knew certain things that were worth knowing. Interested and pleased, I was drawn to her despite her ugliness, and I entered into the experience with ingenuousness and delight. However, those days were short-lived, since it wasn't long before my mother caught us in the act. Seeing the frigid, forbidding look in her eyes, I realized that I'd committed a serious mistake. Grabbing the girl by the hair, she escorted her out and I never laid eyes on her again. I waited, fearful and shamefaced. Then she came back, still looking dour and unforgiving. Describing what I'd done as wicked and disgraceful, she spoke to me about the punishment such things call for in this world and the torments they merit in the next.

Her words stung me like a whip, and I burst into sobs. Then for days I was so ashamed and humiliated, I avoided looking her in the eye.

10

A miracle—or so my grandfather described it—took place when at last I passed my end-of-year examination. Consequently, I was promoted to the second grade after spending two years in the first.

When my grandfather looked at the report card he said to me playfully, "If I were still in the army, I'd bring you the artillerymen's band and have them give you a twenty-four-cannon salute in celebration of your success!"

But although my grandfather hadn't been able to give me a twenty-four-cannon salute, he managed—with the best of intentions—to drop a bomb on my life that nearly did me in. It so happened that one day he was visited by a fifty-year-old retired officer who had worked under his command in Sudan. After the man left, my grandfather came to join us on the balcony and began looking searchingly into our faces. He said nothing, but there was a look of joy and satisfaction on his face.

Then, addressing my mother in a jolly tone, he said, "Follow me, Miss Zouzou. I'd like to have a word with you alone!"

I burst out laughing at this charming term of affection. As for my mother, she followed him to his bedroom while I entertained hopes of pleasant things to come. My mother disappeared for an hour, then returned to me, and as soon as I saw her, I hailed her, saying, "Welcome, Miss Zouzou!"

Then I burst out laughing again. Contrary to my expectations, however, she just smiled wanly, then sat down on her chair looking grave-faced and pensive. Feeling concerned, I leaned toward her and asked her what the matter was.

"Nothing," she replied tersely. "Just trivial things that are no concern of yours."

Her evasiveness only fanned the flames of my curiosity, so I pressed her to tell me what was on her mind. She sighed irritably, begging me to be quiet. So we sat for a long time without saying a word, then half-heartedly exchanged our usual conversation. When we were called to dinner, I only ate a few bites. As we got ready for bed, she stood for a long time in front of the mirror. Then she lay down beside me, placed her hand on my head and recited some short suras from the Qur'an the way she usually did until my eyelids grew heavy with sleep. During the latter part of the night, I woke up to the sound of what seemed to be whispers. When I listened closely, I realized that my mother was muttering, and I assumed she was dreaming. So I called to her until she woke up, and we remained wakeful till daybreak.

The following day, my grandfather was visited by the same retired officer, and the events of the day before were repeated: he called my mother to his room, and the two of them remained alone for around an hour. When they came out to the balcony together, my mother was clinging to his arm and crying frantically, "No! No! It can never be! And I don't want him to know a thing!"

However, he seemed to take no notice. Then, turning to me, he said firmly, "I'm waiting for you in my room."

My mother began begging and pleading with him, but he just marched back to his room with me close on his heels, while my mother proceeded to our bedroom, indignant and irate. My grandfather sat down on his big, comfortable chair and instructed me to come near. I went to him feeling fearful and overwhelmed.

51

Placing his lean hand on my shoulder and looking at me searchingly, he said, "Kamil, I want to speak with you about something very important. You're still young, of that there's no doubt. Even so, there are boys your age who take on men's responsibilities. I want you to understand me well. Do you promise me that?"

"I promise you, Grandpa," I replied mechanically.

He smiled at me kindly, then said, "The matter is that a friend of mine who's an upright, wealthy man wants to marry your mother. I'm in agreement with his proposal, since I want your mother to be happy. After all, a woman needs a man to take care of her. I'm over sixty now and I'm afraid I might die before you've taken on your duties as a man, in which case she won't have anyone to depend on."

He went on about the matter in great detail, but my mind grew weary and shut down, and before long I couldn't make any sense out of what he was saying.

As for the phrase, 'marry your mother,' it buzzed cacophonously in my ears and exploded in my brain. My eyes wide with astonishment, dismay, and revulsion, I wondered: Does my grandfather really mean what he's saying? It was true that my mother had told me the story of her marriage. But that was just a story, and ancient history. I'd never imagined it to be something that had really happened. Then I remembered the ousted servant girl and my heart sank.

"My mother would never get married!" I gasped. "Don't you understand what marriage is?"

Laughing in spite of himself, the elderly man said with a smile, "Marriage is a way of life that God has established, and God prefers people who are married over people who aren't. I married your grandmother, your mother was married in the past, and you'll get married some day too. Listen to me, Kamil. I want you to go to your mother and tell her that you want her to get married just as I do, and that whatever makes her happy will make you even happier. You have to agree to what will bring her happiness. She's suffered enough already for all of you."

I looked at my grandfather the way a felled animal looks at its captor, and my limbs started to tremble with agitation. Then I asked him in a trembling voice, "Do you want that man to take her?"

He smiled and said to me, "Yes. But I want him to take her so as to take care of her and make her happy."

"And me?" I asked petulantly.

Ever so gently he replied, "If you wish, you can go with her, or you'd be welcome to stay here with me."

Biting my lip fiercely to keep back the tears, I suddenly retreated and fled. I ran out of the room, ignoring his pleas to come back, and rushed to our bedroom, where my mother sat red-eyed from weeping. She opened her arms to me and I flung myself into her embrace, still trembling with emotion.

"Don't believe it," she said. "I mean, don't believe that anything he told you will happen. Don't cry and don't be sad. Ahhh . . . what torment!"

Gaping at her in shock and reproach, I shouted, "Didn't you tell me that this was shameful and forbidden?"

She squeezed me affectionately, fighting back a smile. Then she said, "Perhaps your grandfather told you that he wanted me to marry. However, he surely didn't say that I'd agreed to it myself. The fact is that I rejected the idea from the very start, and without the least hesitation. I would have preferred that you not know anything about it. And when he offered me some time to think about it, I said . . . ."

Interrupting her heatedly, I said, "But what he wants for you is something that's disgraceful and forbidden!"

She said nothing at first, but just sat gazing at me, looking startled and dismayed.

Then, disregarding my objection, she continued, "I told him it was no use giving me time to think it over, since I wasn't willing to consider it. And I said that for your sake. For your sake alone. So, don't you be sad or angry. And don't think bad things about your mother."

Her words had brought me out of the darkness of despair. Even so, I went on repeating my objection until, after some hesitation, she said, "I never said that marriage was something evil or forbidden. On the contrary, it's an honorable relationship that God blesses. What I condemned were other things."

My tongue was tied with shame and timidity. Then, patting me consolingly on the cheek, she said with a tinge of reproach in her voice, "What an ungrateful child you are! Don't you think this sacrifice of mine deserves a word of thanks? Do you think you'll remember this in the future? Of course not! On the contrary, you'll get married yourself someday and leave me all alone!"

With an angry grimace I cried, "I'll never leave you as long as I live!"

She reached out and stroked my hair with a smile, though her lovely eyes betrayed solemnity.

11

My school life proceeded with such slowness and tedium it was almost cause for despair. By the time I reached third grade I was fourteen years old. My grandfather used to say to me in exasperation, "When are you ever going to apply yourself to your studies? When will you ever realize your duty? Don't you see that if you keep on at this rate, you'll be retirement age by the time you finish!"

My mother was pained no end by this bitter sarcasm, and she would always ask him not to throw it in my face for fear that it might discourage me and make me even duller.

Or she'd say to him, "Intelligence is from God, and his good character is more than enough to make up for what he lacks. You couldn't find anyone more bashful or better mannered!"

It then happened that my life underwent a critical development. I don't recall when or how it began, and I fear that imagination may have distorted my memory of some aspects of it. A strange sort of restlessness began to course through body and soul. It flowed through my limbs as a kind of disquiet and turmoil, and when I was alone I was accosted by new sorts of dreams. When I was at school, I would be absented from my surroundings by a tendency to daydream that would focus all my sensations on myself. As the carriage took me home from school, I would gaze up at the heaven's horizons, wishing I could soar up among its mysterious-looking blue particles. Enveloped in melancholy and gloom, I would console myself by crying my heart out. I'll never forget the vague longings, the unnamed fears, the hushed groans, and the sprouting hairs. Lord! I thought: I'm a creature that's bringing forth some bizarre, terrifying life force whose demons make sport of me day and night, whether I'm waking or dreaming.

I discovered on my own—under the pressure of this life force—that fiendish boyhood pastime. No one lured me into it, since I was without friends or companions. Rather, I discovered it the way it must have been discovered for the first time in the life of humanity. I received it with wonder and delight, and in it I found a fulfillment the likes of which I found nowhere else. Finding in it a panacea for my weird loneliness, I gave myself over to it to the point of addiction, while my imagination selected womanly images with which to adorn my imaginary table of love.

The strange thing is that in its ardor, my imagination never went beyond the realm of the servant women in Manyal who went about laden with vegetables and fuul. Nor was this merely a passing phenomenon. Rather, it was a hidden secret, or rather, a hidden malady, as though I'd been destined to love unattractiveness and squalor. If I saw a bright, lovely face that emanated light and beauty, I would be filled with admiration, but my animal instincts would grow cold. If, on the other hand, I was confronted with a robust but homely face, it would arouse me and take utter possession of me, and thenceforth I would include it within my store of fuel for solitude's dreams and amusement. I went to excess as one does when ignorant of consequences, and in that consummate ignorance of mine, I imagined that no one but I was familiar with such a practice. Then one day when I was in the school's courtyard, I heard some of the students accusing each other of it in the most shameless manner. Terribly upset, I was seized by an unbearable chagrin. From that moment on, torment was my constant companion, and my erstwhile placid waters were roiled by a troubled conscience. That didn't keep me from persevering in the habit, however. Rather, I would spend my solitude in wild, but short-lived sensual delight followed by lingering misery.

Those monotonous days of ours would be brightened every now and then by visits from families who were either neighbors or relatives. These would include married women and girls of marriageable age, and on occasion one of the women might lightheartedly introduce her daughter, saying, "Here's Kamil's bride!"

My mother would receive such banter with a notable lack of enthusiasm that was lost neither on the woman addressing her, nor on me. Consequently, I felt increasingly timid, estranged, and fearful, especially toward women. Add to this the fact that once the lady visitors had departed, my mother would never fail to criticize their scandalous, decadent remarks. Meanwhile, I went on with my forlorn, friendless life, feeling restive under its constant pressure, yet doing nothing to change it. I would seize upon its covert pleasures in a state of disquiet and despair, then have nothing to show for them but a bitter sense of guilt. Trapped in an isolation that distanced me from life's other spheres, I wondered in anguish how I would ever break free. At the same time, I was vaguely aware that there was a wider world beyond my narrow horizon. I would overhear snatches of other students' conversations about politics, the cinema, sports, and girls as though I were listening to inhabitants of some other planet. How I wished I had a share of their expressiveness and *joie de vivre*. How I wished I could penetrate the solid, thick wall that barred me from their world. I would gaze at them in dejection, like a prisoner looking out through the bars of his cell at those who enjoy their freedom. Yet not once did I try to break out of my prison. After all, I wasn't unaware of the cruelty and humiliation that awaited me in the world of freedom. Indeed, even when I was safely behind bars, as it were, I was vulnerable to a certain degree of harassment, mockery, and aggression. I said to myself: This is my prison, so let me be content with it. Here was where I found my pleasure and my pain, and here was where I found safety from fear. It was a prison with an open door, but there was no way to cross its threshold.

The only release I found, I found in dreams. As I sat in class, I'd be absent from everything around me while my imagination worked miracles: warring, slaying, and vanquishing, mounting the backs of steeds, flying airplanes, storming fortresses, whisking beautiful women away, and inflicting the most grisly, humiliating punishments on the other students. There would even be times when such daydreams would betray themselves in the movements of my head and contortions in my face, while reflections of those phantoms would cause my head to rise smugly, crease my brow in a merciless glare, or evoke a menacing wave of my hand.

My dreams weren't confined to the realm of humanity, but ascended to the realm of the Creator as well. Primal and firmly rooted, my faith filled my heart and spirit with the love and fear of God. I'd begun performing the rites of my religion from an early age in imitation of my mother. Given the unaccustomed sense of guilt produced by my secret pleasures, my religious sensibilities intensified, and along with my faith I experienced a powerful longing for God and His mercy. Never once would I finish a prayer without lifting my palms heavenward and seeking God's forgiveness. My longings knew no bounds and were transformed into an aspiration to know God. I wished with all my heart that God had made it possible for His servants to see Him, beholding the ubiquitous divine majesty that surrounds all things.

One day I asked my mother, "Where is God?"

"He's everywhere," she replied in astonishment.

Casting her an uncertain look, I asked fearfully, "In this room?"

"Of course!" she rejoined in a tone of incredulity. "Now ask His forgiveness for that question of yours!"

So I asked His forgiveness from the bottom of my heart. Bewildered and fearful, I looked about me. Then I remembered with a pained heart the fact that I would indulge in sin under His watchful eye. The thought caused me intense suffering and I was filled with remorse. Even so, I continued helplessly in its grip.

The ongoing struggle was so grueling, I began thinking seriously of committing suicide. I was seventeen years old at the time, and I was preparing for the primary school final examination for the third time after having failed it two years in a row. I was gripped with panic and despair, both of which were even more overwhelming when I thought of the oral examination. I had no speaking ability, nor did I have the heart to face the examiner. During the previous year's test, the English examiner had asked me about the landmarks I'd visited in Cairo. Whenever he asked me about one of the city's archeological sites or attractions, I would reply that I wasn't familiar with it. Thinking that I was evading his questions, he failed me. Fear overcame me, ushering me into the terrifying chambers of desolation. For the first time ever, I found myself taking a kind of bird's-eye view of life. Tracing its over-all trajectory from beginning to end, I no longer saw anything but the start and the finish while disregarding everything in between. Birth and death: this was the sum of life. Birth had passed; nothing was left but death. I'm going to die, I thought, and everything will end as though it had never been. So why go through all this suffering? Why should I have to endure fear, distress, loneliness, exhausting effort, and exami-nations? My head was swarming with distressing memories from the life I was living: a test that was too much for me to handle followed by failure and bitter ridicule, deprivation of the pleasures in life that other students enjoyed, and being called dumb and disagreeable. One day a student standing near the door to the school mosque saw me coming. He cupped his hand over his ear as though he were going to utter the call to prayer, then in a sing-song voice he shouted in my face, "Hey, disagreeable!" against a background of raucous laughter. I remember how a certain teacher had wanted to test our general knowledge one day. When it was my turn and I stood there in a daze, not answering any of his questions, he asked me what the name of the prime minister was. I didn't say a word. So he bellowed at me, "Where do you live? In Timbuktu?" There were innumerable opportunities to go on strike, but during those days. I'd never taken part in a single demonstration. One day the entire school declared a strike and every single one of the students went out on a demonstration—every one of them but me, that is. I stayed behind in the schoolyard, flustered and afraid on account of my being one of the oldest students. I was seen by a teacher who was known at that time for his nationalist views. When he saw me, he rebuked me sternly, saying, "Why did you break with the consensus? Isn't this your country, too?" As a consequence, I was torn between the suffering caused by the teacher's rebuke and the instructions I received every morning from my mother and which she adjured me to follow without question.

Memories like these threatened to rob life of all value whatsoever. And wouldn't death deliver me from all this? Indeed, it would, I thought. So let me die! Such thoughts became my sole preoccupation, and I made up my mind to throw myself into the Nile. That evening I spent a long time in prayer. Then I went to sleep with my mother's hand in mine, considering myself ready to be numbered among the dead. The next morning I began stealing worried, mournful glances at my mother's face. Moved by her tranquility and beauty, I had the urge to cry, and it distressed me not to be able to say goodbye to her. How will she handle the shock? I wondered fearfully. Will she be able to bear it? I'll be responsible for bringing grief to those serene eyes, causing wrinkles to appear in that smooth, youthful-looking face, and destroying her tranquility forever. Suddenly I feared that I might weaken in my resolve, but despair endowed me with new strength and prompted me to flee. I finished my morning tea without taking my eyes off her face. Then I bade her farewell and left the room, my chest tight and my soul full of bitterness, and got into the carriage. Casting a glance back at the house, I muttered, "Goodbye, Mama. Goodbye, dear house." Then the carriage took off. Before long I caught sight of al-Malik al-Salih Bridge, and my heart started pounding so hard I could hardly breathe. Everything would have to end now. Just a few more minutes, then eternal rest. At that time I knew nothing about the torment in the afterlife that awaits those who take their own lives, so I was sure I was about to commence a life of pure serenity. Little by little the bridge drew nearer and the clip-clop of the horses' hooves began pounding on my heart. I glanced down at the Nile and saw pearls scattered over its dark façade. I imagined myself striking the surface of the water as its peaceful, soundless waves cast me indifferently to and fro, confident of the struggle's outcome. Then, readying myself for the act of madness that I'd determined to commit, everything else faded from consciousness and I cried out to the aged driver as he turned onto the bridge, "Stop!"

The man pulled in the reins and the carriage came to a halt. I got out hurriedly and said to him, "Go on ahead to the end of the bridge, and I'll catch up with you on foot."

I waited until he'd gotten several yards ahead of me, then I turned toward the railing. I looked out over the river with my towering height, saying to myself, "They say I'm not good at anything in life. But now I'm going to do something that nobody else would dare to!" I cast a stony glance at the water, and in a flash, what I was about to do appeared in my mind's eye. Everything has to happen within a matter of seconds, I thought. Otherwise, passersby are sure to intervene and prevent me from doing what I intend to. I'll climb over the railing, then throw myself down. As long as I've taken matters firmly in hand, that won't take more than a few moments. My heart shrank as I looked down at the flowing water. When viewed from above, it looked swift and turbulent, and my head began to spin. One . . . two . . . a chill went through my body. What do you suppose it feels like to fall from a height? How does your body collide with the water? How is it when you plunge beneath its watery depths? And how long does it take for the ordeal of drowning to be over? My grip on the railing grew tighter and I said aloud, "Everything has to be over right away." In reality, however, I was retreating, and my resolve was giving out. I'd been defeated by the thoughts and images that I'd allowed to thwart my purpose. Someone who intends to commit suicide mustn't think or imagine. I'd begun thinking and imagining, and I'd been defeated. My heart beating wildly, my hold on the railing went limp. Then I moved away from it with a dazed sigh. My wobbly legs carried me to the end of the bridge where the carriage was waiting for me, and I got back in. Dog-tired, I sprawled out on the seat until I was overcome with sleep.

For years I wondered what it was that delivered me from death on that morning. My heart would say: It was fear! While my tongue would say: It was God, the Most Forgiving and Merciful!

No doubt I'd overstated my reasons for committing suicide, since I graduated from primary school at the end of that year.

12

It was around this time that our little family lost one of its loveliest trappings when my grandfather sold the Victoria and the two horses that drew it, and dispensed with the elderly driver's services. I learned through what I picked up from the family's conversation that one night at the casino my grandfather lost more than the usual amount of money, and had thus been obliged to borrow an amount of cash equal to his monthly pension. Given the fact that he was a man with a penchant for order, he preferred to sell the carriage and the two horses rather than upset his budget. It grieved us sorely to sell the carriage, lose the horses and have to part with Uncle Karim, the driver who'd spent his lifetime in my grandfather's service and who was so advanced in years he'd lost his teeth. I wept bitter tears over all of them, though without saying a word. My grandfather spent more time at the casino than he did at home. It was his only solace and entertainment, especially since he'd left the military. However, what with his innate candor and jovial nature, he never made any attempt to conceal his comings and goings. In fact, he would often tell my mother anecdotes about the things that happened to him during his evenings out.

With a shake of his grizzled head he'd say, "I had bad luck all last night until, just before closing time, I recouped my whole loss with two lucky strokes!"

Or he'd say, "Talk about greed! A single gamble at the end of the night lost me twenty pounds that I'd earned by the sweat of my brow!"

For the most part, though, he was a sensible gambler, if I might call him that, who was captivated by the mad delight of laying a bet without its causing him to forget the limits of what his budget would allow or his responsibilities as our family's provider. I'm sure the matter of my future preoccupied him quite a bit, not for my sake alone—though he constantly showered me with his love and affection—but, in addition, because my mother's fate was tied to mine. Then there was the fact that my schooling had faltered so badly that by the time I finished primary school, I was seventeen years old and he was nearing seventy. Consequently, he began feeling increasingly concerned, knowing well, as he did, that the 'fortune' he'd amassed was hardly worth mentioning. He would always overcome his anxiety thanks to his natural propensity for optimism, an optimism that was due for the most part to the God-given good health that, despite his advancing years, had never left him. Nevertheless, his most recent loss had reminded him of his anxiety and fears, and as such, it had impelled him to deal with them with prudence and caution.

One day, as he and my mother were discussing my future, he said to her after no little hesitation, "It seems to me that Kamil shouldn't be so utterly ignorant of his father."

Her face suddenly pale, my mother stared at him in horror and said, "What do you mean, Baba?"

"I mean," he replied nonchalantly, "that he should get to know him. This is necessary, since otherwise it will look to people as though he has no father."

Her voice quavering, my mother said, "His is a father of whom it's better to be ignorant."

Looking annoyed, my grandfather said firmly, "It's as though you're afraid that if he saw the boy, he'd try to take him back. But this is an illusion that exists only in your head. As a matter of fact, I'm quite confident that he was thoroughly pleased when fate provided someone to raise his son in his stead. Even so, I think Kamil should get acquainted with his father now. I've decided to take him to see him. Who knows when Kamil might need him? Can you guarantee that I'll be there for him forever? And don't forget that Kamil is about to enroll in secondary school, and that I might persuade his father to help me pay for his education."

My mother had, no doubt, been about to raise some objection. However, when she heard the last part of what he said, her fervor abated. A look of sadness flickered in her eyes, and she didn't say a word. As we left the room, her eyes welled up with tears.

Moved and saddened to see her this way, I came up to her and dried her tears, saying, "There's nothing to cry about, Mama."

With a tepid smile, she said unhappily, "There really isn't. I'm just crying over the past, Kamil. I'm crying over the peace of mind I enjoyed for so long. Life was comfortable and pleasant, and there was nothing to disturb us. Now your grandfather is talking about the future, and whenever he does that, he fills me with fear and worry. Let's ask God together not to let us be separated, to grant your grandfather a long life, and to protect us from having to depend on others."

She sat thinking for some time. Then she looked at me strangely and said, "If you do meet with him, be polite to him. He is your father, after all. But in your heart of hearts, never forget that he's the one who's caused us all to suffer."

A faint smile crossed my lips at this veiled warning—a warning of which I had no need. It wouldn't have been possible for me to love someone whom his own father had hated. Then I thought about the anticipated first encounter between us as father and son. I tried to conjure an image of him, or to remember what he'd looked like long before in the picture I'd torn to pieces, but to no avail. I felt entirely unenthusiastic about the visit, and I wished my grandfather would change his mind about it.

However, he decided that we'd make the visit the very next morning.

65

Hurrying me to get ready, he said, "We've got to go see him early in the day, before drunkenness makes him oblivious to everything around him."

We left together and walked to the tram stop. We took the tram to Ataba, and from there to Hilmiya. Then we went to Mubarak Street. As we approached our destination, he began instructing me to be polite and friendly while in my father's presence.

He said to me, "You're very shy and introverted, and I'm afraid he'll mistake your shyness for dislike and respond to you in kind, especially in view of the fact that he's never cared whether anyone loved him or not. So, look alive, and be friendly, gracious, and warm."

We stopped in front of a large two-story house. All that could be seen of the first story was its uppermost part, given the height of the surrounding wall. We knocked on a massive door that opened with a loud creak. From behind the door there emerged an elderly Nubian gatekeeper who welcomed my grandfather in a tone of respect, then stepped aside to let us pass, saying, "Ru'ba Bey is in the men's reception room."

The name roared in my ears. In spite of myself, I could feel the tie that bound me to this house, and I was seized by a sudden urge to retreat. However, it was an urge impossible of fulfillment. I looked ahead of me and saw a large garden, and before long my nostrils were filled with the sweet fragrance of lemons. The garden was striking for the enormity of its date palms, lemon trees, and mulberry trees, and it was congested with boughs and branches that blanketed its floor with dry leaves. Both the garden and the atmosphere that surrounded it exuded an air of gloom and melancholy that made their way instantly into my soul. At the garden's end lay the house, the foremost part of which was taken up by the men's reception room, and atop the wall a wooden barrier had been erected to prevent those in the garden from seeing inside. The gatekeeper went inside ahead of us to request permission for us to enter. Shortly thereafter he returned, inviting us respectfully to follow him. He proceeded before us down a mosaic walkway, and I walked behind my grandfather, gripped by an angst that only grew worse as we made our way farther into the garden. As I began ascending the steps, my throat went dry with anxiety. My father stood waiting for us, and I cast him a quick glance from behind my grandfather.

At that time my father was sixty years old. He was medium height and overweight, though in his white, loose-fitting robe he looked far more portly than he was in reality. He had a fair complexion, with a ruddy face and neck, his jugular veins protruded and his face was congested with blood. As for his facial features, they were large and pronounced, but well-proportioned. Bald, he had black, protruding eyes landscaped by a network of fine red lines that looked like tiny hairs. In his eyes there was a distracted, languid look that served to dispel whatever awe his huge frame might otherwise have inspired. I was possessed by a feeling of alienation, disapproval, and aversion, and I felt angry and resentful toward my grandfather for making me visit him. My indignation intensified when I saw that the only sign of welcome the man had shown was this lethargic stance at the door. The two men shook hands and I heard a deep voice that reminded me of my brother Medhat saying, "Welcome. How are you, Abdulla Bey?"

"Fine," replied my grandfather. "How are you?"

My grandfather stood aside slightly to make me visible and gestured toward me with a smile, saying, "Your son, Kamil."

I came forward, visibly tense, with my eyes fixed on him. As he scrutinized me with intense interest, a faint light glinted in his eyes, and I extended my hand. At that point—as if to forestall some faux pas that he considered me likely to commit—my grandfather said, "Now put away that shyness of yours and kiss your father's hand."

Getting the message, I grasped the hand extended in my direction and kissed the back of it. I looked up at him and found him to be smiling.

Then I heard him say, "Welcome to the son who hasn't known his father! And what a fine boy you are."

Then, addressing my grandfather, he continued, "He's become a man. In fact, he's taller than his father!"

Laughing his grand laugh, my grandfather said, "Yes, indeed, he is a man. But it's no fault of his if he hasn't known his father."

My father examined me from head to toe, then invited us to sit down. We sat down on two chairs that had been placed near one another, while my father sat on a couch in the front of the room. Before him there was a black wooden coffee table inlaid with shells on which a long-necked red bottle, a glass, and a Chinese decanter filled with ice had been placed.

The bottle was nearly full, and the glass was nearly empty. I'd never seen liquor before, but I realized immediately that I was looking at the vile drink that had put my family through so much, and I was filled with loathing and disgust.

"As I was saying," my grandfather continued, "what fault is it of his, poor boy? He's never known his father, and there's nothing he could have done about it. Nor is there any need to bring up memories of things done and gone. However, I saw that he'd grown up, as you say. He finished grade school this year, and before long he'll be enrolling in secondary school, so I hated for him to go on being ignorant of his father. I suggested that I introduce him to you, and he welcomed the idea. And now, here we are, praise be to God."

My father didn't take his eyes off me, as a result of which I couldn't shake off my discomfort and timidity. When my grandfather had finished speaking, a look of skepticism flashed across his distracted eyes.

"Were you really happy about the idea of being introduced to me?" my father asked me.

"Yes," I replied in a voice that was barely audible.

"So," he went on with a crafty look, "would you like to come live with me?"

My heart shrank, and my eyes betrayed a look of indecision. What was I supposed to say? My grandfather's instructions were still ringing in my ears. Yet, supposing I replied in the affirmative and he invited me to stay with him, what would my fate be then? No, I couldn't possibly do that. I looked down, my mouth pressed shut, and didn't utter a word. My father laughed out loud in a voice that caused my grandfather to tremble.

"Go easy on him, Ru'ba Bey," he said, looking at me indignantly. "He's never been separated from his mother, and there's nothing more difficult for someone than to change a habit. However, I assure you that he was very happy to know that he'd be meeting you. Don't hold it against him that he's quiet and flustered, since he's as shy as a virgin."

My father shook his round bald head, his lips still parted following his laugh.

Then, as though he wanted to challenge me, he asked me, "What do you say you come stay with me for part of your vacation? A month, say, or two weeks?"

"Something like that," interjected my grandfather, "could easily be arranged!"

Picking up on the hint that my grandfather's words seemed to convey, I found myself like a mouse in a trap, and I was overcome by such anguish, I thought my chest would split open. I cursed the loathsome resolve that had led my grandfather to herd me into this wretched abode, and despair and obstinacy kept my tongue tied until my father said cynically, "That's what *you* say, Abdulla Bey. But I wonder what Kamil Bey has to say about it?"

His cynicism pained me. By now I was so miserable I neither spoke nor looked up. I longed for my mother the way a drowning man longs for dry land, as I always did when I found myself in distress.

Guffawing sarcastically, my father said, "He may be happy to see me, but only from a distance!"

Then, changing his sarcastic tone, he said forcefully, "Don't you know that if I wanted to keep you here, nothing could stand in my way?"

He paused for a moment to allow his pronouncement to have its desired effect.

Then he continued with a laugh, saying, "Don't worry. I have absolutely no need to do that."

A dreadful silence ensued. My grandfather may have realized that through what he had just said, my father had brought a certain hostility out into the open, and I sensed instinctively that each of us harbored an aversion to the other that there was no way to hide. I was dismayed at the bitter disappointment my grandfather had been met with, and I expected him to give me a thorough tongue-lashing.

69

However, he said softly, "Your son's had bad luck, Ru'ba Bey. He's been deprived of the ability to express what's going on in his mind. He's a timid boy who knows nothing about the world, so show him compassion and don't blame him."

"What's this you're saying, Abdulla Bey!" retorted my father crustily. "Timid? A virgin who doesn't know a thing? What have you done to him? He had a sister who was a virgin, but she ran away with a man! So what stuff is he made of?"

I felt as though someone had opened a gaping wound in my heart. The blood rushed to my grandfather's face and his brow furrowed in anger.

Proudly he said, "His sister chose to go to her husband after despairing of receiving justice from her father!"

His words consoled me. However, my father let out a long laugh, his face more bloodshot than ever. He looked boorish, cruel, and revolting.

Then he said sarcastically, "You say, 'after she despaired of receiving justice from her father'! Allow me first to fill a glass (whereupon he filled the glass and took a swig from it). Would you like to join me? No? As you wish. After all, we all have our vices. And now, back to what you were saying: What did you say, Abdulla Bey? 'After she despaired of receiving justice from her father'? And what about you? Haven't you despaired of receiving justice from her father?"

With a look of reproach and scorn, my grandfather asked, "What do you mean?"

"I mean to say that although the girl may have given up on her father, her grandfather hasn't, as evidenced by the fact that you've brought this boy to me today, not to introduce him to me as you've claimed—since you could have done that at any time in the past—but, rather, to inform me that he's about to enroll in secondary school, which involves certain expenses. Hah!"

Beside himself with rage, my grandfather roared, "I wore myself out trying to reform you in the past, and I'm a fool to try again now! I raised him till he became a man without it costing you a cent!"

My father clapped his hands in derision. Then, his voice rising, he said, "Ah, how crafty men can be! Some time ago you came asking me to leave the boy in your care. And now you're telling me I should be grateful to you for raising him to manhood! Well done, well done! But don't you remember our previous agreement?"

Seething with ire, my grandfather said, "What agreement, you . . . ?" his tone of voice betraying his agitation. "We're not talking about a business deal. We're talking about your son! Where's your sense of fatherhood and compassion?"

"Fatherhood? Compassion?" my father asked. "What noble qualities to have! However, money corrupts them. Let's leave idle talk aside, Abdulla Bey, since it doesn't befit a military man like yourself who fought the wars in Sudan. You know me quite well. So, where on earth did you get the idea of coming to me with this sort of pointless request? Think it over carefully. Either you take care of him yourself as we agreed that you would, or you leave him to me."

When I looked at my grandfather, his face was flushed with rage. I expected him to blow up at my father. However, with a tremendous effort he managed to keep himself under control. Then he said calmly, "If it weren't for my duty toward your son, I would never have asked such a thing of you. I'm not seeking anything for myself. Rather, I want to assure the boy's future, especially in view of the fact that I'm an old man and might die tomorrow."

"If you die tomorrow, I'll take care of him," said my father impatiently.

My grandfather knit his brow indignantly. I was appalled at the cruelty of what my father had said, and I hated him at that moment more than I'd ever hated him in my entire life. Then, as if his patience had run out, my grandfather rose sullenly to his feet, and I rose at the same moment as though I were fastened to him.

Casting my father a haughty glance, he said, "I can't say you've disappointed me, since I never thought well of you in the first place. However, there are mistakes we make against our will even though we know better. Good day."

He took me by the hand and led me out of the room as my father said disdainfully, "And a good day to you, Abdulla Bey!"

Thus ended the first encounter between my father and me. I left it with a sense of loathing that was more than I could bear. No sooner had we walked out of the house and into the street than I breathed a sigh of relief, praying to God with all my heart that I'd never be obliged to darken his door again. As we walked toward Hilmiya Square, my grandfather quickened his pace, his head bowed and his face red. He was mumbling unintelligibly, and I began stealing glances over at him, grieved and remorseful. At the same time, I was afraid, since I felt responsible for what had led to their dispute. Then little by little his speech became more distinct, and I heard him say, as though he were talking to himself, "The barbarian! Why does God let people like that have children? Why didn't He punish him by making him barren?!"

He also said, "What a lout! Isn't there even an iota of fatherly compassion in his heart? He didn't leave the boy to us in response to our request. He sold him in return for the money he would have had to spend on him!"

When we reached the tram stop, he fell silent. Then he glanced over at me harshly and ground his teeth.

"And you, you little . . . ! Will you go on being a mule for the rest of your life? Hasn't God given you the ability to utter a kind word? What would it have cost you to pretend to feel friendly toward him? Did you think he was going to fall all over you, you fool?"

I was terrified by his anger, just as I was terrified by anger in general, and my lips quivered like a little boy who's about to cry. Seeing the state I was in, he began sputtering with rage.

"How quick you are to cry!" he shouted. "What's there to cry about? Have I been unfair to you? Have I done you some violence? I made an idiotic mistake, and all I said was that I'd made a mistake. Is that so unforgivable?"

I didn't utter a word the entire way home. I went on feeling grieved and disconsolate until I remembered that I was going home to my mother and that soon I'd be telling her about everything that had happened. And that made me feel better.

13

One day during the week that followed our meeting with my father, we received a visit from my brother Medhat. When I took a good look at his face this time, I could see that he was the spitting image of our father, and I wondered with some alarm what his lifestyle and morals would be like. Would he resemble his father in those areas the way he did in his physical constitution? I gave him a strange look that day that no one took any notice of. At the same time, I loved him dearly, just as he loved us. When my mother chided him for not visiting us more often, he said to her, "You, of all people, know what madmen's morals are like!"

His quip sent me into gales of laughter, and I looked over at my brother with gratitude.

Then he turned toward me and said regretfully, "I heard about what happened during your last meeting with our father."

"Did he tell you about it?" asked my mother with interest.

"No," he said with a laugh. "Uncle Adam the gatekeeper did."

"The gatekeeper!" I cried censoriously, feeling quite indignant. "Was he eavesdropping?"

"No," Medhat assured me. "He has no need to, since my father fills him in on every little thing that happens to him. Uncle Adam is father's long-time confidant and hears everything that's on his mind, though most of the time he's the butt of his sharp tongue. I can't tell you how badly I feel about the attitude he took toward Grandpa. I wish I could have seen him here today so that I could kiss his hand and apologize to him."

We went on talking for a long time. Medhat was a skilled conversationalist who knew how to communicate with ease and warmth. His laugh was loud like his father's, though without his father's coldness or harshness. Hence, it wasn't long before I'd come to love and admire him, and I wished I had some of his joviality and ease of expression. Eventually the conversation came around to the subject of his future. He'd completed the Intermediate Agricultural Certificate in the summer of that year, and he said, "I went to see my uncle in Fayoum in hopes that he might help me find a job through one of his acquaintances, but he didn't take to the idea of my looking for work with the government. Instead, he proposed that I practice on his farm for a high wage with the idea that he would rent out some land to me in the near future. I saw his offer as a way to start making a good living through agriculture, so I accepted it."

As for my mother, she wasn't so sanguine about the idea.

"Wouldn't it be more respectable to get a job with the government?" she objected.

My brother let forth a long laugh, then said, "My diploma doesn't qualify me for a decent job. But my uncle can give me valuable work opportunities and the chance to make a fortune."

"And live the rest of your life in Fayoum?"

"It's a suburb of Cairo!" he replied consolingly.

"For so long I've hoped for the day when you could be on your own and we could live together!"

He kissed her hand gently and said with a smile, "You'll see me so often, you'll get sick of me!"

Then he bade us farewell and departed.

Heaving a deep sigh, my mother said forlornly, "He spent the first half of his life in that madman's house, and he'll spend the latter half off in Fayoum!"

74

After a moment's reflection, she said as if talking to herself, "His uncle didn't make that offer just because he happens to like him so much. He must be planning to marry Medhat to one of his daughters."

"And what's wrong with that?" I asked ingenuously.

In response, she cast me a strange look. More than once she began to speak, but thought better of it and held her tongue.

My mother's hunch proved correct. It wasn't long before we received a letter from Medhat, informing us of his engagement to his paternal cousin, telling us the wedding date, and inviting us to attend. Scandalized that he would have become engaged without consulting her first, my mother made no attempt to conceal her indignation.

"Do you see how that madman's brother has gone and stolen my son?" she asked my grandfather furiously.

We didn't attend because I fell ill not long before the wedding and was bedridden for two weeks. Hence, my mother forgot all about the wedding with its joys and sorrows. And thus it was that Medhat's nuptials were attended by neither his mother nor his father.

Commenting sardonically as usual, my grandfather said, "God created this family as one of the wonders of mankind. Every family is a unit except this one, which is scattered this way and that and never comes together. O God, Your pardon and good pleasure!"

The summer drew to a close and it was nearly time for the schools to be back in session, so my grandfather enrolled me in Saidiya. We went there together, and on the way he said, "If you were really a man, you wouldn't need me to come with you, but you're seventeen years old and you still don't know the way to Giza. Memorize the route we take to get there. I was an officer at your age!"

My grandfather was putting on a show of discontent and offense. However, in my heart I sensed that he was happy, even overjoyed, and I could feel his affection wrapped about me. Consequently, it shamed me to think of all the trouble he was going to for my sake even though by this time he was a seventy-year-old man.

When we came home, he thumped me gently with his cane, saying, "You're now a student at Saidiya, so do your best and make us proud. I want to see you an officer before I pass away."

And I prayed with all my heart for him to be granted length of days.

He fell silent for quite some time. Then, without any apparent occasion, he said, "Back in my generation, a primary school certificate was a great thing. In fact, it was rightly considered the equivalent of the highest degrees they give out these days."

Then he continued with a nod of his head, saying, "Those were the days! And we were real men!"

14

The summer vacation ended and I was smitten with gloom. School was the bane of my existence, and I genuinely and profoundly detested it. It was true, of course, that I was about to start out at a new school that was associated in my mind with manliness and glory. However, it was still a school, which meant that like any other school, it would have scheduled times, classrooms, students, teachers, punishments, and lessons that were bound to be more difficult than the ones in primary school.

On the first Saturday morning of October I woke up early, four months since the last time I'd had to engage in this wearisome habit. I put on a suit, spruced myself up as usual and chose a necktie out of my grandfather's wardrobe. My mother took a long look at me, then said to me with satisfaction, "You're as beautiful as the moon, I swear to God! You've got your mother's face, but with a fair complexion the likes of which I've never had. May the Merciful One's care protect you."

She instructed me to be careful when I walked, got on and off the tram, and crossed the street, then uttered a long prayer of supplication for me. When I left the house, she stood on the balcony watching me till I rounded the bend and disappeared from view. I kept walking, all the while feeling worried and dejected until I reached the tram station on Qasr al-Aini Street. As I stood waiting for the tram alone for the first time in my life, I had a sense of independence that I'd never had before. The feeling consoled me and afforded me some relief from the distress I was suffering. Then suddenly I began to entertain the hope of beginning a new life—a life untroubled by the misery that had been my constant companion at the Aqqadin School. I thought to myself: Here I am on my way to a new school. I'll be meeting new people, so why can't I turn over a new leaf? Just maybe, if I applied myself diligently, could I avoid the teachers' cruelty? And if I managed to be friendly toward the other students, I could win their affection and keep them from despising me. It's something that lots of other people can do, so why should I be the only one who can't? A joyous enthusiasm danced in my heart, and I said to myself: If I succeed in what I've failed at in the past, I can make a good life for myself.

In this way I endeared to myself the school life I'd been fated to endure whether I liked it or not, and I continued on my way to Saidiya, luxuriating in the new hope that had sprung up suddenly in my heart at the tram station.

However, life at the new school was harsher than hope had given me to believe. My extreme shyness and aversion to people prevented me from making a single friend, while my tendency to daydream made my diligent efforts go up in smoke. And oh, the suffering I endured on account of that tendency! It robbed me of my senses and of all ability to pay attention and focus my thoughts. Hence, it made me easy prey for teachers. During the second week of my new school life, I was jolted awake from a daydream by the teacher's ruler as it struck my forehead, and by his voice as he asked me menacingly, "I said, what borders it on the north?"

I gazed into his face in bewilderment, so terrified I even forgot to stand up.

"Please be so kind as to stand when you answer your father's servant!" he screeched.

I rose to my feet in a fright, then stood there motionless without making any reply.

Slapping me on the cheek, he shouted, "What borders it on the north?"

When I failed to come out of my silence, he slapped me on my other cheek.

Then he said, "Leaving aside for the moment what borders it on the north, what is the 'it' that I'm asking you about?"

My cheeks ablaze, I persisted in my silence. He struck me successively on the right cheek, then the left without my daring to cover my face with my hand until, his rage quenched, he ordered me to sit down. Part of the class broke out in loud laughter, and I sat there fighting back the tears. Once again, then, I'd become the butt of teachers' harassment and students' ridicule. I nursed my wounds in silence, consumed by despair. With hope extinguished and my new effort having ended so quickly in failure, I reverted to my accustomed misery. Even so, clinging to a fine thread of hope, I devoted all my time to studying. I'd pore over my books for hours on end, but the effort was all but wasted. For while my eyes were fixed on the page, my imagination would be soaring through valleys of dreams, and I had no ability to rein it in. Stirred by physical desire and populated by ill-mannered servant girls, my daydreams would generally end with the infernal habit to which I'd been addicted since I reached puberty. Not a night would go by but that I would be melted down in its furnace with an affected pleasure followed by prolonged, painful regret.

I wasn't utterly passive in the face of my desire to make friends, but my efforts in this area met with utter failure. For one thing, the desire for friendship was countered by a genuine predilection for solitude, an aversion to and fear of people, and an introversion that thrust me into an excessive concern for privacy. I didn't like anyone to know my secrets, nor even where I lived or how old I was. This was compounded by an inability to engage in conversation or catch on to people's jokes, still less make up any of my own. Consequently, none of the other students found anything about me to like. They went back to accusing me of being disagreeable, and I lived a friendless existence. At the same time, though, I didn't see myself as I really was. I accused others rather than myself of the faults that had deprived me of friendship, and for some time I believed that I had no friends because there wasn't anyone who was good enough for me. Incredible, the conceit and self-deception a person is capable of: the heavens and the earth aren't vast enough to contain them. Despite my faults and shortcomings, I used to imagine sometimes that I was the embodiment of absolute perfection. Hence, my deadly shyness was good manners, my academic failure was a genius that was slow to develop, and my abject poverty where friendship and love were concerned was a sign of superiority. Psychology—which we studied in the fifth year—supplied me with mysterious-sounding terms that I put to use in satisfying my false pride. Even so, I was weighed down by hours of desolation during which I would almost glimpse the truth.

One day I told my mother, who was the only beloved, friend, and companion I'd ever known, "I don't have any friends. The other students despise me."

In a fit of anger she cried, "Your shoe is worth a thousand of their heads! They only like people who go along with them in their silly pranks and bad manners. They envy you for your shyness and politeness. So don't you be sad. There's no virtue in getting close to other people!"

"I feel alone sometimes," I said dejectedly, "and loneliness is hard for me to bear."

Horrified by what I'd said, she looked at me reproachfully and said, "And where is your mother? How can you say such a thing when your mother is alive? Don't I devote my life to your service and care?"

Indeed, she was devoting her entire existence to me, and she was everything in my life. But who did I have outside our home?

Meanwhile, my academic life hobbled sluggishly along despite being supported on the crutches of private tutors.

My grandfather suffered terribly whenever I failed an examination, and he no longer made fun of me the way he had before. Perhaps the fact that he was getting on in years had caused him to be more fearful than ever for our future.

He would say to me, "Why do you fail this way, Kamil? Aren't you able to pass a grade in less than two years? Don't you realize how anxious I am to see you working before I die?"

His words would fall like a heavy weight on my heart, and I would say, "There isn't an evening when I don't study till midnight."

My mother would be quick to affirm the truth of what I'd said, whereupon he would shake his white head and mutter, "All things are in God's hands."

For this reason, I would anticipate test season with disquiet, dread, and bad dreams. For this reason also, I would be tempted by a combination of shame and conceit to feign exhaustion and illness during the months leading up to the examination so that I could use them as an excuse for my anticipated failure. As for my mother, she would visit Umm Hashim's shrine, make vows, and tie protective amulets around my neck. I'll never forget the time when, not long before my proficiency examination, she brought me a fortune teller, trusting in her ability to bring me success. The woman burned some incense in front of me, then propped a short stick up against the heater and instructed me to jump over it three times. I did as I'd been told, and she said to me confidently, "You'll pass the test, God willing."

When I failed the test, I said to my mother incredulously, "How could I have failed after jumping over the stick those three times?"

Yet in spite of everything, I kept on studying. And eventually I put the era of secondary school behind me and finished the baccalaureate when I was twenty-five years old.

15

Despite my successive failures, I felt proud and manly. Many government employees had nothing but a high school diploma. So, I thought: I'm a man worth his salt! I didn't aspire to work for the government with it, but I did hope it would enable me to get out of the house. In other words, I hoped to be released from the lasso that had bound me so tightly, I feared it would crush me. Indeed, I was gripped by a headstrong feeling that caused my heart to yearn for renewal and release. No longer was I a boy who could be led around by his nose, and life was inciting me to rebellion and revolution. But what rebellion, and what revolution? Against what or for what? I didn't find a clear answer to the question, and the truth is that I wasn't thinking. The turmoil I was experiencing wasn't an intellectual one. Rather, it was an emotional unrest that arose from somewhere deep inside me and longed for release, change, and the unknown. I didn't perceive any particular purpose behind it, but I suffered a painful, nebulous yearning that, whenever it stirred within me, plunged me into sorrow and desolation. And whenever these feelings came over me I would fall prey to anger and lose my temper for the most trivial of reasons.

At that time my grandfather was approaching his eightieth birthday, and my mother was in her early fifties. My grandfather had become a lean old man, but he'd preserved his health and hadn't succumbed to any serious illnesses. He still enjoyed an enviable share of his God-given vigor, and he hadn't lost his kind spirit or his understated wit. He still retained his brisk, dignified military gait and his perfect posture. He did, however, find himself obliged to change his lifestyle, since he could no longer tolerate regular long evenings out. Instead he would go in the mornings to the Luna Park coffee shop to meet with a few of his friends, then go to the casino for a couple of hours in the evening and be home by ten.

As for my mother, she seemed older for her age than my grandfather did. She'd grown thin, and her temples and the part in her hair were visibly gray. She was in good health, however and her face retained its beauty and radiance. There were times when she succumbed to the temptation to neglect her appearance, a development that caused me no little heartache and displeasure. It disturbed me so deeply that once I said to her, "Meet me looking the way you would if you were receiving guests." And she didn't disappoint me, since thereafter she would always appear at the door looking her best, which brought me gratification and joy.

My grandfather supposed that the time had now come to fulfill the hope he had cherished for so long, namely, for me to become an officer. I was now past the maximum age for enrollment in the military college. However, he figured that a bit of mediation could overcome this obstacle, and he approached numerous senior officers in this connection. Unfortunately, though, he was given to understand that the law allowed for no lenience on this point. Gravely disappointed, my grandfather said to me sorrowfully, "If you'd entered the military college, I could have guaranteed you a good future, and I would have set my mind at rest concerning you and your mother."

Shaking his head bitterly, he asked me, "So what do you intend to do?"

I looked at him uncertainly and made no reply.

Again he asked me, "Don't you have a preference for some profession in particular?"

I felt even more uncertain now. Thanks to my grandfather's own influence and his faith in the rightness of my joining the military, I'd never felt a leaning toward any other profession. So I didn't know how to answer his question.

"I'd been hoping to enter the military college," I said. "Now, though, all professions are the same to me."

"My choice is for you to study law, then, since it's the best option we have left. I won't tell you to be diligent, since it's a disgrace for anyone to fail at the university. But God help us with its expenses!"

I regretted having missed the chance to attend the military college. However, I only realized the enormity of my loss when I saw that I'd have to go on studying for at least four more years, or eight years if I kept up the pace I'd been accustomed to during primary and secondary school. By nature I detested studying and school, so I looked upon the future with no little resentment. I didn't know the first thing about university, but I thought it unlikely to be as odious as school. I said to myself: University students are adults, so they couldn't possibly treat me as badly as certain brothers of theirs whom I've known in the past, and who left scars in my soul that have yet to heal. I also thought it unlikely that punishment would be a permissible manner of dealing with men, or those who were as good as men. I thus labored tirelessly to endear to myself my upcoming academic life, glossing over its potential difficulties in order to enable myself to endure it patiently. And in the summer of that year I was enrolled as a student in the Faculty of Law.

16

On a Saturday morning in mid-October, I left home shored up by prayers of supplication and headed for the Egyptian University. I stood on the sidewalk waiting for the tram, the same one that used to take me to the Saidiya School. Despite the resentment I felt over having to go where I was going, I wasn't without a feeling of pride.

As I stood there waiting, I heard the clattering of a window shutter as it opened forcefully and struck the outside wall. I looked up at the second story of an orange building located directly in front of the tram stop where, up until around a month before, there had been a sign advertising a doctor's clinic. My glance fell on a girl who stood on the balcony drinking tea, and I realized immediately that a family had moved into the flat that had been vacated by the physician. Fixing my gaze on her, I began following her movements as she raised the glass to her lips and took a sip, then puckered her mouth and blew on the hot liquid once more. She stood there repeating the process over and over, engrossed in the enjoyment of her drink. She was a tall girl with a slender, svelte figure and a wheat-colored complexion. Clad modestly in a jacket and a gray tailored suit, she looked as though she were about to go to school. She had the side of her face to me, and when she held her head up straight, I saw a round face surrounded by a halo of chestnut hair whose appearance from afar suggested a lovely composition, though I wasn't able to make out its features from where I stood. The sight of her had a joyous effect on me. However, she only remained in view for a short while, and before I knew it she'd turned and gone back inside.

I kept her image in my mind out of curiosity as the tram approached, then I boarded with a sense that, thanks to the agreeable effect she'd had on me, I'd been relieved of the gloom of this day on which my studies were to begin. At the same time, the Faculty of Law possessed advantages that were likely to relieve me of my fears, though they did nothing to detract from the reasons for my overall aversion to studying. One such advantage was that students generally attended classes for only fours a day, their school day ending at around 1:00 p.m. Another advantage was that students were unsupervised, and enjoyed the freedom to choose whether they would attend lectures or not. And most important of all was the absence of the notion of punishments. In fact, I gathered from the general mood of the students that the threats that hung over professors were more fearsome than those faced by the students themselves. All this was cause for delight as far as I was concerned, and I consoled myself with the thought that this period of study, like those that had preceded it, would ultimately come to an end, however bitter it turned out to be. It wasn't new to me to have to drink the bitter cup of academics to the dregs, however much I detested it. And when I came home to Manyal later that day, a sudden elation come over me as I fancied myself to be a man of importance: half a professor, and a quarter of a public prosecutor!

The following morning as I approached the station, I remembered the balcony. Stirred by a quiet, natural curiosity, I looked toward it, but found it empty. My glance then stole inside the flat, where I saw a mirror on the opposite wall and to the left, a burnished silver bedpost and a ceiling lamp covered with a large blue lampshade. There appeared in the center of the room a fifty-year-old man wearing gold spectacles and buttoning his suspenders. Upon seeing him, I lowered my gaze and began pacing up and down the sidewalk. Then, happening to glance over at the stop where the tram heading for Ataba would come in, I saw the girl again. I recognized her by her height and what she was wearing, and this time she had a book in her hand. She had a dignified bearing that was lovely for her age, as she couldn't have been more than twenty. She didn't turn to look at any of the people crowding about or passing by her. Her reserve had a salutary effect on me and filled me with respect and admiration, as a result of which I felt a kind of attraction and affection for her. It was nothing new for me to be affected by women, of course. After all, I would often see beautiful women on the street or in the tram, and in general I would look at them like a passerby tormented by deprivation, loneliness, and desire. After glances of this sort, I would come away with a combination of intense elation and a painful jolt. As for this girl, though, she was something different. My attitude toward her wasn't that of a mere passerby. Rather, it was the attitude of a resident, or someone who's on the order of a neighbor. After all, I was seeing her today, and I'd be seeing her tomorrow, and so on indefinitely, a fact that intensified my interest in her, stirring in my heart imagined hopes and a desire for a happiness that could be renewed every day. It was as if my seeing her were a kind of getting-to-know-one-another, a vague hope, and an object of passive delight beyond which a shy, diffident sort like me would entertain no aspiration.

I went to the university in high spirits, and I wondered: Might she possibly take notice of me? I remembered her again in the heart of the night, in my emotional solitude as the delirium of erotic visions toyed with my imagination. However, I discovered within myself a fierce resistance to the idea of admitting her into this part of my world—indeed, a violent rejection of it. Hence, I banished her from the realm of my vile habit and, turning away from her image, I contented myself there with the lewd creatures that always inflamed the basest of my physical sensibilities.

❖

On the morning of the third day, I set out for the tram stop filled with such anticipation you would have thought I had an appointment to keep. I looked over at the tram stop across the street and saw her standing in the same place I'd seen her the day before, with her tall, slender frame, her moon-like face, and her charming, dignified bearing, and relief coursed through my whole body. Then it occurred to me to find a way to approach her without her noticing, thereby quenching my thirst to get a close look at her face. Fearful that the tram she was waiting for might come along and rob me of the opportunity, I hastened without further ado to carry out what I had in mind. I headed gingerly in the direction of the other tram stop, my heart sinking in my chest from fright, then walked past her with a stealthy look in her direction. In terrified haste, I saw a pair of limpid, honey-colored eyes that were dripping with sweetness, a dainty nose, and delicate lips. She may or may not have felt the warmth of my gaze, but she happened to look up and our eyes met. No sooner had she looked up than I looked away, since it's easier for me to stare at the sun at high noon than to bear the weight of someone's gaze. I strode to the edge of the sidewalk and stood there uncertainly, not knowing how to get back to the other side. It now seemed that I'd committed an act of madness, since I'd gotten myself into a predicament from which it would be difficult to escape. This, however, was how I perceived even the most unthreatening of situations. In any case, I stood frozen in place until the girl boarded the tram and the sidewalk was empty again, whereupon I returned breathlessly to my place. I thought to myself: Who could imagine such loveliness, such grace and modesty?

I lived the rest of that day in the shadow of her presence, hardly taking notice of the lectures I heard. The more I longed to give free rein to my emotions, the more I detested the lectures that stood in the way of my dreams and aspirations. I was filled with the desire to rebel against this academic life that so tormented my mind and disregarded my heart and feelings. It was as though I were taking notice of my heart for the first time, recognizing it as a living part of me just like my other bodily organs: one that gets hungry like the stomach, that grows tender like the soul, and that longs expectantly like the spirit. I wished I could devote my life to its happiness, giving myself over to the warm contentment from which its springs erupt.

I sighed from the depths of my being as I sat at the back of the lecture hall, present in body but absent in spirit. A voice inside me told me that beyond this dreary, narrow, constricted life there lay another that was bright, expansive, and free, and my soul went soaring away, anguished and eager, in search of it. My thoughts returned to the girl. This time, however, my imagination wasn't content with the mere sight of her. Instead, it created whatever suited its fancy. I saw myself attracting her attention. I approached her as I'd done that morning, but I didn't get flustered the way I had then, and I gestured to her with a rare boldness that got a warm smile from her in return. I whispered to her whatever I wanted to, and she whispered back. We got on the tram together, and somewhere along the bank of the Nile, I told her I loved her, and she, her cheeks aglow, said she loved me too. In response, I planted on her cheek a kiss filled with an admiration, respect, and tenderness that were too sublime for bodily lusts. Indeed, my imagination refused to summon her image in anything but a long dress, and surrounded by a halo of modesty and decorum.

On the morning of the fourth day, I went to the tram stop early and found the balcony empty. I shifted my gaze over to a window to the left of the balcony, where I got a side view of the girl's face. Standing attentively the way a person does when he's looking at himself in a mirror, she began arranging her hair and giving it the final, self-indulgent touches. Delighted, I began following her hand with my whole body until I imagined myself actually touching her silken hair and breathing in its sweet perfume. Then I saw her turn away from the mirror and look out the window at the street. Judging from the direction in which she was facing, I concluded that her eyes must be on the sidewalk. Given my instinctive shyness, I was tempted to lower my eyes. However, encouraged by the distance between us, I managed with a slight effort to keep my gaze fixed on her. Do you suppose she sees me? I wondered. Does she remember the young man whose eyes met hers yesterday for an exquisite moment? No, I concluded, she doesn't even know I exist, nor will she ever know it. She tarried slightly, then retreated inside, disappearing from view. I paced up and down the sidewalk, then returned to my place. One tram came, then a second, as I stood there waiting. Meanwhile, a ten-year-old girl whom I knew immediately to be her sister appeared on the balcony wearing a blue school uniform. Then I saw a girl emerge from the building and head toward the tram stop opposite mine. It was the first time I'd seen her walk. She had a calm, measured gait that well befit her delightful poise, her lithe figure, and her tall frame. Admiration and respect stirred within me, and I kept looking in her direction until the tram came and she boarded. Rewarded for my wait with joy and satisfaction, I got on the tram laden with a beautiful bouquet of dreams.

I wasn't unaware of my interest in her and the delight I took in her modesty and dignity. I knew that observing this particular household would henceforth be a regular pursuit of mine, and I said to myself: How badly I need a life companion who's as perfect as she is. My longing was intensified by the fact that thus far I'd lived my life without a single companion. At the same time, it worried me to have given expression to this desire. I also felt terribly embarrassed. It wasn't the first time I'd expressed the desire for a friend, but on previous occasions it had been in the form of a passing comment, and the longing was a general, ill-defined one, that is, a desire without any particular object. This, however, was a dangerous statement that stirred up a sense of shame and fear. It was a particular longing and a desire that might tempt one to hope. Moreover, it was a yearning that was fuelled anew every morning. And the most peculiar thing about it was that it was a homey sort of feeling, if one may speak of such. From the very beginning it focused around the girl and her house, and never once did I think of her without the image of her house also coming to mind. Consequently, the two images merged in my mind's eye; they received the same share of my attention, and they appeared equally in my dreams, where she soon began appearing as my wife. And it was no wonder. After all, I was the type who, if he saw a girl on the tram, would let his wandering mind go to work, and by the time the tram had gotten halfway from al-Malik al-Salih Bridge to Abbas Bridge, he'd already imagined asking for her hand. How, then, could I have failed to imagine the 'morning girl' as my wife? Overflowing with admiration and respect, all I could think about was the sacredness of home, the sentiments it engenders, and the tenderness of conjugal love. These feelings were connected by a thread of heartfelt attachment. Perhaps it was the love my heart had yet to experience.

On the morning of the fifth day, I stood longer than usual in front of the mirror before leaving the house, scrutinizing my appearance with the greatest of care. I must confess here to the fact that I was exceedingly impressed with myself. My egotism wasn't restricted to my behavior, but extended to the way I looked as well. I devoted the minutest, most painstaking attention to those large green eyes, that straight, delicate nose and that long, fair-skinned, well-proportioned face. In fact, my stylishness was legendary both at home and at school. I remember the Arabic teacher once saying to me, "If you mastered Arabic the way you've mastered putting on a necktie, you wouldn't be my worst student!" As I stood there scrutinizing myself at such length that morning, my mother began looking at me admiringly and teasing me with flirtatious-sounding remarks. Ah! I thought to myself, if only she knew who I'm preening myself for! Then I left the house satisfied, confident of the good impression my appearance was likely to make on the girl if fate should happen to direct her glance my way. However, my satisfaction was short-lived, since it wasn't long before I remembered something that for years had robbed me of my peace of mind, and my enthusiasm began to wane. I remembered all the times I'd been accused of being difficult to get on with, and at that moment, I didn't rule out the possibility that this was the reason for my life-long failure to make friends. Consequently, my placid waters were roiled and the whole world looked bleak. With heavy steps I walked the rest of the way to the tram stop. My gaze began searching for her until I spied her drinking tea on the balcony the way she had been the first time I saw her. And there I forgot my grief and worry as delight welled up in every drop of my blood. There, too, I realized that she was my delight and joy, that she was my spirit and my life, and that the world without the sight of her face wasn't worth a pile of ashes!

For two months or more—day after day, and with utter promptness—I faithfully kept this appointment of which the other party knew nothing. I manned my observation post until my eyes grew weary, gladly giving her my admiration and respect until I had nothing left to give. I luxuriated in happy dreams until I'd forgotten truth and reality, roaming about in the world of ardor until it had robbed me of reason and good sense. I memorized her from tip to toe: her every gesture and sidelong glance, the way she stood and the way she walked, her stillness and her movement. Through the windowpanes of her flat I came to know her entire family: her father, her mother, her sister, and her brother. And all of this without her knowing a thing about me, or even sensing that I existed. It was as if, as far as she was concerned, I inhabited another planet. I was tormented by anxiety and weariness, consumed by the desire to prove my existence, but I was helpless to take a step beyond where I stood. In my daydreams I would imagine myself accosting her or following her or declaring my admiration and respect for her. In reality, however, no sooner would she emerge from the door of the building than my heart would shrink in diffidence and alarm. I would even get ready to look down in the event that she happened to look my way. It would probably have been easier for me to throw myself off al-Malik al-Salih Bridge than to endure a single look from her eyes. I wondered in gloom and desperation: When will she notice that I exist? When will she realize that there's a stranger who has far more love for her in his heart than even her mother and father? Isn't it strange that someone can simply brush past a heart that would gladly be the ground on which she treads?

My thoughts during that time focused on my heart, with its sorrows and its hopes, its fears and its joys, and I felt a tremendous need for someone who could give me counsel and advice. My mother was the only friend I had in the world. But I didn't go to her with my crisis, of course, since I sensed that my heart's desires would be met with hostility on her part. However, in some of the magazines my grandfather read I found pages devoted to readers' questions, and I hoped that here I might find the advisor I lacked. To one of them I sent a question that had been keeping me awake at night: "From an unlikable man: Is there no hope that his beloved might love him in return?" The magazine's reply was: "Love is a mystery that has nothing to do with likeability or unlikeability. Love may be blind to ugliness and unattractiveness, so don't worry about your own unlikeability! And if we might be allowed to speculate concerning the woman's nature, it may be accurate to say that she's charmed by strength and valor!" I was happy with the reply's opening, but when I got to the conclusion, I felt let down. I wondered what the writer meant by 'strength.' Oh! I thought, I'm not strong anyway, and if the truth be told, my addiction to a certain despicable habit has turned me pale and made me thinner than I ought to be. When I thought of valor, I couldn't help but laugh bitterly as I enumerated all the things that frightened me in this world, from people and places to mice and cockroaches. And my heart was wrung with despair.

But I didn't lose hope. After all, the fire that blazed in my soul was too hot to be extinguished by a blow from despair's icy hand. I wrote back to the magazine with the following question: "How can I attract the girl I love?" And the reply was: "Go to her father or her legal guardian and ask for her hand, and I guarantee that she'll love you." Lord! I thought, how cruel can you get? The people at the magazine don't know that I'm still a student and that I have four, or possibly eight, years to go before I'm on my own. Besides, they don't know that it would be easier to storm the gates of hell than to knock on my beloved's door and ask her father for her hand. Don't they know what it means to be shy? I guess I'm doomed to go on living with an undeclared, unrequited love while my sweetheart is just a step away from me!

17

Then something happened to me that may have been trivial in itself, but that changed the course of my life. My academic life was a never-ending battle between my slothful mind and my itinerant soul. It was a battle that yielded—as it had in the past—acute suffering but very little fruit. My mind's tendency to wander had become a dominant character trait that had taken over all my mental faculties. I'd even begun worrying that I might be thirty-five years old by the time I graduated from university! At the same time, of the critical things I'd learned about what the study of law involves, there was one thing I hadn't realized I would have to face. This thing—to which other students hardly attached any importance, and which they actually took to with gusto, viewing it as a kind of sport—was the study of rhetoric. Once a week in a large lecture hall, all first-year students attended a lecture on public speaking. During the first two months we heard lectures on the theoretical aspects of the art, after which the practical training was to begin. The professor began inviting students to give extemporaneous speeches on various topics. They would speak fluently, with stentorian voices, courage, and aplomb, and I would listen to them with a mixture of amazement and profound admiration. I was taken by their glibness and guts, and astounded at their ability to handle such a frightening situation in front of such a huge gathering. Hence, I volunteered to be shy in their stead, so much so that my forehead would be dripping with perspiration.

Then one day what should I find but that the professor was calling my name: "Kamil Ru'ba Laz!"

I was sitting in the very back row—my favorite place, since no one would notice me there—and when I heard my name I rose to my feet in a reflex reaction.

The sound of my name aroused derisive attention and one of the students whispered, "That's Lazughli's grandson."

Another asked, "Is 'Lazughli' a noun or a verb?"

Meanwhile, I stood there in a state of shock, my heart pounding wildly. "Come up to the podium," said the professor.

I froze in place, however, too flustered to move. I wanted to apologize, but the distance between the professor and me would have required me to raise my voice loud enough for everyone to hear me, so despite my desire to speak, I kept quiet.

Looking at me in bewilderment, the professor said, "What are you just standing there for? Come to the podium!"

Heads kept turning in my direction until I felt as though I were going to burn up under their stares.

As the professor urged me to come forward with a gesture of his hand, I asked reluctantly, "Why?"

My question provoked quite a number of laughs, and the professor said testily, "Why? So that you can give a speech like the others!"

In a low voice that couldn't be heard beyond the last two rows of the lecture hall, I said, "I don't know how to give a speech."

Since my voice had quite naturally not reached the professor, a student sitting nearby volunteered to relay the message.

"He says he doesn't know how to give a speech!" he shouted sarcastically.

In an encouraging tone the professor said, "This is a training session, specially designed to help people who aren't good at giving speeches. Come."

So, seeing no way of escape, I moved my feet painfully and with what felt like a superhuman effort, as though I were being led to the gallows. I ascended the podium in a stupor, then stood there with my left side to the students, staring at the professor with a look that bespoke both resignation and a plea for mercy.

Seeing how ill at ease I was, the professor said kindly, "Look at your classmates, compose yourself, and speak as if you were all alone. One has to get used to these situations, since a lawyer's life is full of them. Otherwise, it's a farce. How will you stand in court tomorrow, as either a defense lawyer or as a prosecutor? Gather your courage, then deliver a speech to this audience, urging them to contribute to a particular charity."

Everyone looked at me with rapt attention the likes of which even the most eloquent orators wouldn't receive. I gazed into the faces looking at me without seeing a thing, and I was filled with such dismay and such a deadly faintness of heart I nearly swooned. I was enveloped by that acute sense of despair that grips one by the neck in nightmares, and not for a moment did it occur to me to think about the topic. I may have forgotten it entirely, and the only thing that went through my mind was the question: When will this ordeal be over?

Weary of waiting, the professor said, "Speak, and don't be afraid of making a mistake. Say whatever's on your mind."

Lord, when would this torment come to an end? It was clear that no one was going to take pity on me. On the contrary, the students had started winking at each other and cracking jokes at my expense. One of them, as if he were warning the others not to look down on me, said, "This is how Saad Zaghloul started out."

"And this is how he ended!" added another.

A third shouted, "Listen to the eloquence of silence!"

The place was filled with noisy clamor and laughter. My head spun and I started having difficulty breathing. Then, determined to put an end to the miserable situation, I left the podium and headed for the exit without paying any attention to the professor as he called me to come back. And all the while I was pursued by the demons' loud clamor as their derisive laughter rang in my ears. I went out wandering aimlessly, frantic and delirious, till I ended up at the tram stop.

Over and over I said to myself with bitter resolve, "I'll never go back, I'll never go back."

This resolve was the healing balm I needed for the wound I'd received that day. Indeed, I would never go back. They would never lay eyes on me again, and never again would I expose myself to their contemptuous grins. Besides, what was the use of going back to the Faculty of Law if a lawyer's life was full of such situations? It would be better to draw the curtain altogether on the era of academics. I'd been a slave to torment long enough. My new resolve comforted me in the face of all the humiliation and embarrassment I'd endured. In fact, it was like a breath of fresh air to my suffocating heart, and it caused me to forget my pain and bitterness. I returned home with nothing on my mind but this same determination.

After lunch, I told my mother and grandfather about the affliction I'd suffered that day.

My voice choked with tears, I said, "This is an unbearable life, and I'll never go back to the university."

Shocked by what I'd said, my grandfather rejoined, "Are you really a man? If you'd been born female, you would have made the best of girls! Do you want to quit your education when you're on the last lap just because you weren't able to say a couple of words? I swear, if your mother had been in your place, she would have delivered a speech to the people there!"

My mother began clenching her right hand, then releasing it in a kind of spasmodic motion as she said, "They envied him. O Lord, they envied him!"

My grandfather tried to talk me out of my decision, sometimes with gentle persuasion and other times with threats, but desperation had entrenched me in my obstinacy, and I wouldn't bend. When his patience had run out, he said, "So then, the whole year is a loss. There's no point in enrolling you in some other faculty when we're already more than two months into the school year."

Fearful that I might be cast once again into the educational hellhole, I said, "There's no use in my going on with my education."

Interrupting me in a pained voice, my mother cried, "Don't say that, Kamil! You *will* continue your education, whether in this institution or in another one!"

Clapping his hands together, my grandfather said, "He's lost his mind. And this is the end of the pampering!"

However, I was like someone defending himself in the face of certain destruction. Knowing I no longer had it in me to cope with lessons, examinations and other students, I cried desperately, "I can't! I can't! Have mercy on me!"

A fierce argument then broke out which I handled with a strength I hadn't known I had in me—a strength derived from fear and despair. Finally my grandfather fell silent, furious and exasperated.

After a period of enervating silence, he asked me, "Do you want to get a job with nothing but a high school diploma?"

"Yes!" I replied, without looking up.

When I stole a glance at him, he was calm, his brow was furrowed, and he was fiddling with his silver mustache. I then looked over at my mother, whose eyes were filled with tears. Even so, I felt certain that my grandfather's opposition was only half in earnest, and that if he had really wanted to break my resolve, he would have had the last word. The fact was that the matter of our future occupied his thinking a great deal during those days, especially now that he'd entered old age, and he may even have been relieved at the suggestion that he help me find work, since in this way he could set his mind at rest concerning my mother's fate.

Thus it was that my academic life drew to a close barely two months after I'd enrolled in the Faculty of Law. However, I didn't find the happiness I'd dreamed of. It's true, of course, that not for a moment did I consider going back to the cruel experience of academic life. At the same time, though, I felt an intense need to portray myself as an innocent victim, making up hollow excuses for myself for having withdrawn from the pursuit of knowledge and fled its institutions. Although this attempt of mine succeeded to some extent with others or, at least, with my mother—my true-blue friend for right or wrong—I just barely managed to convince myself. I was filled with a bitterness and discontent that triggered within me a desire to discipline and punish myself. This desire took the form of an offensive launched against myself, and I subjected myself willingly for the first time to an honest confrontation with my faults and shortcomings.

I saw my life as it was: childish, fugitive dreams, timidity and fear that put aspirations to death, and an utter self-centeredness that had doomed me to an isolation devoid of a single friend or companion and to an ignorance of the world and everything in it. There was no time and no place, no politics and no sports. As for the large metropolis in which I'd been born and raised, all I knew of it was a couple of streets, as though I'd been living in a cell in the desert. A heavy pall of gloom settled over me, and I mulled over my grief in a deadly, heartfelt loneliness. However, my mother didn't abandon me for a single moment of those dark days, nor could she bear to stand opposed to me for long. Hence, it wasn't long before she abandoned her opposition and came over to my side, pretending to be pleased and content.

One day she said to me consolingly, "The best thing lies in what God has chosen. Do we have the power to do anything for ourselves? Before long you'll become a responsible man, and it will be your turn to pamper your mother and repay some of the debt you owe her."

We spent long hours together in which I basked in her gentle, healing words. It was thanks to her alone that my ordeal passed, my heart was opened anew to life, and I ceased to labor under the weight of scruples, misgivings, and obsessive thoughts.

18

In his efforts to find me a job in the Ministry of War, my grandfather sought the good offices of a high-ranking army officer who had once worked as a petty lieutenant under his command in Sudan. And his efforts were crowned with success. However, the officer informed him that I might be appointed to Salloum. When my grandfather mentioned this, my mother's face clouded over.

"Salloum!" she cried in horror. "Don't you know that Kamil wouldn't be able to live by himself?"

She thought that Salloum was a nearby town like Zagazig, or possibly one as far away as Tanta. When she found out that it was really next to the border with Libya, she let a nervous laugh escape, thinking it was a joke.

"Find a job for him yourself!" shouted my grandfather in frustration. "Or appoint him to work in your lap and give me a break!"

However, continuing to spare no effort on my behalf, he approached old acquaintances of his who had been born in the nineteenth century and who had worked under his command many years before. They may have been touched by his venerable age and his long, active military career, not to mention the memories he stirred up in them, so they promised to do their best. And sure enough, they found me a job in the warehousing section of the Ministry of War's general administrative office. The ministry was only three tram stops and a ten-minute walk from our house. Hence, my mother approved and was visibly pleased. The justifications for the appointment were presented, and I was seen by the general medical committee in keeping with routine procedures. In short, I became an employee of the government. The feeling I had as I left home for the ministry for the first time was a complex one: it included an element of pride, as well as a sense of delight over being liberated from slavery to both home and school. At the same time, it wasn't without an element of anxiety of the sort that would come over me whenever I embarked on some new venture.

My heart aflutter, I proceeded toward the stop where I would see 'my beloved,' since as of this auspicious day, our paths had become one, if only for a few stops. Even if the job had involved this alone, it would have provided me with sufficient happiness and well-being. Taking precautions on behalf of my cowardly heart, I stood at the far end of the sidewalk lest I faint from being too close to her. A short while later she came along, striding by with that dignified but lively gait of hers, and my heart received her with a jubilant throb. I kept my gaze lowered, though I was in a state of elation that turned the world around me into a chorus of heavenly praises. The tram arrived and we boarded together. It was the first time we'd been in the same enclosed place together, and the feel of it coursed through my body like electricity. I wished the tram would keep on going forever without stopping. When I got off, I crossed the street hurriedly to the sidewalk, then looked back at the ladies' compartment, where I caught a glimpse of her back as she pored over a book she was holding. As the tram began to move again, she suddenly turned and looked behind her, and her eyes fell on me. Then she turned her back to me again. A rush of excitement went through me from head to toe. Frozen in place, my eyes clung to the tram until I could no longer make out any of its features. Then I proceeded on my way, oblivious to everything around me, intoxicated by the glance that heaven had so generously bestowed. Puzzled and amazed, I wondered:

Why did she turn around? What would have prompted her to do that? Indeed, what could possibly have prompted her to do so but my spirit's unspoken invitation? A radio picks up sound over the airwaves even from inside our homes. So what would there be to prevent someone from answering the summons of another spirit charged with amorous affection and desire? Enchanted by the thought, I jubilantly embraced the belief that my spirit had an effect on hers. But, Lord have mercy, how I'd trembled under the impact of that fleeting glance! Do you suppose she recognized me as the young man who had looked at her for a moment at the tram stop three months earlier?

By this time I was approaching the ministry, and I gradually began waking from my reverie. Then, as though I were bidding farewell to this passing moment of ecstasy, I said to myself: I love her! This is love, plain and simple.

Then I exited the world of amorous love to enter the world of government. I introduced myself to the director, who introduced me in turn to my nine office mates. This was a small number by comparison to the students I'd had to deal with. Besides, they were full-grown men, so I couldn't possibly expect them to treat me with mockery or disdain. I hoped with all my heart that I was beginning a new, rich life, and since no work had been assigned to me that day, I had some moments in which to dwell on happy thoughts. So I pondered the freedom I'd been looking forward to and which I hoped would rescue me from the prison of home and the slavery I'd known as school, as well as the enchanting look my soul had managed to wrest from the depths of the spirit by dint of its strength and potency.

Embarking on my new life full of hope, I won the first type of friendship I'd ever known in my life, namely, what they term 'office friendship.' It's a kind of compulsory friendship that's imposed on people by virtue of being coworkers in the same office. I delighted in it at first. After all, for someone like me who'd never had a friend in his entire life, it was the only way I could have responded to being in the midst of nine men who called me by name and who received me and bade me farewell in the friendliest of ways. But alas, my severe shyness stood as an impenetrable barrier between us. Then over time, experience demonstrated to me that it was a species of friendship that isn't worth grieving over. It starts in the morning with a greeting and pleasantries, but by noon it may have been transmuted into some unpleasant incident that ends with a warning or a punishment. And the worst thing of all was that I had no real work of my own to do. Rather, there wasn't a single one of them who didn't assign me to mechanical work that I would carry out in servile obedience. It wasn't unusual for them to spend most of the day chattering, smoking, and drinking coffee while I sat bent over a stack of papers in a kind of semi-slavery. Shrewd folks that they were, they'd no doubt picked up on the fact that I was inexperienced and unsure of myself, and they took advantage of my weakness in the worst possible way. So, within a month of the time I'd begun, I'd grown weary of the new life, and I concluded with a certainty that I'd gone from the frying pan into the fire.

To make matters worse, I discovered that my difficulty in keeping my mind on a task hadn't left me. I made careless errors time and time again, as a result of which I repeatedly became the object of derisive criticisms and warnings from my supervisors. It was as though I were back in school with its students and teachers. The bitterness of my past life returned to haunt me, and I concluded that I'd never know true rest as long as I had to have dealings with a single human being. However, I nursed my wounds in secret, and never once did I rebel openly against anything that made me miserable. Rather, it was my wont always to obey with a bleeding heart filled with pent-up rage.

What made my suffering even more acute was the fact that I could see no way to change my life or any hope, even a distant one, of deliverance. When I was in school, I had sometimes derived the strength to endure my misery from the hope that it would be over some day and I'd become a free, independent man. Now, by contrast, I saw nothing before me but a dreary, harsh future from which the only escape would be death. I realized that relief would elude me for the rest of my life,

103

and that I'd always be afflicted with a secret desire to flee. But where would I flee this time? The root of my misfortune lay not only in my helplessness in the face of obstacles, but also in my tendency to blow them entirely out of proportion. I'd pitted my mind against my soul in a terrible war of nerves. I'd never accustomed myself to living in reality or bearing up under its difficulties. Consequently, I knew nothing of the philosophy of being content with one's lot or making light of one's woes. Nor was I capable of living by the philosophy of power or revolution. Hence, whenever I was presented with something that was unbearable—and life in its entirety was unbearable as far as I was concerned—my sickly imagination would go and make a mountain out of a molehill. I faced difficulties with what appeared on the surface to be patient endurance. In reality, however, I would retreat within myself in a deadly state of misery and anxiety. Consequently, no place I went was without an enemy, whether real or imagined. The students and teachers had been my old enemies, and my fellow employees had become my new ones.

But she was my solace and delight! Life was a barren desert expanse, and she alone was the lush, green oasis in which the soul could find refuge. I swear to God, the only good thing about my job was the fact that its path led me to her doorstep. Every morning I would await her appearance the way one awaits the rising of the sun, and when I saw her approach with the sprightliness of a gazelle and the stateliness of a peacock, I'd retreat to the distant end of the tram stop in a near panic, asking God to calm my throbbing heart. Then I'd steal a glance at her while avoiding any direct eye contact between us, since that would have been an event of such moment that only the fittest would have been able to endure it. When the tram arrived, we would both board, though she had no idea what delight I took in its transporting us together. Then I'd get off as it took her to her unknown destination, attended by my prayers for the Lord to grant her happiness and protection. Thereafter her image would remain suspended in my mind's eye, spreading over me a blanket of warmth and intimacy in the loneliness of my new prison. But how long would I be able to go on in this state? Anguish had assailed my heart, and waiting had become a torment.

My agony was made all the worse by the fact that I'd begun seeing her in the afternoons as well as in the mornings, since I'd leave home in the late afternoon the way many other employees liked to do without objection from my mother, who could no longer protest against my doing so. I would rush to my old tram stop across from her house, then stand there with longing in my eyes, waiting to see whether my 'sunshine' would emerge over the horizon. Sometimes I'd see the mother, the father, the brother, or the sister, and other times I would see her in a simple but elegant house dress that would send tremors through me.

I could no longer see any hope for my life in anything but the prospect of an intimate companion. So I fell completely in love with her. I was possessed by a genuine, fervent desire for the happiness which, as far as I could see, would only be realized if I could lose myself in her, and she in me. Even so, I wasn't unaware of the obstacles. (Indeed, had it ever been my wont to do anything but make too much of the obstacles in my path?) I hadn't forgotten, for example, that I was still in the beginning of my career and that my salary was only seven and a half pounds a month. Then, to my dismay, I noticed that there were two other men who stood with us at the tram stop in the morning and who had a habit of regarding the girl's face with marked attention. One of them, whom I would sometimes see coming out of the same building in which the girl lived, was around forty years old and had a dignified, serious look about him. He also had the air of a distinguished employee. As for the other, he was around thirty years old, rather obese, but well-dressed and prestigious looking, and his gestures and way of looking at others gave him an air of smugness and self-satisfaction. I was surprised to find them looking at her in this way. There was no reason for surprise, of course, but I had supposed—and what a laughable supposition it was!—that I was the first person ever to have discovered this treasure. Indignant and annoyed, I found the worm of jealousy writhing in the depths of my heart. She never looked to the right or to the left. Yet I wondered: Is she really as ignorant of them as she is of me? Especially

105

of the neighbor who lived in her building? My heart shrank in alarm and despair, and I glared at her angrily as though she were responsible for people's interest in her.

Meanwhile, my life followed its familiar rhythm, divided between a loathsome job and a peculiar, uncertain love.

At that time our household would have been considered a happy one, since the hearts of those who dwelled there had no reason to fear. After all, its aging patriarch had ceased his fretting, and my mother was content with the lot that had been apportioned to me and to her.

One day, though, my grandfather said to me derisively, "Have some shame, man, and buy yourself your own bed! Do you plan to go on sleeping in your mother's arms forever?"

And in fact, I did buy myself a bed. However, I set it up in the same room—the room in which I'd come into the world—and which went on accommodating the two of us together.

19

It was a historic morning in my life when her glance fell upon me and our eyes met as she came toward the tram stop. My limbs trembled, and as I struggled with my shyness I wondered: Doesn't she remember the young man she saw on the day when she answered my spirit's invitation? I was intoxicated by an excitement that even the arrival of my two challengers couldn't dampen. The tram carried us all as far as the ministry stop. I got off and rushed to the sidewalk, then glanced back at the ladies' car. She was sitting in the last row and facing my direction, and our eyes met once again. I lowered my gaze shyly, but my heart was in bliss. As I walked briskly along, I mumbled to myself: I've been exposed!

That afternoon as I sat in my room not far from my mother, I recalled the happiness I'd known earlier in the day. Stealing a strange glance at her, I thought to myself: Ah, if she only knew my thoughts! Hadn't past experience taught me that this sort of happiness on my part was among the things she viewed as unforgivable sin? This was a fact I'd never lost sight of. Even so, it seemed at that moment to be strange and unfamiliar, as though I were discovering it for the first time. I looked over at her regal, lovely face in protest and indignation, saying to myself furiously:

It would probably be easier for her to hear that some harm had come to me than to discover that I'm in love! I may have been exaggerating, but her past comportment had robbed me of the ability to look at the bright, pleasant side of life without a heavy dose of fear and shame where she was concerned. So, weary of having to conceal my happiness in her presence, I left the house with a sigh of relief, then hurried as usual to the old tram stop. Looking ahead of me, I caught sight of the two sisters behind the windowpane, and I approached with a feeling of elation. With uncertain steps, I slipped into the crowd of people standing at the tram stop, wishing with all my heart that I didn't have to leave until night had drawn its curtains. The weather was extremely cold, and it pleased me to be enduring the harshness of the elements in return for one glance from her eyes. I was certain that my height and my black coat would be sufficient to remind her who I was. Lifting my gaze fearfully, I saw her looking my way, although, given the distance that separated us, I wasn't able to determine exactly what she was looking at. Nevertheless, a rush of delight flowed through my limbs. Although I wished it could be otherwise, the tram arrived, and bashfulness left me no choice but to get on.

My life no longer had any goal but the tram stop and the girl who lived next to it. All I could do was steal timid glances at her, then lower my gaze quickly if the eyes I'd come to love more than life itself happened to look back at me. My girl was no longer ignorant of me as she had been for the four months previous. On the contrary, she knew now that there was a young man who looked out for her wherever she went and that he did this deliberately and patiently, albeit without making a move. In fact, good fortune smiled on me so generously that I began winning a look from her nearly every day, though it seemed to be mere chance that brought it about. In other words, it would be a passing glance cast at the place as a whole and which happened to include me as part of the larger picture. Beyond this, she maintained her usual modesty and decorum. Indeed, she was no longer ignorant of me however much she happened to ignore me, and it was a glorious victory—considering my powerlessness—for her to be aware of my existence after that long, silent struggle. So I persisted in my unwearying surveillance as though I were waiting for the next step to come from her, or from the Lord of heaven and earth.

Those were sweet, happy days, even if they did happen to be devoid of hope. I lived them with a feeling of profound contentment and with dreams that couldn't be contained by mere imagination. They wafted through my heart in purity and holiness, and I was careful to keep them locked securely out of my nightly retreat into seclusion and fiendish pleasure.

After some time it became apparent to me that, despite my caution and attempts at concealment, my well-kept secret was giving itself away. I don't know how it happened. It may simply be that in moments of ardor I would forget myself, as a result of which my eye would fall on something I should have been careful not to look at. To my surprise, one day I found my two 'rivals' looking at me suspiciously, as though they realized that a new competitor had appeared on the scene. On another day, as I stood in my usual place at the tram stop, the servant girl who worked in my beloved's house passed by me and, as she did so, cast me a meaningful glance that made my heart melt on the spot. Joyfully and fearfully I wondered: Do you suppose my secret has reached the household itself? Then, feeling mortified, I muttered to myself, "Oh well, my secret's out now, and there's nothing I can do about it." One time I saw the little sister at the window as I approached the tram stop in the afternoon. When she glimpsed me, she turned and looked behind her as though she were talking to someone I couldn't see. Then the mother appeared behind the windowpane and cast me a scrutinizing glance. Lord! I felt like a criminal who'd been caught red-handed! In any case, there was no doubt that the household recognized me now, and in the days that followed this certainty was confirmed. Whenever any of them happened to look at me—with the exception of 'my lady,' of course— they would scrutinize me with intense interest. As for me, I became more and more unsettled.

Feeling a bit befuddled, I began wondering what they were saying and thinking. I had deceptively impressive appearance, and they may have thought I was some outstanding employee with a bright future ahead of me! Ahhh . . . I was an outstanding employee in my mother's eyes alone. I may have felt some regret then for having quit the university, but I consoled myself with the thought that one day I'd be inheriting a sizeable fortune. Be that as it may, I thought, that's no reason to be afraid of the people in the household. On the contrary, I felt as though it were there that my own happiness lay and I loved it with all my heart: its inhabitants, its furniture, its rooms, and even its servant. I resided there in spirit, and in my mind's eye I would carry on long, fascinating conversations with the people who lived there. As for my beloved, she filled my heart, my mind, and my imagination. If I saw the laundry hanging on the balcony, wafted to and fro by the afternoon breezes, I would gaze at it with eyes of love and affection. I'd look at its various colors and shapes, enchanted by delicate fringes that would send my heart into holy raptures as though it were feasting on the sweetness of celestial refrains. Time and time again I addressed my beloved's room, exhorting it to keep her in its care in both wakefulness and slumber, when dreams soared away with her, or when she uttered words I hadn't had the pleasure to hear.

One day I had an impulse to stay on the tram and escort my beloved to her school, though I was fearful and anxious at the thought of the risk involved. The tram got as far as al-Ataba al-Khadra, and I kept my eyes glued to the ladies' car so that I could see where my beloved got off. The tram took us across streets I'd never seen before until it crossed the Abul-Ila Bridge, and at the next stop, she got off. As I stepped onto the sidewalk, tracking her with my eyes, I saw her veer right with her towering height and her trim figure. Then she turned onto a side street that ran parallel to the mansions located along the Nile. As she turned she happened to look back and see me as I stood there looking at her. Blushing with embarrassment, I shuddered as though an electric current had gone through me. Presently she disap-peared from view, and I took a few steps forward until I was able to see the street. I saw her stepping gracefully away, and then passing through a nearby gate. I stood still for a whle, unsure what to do next, and thought of returning to the ministry, as I was late for work with no excuse. However, I couldn't bring myself to end the adventure without anything to show for it. Hence, I headed in the direction of the school with a timorous heart. As I passed hurriedly in front of it, I saw a sign that read, "The Higher Education Institute for Girls." Then I returned to the tram stop and boarded the tram heading back where I'd come from, wondering about the meaning of what I'd read. When I got to my workplace, I learned from an employee there that this was an institute that trained teachers for girls' primary schools, and that the girls who studied there enrolled in it after finishing their high school diploma. I felt proud to know that my beloved was going to be a teacher. At the same time, I wasn't unaware of the major discrepancy in our educational levels. I cursed the spinelessness that had moved me to flee from the university, and feelings of dread and dejection came over me. Consequently, I resorted again to my old counselor, the magazine, with the following question: "Is it possible for a highly educated girl to love a young man with nothing but a high school diploma?" In its reply, the magazine mentioned the princess who fell in love with the shepherd!

That night I dreamed of my beloved, and it was the first time she visited me in my sleep.

20

My aspirations revolved around two things: having a good income—which was coming eventually—and winning a bride. I to be the type that's tormented by ambition, and if I'd had any ambition at all during the dream days of the past, it had been buried in the warehousing section of the Ministry of War, where a bonus of half a pound was considered a distant hope at best. No, I wasn't moved by high-aiming ambition. However, my soul longed for happiness and peace of mind, a pleasant life, and a loving, upstanding wife. There was nothing new in my life apart from the fact that I'd begun performing the five daily prayers regularly after having neglected them from time to time. Perhaps it was my lovesickness that readied me for such unsullied communion with God five times a day. At the same time, though, my soul experienced no release from its old pain. In fact, given the moments of frenzied enjoyment that I continued to steal by night, prayer actually caused my pain to increase. I was no longer able to give it up. On the contrary, I surrendered to it more completely than ever before, yet regret had no mercy on me even for a day. There's nothing more miserable than to be tormented by regret when you're a person of faith.

It was this ongoing struggle that led me to take a long look at myself and my life. When I did so, I was appalled at first to see what a monotonous existence I led, a day of which was equal to a year, and a year equal to a day. Hadn't an entire year passed since I began work at the ministry without a single new development? A lifetime was passing by in a boring job to which I'd been doomed, and in a forlornness that was dissipated in only two circumstances: when I was at the tram stop, and in conversation with my mother at home. Even these brief moments of happiness weren't without a tinge of misery and pain. When I was with my beloved, I was haunted by the specter of my mother; and when I was my mother, I was frightened by the specter of my beloved. This generated an unsettling angst mingled with remorse, and I was enveloped by a cloud of melancholy that refused to leave me. When I think back to those days, I blame myself, not because there was no good reason for my unhappiness, but rather, due to my usual bad habit of blowing my pains and sufferings out of all proportion, and because never in my life have I faced anything with the required courage and resolution.

As for my mother, she couldn't pinpoint a reason for the glumness in me that caused her so much anxiety. I don't know how many times she said to me sorrowfully, "Why do you seem sad sometimes? For the life of me, I can't imagine what it is that you lack. You wanted to be a government employee, and you've become one. God's blessed you with loving care and concern from your grandfather, who provides a comfortable life for us. And in your service you have a mother who would gladly give you her very life if you asked her to. Not only that, but you have youth and good health, which I pray you'll enjoy for long years to come. So what do you lack?"

I was amazed that she would be asking what I lacked. It was true, of course, that she'd enumerated for me an abundance of blessings. However, the value of these blessings was lost on me. They were, to me, like the air that we breathe every moment of our lives without it ever occurring to us to be thankful for it. Instead, I thought constantly about what I lacked, blinded to what I already had by what I was bent on attaining. I seemed to have been destined not to know anything about life's true wisdom, and I'd never gone beyond the narrow confines of my own soul. And herein lay the secret of my malady. It was this that had cut me off from life's joys and pleasures and all that these entail by way of virtues, meaning, and friendship. Toward others I harbored feelings of alienation and fear. In fact, such feelings caused me to view the entire world as an enemy that lay in wait for me. It may be that the only thing that would have satisfied me would have been for the world to abandon its own concerns and devote itself to making me happy! And since it wasn't able to do that, I shunned it out of a sense of helplessness and fear and declared myself its enemy. I crawled into my shell, ignorant of the people, hopes, and virtues that filled my soul. Even in the face of love, which was the first noble sentiment ever to inspire me, I stood motionless and terrified, waiting desperately for it to make the first move.

Then came my mother's turn, albeit belatedly. I started rebelling against her, although my rebellion remained a smoldering ember that emitted no sparks. It grew out of the peculiar attitude she took toward anything that reminded her of the fact that, sooner or later, I would marry. I'd first picked up on it myself when, during one of her formal visits, my aunt spoke of her hope that I might marry her daughter, who'd become a young woman. I saw my mother receive the suggestion in such an observably bad temper that she wasn't able even to maintain the atmosphere of goodwill and courtesy that ought to prevail between two sisters, and my aunt left in a huff.

I noticed it again when a matchmaker who used to visit us during the clothes shopping seasons suggested that she find me a suitable bride. I saw my mother explode at the woman with such rage that her tongue was tied in astonishment and bewilderment.

I observed these things in horror and speechless indignation, and could find no satisfactory explanation for it. I had no desire for my maternal cousin, nor for any of the brides that the matchmaker might have chosen for me. However, what I sensed was that my mother hated the thought of my marrying at all and, fearing for my hopes, I was enraged.

One day, seemingly apprehensive in the face of my anger, she said to me, "These woman aren't interested in your happiness. They're just looking for a way to make their daughters happy!"

What she said made no sense to me, and in her eyes I discerned the hope on her part that I'd express my indifference to the matter. However, I had enough courage to remain silent.

In an anxious-sounding tone she said, "Marriage is a way of life established by God, and it won't do for someone to marry before he's a full-grown man."

And I wondered to myself resentfully: If I haven't become a full-grown man by the age of twenty-six, when will I? I wished I could say what was on my mind, but my courage failed me, and I didn't say a word.

She looked searchingly into my face, then went on uneasily, "I want you to have a bride who's truly worthy of you, one whose beauty will dazzle people's eyes, whose good morals are praised by all, who's from an aristocratic family, and who'll provide you with a sumptuous mansion to live in."

Concealing my rage, I asked, "And where is such a bride to be found?"

"We'll find her some day, God willing!" she said, biting her lip.

I said to myself: If this isn't setting me up for failure, then I don't know what is. Seething inside, I imagined her face surrounded by a halo of fury, and I thought to myself bitterly: When my mother gets angry, her beauty disappears, and the kindness seeps out of her face.

21

Marriage! Marriage! It was all I could think about anymore. I couldn't imagine my life having meaning unless this dream could be fulfilled. I thought to myself: If we don't marry, what are we living for? In fact, why were we even brought into existence? I ached for it so badly, it made my heart weep. Marriage is the paradise of those who've been afflicted by the fires of hell. Not for a moment did I stop imagining it in those wandering daydreams of mine that would absent me from my surroundings. I'd see myself next to my beloved, her comely face concealed by a silken veil embroidered with jasmine blossoms, and with candles glowing all about us. I'd see myself taking her to a dwelling at the other end of Cairo, though I didn't know why I liked for it to be at the other end of Cairo. Then I'd see her waiting for me on the balcony and, released from the prison of the warehousing section, I'd come rushing toward her. I was blessed with a happiness that transported me so thoroughly, one would have thought I could defy gravity, and which was so wondrous, I couldn't imagine it even in my dreams. However, I didn't enjoy such fantasies undisturbed, for time and time again, the euphoria produced by my imaginary joy would be followed by a vague melancholy that I couldn't explain.

Never was my mother's beloved face absent from my mind. Consequently, I'd be assailed by a shame so devastating that my forehead would be wet with perspiration, and a guilt so loathsome that my mouth would be contorted with revulsion.

There was also the fact that I hadn't rid myself entirely of a certain predilection for the single life. The love of solitude is a kind of malady. It's like a drug from which you'd like to flee, yet you can't give it up. You loathe it in yourself, yet at the same time you long for it. Would I really have the nerve to renounce my long past? At times my soul would pine for the happy married life. Then at other times I'd be possessed by the fear of losing the delight of placid solitude and the tranquility born of being exempt from responsibility. Flight from responsibility was a long-standing sickness of mine. It was such a part of me that I'd even chafe at having to shave or do my necktie. How, then, would I manage the responsibilities of a household, children, and all they'd bring with them by way of social life and its attendant obligations and traditions? The mere thought of such duties made my limbs grow cold. At the same time, though, there wasn't so much as a moment when I didn't long to be married.

I began to feel that I'd fallen prey to two deadly concerns: my indecision and my mother. And for all I knew, my mother was the only concern. Everything in me desired a peaceful haven in which to take refuge. So I made up my mind to face the danger head on, come what may.

One evening as I was sitting with my mother, I said to her suddenly, "I've noticed, Mama, that you'd rather I didn't get married. Is this so?"

Her beautiful green eyes opened wide in astonishment and I could see a flicker of uncertainty pass through them.

Then, her voice altered, she said, "I always want your happiness, and that's my main concern. If I haven't agreed in the past to the proposals made to me in this connection, it was because they fell short of what I want for you. You surely realize this. But . . . ."

She hesitated for a moment, then continued, "But . . . why are you asking me this question?"

I looked away from her as though I were afraid she might read my mind.

Then I said casually, "It was just a question. I always like to know what's going on in your mind."

Her voice trembling, she replied, "There's nothing in my mind but the desire for you to have far more happiness than you could even wish for yourself. However, marriage isn't fun and games. Take your mother's tragedy, for example, which is the most powerful evidence in favor of what I'm saying. Remember that choosing a wife is no easy task. Besides, it's the task of the mother first and foremost, since this is the area in which she has the most experience. She knows her son better than he knows himself, and she places his happiness before her own. Besides, age is an important matter, too, and you're still practically a child. So why do you ask me this question?"

(Here her voice began to tremble even more.)

"Think about your mother's tragedy, which should never be absent from your mind. What pain and torment I've been through, and what insults I've had to bear! Think of all the tears I've shed over my children, who've lived as virtual strangers to me even though we were in the same city! And even you—the possibility that I might have to part with you used to haunt me every minute, and it caused me many a sleepless night. If they'd taken you away from me, I would have died of a broken heart. How many times I've wished I could die and find rest from this worrisome life of mine. . . ."

It seemed to me that she was referring to her present life with this last comment.

"This is why I devoted myself to taking care of you and sacrificed my own happiness for your sake. And . . . ."

Here she hesitated for a moment. She may have been about to remind me of the suitor she had refused on my account, but she thought better of it.

"And don't think I'm trying to make you feel as though you owe me something. Mothers aren't like that. If only sons felt the same kind of compassion that mothers do. How easily you forget. . . . Lord! Forgive me,

118

I don't know what I'm saying. But don't think bad things about your mother. We give everything gladly, and then when our children grow up, all they think about is turning their backs on us and finding themselves some way of escape. Again, forgive me! Unfortunately, I'm not good at controlling myself. But we've had this whole lifetime together, and you're my only hope in this world. If you turn me out, I will have nowhere to go. Our children are our lives in both our youth and our old age. As for you, you love us when you're small, but when you grow up you hate us. Or, you love us when you don't have anyone else to love. What did I say? God forgive me! Forgive me, Kamil, I'm agitated. And I'm no good at talking."

I was astounded at how talking had sucked her into this downward spiral. It had been bearable at first, but then it had spun out of control. I tried to keep her from going on and on, but to no avail. Consequently, I'd had no choice but to drink the bitter potion to the dregs with all the pain and grief it brought in its wake. We exchanged a long look, with reproach coming from my end and consternation from hers. Alas, she wasn't entirely in her right mind.

"So is this what a person gets for asking an innocent question?" I asked glumly.

With tears welling up in her eyes and her glance lowered, she said, "There are times when I'm no good at talking and it would be better for me to hold my tongue. Don't worry about me. And if some day you'd like me to get out of your life, all you have to do is say the word, and you'll never see me again!"

Clapping my hand over her mouth, I shouted, "May God forgive you! That's enough talk! I made a huge mistake by asking my innocent question!"

Then she pretended to make light of the matter. In fact, she let out a long laugh as though nothing had happened, while I nursed my wounds in the privacy of my own heart. Her words had a profound impact on me. Indeed, they shook me violently, and I felt a grief the likes of which I'd never felt before. I wondered how on earth she could have allowed her agitation to get the better of her to the point of hurling such cruel accusations in my face. I wasn't without a feeling of bitterness toward her, not because she'd accused me falsely—after all, anyone could do such a thing in a moment of passing anger—but rather because she'd met my unspoken desires with an outburst that had gone beyond the limits of reason. Giving free rein to my bitterness, I thought: She remembered herself more than she should have, and she forgot me more than she should have. As was my wont, I let my own selfishness have its say by accusing her of the very same fault.

Two days after our bizarre conversation, my mother succumbed to an ailment that left her bedridden, and I stayed by her side throughout her illness except for the times I was at work. Although it wasn't serious, her face looked haggard and gaunt given her natural thinness, and it pained me no end. I couldn't bear to see her deprived of her beauty and health. Her appearance and her self-neglect pained me. She would bind her head in a scarf from beneath which strands of her unkempt, neglected, graying hair would peek out, all of which distressed me greatly and caused the whole world to look dismal to me. Then one day, as I was sitting next to her, strange thoughts—prompted possibly by fear and pity—began running through my mind in a kind of stream of consciousness. I put to myself the following dangerous question: What would life be like if this tenderhearted mother weren't a part of it? A chill went through me as the question presented itself, but my imagination refused to abandon its raving. The scenes kept passing before my eyes in succession and I surrendered to them in a heavy, wordless grief. I saw an abandoned house, and I saw myself wandering aimlessly like someone who's lost his way in a vast desert expanse. My grandfather, disgruntled and bitter, was venting his wrath on the elderly servant and the cook. As for me, I sensed my inability to carry on with this forlorn existence, so I proposed to my grandfather that I marry so that we would have someone to take care of us. I saw my beloved with her lithe physique and her endearing poise as she came to take over the household and its residents with perfect compassion and boundless love. Then I saw all of us—my grandfather, my wife, and myself— standing over the grave of someone dear and watering it with our tears. When I came to myself in a fright, I felt tears in my eyes ready to fall.

Remorse stung my heart and I was filled with resentment and rage. "Forgive me, God," I mumbled to myself, "and grant her a long life." Then I bent over and kissed her face tenderly. The memory of those fantasies haunted me frequently thereafter, leaving deep, painful scars. Even after she'd recovered and her vigor and beauty had returned, worry was my constant companion, and I nearly returned to that unwholesome way of thinking that sees life only in terms of what lies at the start and the finish—birth and death—while viewing everything in between as sheer vanity. This was the kind of thinking that had once led me to make an attempt on my own life and, if God hadn't intervened, would have been the death of me.

22

ummer had arrived, which meant—as far as my heart was concerned—that my beloved would stop going to the institute, as a result of which I'd only be able to see her on the balcony or in the window. She knew me well by now, as did everyone in her household—the young man who was constantly on the lookout for her, who gazed at her with eyes full of admiration and love, and who had persevered in doing so with astounding patience for nearly a year, yet without making a single move. And what was even more astounding was that I would catch her looking back at me from time to time, and I would go mad with delight. I could almost hear her wondering what I wanted. In fact, I could hear all of them asking themselves this same question, which made me happy and miserable at the same time. The fact is that I love you, sweetheart, with everything in me, and if you should ask why I don't make a move in your direction, the answer is that never in my life have I known how to make a move in anybody's direction. I have a mother standing behind me, as it were, and limited good fortune. So how am I to overcome these obstacles? Tell me, my love, and I'll come flying to you without wings!

It was a strange day in my life.

I began the morning with my usual ardor-filled pause and impassioned gazes outside her window, after which I went to the ministry, with bliss and desolation doing battle in my heart as they did every morning. As the employees began the day with their usual chatter, the one sitting next to me said, "I got so plastered yesterday, I didn't know which way was up!"

My interest suddenly piqued, I thought of my father. What the man had said left an impression on me that was lost on those sitting around me. And it was no wonder, since alcohol had written the history of my family and determined its destiny.

Hardly aware of what I was doing, I turned to the employee who'd spoken and asked him in a whisper, "Why do you drink?"

Realizing immediately the error I'd committed in my haste, I was flustered and embarrassed. Never in the entire time I'd worked there had I spoken to anyone in the department about anything that wasn't work-related. In fact, I was so quiet that they'd nicknamed me 'Gandhi,' because he'd been known for his custom of vowing himself to silence one day a week.

Delighted with my nosiness, the man pointed at me and said in a loud voice, "He finally spoke!"

"Who?" one of them asked as they all peered in my direction.

"Gandhi."

"And what did he say?"

"He said, 'Why do you drink?'" replied the man with a laugh.

The other said, "He keeps his mouth shut for an eternity, then when he opens it, he blasphemes!"

They all guffawed as I melted into my seat without a word. Most of them then started talking to me about alcohol and the euphoria, pleasure, and oblivion it brings, and I regretted having asked a question that had made me the butt of their jokes and sarcasm. I thought about the matter for a long time. Then, to my amazement, I woke from my reverie to find myself dying to try it myself! In the days that followed, I continued to be amazed at the uncharacteristic yearning that had come over me after twenty-six years of life on this planet, years that I'd spent in a near-ascetic existence (with the exception, of course, of the secret pleasure in which I indulged, and which subjected me to the bitterness of guilt and remorse). Had this desire really sprung up overnight? On the surface, it appeared that it was the conversation which had taken place among the employees that day that had brought it on. On the other hand, I thought, would it make sense for a scrupulous person like me to fall into temptation in response to such a passing, trivial event? Ridden by a mad impulse, I hoped the day would be over quickly so that I could knock at last on pleasure's closed door and break the chains to which I'd submitted all my life. As though it were a stranger speaking, I said to myself: Tonight I'm going to try women and wine! My resolution brought me a sense of relief, since it was certainly better than anxiety and indecision, and since I held out the hope that in this way I might find release from the terrible pressure that weighed me down. Not once all day was I plagued by hesitation—that odious companion. But when late afternoon rolled around and the tram took me to Ataba, I stood in the square feeling lost, not knowing where the pubs were. Then I saw a carriage, so I hailed its driver and got in.

In a low, diffident voice I said to him, "A pub . . . any pub, please."

The man shot me a strange stare. Then, as he stung the horses' backs with his whip, he said, "I'll take to you Alfi Bey Street, and there you can choose whichever one you like."

As the carriage set out, it reminded me of our old Victoria and its bygone glory days. In my wallet I had twenty pounds and some loose change; although my salary was modest in and of itself, I could keep the entire thing for myself, and it was enough for my needs and more. When I sensed that the carriage was nearing the longed-for destination, my heart began pounding wildly, and I was so agitated that I paid no attention to the streets down which the carriage was taking me. It came to a halt at the head of a long street in the center of which cars and carriages were parked in a long line.

Waving his whip, the driver said, "The bars are on both sides of this street."

124

After paying the driver, I got out and found myself in front of a small tavern that was no larger than a good-sized room, and whose waiters were standing at the door since it hadn't received any customers yet. I had my first twinge of hesitation and thought of going back home. I stood there ambivalently, and there came over me the feeling I'd had on the day I'd run out to the railing of al-Malik al-Salih Bridge to throw myself into the Nile. But I went in anyway. Once inside, I saw a door leading out into a small garden that took up the space outside, and in the center of which there was a fountain. It was shaded by a grape arbor, and there were tables along either side. It seemed like a safe place for someone coming there in stealth, so I went out into the garden area and sat at a table a good distance away from the entrance. My nerves were tense, but I'd stopped thinking of running away. A Nubian waiter clad in black trousers and a white jacket came up to me, smiled politely, and stood waiting for my order.

With the blood rising to my face, I said in a whisper, "Liquor!"

Not appearing to have understood, he asked in a brassy-sounding voice, "Whiskey? Cognac? Beer? Wine?"

Afflicted with the perplexity of the ignorant, I said disconcertedly, "I want liquor."

The man smiled in a way that pained me and asked, "What kind of liquor do you want? Whiskey? Cognac? Beer? Wine?"

More disconcerted than ever, I asked him, "Which kind is best?"

"That depends on what you're looking for. But the weather is hot, so beer is preferable."

Released at last from my indecision, I ordered beer. The waiter disappeared for a few minutes, then brought me a glass of something frothy and set it down in front of me.

Before he'd gone, I asked him, "How many of these does it take to make you drunk?"

After giving me the same sort of look I'd gotten earlier from the carriage driver, he said, "It differs from one person to the next. However, if you're a beginner, it's best that you not go over three."

I took hold of the glass, which was pleasingly cool. I put my nose up to it and sniffed it, and found that it had a pungent smell I didn't

125

like. However, it was too late to hesitate now. I drew my face near, dipped my tongue into it, then took a wary lick of the foam. My nerves tenser than ever by now, I lifted the glass to my lips, then downed its contents in a single gulp, contorting my face in disgust as though I were taking a dose of castor oil. Its coldness refreshed me, and I could feel it churning in my gut and giving forth a strange sort of warmth. As I sat waiting for the magical effect I'd heard so much about, a group of foreigners walked in, laughing and prattling away in some unintelligible language, and sat around a large table. I was distressed, but they didn't look my way at all, so I calmed down and went back to feeling the pleasant warmth that was spreading through my insides. The blood that was rising to my head brought a burst of this warmth to my brain, which stretched like someone receiving the sun's first morning rays as it shook off its anxiety and caution. A delicious sense of relief came over me and my features relaxed. Before long I ordered another glass with a boldness I'd never seen in myself before, and no sooner had the Nubian placed it in front of me than I lifted it to my mouth and gulped it down in two swigs. I waited again, now in a state of perfect repose and with my attention focused inside me, and a wondrous thrill surged through my body and caused me to close my eyes in surrender. It was a thrill that circulated with my blood and danced in my brain, triggering a happiness that was madness itself, and I imagined myself an ethereal creature freed from the trials of its mind, its heart, and its life. With a sense of confidence and importance I'd never experienced before, I lifted my head high in a regal gesture, astounded at this magical bliss that I'd never imagined even to exist. I raised my hand merrily and sprawled out my legs, indifferent to where they happened to land. Then all of a sudden, the image of my beloved materialized before my eyes with her willowy frame and her unswerving, demure gaze, and my heart was flooded with tender affection and longing.

Now I was shaken by an intoxication that went beyond that produced by the alcohol. How enchanting you are, darling! Now I know the secret of wine's intoxication: it's love! Love and wine's intoxication are from a single nectar that flows from deep within the spirit. After all, is a love that flourishes anything more than a prolonged intoxication? So even if I miss out on being loved by you, I won't miss out on the love that wine has to give. Why am I always afraid? Fears are nothing but illusions. If they weren't, how could they have disappeared from my horizon in the twinkling of an eye? Wisdom has been revealed to me, and never will I hesitate again. When I see my beloved I'll gesture or wave to her. She'll blush and be speechless with surprise. Then it will be her turn to be shy: a heartbeat for a heartbeat, "and whoever starts is most to blame." She'll wonder in amazement: Has he finally made a move? Indeed, my love, he has, and nothing can stop him now!

I noticed the waiter hovering around me, so I ordered a third glass and sent it down to join the first and the second. Then I went back to the image of my beloved, my body nothing but hearts and no brain.

As though I were preaching to an unseen companion, I whispered, "If you love someone, declare your affection to her, then let the chips fall where they may!" I remembered my mother, but without fear this time. I was certain that she'd love my sweetheart if she saw her, and that my old fears would be gone forever. As for my grandfather, he was sure to laugh out loud for joy when he heard the happy news. At this point I laughed out loud myself, which caused people to look my way. I cast a glance around me and noticed that the garden was packed with newcomers. Those near me laughed, but I didn't get flustered. On the contrary, I smiled at them and said with a strange sort of audacity, "Laugh!"

So they laughed, and one of them asked with a smile, "Anything else?"

Thoroughly inebriated by this time, I replied with a slur, "Bring me my sweetheart!"

"Where is she?" the young man asked. "Tell me, and I'll bring her!"

"In the house in front of the tram stop," I replied.

"Which tram stop?" he asked with a grin.

I pondered the matter for a little while until I'd thought of a landmark, then said, "The tram stop in front of the public lavatory!"

They all hooted again, then barraged me with jokes and wisecracks, and I laughed with them nonchalantly. Then I thought it best to take

127

my leave, so I called the waiter, paid him, and bade farewell to my drinking companions. As I left, they were still teasing me mercilessly. Staggering, I headed for a carriage in the parking lot. Then, sitting down self-importantly in the middle of the seat, I said to the driver in a loud slur, "To the seat of corruption!"

The carriage took off, and before long I was enjoying its sluggish movement. I began looking at the street in such merriment and delight, I wished the ride would never end. I realized I was embarking on a new experience that was no less dangerous than the one before it, and I was beset by anxiety. However, enthusiasm got the better of me again. The carriage stopped on a noisy street and the driver gestured with his whip, saying with a laugh, "Here's the original seat of corruption!"

After some hesitation I asked him, "Do you have any idea about the prices?"

"The most expensive time would be a riyal!" he said with a chuckle.

Pained by the expression despite my drunkenness, I got out of the carriage and found myself in a world ablaze with bright lights and swarming with drunks and revelers. The sounds of laughter mingled with curses and shouts, and I could hear the beating of tambourines and stale tunes coming from a worn-out fiddle or a tinny-sounding piano. Meanwhile, my nose was bombarded by the aroma of sweet-smelling incense. I couldn't bring myself to mix with the crowds of merrymakers, so I made my way to the nearest door and went in. Once inside, I found myself at the entrance to a spacious, circular courtyard onto which numerous doors opened. Around its periphery were couches and chairs occupied by men and women, and its floor was carpeted with bright yellow sand on which a half-naked woman was dancing. My liquor-induced daring seemed to have dissipated by this time, however and I froze in place, not knowing what to do. I was mesmerized by the dancer, since I was seeing dancing for the first time, and I gaped with revulsion and fear at the writhing, semi-naked body. I was equally disturbed by the state of her face, which was coated with a heavy layer of garish paint. Her lips parted to reveal gold teeth that looked like holiday candies wrapped in shiny paper.

Then suddenly there appeared before me a man wearing a striped, brightly colored tunic whose features bespoke malice and depravity. He invited me to have a seat, but I retreated from him and, as I did so, collided with someone behind me. As I turned to get away from the man, I saw a woman who was undoubtedly of the same type as the dancer, and who blocked the door with her arm. She had an offensive smile on her face and was chewing a bit of hashish, which she popped with her teeth. My limbs went cold and my heart shrank in alarm. Seeing the uncertainty and fear in my face, she let out a shrill laugh. Then in a flash, she reached out and snatched my fez, placed it on her head, and headed with swift steps toward a nearby door.

Still standing in his place, the man said to me, "Follow her and don't be afraid. This is Merry Zouzou, and there's no one like her!"

Not willing to stand there a second longer, I left the place without looking back and without giving a second thought to my lost fez. Getting in the first carriage I came to, I said to the driver, "To Manyal."

I arrived home before midnight, broken-winged and smarting with defeat, failure, and disappointment. I'd never imagined that such a bright dream could end on such a hideous note. The magical intoxication had evaporated, leaving in its wake a thick pall that drained the life out of my spirit. I don't know how, but I wakened my mother as I was undressing. She sat up in bed and looked at the alarm clock.

"You're awfully late," she mumbled with a yawn.

Making no reply, I continued undressing until my legs gave out on me and I flung myself onto the chair. I gathered my strength and got up again, but I was still unsteady on my feet, and if I hadn't grabbed hold of the bedpost, I would have fallen to the floor. My mother slipped out of bed and came toward me, her eyes wide with amazement and alarm. She looked searchingly into my face for a short while without saying a word. Then she sat me down on the chair and began undressing me herself. She lay me down to sleep on my bed, and no sooner had I hit the mattress than I fell fast asleep. And it seemed to me—or perhaps I dreamed—that my mother was sobbing.

23

The next morning I woke up unexpectedly early, and within seconds I'd remembered all the events of the day before. I looked fearfully in the direction of the other bed, and as I did so, I happened to see my mother praying. My face ablaze with chagrin, I got hurriedly out of bed and headed for the bathroom feeling altogether disoriented. When I got back to the room, I found my mother waiting and trying to appear calm. However, those limpid eyes of hers couldn't lie. Avoiding her glance, I said, "Good morning" in a near whisper.

She sighed audibly, then came up to me and, placing her hand on my shoulder, said gently but imploringly, "After my devotions, I said a long prayer specially for you, and God is the One who hears and answers. We don't have much time, so listen to me, Kamil. Listen with your heart, and not just with your ears. What's past is past. Never in my life had I imagined that you would do such a thing. However, government employees aren't the best company to keep, and they could corrupt you and lead you astray. This was a mistake that Satan lured you into, so repent of it to God. Do I need to remind you of your father's tragedy when you yourself have been a witness to it, and your mother one of its victims? Even so, my heart is at peace in spite of what happened.

After all, you're a believer who fears God, and you're your mother's son, not your father's. Someone like you who comes before God in prayer five times a day is sure to do all he can to come into His presence in a state of reverence and purity. Don't forget that yesterday's error was a great evil and that it will go on being like a knife that cuts me to the quick. Alas, I'm no longer able to keep you by my side. So when you go out into the world, meet it with the heart of a person of faith who's conscious of God at all times. You'll go to Lady Umm Hashim's shrine today to offer God your repentance with her help."

My eyes didn't meet hers once that morning, and I went to the ministry grieved. I recalled what she'd said word by word and pondered it thoroughly. I was dismayed that I'd allowed her to discover what I'd done, and I realized what a terrible shock it had been to my poor mother. I remembered the disillusionment I'd suffered in the courtyard of that strange house, and my lips curled in revulsion. At the same time, though, I hadn't forgotten the rapturous bliss that had come with drinking. I hadn't forgotten it despite the hangover, the fatigue, and the scandal it had left in its wake. Even after performing the ritual dawn prayer in all sincerity and faith, I couldn't find it in me to hate it. It wasn't that my conscience was at peace (when had it ever been at peace?), but dreams of that enchanting intoxication swept over me, overruling my conscience, my sufferings, and my mother. The meaning of happiness and contentment had been doomed to remain beyond my reach until that intoxication flowed in my blood, opening its heavenly portals before me. This was what I'd been looking for. God! How could I possibly give it up and ask forgiveness for it? What would remain to me after this but unspoken longing, mortal affliction, and anxiety that would tear me limb from limb? Of course, even if I succumbed to its allure, it couldn't possibly yield undisturbed repose. On the contrary, it would add one more struggle to my conscience that I could well do without. I was already in a constant tug-of-war: between taking the world by the horns and shying away from it, between my sweetheart and my mother, and between addiction to my infernal habit and the desire to give it up. Now I faced a new struggle between my desire for

131

alcohol and the need to repent of it, and it burdened me to the point where I turned into a pendulum in constant motion being pulled one way by demons, and the other way by angels. Angst took such a toll on me that I groaned in distress, wondering: Why didn't God create life as pure ecstasy that lasts from one generation to the next? Why can't we attain happiness without suffering and anguish? Why does love suffocate in our hearts from despair, and why does our beloved come and go, unaware of our existence even though she's just a kiss away?

Come what may, I concluded, alcohol is the key to deliverance. It was the embodiment of consolation, the password that opened the door that would lead to my beloved. I didn't want the world so long as it refused to change itself. My loathing for reality was no less than my loathing for that hideous dancer. In fact, the world itself had been revealed to me in a form similar to that dancer in her writhing and twisting, her phony exterior, and her hidden wretchedness. Why, then, should I resist the allure of this magical intoxication?

That afternoon my mother invited me to visit Umm Hashim's shrine with her, so we went out together. It was the first time I'd been out with her in years. We got into a carriage and sat side by side in a way that brought back memories for both of us of the old Victoria, and her gentleness eased the anxiety that had seized me. My mother was wearing a light summer coat that complimented the loveliness of her slender frame. Her comely face looked placid and acquiescent, and in her limpid green eyes she had a dreamy look tinged with melancholy. Her head was swathed in a black veil that framed her face with a solemnity that revealed traces of the fifty-four years she'd spent thus far of the lifetime apportioned to her. Tender affection for her welled up in my heart and I wished I could kiss her. I thought with profound sorrow about her gradual advance toward old age. Then I remembered the treacherous thoughts that had gone through my head when she'd been bedridden, and I bit my lip furiously. What despicable thoughts they'd been! They'd sprung from the depths of the ache that I sought to escape by any means. However, my emotional agony was mitigated by what I imagined she would inherit from my grandfather, who was nearly ninety years old.

At that moment it would have seemed an enormity to disobey her. At the same time, I sensed in my heart of hearts that I was about to offer a sham repentance to which I had no choice but submit, and it grieved me. How would I come before Umm Hashim with this perfidious heart of mine when nothing could be hidden from her? How could I have been transformed overnight from a good-hearted, devout soul into a rascal enamored of waywardness? We arrived at last at the mosque and entered reciting the Fatiha, and as we made our way toward the tomb, my heart was a mix of love, faith, and fear. Memories of days gone by wafted over my heart—memories of when I would come into the sacred mosque with a happy heart that had yet to suffer a sense of guilt and a tormented conscience. My mother went before me into the sacred place whispering fervently, "Umm Hashim, I've brought Kamil to you to repent of his error, so bless him and guide his steps!" Then she nudged me in the direction of the tomb. I placed my open hand on it and felt a coolness flow into my heart. I stood there silently for quite some time in the presence of a majesty that causes hearts to grow humble and reverent. I imagined the holy tomb to be gazing at me with glistening eyes that hadn't been changed by death, and I called upon Umm Hashim from my heart to inspire me with right understanding, to deliver me from my confusion and misery, and to accept my repentance. Then, after a moment's hesitation, I asked her to watch over my wretched love with her merciful eye.

As we took our leave of the sacred resting place, my mother dried her eyes.

"Have you repented to God?" she asked me.

"Yes," I replied without looking at her.

"I hope it was a sincere repentance," she murmured.

24

I wasn't able to resist the new urge. Nothing could stand in the face of it, and not my conscience, my repentance, or my inborn fear of God did me a bit of good. I felt hopeless about my life: my job was truly abominable, my love life was one long sigh of discontent, and the days passed heavily without consolation or hope. My eyes would behold and my heart would beat, but my will was incapacitated by weakness and fear. Alcohol-induced euphoria was my only consolation, and I gave myself over to it heart and soul. This miserable consolation was short-lived, however, and fate wasn't favorably disposed to my enjoyment of it.

One Friday in the early autumn of that year, my mother and I sat talking as usual. The doorbell rang and the servant opened the door, then came and summoned me to meet a certain 'bey.' I went to the door right away and found a distinguished-looking man who must have been sixty or seventy years old. After a courteous greeting, I looked at him questioningly.

"Are you Kamil Effendi?" he asked.

"I'm Kamil Ru'ba," I replied as I looked searchingly into his face.

"This is the house of Colonel Abdulla Bey Hasan."

Taking me by the hand, he led me outside, then leaned toward me and said, "May God grant you length of days. Your grandfather has died, son."

I stared into his face in shock, too tongue-tied to respond.

Patting me on the shoulder, he said sorrowfully, "Be brave for your mother's sake, son, and be the man we know you can be. Your grandfather was sitting with us at the Luna Park Café the way he did every morning. He got short of breath and asked for a glass of water. A few minutes later his head fell onto the table and we thought he'd fainted, but then it became clear that he'd gone to be with his Maker."

"Where is he now, sir?" I cried hoarsely.

"We've brought him with us in a car," he said softly.

No sooner had the man spoken than I saw four men at the bottom of the staircase carrying my grandfather. As they slowly and cautiously ascended the stairs, I rushed toward them in a daze. With trembling limbs, I helped them carry him the rest of the way and we brought him into the flat. I saw my mother at the other end of the living room as she screamed in alarm. Rushing toward us, unfazed by the presence of strangers, she asked us apprehensively, "What's wrong with him? What's wrong with him?"

However, she heard no reply. Or rather, in the silence she heard a reply.

Then she let out a loud shriek.

"Baba! Baba!" she wailed in lament.

We laid him down on the bed, after which the men came up to him one after another and kissed him on the forehead. They extended their condolences to my mother, then withdrew silently from the room. Some of them asked me if I needed anything, and I thanked them. Then the man whom I'd met at the door volunteered to tell me about the usual procedures in such situations. He told me he would inform the Ministry of War and that it would be preferable for the funeral to take place at ten o'clock the next morning. I rushed back to my grandfather's bedroom, where I found my mother in bitter tears, and I broke into tears with her. However, she wouldn't allow me to stay in the room.

135

In order to distract me from my grief, she instructed me to inform my maternal aunt and my brother by telegram, and to deliver the news to my sister. I left the house to carry out these duties, then came back accompanied by my sister Radiya and her husband. Radiya's husband was the best of helpers in taking care of the necessary procedures, or rather, he took care of them himself, while I contented myself with tagging along in a daze.

No sooner had darkness fallen than the house was filled with family members. My maternal aunt and her husband came, as did my brother Medhat, his wife, and my paternal uncle. The only person who didn't come was my father. When Medhat informed him of my grandfather's death, he said, "May the remainder of his days be added to yours. Please convey my condolences to your mother, your brother, and your sister, since I don't attend funerals or weddings."

Of all the family, my mother was the most grief-stricken by my grandfather's loss. After all, she'd never been apart from him in her entire life, the only exception being the three months she'd spent grudgingly in my father's house.

And that's how my grandfather died. He'd enjoyed a long life and hadn't been debilitated by old age or illness. He passed away in his cozy perch at the coffee shop surrounded by his loyal, loving friends, and with an ease only rarely enjoyed by those who depart from this life. Whenever he came to mind, I would bow my head in reverence for his memory, calling down God's mercy and forgiveness upon his great soul. He was my grandfather, and he was my father. He was the wing of compassion that had sheltered me, and beneath that wing I'd enjoyed a life of abundant provision. I hadn't forgotten that once, during certain dark hours of my life, I'd accused him of having raised me badly, or of having allowed my mother to ruin my life with her coddling. But when I reflected on the matter, I couldn't help but excuse him, since I'd come into the world when he was over sixty years old. Besides, it's a very difficult thing indeed to know one's grandfather as he really is. In general, grandfathers appear surrounded by a halo of veneration and sanctity due to the fact that the family members who preserve their histories tend to be among those who hallow and revere them. However, even based on what I myself had observed of his life, I could praise him to the skies. His good health, his love for order and military precision—though without being harsh or overly strict—had always been things I admired intensely, and his tender solicitude toward us had softened the blow of many an affliction. Suffice it to say that I never tasted life's bitterness until we'd escorted my grandfather to his final resting place. No matter how long I live, the image of him during his final days will never be erased from my mind: old age had crowned him with a head of snow-white hair, bestowing upon him an air of dignity and splendor and causing his green eyes to twinkle with humor and compassion. I wasn't surprised at his friends' grief over him, and I realized—although I may have missed it myself—that he was one of those people who love and are loved in return, who know others intimately and who are known intimately in return. It was a God-given aptitude of which I'd been deprived, and which I've longed for all my life.

His funeral was scheduled for ten o'clock in the morning, and when it came time for the inevitable leave-taking, the balcony was filled with weeping women and the cannons were fired in a salute to his tomb. His bier was borne atop a cannon in front of which a military band marched. As he disappeared into the grave, I cast his body a parting glance and sobbed like a little boy.

25

"All we have is God," she said to me sorrowfully. Experiencing a kind of fear I wasn't familiar with, I said, "He's the best Protector and Helper of all."

The facts then began making themselves clear to me. I learned that my grandfather's pension was cut off when he died. I figured up how much his bequest came to and found that he'd left four hundred pounds in the bank. Since my mother and my maternal aunt were his sole heirs, each of them had been allotted two hundred pounds, which was now all we had apart from my paltry income. Thus, I'd become the head of a household, a fact to which my paternal uncle drew my attention as he bade me farewell. Then, reiterating his condolences, he instructed me to take good care of my mother, saying, "Honor your mother to the best of your ability. You're the head of the household now, and you're your grandfather's successor!"

I received his words with fear and gloom, and looked to the unknown future with unspoken apprehension and resentment. It pained me to find myself responsible for someone else—I who'd grown accustomed to having someone else be responsible for me. When those who'd come to offer their condolences had gone their way and the house was empty again, my mother and I sat alone discussing matters.

"Lord help us!" she said in a tone of distress.

Full of fear and melancholy myself, I looked up at her uncertainly and asked, "What do you think, Mama?"

"Life won't be easy the way it has been for us," she said dolefully. "But this is God's decree, so we have to submit to His will and be patient and thankful. I hate to be a burden to you, but what can I do?"

"Don't say that," I rejoined fervently. "You're all I have left in the world, and if it weren't for you, I wouldn't have anywhere to call home."

Her lips parted in a mournful smile and she uttered a long prayer of supplication for me.

Then she said, "The little bit of money I've inherited will be at your disposal. You can make use of it when the need arises until your salary increases."

As she gazed steadily into my face with her mournful eyes, I took refuge in a pensive silence.

Then she went on, saying, "This house isn't suitable for us anymore. As you can see, it's large, and the rent is equal to your salary. Maybe we can find a small flat in the neighborhood for just a hundred fifty piasters."

Silence reigned again, and I began wondering what had blinded me to this eventuality, which I surely could have anticipated.

Then my mother said in a low voice, "We'll have to let the servants go. In the future all we'll need is one young servant."

The distress I felt was so overwhelming, I didn't know how my heart would bear it.

I knew nothing whatsoever about the struggle people go through to survive. Eyeing my mother with a look that was tantamount to a cry for help, I asked, "What do you estimate our living expenses to be, including rent, food, a servant, and so on?"

She sat thinking for some time. Then she said softly, "They'll come to at least six pounds."

Then, as if to mitigate the impact of what she'd said, she added, "I'll set aside my money for clothing and whatever we need beyond daily expenses."

But I paid no attention. Instead, I began thinking about what I'd have left of my salary once we'd covered living expenses, namely, one and a half pounds, how much of that would go toward transportation, and how much I'd have left to spend on entertainment for myself. My thoughts were filled with bitterness and gloom, and my heart shrank in loathing from this ridiculous, meaningless life. Hadn't I been spending my entire salary on food, drink, and carriages? And hadn't I, in spite of this, been irritable, unhappy, and full of complaints? Lord! The past had been an era of undeniable ease and comfort, but I'd only woken up to what a blessing it had been now that nothing was left of it but memories. I'd been blind, of that there could be no doubt. I'd been blinded to what I had by frivolous dreams, and people like me are doomed never to know happiness in this life. The whole world looked gloomy in my eyes, my sense of purpose began to fade, and I was filled with such pessimism that I expected evil to come from every step I took. After all, might not the government dispense with my services for one reason or another, thereby depriving me even of the meager salary I now earned? Might I not have a road accident that would leave me handicapped and unable to work for a living? Why were we put on earth in the first place?

It may have been black thoughts like these that led me to ask my mother, "What am I expected to inherit from my father when he dies?"

Not pleased with my thoughts, she replied indignantly, "Don't build your hopes in life on someone's death. How long people live is in God's hands, and I beg you to get these thoughts out of your head."

However, making light of her fears, I pressed her to answer my question.

Yielding to my persistence, she said, "Your father has family endowments that bring him an income of forty pounds a month. That's in addition to the house he lives in."

Through some simple calculations I estimated that my share of the house would come to sixteen pounds a month. If this were added to my meager salary, it would amount to quite a bit, and as usual, I gave myself over to dreaming. However, my dreams didn't do a thing to change reality.

"How old is my father?" I asked her.

"He's at least seventy," she replied grudgingly.

Would he live a long life the way my grandfather had? I wondered. What state would I be in if he lived a long life and deprived me of my inheritance for the next ten to twenty years? I recalled what I'd been told about how he'd once been anxiously awaiting his own father's death, and how anxiety over his future had led him to attempt the crime that doomed him to be deprived of a vast fortune. I was suffering the same feelings he'd suffered thirty years earlier, and perhaps if I'd had some of his pluck, I would have gone the same route he had.

My mother summoned the elderly cook and Umm Zaynab. Then, sorrowful and ashamed, she informed them that we'd be moving to my brother's house (she preferred to lie rather than admit to poverty) and that she would have to dispense with their services. She expressed her regret for having to bring their long term of service to an end, commended them highly, and prayed for their future success. Then she presented them both with something to tide them over until they could find other work. Umm Zaynab burst into sobs and the old man's eyes welled up with tears as he called down God's mercy and forgiveness on my grandfather.

Then he said earnestly, "Madame, I would rather have died before this noble household closed its doors."

Unable to contain her emotions, my mother cried and, infected by her sorrow, I cried too. I was going through a time of pain and ignominy the likes of which I'd never felt before. Before the month was out we'd moved into a small flat on the second floor of an old three-story house on Qasim Street just off Manyal Street. The house was located halfway between Manyal Street and the Nile. As for the flat, it consisted of three small rooms that we fitted out with some of our old furniture, the rest of which we sold for a pittance. I wondered apprehensively: Will my mother be able to handle the burdens of household service after a lifetime of leisure and comfort? She was approaching her mid-sixties, and all the domestic help she had left was a young servant. How would she endure this new life? As for me, my existence was growing all the more troubled, and I was bitter and angry at everything. Even so, my mother took to her new domestic chores with such gusto that she succeeded in making me believe that she was happy with our new life, as though all her days she'd been suppressing a fervent desire to labor and be of service.

With a satisfaction that I could sense in her tone of voice and the smile in her eyes, she said, "There's no greater happiness for me than to serve your household."

I drank in the new life drop by drop—this life that had added a new longing to my old ones, namely, the longing to return to the life of ease and, in particular, to drinking. I made up my mind to stint myself enough to be able to afford to get drunk even just once a month. And it's no wonder, since to me, liquor wasn't mere amusement and frivolity. Rather, it was an imaginary existence into whose arms I would flee from the pain of odious reality.

One day when my mother sensed that I was receptive to what she had to say, she commented, "Perhaps you realize now why I've refused any marriage that wouldn't be fitting for you."

I understood immediately what she meant. It was as if she were saying, "What would you have done with your life if you'd been the head of a family!"

I didn't doubt for a moment the accuracy of her observation. For truly, if I'd been the head of a family, I would have been several times more miserable in life than I was at present. Even so, I didn't like what she'd said. To my broken spirit, her words sounded like a gleeful 'I told you so.' Consequently, I was gripped with bitterness and anger, and it was only with great difficulty that I kept my emotions in check.

26

nother autumn rolled around. Autumn was the season I loved, since it heralded the opening of the schools, which meant that my beloved would return to our usual meeting place at the tram stop. My beloved was the only flower that bloomed in the autumn, when trees were stripped bare of their leaves and flowers withered and faded. I noticed that the times when she left the house weren't regular the way they had been before. Was it possible she'd begun her life as a teacher? The thought gave me pleasure, and my body trembled with joy. At the same time, though, I couldn't forget that the course of my life had changed and that I was languishing under the burden of poverty and despair. Consequently, my beloved was a lost cause. But hopelessness only caused me to fall more passionately in love, kindling grievous longings in my heart. How quickly an impossible love turns into an uprising against life! Isn't it a kind of mockery that we should be created for a certain life, only to be prevented from living it? And what made me even more lovesick was that there were many times when I imagined her eyes to be casting me a look filled with life. What life? I didn't know, but it was sufficient to drive my imagination wild. One such look would inebriate me with a magical intoxication that would stay with me until I was shocked awake again by some bitter reality in my life.

Meanwhile, the people in her household had begun scrutinizing me with such intensity that I could almost hear them wondering aloud: What do you want? Why do you devour her with your eyes? What kind of a man are you? Isn't a year and a half enough for you? You're right, by God. You're absolutely right. But what can I do? Put yourselves in my place, and tell me what you'd do. Do you have a solution to help-lessness and indigence?

My girl's two other admirers gave me no rest. On the contrary, they kept hovering about her until I'd come to fear them as much as I feared helplessness and poverty, and until I loathed them as much as I loathed the wretchedness that was tightening the noose around my neck. The most enjoyable thing about this sort of life was running away from it. As a result, I found a way to get to the pub no matter what it took. Alfi Bey Street wasn't a suitable haunt for me anymore. Hence, I sought assistance from my carriage driver—my number two advisor on worldly affairs after my mother. I asked him to take me to a modest sort of pub, and where should the man take me but the vegetable market! He himself, or so he told me, used to go there from time to time, and as evidence of the appropriateness of his choice, he said to me, "The big pubs are just showy places that steal people's money. But booze is booze, and the best booze is the type that gets you drunk for the cheapest price!"

I listened to his lecture in a state of pained embarrassment that was echoed by a profound sorrow in my soul, as though he was lamenting my end and consoling me over the loss of times gone by. Taking my leave of him hurriedly, I proceeded in the direction of a small pub at the head of one of the side streets leading to the market. As I did so, I got the distressing feeling that I was descending into the abyss that had swallowed up my father before me. However, neither this nor anything else was going to stop me from doing what I was destined to do.

The run-down, dingy-looking pub was a small, square-shaped place with just a few tables in it. Its waiter was an old, bleary-eyed

Greek, and its clientele were lower-class folk and some down-and-out government employees. But, as the carriage driver had said, booze is booze, and I can't deny that I brightened at the sight of the bottles that lined the long shelf. In fact, I was so happy to see them, I forgot the sting of the lowliness to which penury had bound me. I also saw a new type of container for liquor. A carafe of cognac sold for ten piasters, a price so negligible that I'd be able to come to the pub twice a month or more. I drank and yielded to wandering dreams in longing and delight. Then coincidence supplied me with new fuel for my dreams when I was approached by a man peddling lottery tickets. "A thousand pounds!" he cried as he waved a piece of paper at me. I reached out and took it from him, paid him for it, then folded it up and slipped it into my pocket. Indeed, new fuel for dreams on a par with liquor's intoxication. Lord! What would the world be without dreams! I was now the exclusive owner of a thousand pounds! The earth was solid under my feet, unshaken by fear and poverty. The world was smiling, and it was sure to laugh out loud if my father bit the dust! From now on it wouldn't do to hesitate. I'd meet my sweetheart's venerable father and tell him straight from the shoulder, "I'd like the honor of being your in-law." Then I'd give him my card. After all, I thought, who doesn't know the Laz family? It's true, of course, that my job is a humble one, but I own a sizable fortune, and I'll be inheriting another one as well. The man would have no choice but to welcome me. I saw myself being escorted down a candle-lined aisle, my bride promenading alongside me like the moon.

I couldn't bear to stay any longer once I'd downed the carafe's contents, so I left the pub and went wandering aimlessly through the streets, looking about me dreamy-eyed and pleased with myself and the world. I wouldn't go home until I'd sobered up again. However, before the intoxication had worn off completely, I found myself in front of my beloved's house, so I didn't head for Manyal. It was nearly two in the morning. The deserted street was enveloped in thick darkness, and there was a silence so deep you could almost have heard the thoughts going through someone's head. I stood on the sidewalk looking at the sleeping household. My gaze settled on her bedroom window, my spirit slipped through it, and I imagined myself feeling her rhythmic, fragrant breaths. My faith in the spirit knew no bounds. After all, hadn't it drawn her glance my way in the past? If so, then it could insinuate itself into her dreams and cause her to see me, and even to hear me if I called out to her.

So I spoke to her, saying, "I love you, my life! I love you with a love that's no less a wonder of the universe than the rotation of the heavenly bodies in their orbits. How I long to say, 'I love you' when I'm sober, but I can't. Shyness is dumb, my love, and poverty is a high-walled prison. Someone who owns no more than a pound and a half of his monthly salary has no right to declare his love to a precious angel like you. Yet in spite of it all, I love you, and I can't bear for you to spurn my affection. I nearly go mad when I see those two nasty men looking at you. So encourage me, my darling. Make some gesture toward me. Smile in my face. There's nothing wrong with your doing that as long as I'm sincere in my love for you (as you surely know me to be), and as long as I'm helpless and hopeless, as you also, no doubt, realize. . . . Ahh!"

I stood there for a long time without taking my eyes off the closed window. Eventually my eyelids grew heavy and I was overcome by a feeling of dizziness and fatigue from my hangover and the strain of walking. Then suddenly I heard the sound of heavy footsteps. Turning fearfully in their direction, I saw the shadow of a policeman approaching. So I stepped back from where I'd been standing and went quickly on my way.

27

What was standing between my beloved and me? Poverty. I could see no other answer to my question, since it was the only obstacle I couldn't be considered responsible for. At least, this was what I believed. How could I get money, then? I pondered the matter glumly. Then where should my thoughts take me but to my father! This was the person whose death I'd long wished for, but wishing had gotten me nowhere. So why not visit him? Why not ask him for the money I needed? The thought seemed bizarre, unbelievable, especially for me, who feared him more than anyone else. Never in my life had I expected anything from him. However, during those days anxiety and fear were taking me to the limits of my endurance, love ran in my blood, and I had a growing, increasingly dismal sense of life having passed me by. I feared that if I got to be thirty years old without marrying, I'd be a goner. Such worries tormented me, and the sweet glances bestowed on me by my beloved brought with them both happiness and a silent rebuke. So in the end I felt I had no choice but to think seriously of visiting my father.

I went without announcing my intention to my mother, and I found my way to Hilmiya with the help of the tram conductor. When

I reached Ali Mubarak Street, I recalled immediately the way I'd come with my grandfather nine years earlier. I glimpsed the large house with the tall treetops looming up behind the wall that surrounded it. I also saw the gatekeeper, so aged now that he was little more than a black specter, sitting in front of the gate. But when I was two steps away from him, my courage failed me, and instead of turning to go in, I kept on walking. Gripped by a sense of futility, I told myself to go back where I'd come from. After all, what was the use of making an attempt that was doomed to failure! I didn't flee far, however, and perhaps it was despair itself that shored me up with an unanticipated strength. Hence, I headed back toward the gatekeeper with renewed determination, reproaching myself for the weakness of will that would deign to come between me and a house to which I had an undeniable right. I hailed the gatekeeper, and he returned my greeting without rising to his feet.

In a tone not altogether lacking in self-importance, I said to him, "Kamil Ru'ba Laz. Inform the bey, please."

The gatekeeper rose with a smile and invited me into the garden, then left to announce me to the bey. It was the same garden, still redolent with the fragrance of lemon, still roofed with date palm crowns, and still able to infect one's soul with a sense of melancholy and forlornness. I looked toward the veranda at the end of the garden and saw the gatekeeper beckoning to me, so I came forward, fighting off my tension. As I ascended the steps, I was met with the familiar scene: the man, the ornamented coffee table, the long-necked bottle, and the glass. He extended his hand with a half-smile on his face, and I greeted him. Then he invited me to have a seat, so I sat down on a chair to the right of the coffee table. Casting him a quick glance, I saw that his portly body had grown flaccid and that his full face had grown more bloodshot. His eyes had an absent, dazed look about them, while old age had etched furrows across his forehead and around his eyes and left his cheeks looking withered and limp.

I wasn't pleased by his appearance. However, I made sure that nothing of what I was feeling showed on my face. I looked strangely at the half-full bottle. As I recalled how it had looked to me during the first visit, I said to myself: How quickly corruption finds its way into a person's heart! He was wrapped in a silk robe to ward off the autumn dampness that would descend at that time of the afternoon, and I was certain that he was up to the gills in liquor. I felt worried, wondering what sort of madness had moved me to undertake such a futile visit. He began looking over at me with interest, or perhaps it was just curiosity. Amazed at this peculiar encounter between father and son after a lifetime of separation, I wondered in bewilderment and disbelief what's said about the love between parents and children.

Quite naturally, I didn't know how to begin the conversation. However, he saved me from my dilemma by starting to talk first.

In a thick voice he said, "So, how are you? Your grandfather has died. He was a nice man, and I have pleasant enough memories of him in spite of the things that happened. I didn't attend his funeral, which many would consider unforgivable. But someone my age should be exempted from obligations. The same thing applies to both the elderly and children in that respect. Don't forget, though, that nobody's expected to attend my funeral—except, perhaps, Uncle Adam the gatekeeper. And it isn't unlikely that he himself will be too busy searching my pockets and stealing whatever money he thinks he'll find there. Will *you* attend my funeral?

His question took me by surprise after an anxiety that had gripped me in response to his drunken tone of voice, and I could see that the task before me was going to be arduous and fearsome.

Nevertheless, I said to him, "May God grant you a long life."

He guffawed, and I saw that he'd lost his molars. I was offended by both his appearance and his laugh.

Then he went on, saying, "What a loyal son you are! It's a lovely thing indeed for you to love your father and pray for him to have a long life! Kindness to one's father is a virtue I didn't have much of myself, unfortunately, and if I'd been a bit hypocritical or a bit more patient, I'd now be among the country's well-known and well-to-do—like your paternal uncle, damn him. Have you noticed how he wasn't content with the money he'd inherited (may God preserve it!)? No, he had to

149

monopolize your brother Medhat, too—that bull—and marry him to his daughter! I used to think he'd be the divorcing kind like his father, but he seems like the type that bows and scrapes for women. And now he's turned into a peasant farmer who lives the same sort of life his flocks do. He may be dreaming of a vast fortune after his uncle dies, but he'll be disappointed. After all, his wife has six sisters, and every one of them would be considered a great catch for some stud enamored of money and women. That's why I say it's a miserable thing to have daughters. It's a huge shame, no matter what they say about how marriage is half the religion. Unless, of course, the other half is divorce!"

Then, changing his tone, he continued, "Why don't you propose to one of your paternal cousins? Don't you know that every one of them is due to receive an inheritance of at least a hundred pounds a month? But enough of all this. Let me look at your face a bit, since I hardly recognize you. My, my, what a fine young man you are. All you lack is a mustache. Why haven't you grown one? Besides, you're handsome. But you're thin and pale, as though you don't get enough to eat. It's a shame for a young man your age to be skinny. Even so, it makes a father happy beyond words to see his son a man, and especially if he's only seeing him for the first or second time. Don't you think I'm an extraordinary father? I've got three children, yet I'm abandoned and alone. But I'm not bitter about my luck, since it's a happy thing to be alone. Not once have I ever spent time with anyone but that we've parted as enemies. They usually say I'm at fault, and I say they're at fault. In any case, God will judge between us on the Day of Resurrection. Now, don't be surprised if you hear me quoting from the Qur'an. That's thanks to the radio. I've distanced myself from the world, but the world insists on invading my house through the radio. Welcome, welcome! You're a loyal son, Kamil. But you should take care of your health and eat enough so that you can put on some weight. Didn't your grandfather leave a fortune?"

I was apprehensive and discouraged, not knowing how to broach the subject I'd come to speak about in the wake of all this wild prattle. And my apprehension and misery intensified when, during his harangue, I saw him filling the glass again. However, taking advantage of the opportunity afforded by his last question, I said definitively, "My grandfather didn't leave anything at all."

He nodded his flushed bald head as if to say, "That's what I'd expected."

Then he said, "A high salary, few dependents, and a huge pension. And then he doesn't leave anything. He was a gambler, God have mercy on him, and the gambler prefers to lose his cash at the table rather than save it up in the bank. Deep down he was nothing but a child who loved to play. And I don't blame him, since I for my part am a drunkard. The difference between the gambler and the drunkard is that the former is a practical man who speculates, cheats, wins, and loses, whereas the latter is the theoretical type who dreams and dreams and dreams. If the gambler aspires to wealth, he gambles with his fortune by playing, then usually loses it. He consoles himself with the hope of recouping his loss, but all he does is lose more and more until, when he dies, he leaves nothing but a heavy debt. And the strange thing about it is that all gamblers lose, so I don't know who wins! As for the drunkard, if he aspires to wealth, he finds it ready and waiting for him without it costing him more than thirty piasters, namely, the price of a bottle like this one. Do you say it's just an illusion? So be it. Is there anything in this world that isn't an illusion and a fantasy? Where's your grandfather? He was a concrete reality, but where is he now? Roll up your sleeves and look for him, but you won't find a trace of him. Look for him in the house, at the coffee shop, at the casino. Look for him in the grave itself, and I bet you my life that you'll find neither hide nor hair of him. So how could he have been real? God have mercy on him! And what have you all done since he died? Are you still a student?"

Concealing my rage and distress behind a wan smile, I said, "I got a job at the Ministry of War."

He raised his glass with a chuckle, saying, "To your future! Well done! Our family is an illustrious one, but we haven't had a single government employee. So you're the one blazing a path for us into government circles!"

Feeling cornered, I said wearily, "I'm just a petty employee, and I don't get a salary worth mentioning."

He shot me a wary look from beneath his gray eyebrows, then said indifferently, "Don't worry. A child always grows up. The wisdom of the world decrees that children grow up and that adults turn back into children. It seems that God created a single limited fortune that neither increases nor decreases. However, people's shares in it may change. Otherwise, everyone would get rich. So be patient, son, and don't busy yourself thinking about money. Thinking about money is a perilous thing that was nearly the death of me once. I find it amazing that people love money the way they do. At present I'm not a lover of money. The only thing I love is liquor. If everyone loved liquor the way I do and made light of money, the world's problems could be solved with a single word. Imagine with me a happy town. They divide it down the middle, then build houses on the right, pubs on the left, and government buildings in the center. And people's sole duty is to drink. Now that's a town that lives and lets live. Won't you have some, son? No? So what vices have you taken up? A man's true value consists in the evil he does. Suppose I died tomorrow and hadn't been a drunkard. What might people say about me? Nothing! However, being what I am, they're sure to say, 'He was a drunkard!' In fact, even if I gave this money of mine away in charity, no one would say a word about me. People forget good things quickly, even if they're the ones who did them. The only thing that immortalizes you is evil. What do you say?"

Having no choice but to reply, I said, "We should fear God and obey Him."

He affirmed what I'd said with a feeble-looking nod of his round head.

"Right you are!" he continued. "That's the secret of existence. However, if what they say about God is really true, we're all in for a black fate! Even so, I have great confidence and assurance. I only feel otherwise if I get indigestion, and when that happens, the whole world looks cold and dismal. In any case, I don't believe God torments His servants. How can I believe that a great God, glory be to Him, would burn a creature like me in hell just because he loved liquor! Don't you like what I'm saying? You've come to keep me company, yet I can see the boredom in your face. What do you suppose caused you to remember your father now after forgetting him for a lifetime?"

My heart was beating wildly and I couldn't bear to keep quiet any longer. It may not have been prudent of me to broach my topic after that particular question. However, I said unthinkingly, "I find myself in hard straits, and if bad circumstances were what separated us, you're still my father in spite of those circumstances."

He burst out laughing, and for the second time I hated the way he looked. Then, in that crazed tone of his that robbed his hearer of all confidence in what he was saying, he continued, "You're right. This whiskey contains a precious wisdom. Like the world, it's bitter. However, the wise man is the one who gets used to it and cultivates a taste for it, just as wise men grow accustomed to the world and cultivate a taste for it. Woe to those who shrink from its bitterness, since they won't be able to endure life. As I said, son, you're right. By God, I'm pleased by your tact and the fine way you've prefaced what you have to say. You've boycotted me willingly for thirty years or nearly that, so don't call me to account for my mistakes, since drunkards put no store by such reckonings. After all, one plus one doesn't necessary equal two. One may be equal to ten. As I said, you stay away from me a lifetime, then you come to me apologizing with polite words. In any case, I accept the excuse. And why shouldn't I? The fact is that I don't regret people's staying away from me. As for the straits you're complaining of, they're very important to me. Whatever distresses my son, distresses me. So, what do you mean, son?"

Something in me told me to leave, since I couldn't see any benefit in his delirious ranting. But I rejected the idea angrily. After all, it pained me to think of turning on my heels after having come this far. So I gathered my strength, exerting a greater effort than I could usually endure to keep my timidity and nervousness at bay.

Then I said softly, "I want to get married."

In response, the drunk man resumed his odious guffawing. Then he said in astonishment, "Why doesn't our family ever get over this pernicious malady? Your sister was on pins and needles for me to

153

choose a husband for her the way I ought to. Then she ran off with a strange man and married him. And that brother of yours had hardly started to sprout whiskers when he found himself in his bride's arms. I'm not trying to justify myself, since I tried to be a husband once, twice, and a third time. What a strange family! Maybe you need money in order for this marriage you want to come about? I wouldn't rule it out, since marriage, even if it is a malady as I've said, is something we spend huge sums on. This alone is sufficient evidence of human beings' madness. And maybe you've put yourself through the disagreeable experience of seeing me in order to ask me for money that you can use to tie the knot. I don't think it unlikely. But where will I get the money you're asking for? Have people told you that I'm rich and prosperous? I don't deny that I have a monthly income of forty pounds in addition to the rent I get from the second floor of the house. However, don't lose sight of my expenses. Take the cook, for example, who robs me of twenty pounds a month. If it occurs to me to check up on him, he makes my head spin with a long bill that I can't make heads or tails of. Then there's liquor, too, of which I need two bottles a day, and that comes to more than fifteen pounds a month. What's left after all that is just barely enough to pay for other necessities such as clothes, cigarettes, salaries for the gatekeeper and the servant, and fare for the carriage that takes me down some nearby streets when I get tired of staying at home. I've got nothing in the bank. In fact, I treat my indigestion with folk remedies. Don't ask me for money, son. God knows I say this to my regret. Why don't you follow your brother's example and marry without having to pay a cent? And if you really want my advice, don't get married at all!"

As he glanced over at me with his drifting eyes, he looked repulsive and detestable. He got out his pack of cigarettes, took one out and lit it, then began smoking it with relish. He began watching the cigarette smoke with his lackluster eyes, and it seemed as though he'd forgotten me. Then it occurred to me that he was deliberately tormenting me. I was filled with bitterness and anger, but I sat there motionless, all the while feeling more and more desperate and disappointed.

A long silence ensued, during which he turned toward me and cast me a vacuous look. Then his broad mouth broke into a smile.

"Won't you have a smoke?" he asked.

"No," I replied.

We fell silent again. Wouldn't it be best for me to go? I wondered. And indeed, I would have jumped up to leave if it hadn't been for something unexpected that happened just then. As I gazed at him in bewilderment and alarm, a look of fatigue came over him, his forehead began dripping with perspiration, and his eyes roamed the place as though they didn't see a thing. I saw a nervous twitch to the right side of his mouth, after which his right eye teared up. I expected something frightening to happen, the nature of which I couldn't identify. However, the condition passed quickly. His face relaxed and his eyes recovered the negligible bit of life that generally appeared in them. Then he looked my way again. The vague fear I'd felt left me, only to be replaced by a return of the desperation, disappointment, and hatred I'd been feeling before. I pondered with incredulity the reality before my eyes, namely, that this man was my father, the man who had brought me into the world. This called to mind other, related, realities that appeared to me in concrete images which caused me pain and grief. I hurt so much, I was in a near-daze for a while. Then, unaware of myself, I heaved an audible sigh.

Awakening anew to my presence, he asked me for the second time, "Won't you smoke?"

I shook my head in the negative.

"What a good boy you are!" he exclaimed mockingly. "Your only fault is that you want to get married. Talk to me about this idea of yours. Is it just a desire to marry, or have you got a particular girl in mind?" (At this point, my heart beat wildly, and I almost got tears in my eyes.) "That's how it seems to me. So, how is love these days? No doubt it's still treated with the greatest of seriousness, and still has same power to pull the wool over people's eyes. Nevertheless, I'll say it again as a man with experience: marriage is bondage. Imagine a woman owning you. My advice to you is not to get married at all. Take it from me as a man who's been there. Marriage is bondage. Imagine a woman owning you, and never mind what you've been told to the effect that you're the one who'll own her, since it's a stinking lie. She'll wear you out, rob your money, take away your freedom. And as if that weren't enough, she'll gradually take control of your spirit and everything you own to take care of her and her children! Then if you die, she'll go looking for another man even before her tears have had a chance to dry. Marriage is a ridiculous affair that I couldn't bear for more than one night!"

My heart reeled at the force of the thrust, which pierced to the quick, and in spite of myself, I uttered a groan from the depths of my being. He looked at me stupidly, and I glared back at him. I was so enraged I nearly threw the bottle in his face. However, I wasn't the type of person who acts on such thoughts, and I felt defeated by my weakness. I also felt an urge to cry, which I resisted as best I could.

"Have I hurt you, son?" he asked in astonishment.

"Good day!" I shouted at him as I rose to my feet in a rage.

The very next moment I regretted having let these words escape. Even so, I left the place without looking back. I headed for the street, fuming and cursing all the way: I couldn't bear it for more than one night! God! If a thousand blows had come down on the back of my neck in a public square, they wouldn't have hurt me the way that one statement had! I was so distraught, my eyes welled up with tears and I let myself cry, taking cover in the darkness that had fallen like a pall over the universe. There was no hope of his helping me in any way. His death alone would be able to change my life. Indeed, there was no hope whatsoever in anything but his death. As I got on the tram, my wandering mind went to work as usual, dispelling my anxieties with its unruly dreams. I saw myself sitting with Medhat and my sister Radiya dividing up my father's estate after his death. I suggested that we sell the big house, to which they agreed immediately, and in the twinkling of an eye I became the owner of a thousand pounds. Yet my mother didn't appear in the dream even once. I met with my sweetheart's father and spoke to him courageously of my desire to marry into his family, and everything went without a hitch. Thoughts like these brought me a satisfaction that relieved the tension that had been generated by that frightening, ill-fated visit. However, I quickly recalled how the dream hadn't even acknowledged my mother's existence. A tremor of fear and revulsion went through my body and my heart shrank in bitterness and remorse. How could I have allowed that satanic thought to pollute my soul again? The feeling of indignation and anger stayed with me the entire way home, and I repeated over and over, "O Lord, bless me by granting her a long life!" But it did me no good. I returned home divided and troubled, and I didn't feel at peace with myself until I'd planted a long, fervent kiss on her forehead.

28

The following afternoon I went to the tram stop to enjoy the sole moments of happiness my day afforded. The morning rendezvous was rarely possible anymore. My beloved was sitting on the balcony talking to her sister, and I stood there looking at her, awaiting the sustenance that consisted of a look from her eyes. This, for me, was the water of life. My beloved's head turned in my direction. However, no sooner had she seen me than she turned away from me in a kind of fury. Then she got up and left the balcony. I lowered my gaze in dismay, my enthusiasm now dampened. What had made her angry? Had she decided she couldn't tolerate my inaction any longer?

Was I doomed to be deprived of her sweet glances? Had she decided to counter my inaction with rejection and disregard? I was overcome with grief, despair, and shame. My position was embarrassing, of that there was no doubt. Then something occurred to me that made my limbs grow cold. I wondered fearfully: Might one of the men who were vying with me for her affection have something to do with this new turn of events? If so, then what would I have left in life? Tell me, my love, by your tender youth: is this estrangement spawned by an affection that could bear to wait no longer, or rejection by a heart that's attained its desire elsewhere? Never will I forget the misery of that day, nor of the days that followed. My beloved vanished from my life's horizon. She avoided appearing on the balcony when I was at the tram stop, and on the rare occasions when we happened to meet in the morning, she made certain not to allow her glance to fall on me. I began devouring the balcony and the window with ravenous, weary eyes. I'd sometimes see the mother scrutinizing me, the brother eyeing me strangely, and the little sister looking at me with interest. As for my beloved, she'd disappeared from view, leaving the tree of life bare, its bark yellowed, and its roots withered and dry. Lord! This wasn't simply indifference. If it had been truly indifference, it wouldn't have required such vigilance, and her glance would have fallen on me the same way it would happen to fall on other people and objects in the street. She was avoiding me consciously and deliberately. She was displeased and angry. The story of the young man who seemed to be in love was sure to have filled the house. Nor was there any doubt that his peculiar inaction had become the subject of commentary, criticism, and inquiry. How could I have failed to anticipate the embarrassment and confusion I was causing my beloved? Ashamed and humiliated, I heaved a deep sigh and my forehead was moist with perspiration. I was bitter and angry over my miserable luck, and the flames of my rage extended to my mother, who stood invisibly behind everything! So vexed was I, it was as though a hot, beastly wind had scattered its dust over my soul, and I could find no one on whom to vent my resentment, anguish, and rage but myself. It was a long-standing bad habit of mine, when I was at my wits' end, to rake myself over the coals, criticizing and satirizing myself and exposing all my faults and shortcomings. Hence, I denounced my utter helplessness, my all-encompassing fear of the world, people, and all other creatures, and the phony pride that made me act the tyrant for no reason at home and then, the minute it encountered the lowliest government employee, would turn me into a spineless, dutiful yes-man. I gave myself over to this type of morose thinking until I looked to myself like nothing but a mass of ugliness and ignominy. I was someone who didn't deserve to live. The most trifling task filled me with such terror and foreboding

159

that I found myself wishing there were some way besides a promotion to get a raise so that I'd never find myself responsible for any assignment of importance. I'll never forget the fact that I did my best to make sure that the folks in the warehousing section assigned me the typewriter as a way of avoiding menial tasks that didn't go beyond multiplication, addition, and subtraction. I was nothing but a bizarre, outlandish creature that had deviated from life's true path, as evidenced by the fact that I paid no attention to anything in the world but myself and whatever happened to concern me directly. In fact, I didn't even read the newspapers. Imagine my colleagues' amazement when they found out by chance that I still didn't know the name of the prime minister months after he'd taken office. They started making wisecracks about my ignorance while I sat there in morose silence. It's as though I weren't part of society, since I didn't know a thing about its hopes and sufferings, its leaders and rulers, its parties and organizations. I don't know how many times I heard the other employees talking about the economic crisis, the decline in cotton prices, and the change of constitution without making any sense of what they were saying and without it registering any response in me. I had no homeland or society, not because I'd gone beyond patriotism, but rather because I hadn't yet realized what patriotism meant! I may have felt at times that I loved all people—people as a general, spiritual entity—but there wasn't a single person who'd come in direct contact with me but that he'd aroused in me a feeling of alienation and dislike. Even my deep faith hadn't been able to deliver me from this frightening savagery. Rather, all it had done was burden me with anxiety and a troubled conscience over the crazy habit that had such a hold on me.

Hence, when dream day came, I'd take off straightaway for my new pub in the vegetable market, then order the infernal carafe that had become my only consolation in life.

29

As I stood at the tram stop before sundown, I still peered up at the balcony and the window. However, from the time she'd spurned me, my beloved had shown me no mercy. On the contrary, she'd shunned me cruelly, and my life had been consumed with grief. Winter was at its coldest, black clouds cast their heavy shadow on the ground, and a frigid wind was blowing. Standing there wrapped in my black coat, I would cast the beloved house an occasional look of longing and despair.

Then suddenly I heard a gentle voice saying, "Excuse me, sir. . . ."

I turned around in surprise, and my surprise intensified and mingled with dread when I saw before me one of the two men I suspected of loving my sweetheart. It was the dignified-looking gentleman who lived in her building.

"Pardon?" I muttered disconcertedly.

In a calm, placid voice and with an air of solemnity he said, "Would you mind if we walked together for a bit?"

"What for?" I asked uncertainly, though my heart sensed what he wanted to say to me.

"There's something I'd like to speak with you about," he replied with a smile.

"Of course," I said, seeing that I had no real choice in the matter. Looking up at the sky, he said, "It's quite cold. What do you say we take the tram to Ismail Square and sit in the café? I'd just like to speak with you for a couple of minutes? Do you mind?"

So we got on the tram, got off, and sat down. Realizing beforehand what the subject of conversation would be, I felt afraid. However, my sense that the conversation would revolve around my sweetheart left me no choice but to accompany him without hesitation. In fact, I went with him out of an irresistible longing. I kept wondering what he was going to say and what he hoped to accomplish. As we sat together at a small table, I got a close look at him for the first time. He was around forty, with a thin face and delicate, small features. One of his fingers was adorned with a diamond ring, and his thick spectacles made the look in his eyes appear sharper than it really was. Fiddling with the chain to a gold watch that dangled from the buttonhole in his vest, he asked me politely what I preferred to drink, and when I made no reply, he ordered tea.

"Pardon me for this intrusion," he said, "but you're certain to appreciate my position once you know what's led me to extend you this invitation. But first of all, allow me to introduce myself: Muhammad Gawdat, director of operations at the Ministry of Works."

The word 'director' struck terror in my heart.

"It's a pleasure to meet you, bey," I replied. "I'm Kamil Ru'bah Laz, an employee at the Ministry of War."

As the waiter brought glasses of tea, I was thinking about the huge disparity between us as employees: he a director of operations, and I a typist in the warehousing section. Behind him I caught sight of a mirror on the wall, and I saw my image reflected on its surface. As I looked at my rectangular face and green eyes, I was consoled by a sense of satisfaction and admiration.

As for my companion, he said to me, "Mr. Kamil, I've invited you to a brotherly consultation, and I hope you'll appreciate the desire of a man like me—whom you can count as your older brother—for honest mutual understanding. I'm not one to accuse others for no reason. However, I hope we can be frank."

Feigning surprise, I said, "I hope you'll tell me what's on your mind, sir, and you'll find me at your service."

He chuckled softly. Then, after some hesitation he said, "Will you forgive me if I ask a question I have no right to ask?"

Lord! I was dying to hear it. True, I was certain that his question wouldn't bring glad tidings. Even so, to me it seemed like the one thing most to be desired.

"Of course," I replied with an awkward smile.

Resting his elbows on the table and weaving his fingers together, he said, "I've noticed that you take special interest in a particular person. Perhaps you know who I'm referring to." Here my heart pounded violently. "I hope you won't hold it against me if I ask you about the true nature of this interest of yours. Is there a particular desire or intention on your part, or some bond between you?"

I nearly pretended to be surprised again and claim ignorance of the matter. However, I thought better of it. How many times had our eyes met at the tram station, and how many times had I seen him watching me as I looked up at the balcony? Similarly, he'd seen me watching him as he aimed his gaze at the same target. Hence, he knew everything, and he knew that I knew. So what would be the use of claiming ignorance if he was going to expose my lies?

Consequently, I forced a smile and said, "You've misunderstood, sir. You've concluded that I'm interested in a particular person, when in fact, I look at her the way I look at everyone else. It's nothing but a bad habit!"

I laughed, pretending to think the whole thing an amusing joke. He smiled at me and in his eyes I could see a look of disbelief.

Then he added, "You're a gentlemen as I'd expected you would be. So I ask you please just to tell me honestly: Do you have a relationship with this girl? If you answer me in the affirmative, I'll shake your hand in congratulation and go my way."

My heart breaking inside, I said, "I have no relationship with her."

He hesitated for a few moments. Then with no little embarrassment he asked, "Haven't you thought of asking for her hand?"

A succession of conflicting emotions came over me. At first I felt indescribable torment, after which I felt a kind of covert pleasure because I was sure that the man addressing me was a coward like me, since otherwise, he would have made his way to my sweetheart's house without thinking twice about me. In fact, I was convinced he must be afraid of me, which satisfied my pride in a way that mitigated some of my pain. Then, feeling myself compelled to make false claims for myself, I said unequivocally, "If I'd thought of doing what you've suggested, there would have been nothing to prevent me from doing it long ago."

Silence then reigned. He began looking searchingly into my face with a gleam of satisfaction in his eyes. What would have prevented me? How ironic. Everything seemed like a bizarre dream. Were we really talking about my sweetheart? And had I truly never thought of asking for her hand nor felt a desire to do so? Lord! What a cruel torment this was! I was gripped by a despair the likes of which I hadn't known in all the years of my despair-ridden life.

Then at last the bey emerged from his silence, saying, "I apologize again for my intrusiveness. The fact is that, now that the considerations that have kept me for so long from thinking of marriage no longer apply, I've finally decided to ask for the young woman's hand. I thought it best to speak with you about the matter for fear of trespassing on someone else's territory. And now, all I can do is thank you."

He was the weak type, or so it seemed to me. However, he happened to have met someone weaker than he was, so he was lucky, of that there was no doubt. Seeing that there was no more reason for me to stay, I got up to leave, saying, "Congratulations."

He rose politely and extended his palm. As he squeezed my hand gratefully, I imagined him squeezing my neck, and toward the joy that danced in his eyes I felt a burning hatred. Then I bade him farewell and left the café. My feet took me aimlessly hither and yon and I let them take the lead, since I had nowhere in particular to go. Taking a deep breath, I said to myself, "Praise be to God." Then I said it again out loud as though I were congratulating myself. Perhaps I was really congratulating myself on my despair, while holding out the hope of deliverance from the anxiety, torment, and pained longing that had been my constant companions over the long months since love had taken up residence in my heart. I'm happy, I said to myself, and no one deserves happiness more than I do. My sufferings are over for good. It seemed to me that if I'd thrown myself off al-Malik al-Salih Bridge the way I should have done that day in the past, I would have flown rather than fallen, so happy was I! I tasted the sweetness of despair with a kind of weird, frenzied pleasure, and I passed through moments of madness. Now I knew why it was that my sweetheart had disappeared from view. I began coming out of my ludicrous, ill-founded rapture as jealousy plunged its venomous fangs into my heart. Could this really be happening? I couldn't believe it. Why? Maybe it was on account of my unshakable faith in the merciful God and His providence. Yet who could have believed that fortune would lead me to the state I was in now? As I heaved a bitter sigh of despair, a shiver went through me from the biting cold. It was the first time I'd noticed the chill in the air since I left the café, and I wrapped my coat more tightly about me for fear of catching cold as I tended to do during the winter. Then a strange desire came over me, namely, to be bedridden. With a kind of satisfaction I imagined myself lying there, surrounded by tender, loving care. Then without warning, my nerves collapsed under the terrible pressure I'd endured, and I had a dreadful urge to cry. Encouraged by the darkness that surrounded me on all sides, I surrendered to it and wept. I gave in to the urge more and more until I began to gasp and sob like a little boy.

30

A t ten o'clock the next morning, I was on my way to Hilmiya to see my father. How had I come to this, especially given the fact that not even a month had passed since my last, harrowing visit? It was desperation. I'd had a miserable, sleepless night in which I hadn't so much as closed my eyes. I'd pondered my situation long and hard until my thoughts took on human flesh and shouted at me, "Go to your father no matter what, no matter what it costs!" Hesitation wasn't an option in a situation like mine. I'd lost my senses, and pain had distracted me from my usual feelings of hesitation, shyness, and fear. Besides, my father—despite everything—was the only hope I had left.

I'd chosen to visit him in the morning since, if he wasn't drunk yet, I might find him in a better state than the one I'd found him in on the previous, ill-fated visit. Besides, I didn't have the patience to wait till late afternoon. I put in a call to the warehousing section explaining that I wouldn't be coming in, then headed for my destination. A headache was pounding on my skull with its hammer after a night of sleeplessness and worry. I maintained my composure, however, drawing an unaccustomed strength from my desperation. I reached the house a little after ten in the morning. When I arrived, Uncle Adam rose respectfully. I greeted him, then went in without requesting permission, either because I refused to request permission to enter a house which I considered my own, or simply because, in my anxiety and distress, I'd forgotten to. I proceeded in the direction of the veranda, clearing my throat as I ascended the steps, but I found it empty. As I stood there feeling ill at ease, Uncle Adam caught up with me, opened a door that led inside and walked ahead of me, saying, "Kamil Bey is here."

He stepped aside to let me pass and I crossed the threshold with a self-assured gait. I found myself in a large, rectangular room at the far end of which were two doors. Between the doors there hung a life-sized picture of my father in the prime of his youth. The floor was covered with a costly, ornate carpet, and along one side of the room there was a row of couches. The curtains on the windows and doors were all drawn. I saw my father sitting cross-legged on a couch in the center of the room's left wing, and on an elegant table in front of him I saw his drinking paraphernalia which, given the fact that it had never been parted from him, seemed like an extension of his body. But he wasn't alone. The barber, who was standing nearby and gathering his instruments into his satchel, bade him a courteous farewell and went his way. Once the barber had left, Uncle Adam withdrew and closed the door behind him. As I walked up to my father, my eyes gravitated toward the bottle, and I found that it hadn't been touched. Feeling relieved and hopeful, I extended my hand to him, and he took hold of it with his thick, coarse hand.

A wan smile crossed his lips. "Welcome. Are you on vacation?"

I didn't like the way he'd received me, but I overlooked it. The truth is that the sufferings of the previous night, the headache that was digging its nails into my head, and my deep despair had overruled my natural tendency to be shy, fearful, and spineless, and I said, "Yes, I've taken a day off especially to meet with you."

He cast me a worried glance without any attempt to conceal what he was feeling, and I for my part felt angry and resentful.

"Is it something important?" he asked me tersely.

Oblivious to everything but my excruciating pain and my lingering hope, I said with an irritability that was betrayed by my tone of voice, "Very important. Or rather, it has to do with my life and my future."

Repeating my words after me, yet without coming out of the lassitude and stupor that had become second nature to him, he said, "Your life and your future!"

Imploringly I said, "My marriage that I talked to you about. There's a man who's about to ask for the hand of the girl I want to marry. So if I don't propose right away I'll miss my chance, and my life will be lost."

My heart shrank in dread. Will he shoot back some sarcastic reply the way he usually does? I wondered. He wasn't delirious or quarrelsome, but he seemed lethargic, sickly, and dazed. In fact, he seemed dead. I had every reason to despair, but I refused to despair. My overworked mind was fixed on a single idea and I was blind to all else in the mad race in which I'd embroiled myself.

I waited apprehensively until he said, "Don't worry. No one's life will be lost by losing a woman."

"I know better than anyone else about my life!" I shouted fervently.

"That's your business, son," he replied nonchalantly. "I don't interfere in what doesn't concern me."

I retorted stubbornly, "As I've told you before, I'm in desperate need of money."

"And what did I tell you?" he asked in a bored-sounding tone of voice.

Gripped with rage, I concluded that he was more despicable sober than he was drunk.

"I've got to get the money I need," I said, defending myself with an anguished tenacity. "I ask you to recognize the terrible straits I'm in. If I miss this chance, I'll have no more hope in life."

He glanced over at the bottle, then furrowed his brow slightly and said, "You're asking for money, but I don't have any!"

"That's ridiculous."

"It's an indubitable fact!"

I concluded from his tone of voice, his indifference, and his impatience that it would be easier for me to reach the heavens above than to arouse his concern and compassion. With my despondency, my headache, and my indignation all conspiring against me, I said in a loud voice that filled the huge room, "Never in your life have you spent a red cent on me. So what harm would it do you to give up a few hundred pounds for me now?"

Glowering, the man snorted and his face got redder than usual.

Then he said in a gruff voice, "You seem not to understand what you're told. Nor do you mean what you say. I've told you that I don't have any money. I don't have any money. I don't have any money!"

Losing all self-control, I balled up my fist, struck my thigh and screamed, "Is there no mercy in your heart?"

He looked at me as if to say: I'm worn out from trying to convince you. Then he replied with terse indifference, "No."

I gave him a hard look that must have betrayed the feelings of hatred and bitterness that had welled up in my heart, since I saw him grimace and his face clouded over in anger.

Then, in a voice that sounded like the lowing of a cow he bellowed, "Won't people leave me alone so that I can live what's left of my life in peace?"

I bellowed back madly, "And when have we disturbed your life? You're the one who's disturbed *our* lives! I need some of the money you spend on booze without a thought for how much it costs, and I *will* get what I need."

Grasping the empty glass with twitching fingers, he screeched, "You've gone mad! Are you cursing me to my face? Are you threatening me? Get out of my sight, and don't come back to this house as long as you live!"

More furious and agitated than ever now, I screamed, "This is *my* house! And whatever money is here is *my* money, and no power on earth is going to keep me from getting what I want. Do you understand? Do you understand?"

He rose to his feet with sparks flying from his eyes. Then he clapped his hands violently and roared, "Get out of my face, boy, and don't you dare come back to this house ever again. Adam! Adam!"

The door opened and Uncle Adam came in as though he'd been waiting to be summoned.

"Yes, sir!" he said as he came up to us. "I hope everything's all right."

Then suddenly I felt chilled as though someone had turned a cold shower on me. My anger abated, my agitation ceased, and my heart turned on its heels and fled. Fear's frigid hand had taken hold of my neck and I froze in place, confused, panicky, and unable to focus my gaze on anything. Gone was the Kamil that had been brought into being by rage and desperation, and all that remained was the other Kamil as he existed in his natural state.

Showing me no mercy in my weakness, the enraged man shouted at the gatekeeper, saying, "See this good-for-nothing to the door, and never let him in again! He's threatening to kill me!"

I stared into his face in bewilderment and dismay, hardly able to believe my ears. In his wild outburst he seemed like an accursed demon.

Then he shouted in my face, "Get out of here!"

But I didn't budge. Or rather, I couldn't budge. I wished the floor would open up and swallow me. I was dying of fear, heartsickness, and shame. The man waited, scowling, and when he saw that I hadn't made a move, he turned his back to me and exited into one of the house's inner rooms while the gatekeeper withdrew to the veranda. Thus, I found myself alone. Biting my lip, I regained my composure and managed to get up in speechless indignation. Then I left the room, doing my best not to look in the gatekeeper's direction. As I walked hurriedly through the garden, the gatekeeper followed me, mumbling an apology and making excuses for his employer, saying, "He's always like that."

I left the house without uttering a word.

31

I spent the first half of the day loitering in the streets, so full of despair, rancor, grief, and shame that I could hardly breathe. I went home at the usual time so that my mother wouldn't wonder what had brought me home early. After lunch I felt drowsy and fell into a deep slumber that lasted until early evening. Then I left the house, my soul so heavy it was as if I were carrying the weight of the world on my shoulders. I wondered where I should go, and I could find only one reply. The pub beckoned to me in the most tempting way, and my heart urged me to obey its summons. However, I hadn't forgotten the current reality, namely, that if I went on the much-desired drinking spree, my budget that month was sure to be broken, and I wouldn't have enough spending money to last me until my next salary. At the same time, the summons was impassioned and irresistible. It seemed to me at that wretched moment that an hour's bliss was better than a life devoid of good. I ran my hand over my gold watch, and suddenly it occurred to me that I could sell it if I needed money. The thought brought me a sense of relief, and I smiled for the first time that day. The following moment had me wondering what I'd say to my mother if she happened to miss my watch—and she was bound to miss it sooner or later. I groaned irritably at the thought. My mother! My mother! Always my mother! I said to myself angrily. I'll do what I want. I boarded the tram without hesitation, and on the way, my mind was drawn back for no obvious reason to a memory of my grandfather. I thought back to the days of ease and luxury that I'd lost when he passed away, and I found myself wishing that, rather than being so generous toward me, he had raised me instead on parsimony and the bare minimum. If he had, I wondered, might I not be better at coping with my present circumstances? I recited the Fatiha over his beloved spirit, then got off the tram at Ataba and headed for the vegetable market where my humble pub was located.

No sooner had I taken off my coat and sat down at an empty table than the Greek waiter brought the carafe. My pub was a plebeian sort of place, of that there was no doubt. However, it was rather respectable, too. For alongside the carriage drivers and working class folk, you'd find a gathering of middle-aged government employees whose life circumstances and family obligations didn't permit them to frequent expensive pubs. Among the latter was an elderly man who was fond of singing and merrymaking. The minute he got tipsy he'd wax eloquent, repeating old tunes like "Over Love How I Used to Weep" and "How I Miss You!" His voice wasn't without a touch of sweetness, and his performances always put a smile on everyone's face. In fact, a group of those present would always volunteer to sing the refrain in a sweet harmony.

I started drinking, and as usual I was filled with a feeling of contentment and joy—the feeling I found nowhere but among fellow drinkers at the pub. The pub was the only place where I experienced relief from the ponderous burden of timidity, halting speech, anxiety, and fear. While there I enjoyed such happiness and peace of mind, it was as though I'd just returned to my kith and kin after a long, burdensome sojourn among strangers, and I wished I never had to leave them. It wasn't long before I was flooded with that magical bliss and my being was filled with rapture. The employee entertainer hadn't begun his singing yet, and he was talking to his friends in a loud voice that was

172

audible to everyone sitting around him. After all, why shouldn't they all share in the conversation just the way they shared in the singing?

"Just imagine, folks," he said. "The doctor advises me to give up drinking!"

"Why, for heaven's sake?"

"He's found that I've got high blood pressure and hardening of the arteries."

"Drink fenugreek tea first thing in the morning and you'll be healthy all your life."

"He told me if I kept on drinking, I was sure to die."

"How long one lives is in God's hands!"

"And I said, 'Even if I stop drinking, I'm sure to die some day too!'"

"For an answer like that, you deserve a carafe of cognac, provided it's on you!"

"Would you believe I saw that same doctor one evening sitting and drinking whiskey at the St. James?"

"They're all like that! They snatch your money and tell you, 'Stay away from the booze,' then they take it to the St. James and buy themselves a couple of bottles."

The aging employee straightened up in his seat slightly, then began tapping on the table and shaking his head. Then he broke into song: "Treat the one you love right, good-lookin'!" People looked his way and the chorus made ready to repeat the refrain. As for me, I was drinking, talking to whoever engaged me in conversation, and laughing to my heart's content. My head spun fast as usual, bliss danced in my heart, and I went flying off into the firmament of pleasure and indifference. I went on this way for a long time, or maybe a short one—I can't really tell, since a drunk man loses his sense of time. Then I bade farewell to my friends and left the pub with the music still ringing in my ears. I went wandering aimlessly for a while, then hailed a carriage and got in without a thought for my suicidal budget. After telling the driver to take me to Manyal, I smoothed down the back seat and spread out my legs in a pompous, sultan-like posture. I didn't feel the chill in the air, and I found the carriage's dreamy movement relaxing and delightful.

173

Then, responding to a playful urge, I said to the driver with feigned circumspection, "A woman is waiting for me on the street, and I'm going to take her with me."

"I'm at your service, bey," he replied.

Meanwhile I thought to myself sardonically: Everything's just fine! A comfortable carriage, an amenable driver, and the cover of darkness. All we need now is the woman!

Then, capitulating again to an urge to mislead, I said, "She's a high-class lady, so let's find ourselves a safe street."

He rejoined with a laugh, "I think Garden City is the safest place nearby!"

"You're wrong!" I exclaimed, "Her villa is in Garden City!"

"We've also got Roda Island coming up," he replied with interest, "though the weather is chilly and I'm an old man who can't stand the cold."

"Not to worry," I said reassuringly. "I'll pay you a whole pound!"

The man thanked me enthusiastically, thinking he'd fallen on an unanticipated treasure. I laughed to myself as I ran my fingers over the one riyal that was all I had left till the end of the month. Some time passed, then I saw the beloved apartment building—my sweetheart's building—approaching. A strange sort of wakefulness stirred in my heart, and I couldn't take my eyes off the place. I wasn't free to look at her anymore—though looking at her had been my sole consolation in life—since what had transpired between me and her would-be suitor. I could no longer look up at he balcony or the window. Do you suppose His Eminence the director of operations had spoken to her father yet? Had my beloved really become engaged? Didn't she remember her other devotee—silent and pathetic though he'd been—as she moved into her new world? Didn't she feel the slightest bit of sorrow over him? Wanting to get even with the whole world, I was gripped with dismay and dejection, and I sat motionless until the carriage reached our street. I instructed the driver to stop, got out and paid him eight piasters.

He took them from me in astonishment. "And what about the other trip?" he mumbled questioningly.

I chuckled softly in spite of myself, then went my way. I ascended the staircase wearily, then opened the door with a key that I had in my pocket and closed it carelessly behind me. I proceeded to the bedroom and turned on the light, and my eyes fell on my mother as she slept. The depth of the slumber to which she'd succumbed was clear evidence of the effort she'd been expending in her long, arduous days. I stood there for a moment looking searchingly into her face.

"Mama!" I called out to her.

"Who is it? Kamil?" she murmured as she opened her eyes.

Then, calmly and nonchalantly I said, "I'm drunk."

She stared uneasily into my face, then sat up in bed, distraught, and said, "You scare me to death with that kind of joke."

"It's no joke," I said indifferently. "I drank two carafes of cognac."

She slipped out of bed and came up to me in alarm, not taking her eyes off mine for a second, until I could feel her breath on my face. Then she went pale and said with a trembling voice, "Why have you done this to yourself? How can you obey Satan after having repented to God?"

I didn't utter a word, and fell even deeper into my stupor.

"Take off your clothes," she said. "Let me help you."

As she proceeded to undress me, I was silent and perplexed. Why had I exposed myself in this odd way? I wasn't so drunk that I wouldn't have been able to control myself. On the contrary, I knew I'd come home on previous nights in a far more drunken state, and in spite of this, I hadn't done anything untoward. In fact, I'd taken the greatest of care not to waken her. So what had come over me on this particular night? The strangest thing of all was that my mind had been clear even after I'd entered the flat, and it hadn't occurred to me to waken her until I'd caught a glimpse of her. When she answered my summons, I'd said what I said without hesitation and, perhaps, without realizing what I was doing. Yet I'd been moved by an irresistible force! At the time I hadn't felt any remorse. I'd just stood there inert as a stone, scrutinizing her face with its pained expression as she took of my clothes. Then I moved away from her toward the clothes rack, got my pajamas, and put

175

them on without saying a word. I got into my bed and slipped under the covers. She came up to me and put her hand on my forehead.

Her voice still trembling, she asked me, "Are you all right? Shall I make you some coffee to clear your head?"

"No, thanks," I said. "I don't want anything at all."

32

I t was a week—or maybe more, I don't recall exactly—after that
event and the grief it had left in its wake. I'd finished my daily duties
at the ministry and sat waiting, bored and weary, for our work
hours to end. Then, a little before two in the afternoon, I was called to
the telephone. I answered the summons in astonishment, since no one
had ever called me on the telephone before, and since I wasn't expecting
a call from anyone. It was my brother Medhat, who said curtly, "Our
father has died. Come to Hilmiya."

My tongue tied with disbelief, all I said was, "I'll be there right away."

I hung up the receiver and stood motionless for a few moments.
People began looking my way, and my colleagues asked me what was
going on.

"My father died," I replied in a stupor.

I received the usual condolences, and before I knew it, my astonishment and disbelief had turned to fear, since death always frightens me.
I left the ministry and headed for the tram stop. So, my father had died.
It was an indubitable fact. As I began to get over the initial shock, I felt
waves of deep relief wash over my soul. At the same time, his image
appeared to me clearly with the rounded bald spot on his head and the

177

absent look in his eyes, and for a moment I imagined myself hearing his gruff voice and his sarcastic guffaw. When had he died? I wondered. And how? What a strange thing, death. It doesn't lose its tragic character even in the case of someone like my father, who'd lived most of his life as though he were dead, cut off from people and the world. After all, to live as though one were dead is one thing; death itself is another. I wondered to myself: Who might grieve over my father's death? Medhat? Radiya? He seemed to have left the world without anyone who would grieve his loss, and this, to me, was a tragedy more terrible than that of death itself. Isn't it a strange thing for someone to live in this world for more than seventy years, then die without leaving a single person to mourn his departure? The thought stirred a feeling of pity and sorrow in me. It was a strange emotion that had never stirred in me before. Perhaps it was born of relief rather than regret, since in a case like mine, the soul might pretend to be grief-stricken in order to conceal its delight, or in order to express this delight in a twisted sort of way. Or it might have been a sincere sentiment that expressed itself after the hindrances that once kept it in check had been removed by death. I betook myself to Hilmiya, and as I arrived at the old house, I saw a number of family members sitting on a row of wicker chairs. In the center was a man I was seeing for the first time, and whom I learned later was my paternal uncle. Medhat was seated to his right, and next to Medhat sat my sister's husband. I greeted them feeling despondent and flustered. Then my brother got up and took me into the garden.

"It's been an exhausting, difficult day," he said, "but everything's over now."

"Why didn't you call me earlier?" I asked.

Sighing, he said, "We were too busy even to think. And if it weren't for the fact that Radiya went herself to see our mother and came back here with her, she still wouldn't have heard the news herself. Don't you know what happened? I received a telegram in the early morning from Uncle Adam, asking me to come right away because my father hadn't returned home since last night. So all of us came. Uncle Adam informed us that our father had left the house before sundown yesterday and

178

that, unlike usual, he hadn't come back. The man had waited for him anxiously until a little before dawn. He sent us the telegram in the early morning. Our father used to like to go out from time to time in the late afternoon—drunk, of course, as you know. He would set out on foot for a little while, after which he'd board a carriage that would take him around here and there. Then he would come back to the house an hour or two later. But he would never spend the entire night out. Consequently, his absence worried Uncle Adam, and threw us into a terrible confusion. We didn't know of a single friend of his that we could contact and had no idea which direction he might have taken. It occurred to us that he might have gone to Radiya's house, so we went to see her, but she hadn't seen him since she'd left home. Not wanting want to lose time, we agreed that she would go see our mother as a way of gathering more information, and we—your uncle and I—would inquire about him at the Khalifa police station. When we got there, the master sergeant informed us that yesterday, a carriage driver had brought in a man who had passed away and who fit our father's description. The driver said that the man had boarded his carriage at Bab al-Khalq Square and that he'd taken him at his request in the direction of Imam. When the driver turned around to inquire of him exactly where he wanted to go, he found him apparently asleep. He called to the man to wake him up, but got no response, so he stopped the carriage, got out and shook the man gently. It was then that he realized that the man had passed away. He'd had no choice but to bring him to the station. They arrested the driver as a precautionary measure, and our father was taken to Qasr al-Aini Hospital, where it was confirmed that he'd died a natural death from a heart attack. We went then to Qasr al-Aini, where they allowed us into the morgue."

Medhat fell silent, his eyes betraying signs of pain and distress. Then, in a kind of suppressed outburst, he continued, "What a sight! I don't know how we recognized him! It was something else."

His eyes welled up with tears. I'd never seen him without a smile on his face, so I became more distressed myself, and tears came to my eyes as well.

He remained silent until he'd regained his composure. Then he told me it had been decided to have the funeral at four o'clock.

"He's in his room now, so you can go and look at him for the last time."

My heart pounded violently at the thought, and I was gripped by a terrible fear. However, I couldn't bear to look up at my brother, and so I had no choice but to pretend to welcome his idea. I headed toward the veranda, stumbling along in my fear and confusion, then ascended the staircase with a gulp. As I was on my way up, my sister and I caught sight of each other at the same moment. She seemed to have informed my mother of my arrival. In any case, she came forward hurriedly and met me on the veranda, asking me nervously where I was headed.

"I want to see my father," I said.

"I wish you wouldn't, Kamil," she said imploringly. "Your heart is too weak to bear the sight of someone whose spirit has passed on."

I heaved a sigh of relief and a heavy burden was lifted from my shoulders. The only thing I was feeling by now was fear. After all, will a heart that trembles at the sight of a mouse or a dung beetle be able to face death in its most hideous, fearsome manifestation? I went back outside and sat down between my uncle and my brother without saying a word. Then, half an hour before the funeral procession was to begin, those who'd come to offer their condolences began arriving. Some neighbors came, as did some employees at the warehousing section. Given the fact that my father hadn't had any acquaintances and my uncle had no friends in Cairo, the number of those who came to pay their respects numbered no more than twenty. Visibly moved, my uncle said he would hold the wake in his house in Fayoum. We then came to the final moment, at which point my sister Radiya lifted up her voice in a lament that shattered the heavy silence, causing my heart to quake with emotion and my eyes to well up with tears.

Before long we'd assembled ourselves for the funeral procession. As it began, a heavy gloom descended upon me in response to the sight of the bier, the shadow of death hovering about us, and the memories that had been stirred of my grandfather and his passing. Then the cloud began to lift and I recovered some measure of equanimity. As I looked furtively at those around me, I saw some faces that were serene and others that were smiling for one reason or another, a fact that consoled me and caused me to come back to myself. Suddenly I remembered how I used to walk to the ministry in the morning without a thought for the events that lay in store for me. Yet here I was now, walking behind the bier, and I marveled at this strange life of ours. At that moment, I imagined life sticking out its tongue with mischievous derision and rolling on the floor with laughter, and I wondered to myself which of the two states was better: that of the morning, or that of the afternoon? As the comparison came to mind, I couldn't resist a subtle wave of joy and relief. However, my profound religious sense objected vociferously, sending a wave of fear and anxiety through the depths of my being till I sought refuge in God from the accursed Satan. Trying now to ward off the feelings of joy and relief that kept pursuing me, I unwittingly furrowed my brow and put on a gloomy, sorrowful face. But it was no use, and it wasn't long before my mind began mocking these childish antics and I started thinking instead of the anticipated fortune. I remembered the dream I'd had of selling the house and I wondered: Will the dream come true? Will I become the owner of a thousand plus pounds? Has my rival been slow to take the decisive step, or has the matter been settled so that there's no more hope? And will the awaited fortune be my ticket to happiness, or a new tool in the hands of fate for making sport of weak, helpless creatures? It's made sport of my poverty and my powerlessness, and it's no doubtless capable of making sport of my wealth and power. In other words, it may show me that whichever way things go, I'm doomed to misery and affliction. My enthusiasm waned at the thought and I was gripped with worry and distress. Yet I beseeched God to grant me the good fortune of winning my sweetheart.

I wakened from my reverie to find that the funeral procession had come to a halt in front of the mosque. The bier was taken inside to be prayed over, and those who had kindly come to offer condolences went their way. Then the bier was placed in the hearse that took us and the deceased to Imam, and the occasion came to an end.

The family gathered that night in the large room where I'd met with my father for the last time. I sat with my uncle, my brother, and my brother-in-law on one side, with my mother, my sister, and my aunt and sister-in-law on the other. My uncle was a practical man whose appearance reminded me of my father, and he talked about the procedures that would have to be followed in order to demonstrate our respective rights to inherit. He offered to introduce us to a friend of his who worked in the Ministry of Religious Endowments and who could help facilitate matters for us in receiving our monthly allowances. My brother Medhat spoke as well, saying that since none of us wanted to live in the house, he thought it would be best for us to sell it. His proposal met with my approval, and I voiced my agreement with an enthusiasm that I forgot to conceal. As for Radiya, she had no objections to the idea.

Then my uncle said, "It's a huge, old house that couldn't be sold for less than four thousand pounds. Consequently, it would only be attractive to a wealthy buyer, who would tear it down and construct some big modern building in its place."

Four thousand. Oh, how I hoped my rival had been delayed! It was hard for me to imagine God disappointing my hope after having fulfilled my dreams in this dazzling way. My trust in the omniscient God knew no bounds. I glanced over at my mother and found her silent and immersed in her thoughts. Her thin eyebrows were raised and her lips were parted, revealing her small, glistening teeth. What's she dreaming of? I wondered. And what are her true feelings toward the deceased? Had this old house taken her back to the past eras of her life? I felt compassion and love for her. Then I remembered the thoughts that had taken hold of me not long before, and my feelings of compassion and affection gave way to anxiety and fear.

As the hour was approaching midnight, my brother suggested that we all spend the night in the house, but my mother preferred for us to go home and come back the next morning. Hence, we left the old house and walked side by side in the direction of the tram stop.

As we were on our way she said, "Wouldn't it have been better for you all to keep the house?"

Startled, I said, "And what would we do with it? I'm in desperate need of my share of its price."

"Your monthly salary is enough for you. As for this huge amount, what in the world would you need it for?"

A feeling of unease and indignation came over me. Was it possible that she was afraid? I stole a glance in her direction, but it was so dark I couldn't make out the expression on her face.

Then, in a fearful-sounding tone of voice she continued, "Don't you dare rejoice over anyone's death! Whenever you remember your father from now on, you should say a prayer for God's mercy on him. I don't want you to find pleasure in anyone's death no matter who he happens to be!"

I was amazed to hear such words coming from the very person who had taught me to hate my father, but it didn't occur to me to remind her of this fact. Then we returned home without either of us uttering another word.

33

I was no longer the indigent, destitute person I had been, and the burden of need and deprivation had been lifted from my shoulders. I now had a reasonable income in addition to the fortune that would begin coming to me within a month or two. Now, however, I'd been afflicted with madness of a kind I'd never known before—the madness of someone in love who isn't rendered helpless by poverty. Poverty had been a deterrent that put a damper on my ambition and turned my love into a prolonged affliction locked deep in my soul. Consequently, I'd conceded defeat to my rival Muhammad Gawdat without even a show of resistance, then gone sobbing down the street like a little boy. However, now that poverty had been dealt the death blow, love was no longer an unattainable desire. So I put other obstacles out of my mind and was afflicted by a new kind of madness, namely, the madness of someone for whom happiness appears as a genuine possibility and for whom all that remains is to overcome his timidity, storm the gates, and try his luck.

The afternoon after my father died I lingered at the tram stop for an unusually long time. I looked up at the dearly loved window with fervent longing. I no longer saw my sweetheart, and I didn't know

whether what I feared had come to pass. If it had, then all I stood to
gain from my fortune was so much deadly poison. If she appeared in the
window, what would I do? Would I have the nerve to gesture to her in
some subtle way? On the contrary, my heart shrank with fear and alarm.
I wasn't the type to do that sort of thing. If I'd had an iota of courage,
I would have stormed the building without further ado, requested a
meeting with my sweetheart's father, and told him what was on my
mind. Was such a thing dangerous enough to warrant such awful
dread? Supposing, as a worst-case scenario, that he declined to meet
with me: Why did I think of such an eventuality as a fate worse than
death? Why was it that the minute I so much as thought of taking such
an initiative, I broke out in a sweat and my heart nearly leaped out of my
chest? O God! Didn't scores and even hundreds of people get married
every day? How did would-be husbands find ways to go after what they
wanted? The only thing that stood between me and the object of my
desire was to knock on that door. Once that was done, it would either
be the bliss of hope or the solace of despair. So why hesitate and shrink
from the task at hand? After all, it was a house, not a fortress, and I was
a suitor, not a foe. Why was I so terrified? My aim wasn't to invade a
continent or even to go into battle. I wasn't required to be Napoleon
or Hannibal. On the contrary, all that was required of me was that I
introduce myself and pose my question. In the meantime, I'd be surrounded by the solicitous attention that's always afforded a guest by a
gracious host. Then let the answer be whatever it was meant to be, since
at the very worst, it wouldn't be more than a polite refusal. This is what I
told myself reproachfully, but the minute I imagined the concrete situation
before me, my forehead would get hot, my heart would race, and I'd
feel a shudder go through my limbs. Suddenly I had a flashback of the
ill-fated rhetoric class at the Faculty of Law that cast me beyond the
pale of the university, and I heaved a deep, hopeless sigh. It was too
much for me. I might easily spend my entire life crying on this sidewalk,
I thought, but as for crossing the street and knocking on that door, it's
more than I'm capable of. I worked up such a dread, in fact, that the
anxiety that tormented me turned into a fever that burned both heart

and head. A few days passed, days spent in a kind of delirium. I forgot about the fortune that had fallen to my lot, and my hope and enthusiasm for life were extinguished. My thinking focused instead on one thing and no other, and I danced around it over and over without daring either to approach it or to move away from it. My mother found me in a state of agony that I made no attempt to conceal, and I said to myself furiously, If I weren't afraid of her, I'd ask *her* to go ask for the girl's hand on my behalf and spare me this ordeal!

When will this misery come to an end? I wondered. And, indeed, I never would have seen an end to it if it hadn't been for a certain fortuitous event. I was on my way home from Hilmiya and I got off the tram at Ataba at sunset. Then, as usual, I boarded the tram that goes to Giza via Roda. The tram car was packed with passengers, some seated and others standing, so I made my way through the crowd until I was able to rest my back against the door that led into the first-class compartment. Just after the tram had left the square, I heard a tapping on the door and realized that someone was asking permission to open it. I stepped back from the door slightly, turning on my heels to make room for the person getting on. And when the door opened, who should I find before me but my sweetheart, in the flesh! My heart jumped so violently, my whole chest quaked. I became oblivious to everything in the universe but the happy sight, which caused me to tremble all over in joy and fear. She happened to look into my face, so our eyes met for a brief moment. She seemed to hesitate slightly on the car's threshold between the two compartments, but she had no place behind her to place her foot, so she had no choice but to come forward. She looked around behind me for a place to stand, but the car was packed wall to wall. People were standing so close together, there wasn't so much as an inch of space unoccupied. Consequently, she was obliged to occupy the place where I'd been standing, and she rested her back against the door. Meanwhile, I stood in front of her—only a breath away—holding on to the door handle. There she was—she and no other—as though heaven had granted her to me as a balm to my soul. There are realities that are more wondrous than dreams, and this was the most wondrous of them all. What was I feeling? Was it joy, or fear, or a blazing fire? If it hadn't been for the delicacy of the situation and my appalling timidity, I would have liked to cry! I was insensible to everything, and I no longer felt the people around me despite the fact that they were pressing on me from all sides. I don't even recall what color dress my beloved was wearing or what she had in her hand. It seems that the heart has its own kind of vision that, when it focuses in on something, so obscures physical vision that one becomes blind even though one is sighted. I don't know where I got the courage, but I stole a glance at her, and when I saw her, my heart fluttered mercilessly. It seemed to me that my presence was what had produced this charming friendliness and delightful discomfiture. I sighed in spite of myself, and a lock of her hair undulated under the force of my breath. She looked up at me, then quickly lowered her eyes in flight from my gaze. Ah! I'd finally found someone who ran away from me! An intoxication warmer and more delectable than wine's flowed through my head. Gripped by a madness the likes of which I'd never known before, I fixed my gaze on her face with an extraordinary—and, for me, outrageous—daring. Suddenly I became conscious of a peculiar urge to give voice to what was pressing in on me, and I gulped with a violent nervous tension. Then, in a terrible, angst-filled uproar, I began making ready for the anticipated leap, aided by the madness that was churning inside me and propelled forward by the anxious longing and near-despair that I'd suffered in the preceding days. Then, possessed by a feeling similar to that experienced by someone who's about to commit suicide as he gathers courage for the final leap, my lips moved with a sound that came out in a whisper as I said, "I want to tell you something."

Lord! Do you suppose she'd heard me? Yes, she had! Blushing and blinking her eyes, she stared at me in disbelief.

A harsh, arduous time ensued. My throat went dry and my heart-beats came fast and furiously. What sort of abyss had my lunacy plunged me into? The suicidal maniac had jumped, and now it was time to cry for help. Even so, I felt a profound relief, since I'd managed to budge the hugest barricade on my life's path. I'd spoken! The rock had spoken, albeit belatedly. At the very least, I wouldn't die with my secret still undisclosed. However, the tram wasn't going to give me much more time, since it was about to reach my sweetheart's stop. She was looking out the window by now, her hand was on the doorknob in preparation to open it, and once she did that, it would be all over. With madness coming over me once more, I took hold of the doorknob to keep her from opening it. Where on earth had I gotten such nerve? Her pretty face registered a look of indignation and she looked daggers at me.

Nearly in tears, I whispered imploringly, "Just one thing. . . ."

For a few brutal moments, I expected the thunderbolt to descend upon my head and for her to rebuke me or send me away with angry words. This, of course, would have turned the people around us against me, and that would have been the end of me. If it had happened I wouldn't have had the strength to bear it, and I would have perished on the spot! When the tram stopped, I still had hold of the door, and when it moved again she was still standing there, frowning and disgruntled, though without making any serious objection. A wild rush of satisfaction coursed through my body, so pleased was I with my conquest, and I imagined myself being transformed into an invincible giant before whom death itself falls prostrate after being dealt a single blow. I waited two more stops, then I opened the door and whispered, "After you." She turned around edgily, then made her way through the crowd with me close on her heels. It was then that my elation was dampened by a troubling thought: Might she have simply capitulated out of shyness, embarrassment, and the desire to avoid a scene? Wasn't it most likely that she had restrained her anger on the tram so that she could unleash it on me in the street away from people's inquisitive stares? My strength about to give out, I got off the tram behind her feeling worried and distraught. Darkness had fallen, and the street was virtually deserted except for cars coming and going. She hastily moved away from me and began to cross over to the sidewalk. Propelled by the fear of letting the opportunity slip out of my grasp and emboldened by the darkness, I came up to her.

"Pardon me," I said with a trembling voice. "Please don't take offense at my forwardness."

"What do you want?" she retorted. "And what is this that you did in front of everyone?"

Now I was more flustered than ever. I was hearing her voice for the first time, and I was stirred by her lovely accent despite the sharpness and anger in her voice.

"I ask you to forgive me," I said. "I've wanted to say something to you for a long time, but I never had the chance until today."

I was finding it terribly difficult to express myself, and it seemed that my fervent emotions couldn't be put into words. I was grieved and distressed, and to make things worse, she turned her back to me indifferently and hurriedly crossed the street to the other sidewalk.

I followed her in no less of a hurry, saying, "Please, one moment. Listen to me. I'll say just one thing, then we'll go our separate ways."

Without stopping or looking at me she said, "By what right do you speak to me, you . . . ?"

Forgetting myself, I cried, "I've known you for more than two years!"

"What nonsense!" she said irritably.

Could she possibly not have recognized me?

How stupid could I be! Hadn't she complied with my wishes, with the result that we'd gotten off at this particular stop? This seemed to indicate that she wanted to hear what I had to say. The opportunity was before me, but I was ruining it with my inarticulate, bumbling speech.

I mustered my strength and, in a tremulous voice, I said distraughtly, "For months and months I've been dying to say something. So what harm would it do for you to listen to me?"

Why didn't I just speak rather than making these endless introductions? O Lord, loosen my tongue! It seemed to me at this point that my beloved became aware of my deadly shyness. I don't know what caused her to stop, but I saw her turn toward me and look at me with her beautiful eyes, those eyes that I loved more than life itself.

"What do you want?" she asked me testily.

What did I want? Had I not said it yet? Here she was waiting for the word that I'd sought her permission to speak, wearying her in the process. Had I not rehearsed it? I drew a huge blank as though I'd lost

189

the ability to speak. What was one to say? I swallowed my nonexistent saliva in near despair.

Then, seeing her make a gesture that indicated she was losing her patience and about to leave, I broke out of my silence and cried, "Wait, please! I wanted to say . . . I want . . . ." The words, 'to ask for your hand' got stuck in my throat. "You understand, I'm sure. Don't you? Is this possible?"

"Oof!" she said. "I have to go home, and don't follow me, please."

Seized by a panic that impelled me to speak, I said without hesitation this time, "I'm thinking . . . I mean, I want to ask you to marry me, if you please!"

And with that, I sighed audibly as a sense of relief and surrender flooded my being. At long last I'd spoken and gotten things off my chest. And now, let come what may.

A moment of deep silence passed, like the calm that follows a raging storm. Then she began walking with short steps without saying a word. Feeling uneasy again, I followed her.

Like someone begging for a reply, I said, "That was what I wanted to say."

In a low voice that seemed to reach my ear placidly, without a trace of harshness or anger, she said, "It isn't proper for you to follow me this way."

Stumbling hurriedly over my words, I said, "I asked for your permission, so don't leave me without a reply."

"I'm not the one to be addressed concerning this matter!" she said impatiently.

My heart was beating passionately, overflowing with unspeakable joy.

"I realize that," I said. "However, I was afraid someone else had asked first."

Her voice barely audible, she said, "Suppose someone had . . . ."

"Have I missed my chance, then?" I cried miserably.

With an exasperated sigh she said, "Don't follow me any farther. I'm getting close to the house."

"Is there no hope?" I asked her as my heart strove with all its strength to break free of despair's grip.

Walking even more quickly now, she replied, "I'm not the one to be spoken to about this matter."

I stopped walking and stood still for a moment in a daze.

Then I cracked my knuckles, crying, "What an idiot I am! If she'd wanted to refuse me, she could easily have given me a definitive reply. Didn't she go along with me on the tram? Didn't she listen to me a few minutes ago? Didn't she tell me that she wasn't the person to be spoken to about this matter? So what more could I ask? It was a polite, indirect invitation!"

Once these facts had sunk in, my soul was suffused with a dream-like bliss, and I felt as though I were reeling like a drunken man.

34

I came home with the memories of the past hour singing the most dulcet of tunes in my heart. I was possessed by a feeling of boundless strength, not to mention a fair measure of pride and conceit. In a single minute I'd bidden farewell to a long era of passivity. "I'll tell my mother about everything," I announced to myself. I said it without fear or hesitation—and perhaps without mercy as well. I knocked on the door and she opened it for me herself, murmuring with a smile as she typically did, "Welcome, light of my eyes."

I found her looking her elegant self, which was the way I liked her to receive me. As I peered searchingly into that demure face of hers, now lit up with a smile of welcome, I sensed the gravity of what I was about to embark on, and a feeling of gloom and dread came over me.

With a hesitancy whose reasons she didn't know I said, "Let's move soon to a more suitable house, and I'll restore to you your servants and entourage!"

She smiled and said, "These are the happiest days of my life because I'm serving you."

I took off my clothes and went back into the parlor, where we sat side by side on a couch. O Lord, Your succor and mercy! I said to myself as angst and timidity took hold of me. It was going to be an arduous, unhappy task, but there was no avoiding it. I stole a glance at her and found her looking tranquil and secure, blissfully unaware of what I had in store for her. I felt a pang of remorse, and the strength of my resolve nearly melted away. However, I also feared the consequences of being indecisive and capitulating to weakness.

So I flung myself into the abyss, saying, "Mama, I want to speak with you about an important matter."

She shot me a peculiar look that I took to be one of wariness and apprehension. In fact, I even suspected that she'd intuited the nature of the subject I intended to broach by the force of some supernatural inspiration. Had my tone of voice betrayed what was going on in my mind? Had I given myself away by the look in my eyes? Or was I just imagining things?

As for her, she said in a calm, inquisitive tone, "I hope everything's all right."

Determined to pass through the danger zone once and for all, I said fearfully, "I'm going to put my trust in God and get married."

The phrase 'get married' sounded strange to my ears, and it aroused a sense of shame in me as though I'd uttered an obscene, hurtful word. She looked up at me in astonishment. Her eyes grew big as saucers, and in them I saw a look of bewilderment and incomprehension as though she hadn't understood a word I'd said.

"Get married?" she asked.

Having cleared the biggest hurdle, I was able to say, "Yes. That's what I intend to do."

She let forth an abrupt laugh that sounded less like laughter than like a cry of perplexity and distress.

Her voice trembling, she said, "How happy that makes me! This is happiness indeed. Did you just decide on this today? Now? Why haven't you told me before? Congratulations, son."

I was upset by the tremor in her voice and her obvious agitation.

"I'm asking for your permission," I said, "Because I always like you to approve of me."

"Can you imagine me withholding my approval from you for a single moment?" she exclaimed theatrically. "O God, after all the love I've given you, am I rewarded for it by your casting doubts on my sincerity? I'd approve of you even if you killed me. Have you forgotten that my entire life belongs to you?"

Swallowing with difficulty as I stole an uneasy glance at her, I said, "I know all that and more, Mama."

A grim look appeared on her face and she seemed to be trying in vain to keep her emotions in check.

"That's something everyone knows," she went on. "After all, what mother isn't going to rejoice over her son's marriage, even if she's all alone and he's all she has left! This is life's wisdom: for me to hold you close for a lifetime, then deliver you as a wonderful young man to your bride. I'm weeping for joy!"

She began to cry as she spoke, and she looked at me though her tears as though she were alarmed by my silence.

Then she said apologetically, "Forgive me, Kamil. These aren't tears of sadness. They're tears of joy. It's just that you took me by surprise and didn't inform me in the gentlest way. Of course, there's no need to be gentle. Don't you think I'm apologizing in a way that's worse than the original offense? May my guilt be forgiven for the sake of my great love, my good intentions, and this heart of mine that I've given you even though you're no longer in need of it. You know that when I get emotional, I can't control my tongue. I congratulate you on what you've chosen for yourself. But, is it only now that this desire has come up? I can't bear to think that you've wanted to marry before and weren't able to. Have you wanted to do this for a long time?"

Masking my feelings with a lame smile, I said, "No, Mama. I only started thinking about it recently, when it seemed to me that I'd grown up."

Laughing hysterically, she cried, "Listen to this, folks! It seems that Kamil has grown up! I must have lived too long, then!"

"Mama," I groaned, "you're grieving me."

"Death to whoever would grieve you! A mother who makes her child sad doesn't deserve to live. But you misrepresent yourself when you claim that you've grown up. What a contrary child you are! I can still see you crawling, riding on my shoulder, and prancing around wearing an officer's uniform with that braid of yours hanging down your back!"

"I'm nearly twenty-eight years old!" I said in distress.

"My youngest child is about to turn twenty-eight! What an old woman I am! Have it your way. No matter how old you are, you'll be the youngest of husbands, but I'll rejoice over it like nobody's business. Why are you looking offended? Have I said something to hurt you? God knows I'm not good at talking, but I'd rather die than hurt you."

With a heavy heart I said, "May God forgive you, Mama."

Then she smiled. Yes, by God, she smiled. Then she said with feigned happiness, "Let's leave all this aside and put first things first. Listen to me, Kamil. Marry with my blessing, and I'll choose a bride for you if you tell me to."

I hesitated for a moment. Then, too distressed to keep quiet I said, "There's no choice to be made. I've already made my choice."

She stared at me in disbelief, then fell into a long silence.

"When did this happen?" she asked.

"Not long ago."

A look of reproach flashed in her eyes, as though it caused her pain for me to withhold such a serious matter from her. Then she looked down in resignation.

In a calm—exceedingly calm—voice she asked, "Who is it?"

"I don't know exactly. Most likely she's a teacher, and she lives in the orange building across from Qasr al-Aini."

Astonished again, she asked, "Haven't you spoken to anyone about her?"

"Not at all."

She thought at length, then continued, "Isn't it possible that she's engaged already?" Here my heart beat violently. "And don't you know anything about her family! Who is her father?"

"I don't know."

"Didn't I tell you you were a child? Marriage is a more serious matter than you think. You may be taken by her face, but you can't put any store by that. What matters is for you to know what kind of girl she is, what sort of people her family are, her status in society, and what their morals are like. When a young man marries, he's marrying a family, not just an individual, and before he takes the final step, he needs to make sure who the mother of his children will be, and who their maternal uncles will be."

Flustered now, I felt angry for the first time.

"She comes from an honorable family," I said with certainty. "I have no doubt of that."

"But how do you know?"

With the tone of someone who'll brook no discussion of the point at hand, I said, "I'm just sure of it, that's all."

With an indignant look on her face she retorted, "A teacher! Girls who come from nice families don't work as teachers. On the whole, a teacher will either be homely or some reckless girl who tries to be like a man."

Stung to the core, I cried impatiently, "Talk about warped ideas! You don't know a thing about the world we're living in. Everything's changed, and I have no doubt that she's a wonderful girl from a very respectable family!"

Agitation overcame her feigned tranquility and she said edgily, "There's no need for you to insult me on account of some young teacher you don't know a thing about! All I'm trying to do is guide you to what's in your best interest."

I was more furious than ever now, and if I'd given in to how I felt, I would have said something I was sure to regret. However, I controlled myself and said imploringly, "God forbid that I should deliberately insult you. And I ask you to stop saying things that hurt me."

Concealing her agitation with a smile, she regained her composure again and said in a resigned tone of voice, "Whatever hurts you, hurts me, and whatever makes you happy makes me happy. However, my advice to you, if you're willing to accept it, is to watch your step. And may God grant you success in whatever will bring you blessing and happiness."

Squeezing her hand gently I said affectionately, "Your approval of me is worth the world and everything in it."

She smiled, saying, "I'll pray for you from my heart night and day."

Such a long silence then ensued that I thought the matter had been settled. However, she looked pensive and troubled, as though there was a thought she felt an urgent need to express, and she shot me more than one furtive, anxious look.

Then, overcoming her hesitation, she broke out of her silence and said carefully, "Don't you think it would be best for you to postpone getting engaged until a year has passed since your father's death? The thing I fear the most is for it to be said that you got engaged before the period of mourning over your father had ended, as though you'd been anxiously awaiting his death."

I could hardly believe my ears! Her words sounded to me like a kind of subtle trickery that I couldn't bear. I went back to feeling resentful and angry and I nearly exploded in a rage. However, I kept quiet until the storm had passed.

Then I said, "In any case, the wedding wouldn't take place before a year had passed."

The conversation ended at that point, as I'd hoped it would. I felt as though I'd overcome the greatest obstacle in my path. I should have been happy, and I *was* happy, no doubt. At the same time, my happiness was tinged with the feeling of disquiet that's tormented me throughout my life. It's haunted me even in my happiest hours, and whenever I make a decision, I find its whisper sapping my strength and destroying my peace of mind. However, my happiness on this particular occasion was too great to be influenced by anything.

35

The next morning I went to the tram stop with a new, intoxicating hope. It was as if she'd been waiting for me. I saw her
through the window with her head wrapped in a white scarf.
Beside myself with happiness, my mouth, my eyes, and my heart all
smiled together. I lifted my gaze in her direction with unaccustomed
courage, and I rejoiced to see a smile on her lovely face. The era of
misery and deprivation had drawn to a close, the darkness in my soul
had dispersed, my beloved's countenance had appeared after a long,
tormented absence, and we'd actually become friends who exchange a
smile! What an incredible reality! Up until that morning I'd still been
afraid that the previous day's conversation might have meant something other than what I'd understood it to mean. However, after this
challenging wait and this radiant smile, I could respond to the call of
bliss with an assurance untainted by even the shadow of a doubt. I
went to the ministry drunk with ecstasy. How strange the world is.
Someone who's been destined to see its look of displeasure can't imagine that it would ever bestow such a smile. I drank in the unbelievable
reality, my beloved's smile, and I said to myself: What this means is
that the doors of heaven have opened and are showering my heart

with consolation. However, it won't do anymore for me to remain idle or silent.

That afternoon I won a second smile, and the following morning a third, so I felt as though I had to overcome inertia through decisive action. The following Friday morning I left home in my black coat, looking smart and filled with determination and resolve. I found my sweetheart sunning herself on the balcony. After we'd exchanged a smile of greeting, I cast a cautious glance around me and gestured to her to come down and meet me. What audacity! Who would have believed it? I focused my gaze on her in trepidation. She looked back at me serenely, then a sweet smile crossed her lips and she retreated inside. Was she coming to meet me? Lord! I'd spent the entire previous night rehearsing for this hoped-for rendezvous. The younger sister appeared on the balcony and was followed shortly thereafter by the mother, and the two of them began looking in my direction. Did they know? This was what I hoped, since in this way I was more likely to ward off the danger posed by Muhammad Gawdat. My sweetheart appeared in the window as she put on her coat. My heart made a violent leap as I stood there, waiting like someone in a dream. Strangely, though, my feeling of happiness suddenly changed and grew tepid, like a beautiful voice that's interrupted by a cough. I was gripped by an unnamed fear and a painful confusion, as though I were trying to recall something important that my memory refused to yield. Realizing the seriousness of the step I was about to take, I was overwhelmed with uncertainty and fear and had the urge to flee. The moment passed quickly, however, and I recovered my former confidence and joy. Heaving a sigh of relief, I crossed the sidewalk feeling merry and gay to wait for the love of my yearning heart. Then I saw her emerge through the door of the apartment building—lissome, stylish, and lovely—in a squirrel-gray coat. She walked to the tram stop with her usual dignified gait and stopped some distance from me. Her mother was on the balcony as if to bless the tryst and lend it propriety. Hence, in addition to the happiness I felt, I had a sense of responsibility. The tram that was to transport us arrived and I looked at it with gratitude, praying for its well-being,

199

and asking God to grant its driver happiness and a raise! We got on together and I saw her proceed, contrary to her usual custom, toward the first-class compartment, so I followed her. There was no one in the compartment but a man and a woman, so my girl sat down, blushing with embarrassment. She may have expected me to sit down beside her and greet her. However, my courage failed me, so I sat down on the opposite seat feeling awkward, shy, and annoyed with myself. As the tram took off down the street, I stole mute, patient glances at her until we passed the Abbas Bridge. She rose and left the compartment, with me following close behind, and we got off at the next stop. Then she proceeded in the direction of a street that ran parallel to the Nile and I tagged along. My heart aflutter, I came gradually closer to her feeling desperately shy.

Then, in a voice that was just barely audible I said, "Good morning."

She smiled without looking at me and murmured no less shyly, "Good morning."

Her response to my greeting overwhelmed me with delight, and as we walked along side by side I thought fervently: O Lady Umm Hashim, look down upon us! I was truly afraid, and intensely flustered and inhibited. I tried to remember the things I'd rehearsed the day before, but I was feeling so muddled that my mind went blank and I couldn't find my tongue. We walked quite some distance without my saying a word. How was I supposed to begin the conversation? What could I say? A terrible anguish came over me since I realized, of course, that I was supposed to speak and that it wasn't fitting for me to be so quiet. Nevertheless, God didn't inspire me with a single word, and it seemed as though speech were an art I'd never practiced. Then, as if she realized how ill at ease I was, she looked at me with a gentle smile on her lips, and I smiled shyly back.

The only thing I could think of to say was another, "Good morning!"

"Good morning!" she replied, her smile broader this time.

Lord! Had my vocabulary gone bankrupt? And I fell back into the same torment once again. I felt as though a couple of iron hands were squeezing my neck and that I couldn't bear this miserable situation a single moment longer. Hopelessness and timidity had such a hold on me that I cried out to her for help, saying, "I'm sorry. I don't know what to say. This is the first time I've talked to a girl!"

She let a short laugh escape in spite of herself and, as though my very shyness had emboldened her, she said playfully, "Actually, it's the second."

Ah! She was referring to my pursuit of her three days earlier. I remembered it in astonishment, as though I weren't really her courageous hero. Be that as it may, her playfulness emboldened me and alleviated my awkwardness and shyness. It also enabled me to say, "Please don't think badly of me. I swear to God, if my tongue weren't tied, I'd have a whole world of things to say."

She laughed, looking up and aiming her glance more fully at me.

Then she said, "Do you realize we haven't introduced ourselves yet?"

Here was a question I could answer. If only the conversation could have been questions on her part, and answers on mine.

Feeling relieved, I said, "Kamil Ru'ba Laz, employee at the Ministry of War."

I wished I could tell her about my monthly income and my anticipated fortune.

As for her, she said, "Rabab Gabr, teacher at the Abbasiya Kindergarten."

I loved the name just as I'd loved the person to whom it belonged.

"Rabab!" I said, as though I wanted to hear the way it sounded one more time.

Feeling heartened and more familiar with her now, I said simply, "Imagine! I've been stealing glances at your face for two years now, and I still didn't even know your name!"

"Two years!" she exclaimed as a look of astonishment came over her pretty face.

Pleased by the fact that she was so surprised, I said enthusiastically, "Yes, it's been nearly two years. Hadn't you noticed?"

I listened intently so as to drink in the voice that I'd longed to hear for so long.

201

"I only noticed a few months ago!" she said with a laugh. "How patient you are!"

There was a barb in her words, of that I was certain. It was as if she were saying, "What kept you quiet for so long that you nearly missed your chance?" Taking advantage of the opportunity to declare what I wished I could have declared long before, I said, "I was prevented from saying anything by difficult circumstances. I couldn't propose to you when I wasn't qualified to do so. Then the circumstances changed and my situation improved. It wasn't long after that that I approached you on the tram, though I was so crazy, I acted in a way that was out of character for me. The fact is that once I was able to come forward, I only waited a matter of days, even though I . . . ." I nearly said, "even though I'd loved you for two years," but the words wouldn't come out. . . . "Even though what you know to be the case had been so for two years."

She looked straight ahead with a faint smile on her face, saying, "And what is it that I know to be the case?"

I fell silent for a few moments as I gathered my strength. Then I said, "You know that I . . . ."

My lips formed the words, 'I love you' without uttering them aloud. However, she saw and understood without a doubt. As my heart nearly beat out of my chest, I lowered my gaze bashfully and went into a passing stupor that absented me from everything around me as though I'd momentarily exited the universe. I looked over at her furtively and found her blushing, with a pensive, serious look on her face. This was a sacred moment. Indeed, time labors under the burden of the weighty moments that have been witnessed by humanity in the course of its history. However, this kind of moment remains among the most glorious of all that time has known. Nor is its weightiness diminished by the fact that it takes place thousands of times every day all over the world. It's the only thing that's repeated time and time again without ever becoming wearisome. After all, how could it—love—become wearisome when it contains the very secret of existence? I couldn't take her into my arms—not because of the orange-laden caravan of camels that happened to be passing by, but rather because I wasn't allowed to touch her at all. We walked some distance without saying a word, my timidity preventing me from elaborating on this particular point. Rethinking the matter from its other angles, I said with a smile, "What happened with Muhammad Gawdat?"

Staring at me incredulously, she asked, "How did you know about him?"

She listened with rapt attention as I told her the story of the meeting that had taken place between the two of us.

Then she said, "He's a virtuous, respectable man and a high-ranking employee, and my father welcomed him. As for my mother, she wasn't terribly enthusiastic about his proposal since he's so much older than I am. Besides, he's been married before and he has a fifteen-year-old daughter. I told my mother about our meeting on the street three days ago, and she stipulated that they need to know everything about you before she says what she thinks."

My heart fluttered with a combination of trepidation and joy.

Though there was no need to inquire, I asked her, "And does she know about this meeting of ours?"

She smiled without making any reply. I remembered my job uneasily and with embarrassment. However, it didn't even occur to me to lie or change the facts.

I said, "As I've told you, I'm an employee at the Ministry of War. However, I have a monthly income of sixteen pounds from family endowments. In addition, I own more than a thousand pounds. I have nothing to be ashamed of in my past, and if they should inquire about me, you'll see that I've told nothing but the truth."

She smiled and said earnestly, "Of that there's absolutely no doubt."

I gazed over at her with profound gratitude. At that moment I thought back on the longing and misery I'd endured on her account, and I was flooded with a joy that defies words. At the same time I wondered fearfully: Will I come up to her mother's standards? Won't she despise my lowly position, or not find me worthy of this lovable teacher? My heart shrank in terror, and I thought of telling her what was troubling me, but timidity got the better of me.

Then a new thought occurred to me and I asked her without hesitation, "Will you continue in your job if things turn out the way I hope?"

"Why not?" she replied. "I adore my work, and lots of my colleagues . . . ."

Realizing what she'd been about to say, my heart fluttered joyously and I cast her a timid look filled with hopefulness and affection.

"That's good," I said approvingly.

Silence reigned briefly, and the sound of our footsteps on the sunlight-strewn boulevard seemed to grow louder. I glanced over at the Nile and saw its dark surface rippling beneath the scattered pearls of light. I began peering nervously and warily into the faces of the few passersby. The sun had tempered the chill in the air, causing a joyous energy to flow through our beings. I could feel life's goodness in a way I'd never felt it before, and I was filled with such gratitude I wished I could kneel down and kiss the earth in thanksgiving. However, I hadn't forgotten the serious matters that were preoccupying me, or what appeared to me to be serious matters.

So I asked her, "Tell me now what I'm supposed to do."

"What do you mean?" she asked in bewilderment.

"I'm supposed to ask for your hand," I said uncertainly.

She looked straight ahead, puzzled, and said nothing.

At a loss, I asked her, "How . . . how do people usually get engaged?"

She giggled and said gently, "Through matchmakers, or through personal contact. Don't you know about these things?"

Her mention of matchmakers reminded me of my mother, and my heart shrank in terror. Then I wondered to myself: Do I have the tact and courage it takes to make the needed personal contact?

It was then that I realized I didn't know a thing about her father, so I said, "Could you tell me something about your father?"

Eyeing me doubtfully, she murmured, "Don't you know anything about him?"

Simply and honestly I replied, "Unfortunately, I don't."

I realized then that she thought I'd been busily finding out everything I needed to know about the family I aspired to marry into, and she was wondering why on earth I hadn't lifted a finger throughout the entire time I'd loved her, content with nothing but gazes, longing, and despair.

In a tone not without a touch of pride, she said, "Gabr Bey Sayyid, irrigation inspector for the Ministry of Labor."

"I'd be honored to make his acquaintance," I said reverently.

I was aware of the weight of responsibility that now lay on my shoulders. However, I had no choice but to say, "I'll meet with him myself. When would be a convenient time?"

"Sometime next week, since he'll be going away after that on a routine inspection tour. But after he comes home from the ministry he rarely goes out."

We'd walked quite a long way by this time, so I suggested that we turn back. So we turned around and started heading back. We exchanged only a few words during our return. I was so happy, I thought I must be dreaming. However, not for a moment did I lose sight of the seriousness of the step I was about to take.

36

I was overwhelmed with fear and anxiety, and once again I experienced that stifling feeling that had come over me on the day when my professor at the Faculty of Law called me up to the podium. Would my feet be able to carry me to Gabr Bey's house? Would I be able to speak to the man about what was on my mind? O God, grant me Your mercy, for love is afflicting me with torments that are more than I can bear! When I tasted the frightening reality and consoled myself with dreams, I found myself on a deserted island where the only other living being was my beloved. In a place like that, love doesn't require the lover to deliver a speech, or even to say a word or communicate with anyone. So in the midst of my ordeal, my soul would go flying away to that deserted island.

I spent Saturday and Sunday in a violent inner torment. Hence, I decided to seek refuge from the torment of my thoughts by meeting the danger head-on. That afternoon I spruced myself up and left the house. Reciting the Throne Verse, I crossed the street with a quaking heart. When I crossed the bridge and the building appeared in the distance, my feet grew heavy and I nearly returned home. However, my resolve was marvelous, and the fear that my sweetheart would think me slow in coming left no room for vacillation. I began encouraging myself by saying that if there were no hope, she wouldn't have agreed to meet me on Friday, and she wouldn't have prepared the way for me to meet with her father. Pushing my heavy feet forward one after the other, I began approaching the building little by little. There was no one either in the window or on the balcony, which was a relief to me since I feel awkward walking when people's eyes are on me. Then I found myself coming up to the doorman.

The man rose and looked at me questioningly.

"Gabr Bey Sayyid," I said.

"Second floor," he replied.

I ascended the stairs in fear and trepidation, stopping at every landing to catch my breath. When I found myself outside the flat's closed door, I grew weak in the knees and was tempted to turn and flee, to postpone the critical visit until another day. However, I heatedly rejected the idea. It occurred to me to go back down and calm my tense nerves by walking around for a while and reorganizing my thoughts, and again, I nearly retreated. However, the next moment I began wondering: Might not the gatekeeper be suspicious of me if he saw me coming down right after I'd spoken to him, then saw me come back to the building just a few minutes later? Thus I thought better of going back down the stairs. Even so, I stood there without moving a muscle. I gazed steadily at the door until I imagined its keyhole to be an eye staring mockingly into my face. I shifted my gaze to the doorbell, and my eyes fixed themselves on it in fear and panic. What would happen to me if the door opened suddenly and I saw someone I recognized and who would recognize me? I wished at that moment that my life had maintained its usual, unhurried pace rather than crashing headlong into this love that had turned it upside down. Then suddenly from inside the house I heard a shrill voice shout, "Turn on the radio, Sabah!" Trembling all over, I listened intently, feeling more frightened than ever. Shame on you, Mama! I thought. Wouldn't it have been better for you to be in my place now? Then I heard the sound of footsteps coming up the stairs, and although I was more agitated than ever by now, I had no choice but to keep on going. I approached the door and brought my hand up to the doorbell. I hesitated for a moment, feeling myself in an uproar. Then I pressed the button and heard a loud, obnoxious ring. Having worked myself into a pathetic state, I stood aside and waited.

The door opened to reveal a coal-black face belonging to a servant woman who looked to be around fifty years old.

"Yes?" she said, peering at me with sparkling eyes.

Hoping the bey would be out for some reason, I asked, "Is Gabr Bey home?"

"Yes, he is," she replied. "Who wishes to see him?"

Taking a card out of my wallet, I presented it to her and said, "I'd be obliged if the bey could grant me a brief interview."

The servant took the card and disappeared while I waited, my heart aflutter and my soul in turmoil. I imagined the bey reading the card aloud while everyone around him exchanged smiling glances, then rushed to hide in some safe place whence they could observe me when I came in. My face flushed with embarrassment at the thought and I became more distraught. Then the servant's head popped out of the door again as she said, "Come in."

I went in with my head bowed, and she led me to a door immediately to the right of the entrance. I entered the parlor, which was an elegant room with navy blue furniture, then betook myself to a chair between two sofas some distance from the door and sat down. I could hardly believe I was actually sitting in their house, and I began listening intently, feeling fearful, apprehensive, and restless. At first I hoped the bey would be delayed so that I could have time to compose myself. Then, given the torment of waiting, I started to hope he'd arrive quickly so as to put an end to my suffering. I don't know how long I waited before I heard footsteps approaching. The bey entered and I rose to my feet. He welcomed me politely and gestured toward the chair, saying, "Make yourself comfortable."

He sat down on the sofa not far away. Around fifty years old, he was tall and slender, with a physique and eyes similar to my sweetheart's, and I liked him right away. He was wearing a loose, reddish woolen wrap, and his hands were redolent with a fragrant cologne.

He smiled at me warmly and said, "Welcome, Kamil. We're honored to have you here."

"Thank you, sir," I said appreciatively.

Did he know the purpose of my visit? Had he heard previously of the name he'd read on the card?

Whatever the case may be, I thought, I had no choice but to broach the subject with him as though he knew nothing about it. I'd written down an outline of what I thought I ought to say, and I'd read it over and over again until I'd memorized it before leaving the house.

In a low voice I said, "I'm sorry to inconvenience you with this visit from someone you haven't met before."

"It's an honor to meet you, Kamil," he said, the gracious smile never leaving his fine lips. "Are you from around here?"

"Yes, sir," I replied, happy to have been given a reason to speak. "I live in Manyal."

"It's a nice, peaceful neighborhood."

Taking more and more of a liking to him, I said, "I was born there, too. My grandfather, Colonel Abdulla Bey Hasan, moved there more than seventy years ago."

"Abdullah Bey Hasan," he said thoughtfully. "I think I've heard that name before. Was he your grandfather on your father's side?"

"No," I said, feeling distressed. "He was my maternal grandfather. My father was from the Laz family."

"Was he an officer, too?"

Feeling increasingly anxious, I replied, "No, he wasn't, may he rest in peace. He was a notable."

Still smiling, he said, "I thought he might have been an officer, since people of the same profession often marry into each other's families."

I affirmed what he'd said, then he fell silent, and I couldn't think of anything else to say. As I went over the things I'd memorized, I recalled the critical statement on which my fortune in life hung. However, my tongue was tied and I said nothing. It wasn't long before I'd gone back to feeling muddled and anxious, and my head was ablaze with embarrassment. At that moment the young servant—the one who knew me well—came in carrying the tea tray. She set it down on a table whose surface was plated with a polished mirror. Then, concealing a faint smile, she withdrew. I welcomed her arrival with the tea, since it rescued me from the awkward silence that was weighing on me almost unbearably. The bey filled two glasses and invited me to take one. I picked up my glass with gratitude and began sipping it unhurriedly while my mind raced. Then, having reluctantly finished my tea, I found myself faced once again with Gabr Bey and the mysterious, cordial smile with which he encouraged me to speak. What had to be done, had to be done. Otherwise, the session would turn into a ridiculous joke. So, I thought: let me feign a bit of manliness in the presence of the person whose son-in-law I aspire to be before I lose his respect.

Gathering my courage, I said in what was, admittedly, a tremulous, unsteady voice, "Sir, I wanted . . . I mean, the fact is that I'd like to have the honor of becoming your son-in-law."

The statement I'd written out and memorized wasn't much different from what I said. I felt muddled after I'd opened my mouth. However, God came to my rescue, and I managed to express what was on my mind with a fair degree of success. I looked over at the man and found him still smiling.

He paused a few moments that were a source of agony to my terrified soul.

Then he said ever so graciously, "I thank you for your high opinion of us."

He fell silent for a few more pensive moments, then continued, "However, I ask you to give me two weeks to consult with other concerned parties."

"Of course, of course," I said. "I can only thank you for your generosity and hospitality."

I rose to my feet in preparation to leave. He invited me to stay longer, but I declined apologetically, thanking him for his gracious offer. Then I bade him farewell and left. Once outside, I heaved a deep sigh, feeling as though a heavy burden had been lifted from my shoulders. Now that the ordeal was over, the task looked like a simple one that shouldn't have caused me such fear, anxiety, and dismay. I smiled in relief, then burst out laughing.

37

I enjoyed the intoxication of relief and victory until evening. Then back came angst, that old cohort that never tires of my company. Would Gabr Bey agree to let a petty employee like me marry his daughter? Wouldn't Muhammad Gawdat be the more likely candidate despite my income from our family's estate? After all, he was an engineer like Gabr Bey, not to mention his being a neighbor and a friend. As for me, I had no such qualifications. On the other hand, Rabab hadn't taken to him, and if she'd had any interest in him, she wouldn't have met with me and encouraged me to meet with her father. This thought cooled my burning heart and brought back my intoxication. However, it wasn't sufficient to eradicate the doubt and anxiety that lurked deep inside me. As the days of waiting passed one by one, I only grew more depressed and pessimistic. Consequently, I kept the matter a secret from my mother, enduring the wait and the bitterness of doubt in a fearsome solitude lest she learn of my failure if that was to be my fate. Strangely, we'd never returned to the subject of marriage since that tempestuous evening. Her behavior reflected an unaccustomed reserve that wasn't lost on my sensitive radar. There were numerous occasions when she seemed like an angry child who's gone off to pout.

Whenever I came to her with something to talk about, she would receive me with a kind of suspicion that wouldn't leave her until she'd assured herself of the nature of the subject to be discussed. I was annoyed by the change in her, but I continued to treat her with courtesy and affection.

During this same period of time, a fellow employee at my workplace whispered in my ear that, according to an employee in the personnel department, 'somebody' had been inquiring about me. Hence, news quickly spread in the warehousing section that I was planning to marry. Accordingly, they began jovially offering me personal advice, which caused me to feel even more resentful and angry. When the waiting period was over, I went to see Gabr Bey Sayyid. However, I didn't go to his house this time for fear that the answer I'd receive would be a disappointment. Instead, I went to meet him at the Ministry of Labor, where he gave me a warm welcome and announced his agreement! Thus my torment came to an end and I was reinstated in the land of the living. During this meeting we agreed on a date for the engagement party. If a person's life is a mixture of misery and happiness, it seemed to me then that my days of misery were over, and that I would be rewarded for my patient endurance, misery, and fear with untainted bliss for the rest of my days. I went home, summoned my mother, and informed her of what had happened.

After listening to me in resignation and astonishment, she asked, "Why did you keep all this from me?"

"I didn't expect it to turn out the way it has," I said with a nervous laugh.

"My Goodness!" she said testily, "Did you really think they'd refuse you? What a naive child you are! Don't you know that there are countless girls out there a thousand times better than yours who'd be more than happy to marry you?"

In a tone that made clear that I had no desire to pursue the discussion, I said, "I'm waiting for you to congratulate me, Mama."

Leaning toward me and kissing my cheek, she murmured, "I'm the one who ought to be congratulated." Then she uttered a lengthy prayer of supplication for me.

Being someone who found it difficult to hide her feelings, my mother's face was an open book. As such, the look in her eyes betrayed a profound disappointment that roiled my peace of mind. I ignored it, however, pretending to believe her words, and before long I'd become too engrossed in my own happiness to worry about her. On that same day I wrote a letter to my brother, informing him of what had happened and inviting him to the engagement party. I visited my sister Radiya as well and invited her too. On the appointed day we all went together, though I honestly don't know how I got the courage to attend. Linking arms with my brother Medhat, I asked him to be my escort, and I wore him out with my awkwardness, passivity, and shyness.

I didn't utter a word the length of the entire party. I didn't even take my eyes off the floor. I was surrounded the whole time by curious onlookers, both men and women, and I didn't get over my fright until after the relatives had gone and the only people left were immediate family.

Gabr Bey's wife said to me with a laugh, "You're so shy, Kamil! Now I know why you hovered around your bride for months as though you were afraid to make a move!"

My heart skipped a beat in response to what she said, and I glanced furtively at my mother to see what impact the woman's words had had on her. However, I found her engrossed in a conversation with Gabr Bey. I sat the entire time beside Rabab without being able to bring myself to look at her, badly as I wanted to. All I managed to do was to cast a quick, diffident glance at her as she entered the room surrounded by a halo of light and splendor. Then, flustered and self-conscious, I reverted into a stupor in which I absented myself from everything around me. When the family celebration had dispersed and we were on our way home, my brother Medhat chuckled out loud, saying in amazement, "You need to find a cure for your shyness. I swear to God, I've never seen anything like you!"

As for me, I took no notice of his ribbing and criticism. I was too happy.

38

After this, visits became easier for me. In fact, I got used to them and even came to enjoy them. Now I could ring the doorbell without my heart being wrenched out of my chest. I could walk to the sitting room without tripping on the edge of a carpet or piece of furniture, and I could meet with my new family without staring at the floor the entire time and stammering when I spoke. In fact, I could make conversation within the limits of my ability and even laugh if the occasion warranted it. My new family was an amiable and lovable family of which my sweetheart was the embodiment, and this alone was sufficient testimony to its goodness. My relationship with Gabr Bey Sayyid grew into a friendship, and there came to be such warmth and familiarity between Madame Nazli and me that we were like mother and son. The little ones, Muhammad and Rouhiya, charmed me with their bounciness and wit, and even the young servant girl and the black maid won a share of my affection. I loved all of them with a love that reflected the passion in my heart for my beloved, and an unspoken longing for intimate, loving companionship.

Gabr Bey Sayyid was one of those men who only leave home given some urgent necessity. Hence, if he wasn't at the ministry or on an inspection tour in the countryside, he would be at home with his wife and children. From the first day we met, he struck me as a gracious, likable man. Nor did I fail to notice—despite the fact that I wasn't the most observant of people—that he was a dutiful, submissive husband and that his wife was the one who ruled the roost. However, this did nothing to undermine his status, and in fact, he may have enjoyed more of his children's affection than did the mother herself.

Gabr Bey wasn't without a certain penchant for boasting despite his having passed the half-century mark. This was easily observable if you heard him speaking about his work, his position, and his dealings with peers and subordinates, or making reference to his inspection tours and the things he had observed. He was quite critical of young engineers who had received their educations in England and Germany. He would say that engineering studies were the same in Egypt as they were in Europe and that one could only become well versed in the field through practical experience, which was something young people didn't understand. During those days he was worried about his position at the ministry. He would complain constantly about the political persecution he was suffering, which, as he saw it, was due to his connection with the former minister of labor, who belonged to the Wafd Party. Once he even went so far as to declare that he was thinking of applying for retirement and getting involved in political activity. However, he didn't have the chance to expound on his point of view, since his wife object with a decisiveness that left no room for discussion. All in all, I was ambivalent in my feelings toward him. On one hand, I felt dwarfed by him given the insignificance of my position in the government and my limited education. On the other hand, I felt proud to be related by marriage to a man of such stature, prestige, and professional expertise.

Unlike her husband, Madame Nazli was rather short of stature and exceedingly plump. She was nearly fifty years old, but she was still quite attractive, a fact that indicated, no doubt, how beautiful she'd been in her youth. And in spite of her obesity, she was in a state of constant motion, so vigilant and tireless was she in caring for her household, her children, and her husband. Once her husband complained to me of her extreme concern—a concern that bordered on obsession and exhaustion—for arranging and cleaning the house and overseeing the servant and the cook. However, his complaint wasn't without a hint of admiration and approval.

Madame Nazli struck me as being charming and unaffected, and she laughed when she thought back on the days I'd spent peering silently up at the balcony and the window. She compared my shyness to the lack of respect shown by other young men, then commented, "Rabab is lucky to have you, and you're lucky to have Rabab, since she, also, isn't like other girls these days."

And it was true. There was nothing and no one like my sweetheart. She was vivacity, intelligence, and beauty all wrapped into one, and with every passing day I grew more attached to her, more enamored of her, and more filled with admiration for her. How sweet her voice was, how graceful her gestures, and how lovely her seriousness and poise. And besides all this, she was the epitome of ideal womanhood. She would look at me with devotion, affection, and candor without any need for some feigned levity or studied affectation. I'd never had the chance to be alone with her since our engagement was announced, though I longed badly to do so. I wanted to be able to take in the sight of her radiant face far from others' watchful eyes. At the same time, it was a bit daunting to think of this hoped-for solitude given the difficulty I was likely to suffer in such a situation when it came to expressing myself, and the resultant awkwardness and distress. Hence, I contented myself with what had been allotted to me within the family circle, where I was happy and safe, satisfied for the time being with the occasional fleeting glance or brief chat, and with the bliss that filled my heart and soul simply from being in her presence. Contrary to what I'd feared, her way of speaking to me was genial and spontaneous, without a trace of the condescension, philosophizing, pretentiousness, or pedantry that one might find in someone with her education.

It was agreed that the wedding would take place during the summer vacation, and they spared no effort in preparing her trousseau. Madame Nazli suggested that they move to a larger flat so that I could live with them. However, I was put off by the proposal, which reminded me of my mother. When I explained that I wouldn't be able to do so because I couldn't abandon my mother, Madame Nazli said, "Your mother is a good and thoughtful woman. However, she doesn't seem to enjoy other people's company!"

I understood what she meant. As a matter of fact, my mother had only visited my fiancée's house once since our engagement, and then only under duress.

With no little chagrin I said, "My mother's gotten used to being alone, and she's never really enjoyed visits."

I had told them parts of my life story, leaving gaps when it came to things that weren't pleasant to remember.

I can't deny that Madame Nazli's observation bothered me, since it reminded me of things I was afraid of, and I entreated God earnestly to spare me the evils of discord both then and in the days to come.

Once when I was sitting with my sweetheart and her mother, I got up the courage to mention the days when I'd been keeping my eye out for Rabab without saying a word, and I expressed my amazement that things had come to this happy conclusion, a conclusion I could hardly have dreamed of.

Laughing, my beloved said, "Even so, you'd hardly taken a single step before everything fell into place in the twinkling of an eye!"

Madame Nazli added, "For so long we wondered what this young man wanted! I used to warn Rabab that you might be one of those fellows who stalk girls in the street. At one point we concluded that you must be busy making inquiries about us the way prospective suitors do. Then when you kept on hesitating, I took offense, and I wondered what it was that you hadn't liked about us."

Pained and flustered, I said, "Actually, I didn't do anything at all. I didn't even know your names until the last minute!"

In terms of money, I had what to me seemed like a veritable fortune, and I showered my beloved with gifts. I sought out my sister Radiya for advice in such matters while keeping them a secret from my mother. She gave me the sincerest of counsel and guided me in discerning what 'duty' required, especially during special seasons like Eid al-Fitr and Eid al-Adha, and thanks to her wise input, I became a model fiancé.

The relationship between my mother and me remained very good, to all appearances, at least, and I took care to include her in the task of making preparations for our new life so that she would appear to be giving it her blessing. So, for example, I assigned her to look for a new flat for us to live in, and her choice fell on a building on Qasr al-Aini Street three tram stops away from my beloved's house. She neither said nor did anything that would have upset me. However, she seemed like someone who feels helpless and who's been relegated against her will to life's periphery. In fact, she withdrew within herself so completely that I was at a loss to know what to do about it. It broke my heart, yet there was nothing in all of existence that could have dammed the stream of happiness that was flooding my being day and night. And if the truth be told, those were the happiest days of my life.

39

One day after the family had made preparations for the wedding, Madame Nazli said, "Rabab is the first of our children to marry, so her wedding celebration has to be an especially festive one."

When I heard what she was saying, I was terrified. However, I no longer had any choice but to face the critical issue that I'd avoided for so long out of fear and cowardice.

"Do you really think it's necessary to celebrate the marriage with a party?" I asked nervously.

She shot me a disapproving look as though she were taken aback by my question.

"Of course!" she said.

"Singing girls, a wedding procession, dancing, and all the rest?" I muttered in dismay.

"It has to be a lavish, unforgettable, evening."

Gripped with fear, I looked up at her like someone begging for mercy.

"I couldn't bear to be escorted in some sort of solemn procession in front of a crowd of guests!" I said hopelessly. "It's more than I could take."

Looking bewildered and irritated, she said, "I don't understand a thing! Are you really that shy?"

With the fervor of someone defending his very life, I said imploringly, "I can't, I can't! Believe me, Madame, I'd rather die than have to walk in a public procession surrounded by guests and singing girls!"

"This is incredible," she said. "You'll be the first man who's ever wanted to run away from his own wedding!"

"Maybe," I said sorrowfully, my forehead and cheeks burning with humiliation. "But there's nothing that can be done about it. I beg you in God's name to have mercy on me!"

"So what are we supposed to do?" she asked reproachfully.

"We can write up the contract with just family members present," I said earnestly. "And then I take the bride home with me!"

"How could you call that a wedding celebration?"

If the issue had had to do with something other than my timidity, I would have given in without a fight. After all, I'm quick to go along with other people's wishes no matter what kind of sacrifice is involved— unless, that is, I'm defending my very life, in which case I turn into someone who'll fight to the death. Drawing strength from my fear and despair, I begged, I pleaded, and I insisted until, shaking her head in amazement, the woman gave up trying to convince me. Given the fact that up to that point I'd been the proverbially generous suitor, I had no reason to fear that they'd think I was trying to avoid the expenses involved in a wedding party. However, Gabr Bey Sayyid informed me after this that he'd decided to invite a group of his closest friends and that he was going to host a sumptuous dinner banquet for everyone. Not long after this he told me that a friend of his was an amateur singer and musician who'd volunteered to provide entertainment that evening for the limited circle he was planning to invite.

As if to make the news easier on me, he said, "This way a senior employee will be providing the entertainment for your wedding!"

"I really, truly regret that I can't comply with your wishes to put on a huge, impressive wedding party," I said dismally, "but I just couldn't bear to be part of a public procession."

Shrugging his shoulders nonchalantly, he said with a smile, "I don't like to upset you, so have it your way."

The bride's trousseau was taken to the new flat, a special room was prepared for my mother, and we moved from Manyal to our new abode a week before the wedding day. The bridal suite, preparation of which was overseen personally by my sister Radiya, left me speechless. I began making the rounds of the rooms in a state of blissful delight. When I came to the bedroom, I went in after some hesitation, and then only with the greatest circumspection and awe. What a sight! It was enough to take one's breath away! I began looking all around me, half awake and half dreaming: A bed that looked as though it were made of gold, silk covers the color of pink roses, and a polished, sparkling mirror. The furniture seemed to pulsate with life, its beautiful colors reminiscent of blushing cheeks and glistening eyes, and its drawn curtains emanated soft, melodic whispers that made one's heart race.

On the morning of the solemn day I wondered to myself: When will I take my bride home with me, leaving all the people and hubbub behind? If only tradition dictated that the man wait for his bride at home, without having to go through all this agony! It looked as though it was going to be a trying day, the sort of day people like me weren't cut out for, and not for a moment was I free of a sense of fear and dread. The first half of the day was spent getting me ready, and my brother Medhat took me to a famed barber who sent me away looking fit to kill.

When my sister saw me she said mischievously, "You're better looking than your bride! Don't you think so, Mama?"

My mother began to say something, then sealed her lips without uttering a word, and I kept wondering what it was she'd been planning to say. I put on the black tuxedo in spite of the hot weather. Then shortly before mid-afternoon I went to the bride's house accompanied by my mother, my brother, my sister and her husband, my uncle and some of his daughters, as well as my maternal aunt and her family. As we approached the entrance to the building I saw that the ground had been spread with bright-colored sand and that large light bulbs were hanging from brightly colored poles. Filled with distress, I said to myself:

This isn't what we'd agreed on! When we went up the stairs I insisted on walking in the rear with my arm in Medhat's. No sooner had the first of us stepped into the flat than we were received with a storm of shrill ululations. I squeezed my brother's arm, wishing I could disappear. But where could I go? I lowered my eyes and walked—or, rather, was dragged by Medhat—to the reception room without seeing a single thing around me, though I could sense with my ears and nose that the house was packed with well-wishers.

As I was seated, still clinging to Medhat's arm, I whispered in his ear, "Please don't leave me."

"Buck up," he whispered back. "Otherwise, your bride will seem less shy than you are!"

Hardly had the harrowing moment of reception passed when Gabr Bey Sayyid came up to introduce me to his coterie of specially invited guests. As I stood there, flustered as usual, I went to work shaking hands as my tongue repeated mechanically, "Nice to meet you. . . . Nice to meet you." I sat down again without having memorized a single name. There then ensued a lengthy exchange that I couldn't comprehend, still less take part in. Still my usual shy self, I grew more and more self-conscious, and everyone seemed to be winking at each other mockingly or laughing at me in their hearts. Time dragged on until I was invited to sign the wedding contract, an event which, much to my relief, was to take place in a room that was nearly empty. On the way there, however, there was an explosion of joyful ululations as if the guests were engaged in a fierce competition to see which of them could outdo the rest, and again I had the urge to disappear.

I returned to my seat and to my muteness and time continued to pass, though to me it was a time for nothing but silence, frenzied thoughts, and a wild desire to flee. Then we were invited to a meal that was being served on the roof in the open air. For someone like me, dinner would just be one more ordeal. Unlike conversation, however, it was at least tolerable, since the guests would be too busy eating to do anything else, and that would give me some peace and quiet. After the meal we returned to our seats, my arm still locked in my brother's, and then the singing began. The amateur vocalist and his band—who were amateurs as well—took their places at the front of the reception room. He belted out "Oh, How I Miss You!" in a reasonably pleasant voice that, in my opinion, was better than that of the singer at the vegetable market pub. Gabr Bey Sayyid brought the band a couple of bottles of whiskey, while others were served brimming glasses.

"Won't you have a drink or two?" my brother whispered in my ear.

I gave him a look whose meaning he didn't comprehend and said curtly, "Impossible."

I said it as though I were shocked at the mere suggestion, then retreated into silent recollections. How I'd adored getting drunk! So wasn't it amazing that I hadn't tasted a drop of liquor since the day I'd mustered the courage to speak to my beloved? I'd abandoned it without the slightest difficulty as though it had never been, and I hadn't been tempted to go back to it even once. The singing and conversation continued and the laughter grew louder. If it hadn't been for my awareness of the critical moment that awaited me, I might have taken to the atmosphere and gotten over my discomfort and tense nerves. As it was, however, I couldn't stop wondering: When will I receive my bride? Where? And will it take place out of other people's sight?

More time passed, then suddenly I was roused from my reverie by Gabr Bey Sayyid, who was standing in front of me and placing his hand on my shoulder.

"Let's go, Kamil," he said in a low voice. "The time has come!"

Looking up at him apprehensively, I murmured, "Is it time to go?"

"Not yet!" he said with a laugh, "But after a simple procession."

"No! No!" I cried in horror as a shudder went through my body. "We'd agreed that there wouldn't be any procession!"

"It isn't what you think," he said. "In the big parlor we've set up seats of honor on a dais for the bride and groom, so you come in with your bride and the two of you sit down on it. After all, everybody wants to see the newlyweds. And what fault is that of mine?"

His words were transformed in my imagination into fearsome images. I saw myself walking out past everyone to the bride's room, then bringing her back with guests surrounding us on all sides with applause and cheers. Then I saw us sitting there at the mercy of everyone's stares! O Lord! I thought. I'm sure to faint!

"But this is a procession!" I said heatedly. "And I can't do it! Please don't make me do it, sir! I can't."

"It's easier than you think. And what has to be done, has to be done. Otherwise, what will the guests say?"

Panicking, I cried, "Let them say whatever they like. I can't. I'll wait for the bride on the landing, then she and I will go home.'"

The man laughed in spite of himself. Then, raising his voice so that he could be heard over the singer, he shouted, "The landing! What an odd groom you are!"

Medhat, who'd been listening to us without saying anything, squeezed my arm and said firmly, "What kind of childish thinking is this? Don't you want to come out with your bride? Aren't you capable of making your way down an aisle in front of a selected group of respectable ladies? Do you want Gabr Bey to have to apologize to everyone on your behalf that you're too shy to appear in front of the female guests? What a scandal!"

Gabr Bey was heartened by what my brother had said. As for me, I stared at my brother in disbelief. I'd never imagined that the fatal stab would come from the very person I'd been counting on! My brother chuckled at my panic and bewilderment and was about to speak when I interrupted him, grieved and desperate, saying, "How can you push me to do something I'm not capable of? Do you want to make me a laughingstock in front of the women here?"

Moved by my desolate, pitiful tone of voice, Gabr Bey said gently, "All the ladies who've been invited are members of the family. You met them on the day of the engagement. And you'll see that I'm telling you the truth."

Still terror-stricken, I said imploringly, "I beg you in God's name to have mercy on me!"

As if he could see that words would get them nowhere, my brother addressed himself to Gabr Bey, saying, "We might agree on some sort

225

of compromise. The bride can come up to the dais escorted by her girlfriends, then I'll escort my brother to her and the two of them can sit there for a while surrounded by family before they leave."

Gabr Bey gestured to me not to raise any further objections, then left.

As for me, I turned to my brother in a fury and said, "What a traitor you are! How can you call this a compromise when all it is a way of torturing me?"

With a resounding laugh that reminded me of our father, he replied, "You'd disgrace an entire country! Now quit your arguing and we'll go together. As for me, I'd be happy to be escorted down an aisle of pretty ladies any day!"

He fell silent for a moment, then thumped me on the shoulder and said, "If you've got cold feet, then run away and give up the bride!"

And with that, I resigned myself to reality, feeling hopeless, weary and dismayed. As the band played "Here Comes the Bride," my heart throbbed with dread, and I could feel the danger drawing near. And as I heard the ululations coming from the parlor, my strength gave out on me.

I turned to Medhat, saying, "Isn't there any way out of this?"

Pulling me by the arm, he rose to his feet as he replied, "There's one way, and it's the way that leads to the dais in the other room. I swear, you're like a little boy being dragged in to be circumcised!"

He started walking. Meanwhile, my feet moved while my heart sank.

As we came through the door, he whispered to me, "Now look up. Stare into those pretty ladies' faces until they look down in embarrassment!"

However, I advanced slowly, my head lowered the entire time. I was certain that my appearance would make anybody want to laugh. I heard a woman's voice asking, "Which one is the groom?" "The tall one!" another voice replied. The place was packed, and I saw innumerable legs and white shoes along either side of the path that had been cleared for us.

Then I heard my brother whisper in my ear, "We've arrived at the dais. Get up there and greet your bride, then sit down."

After ascending a couple of steps, I lifted my eyes cautiously and fearfully and saw my beloved sitting beneath an arbor of flowers. She was decked out in a white bridal gown, and on her head there was a tiara of sweet-smelling jasmine blossoms from which silk ribbons cascaded down her back. She herself was splendor and light, jasmine and roses. When she saw me, she lowered her gaze and a faint smile appeared on her lips. By now I was just a step away from her, and I remembered my brother saying, "Greet your bride and sit down." But how was I supposed to greet her? By shaking her hand? Or by saying, "Good evening"? I hesitated, confused, and in her gentle, demure smile I could see that she was, in fact, awaiting my greeting. Then I remembered anew what I'd forgotten about for a few short moments: I became aware once again of the eyes that were staring at me and nearly burning a hole in my back. And with that I lost my composure and sat down on the empty seat without saying a word or moving my hand.

I'd made a mistake, of that there was no doubt. What would the women say? What would my beloved think? Ugh, what a situation! If I'd known earlier what I knew then, I would never have even thought of getting married. The music was playing, the ululations were ringing out, and the air was redolent was sweet perfumes. To die would be easier than to marry! Was I doomed forever to be the victim of platforms and podiums? The lecture podium at the Faculty of Law had put an end to my future, and this evening, the bridal dais was about to put an end to my life!

And, I wondered, what will the women say about the fact that I kept my eyes glued to the floor the entire time?

Then suddenly I thought of my mother. I wondered where she was sitting, and knew she must see me at that moment. The thought of it made me several times more bashful than before, and I felt like someone who's been caught doing something wrong. Responding to an irresistible urge to see where she was. I looked up cautiously, only to find that she was closer than I'd imagined her to be. She was sitting in the first row, directly in front of the dais. Our eyes met and we exchanged a faint smile. Then my imagination carried me back to an image from the distant past. I saw myself standing behind the fence at the primary school as she stood on the sidewalk on the other side of the fence sending me a look of encouragement and farewell. The memory caused an ache in my heart.

I sighed with relief when Madame Nazli came up to us and said with a smile, "And now, home with the two of you. Adieu!"

Then she said to me in a whisper, "The servant woman, Sabah, will be coming with her young mistress because she can't bear to part with her. So be good to her, and you'll find her to be the best of cooks."

Then she stepped aside with tears in her eyes. We rose from our places, I took my bride by the hand and we made our way for the door at a measured pace as well-wishers bade us farewell with ululations and song. A friend of Gabr Bey's had placed his car at our disposal for the evening, so we disappeared inside the vehicle and it whisked us away.

Turning toward her with a sigh as though I were seeing her for the first time, I said contentedly, "What an ordeal that was!"

"And what a bashful guy you are! Was it really that bad?"

I laughed to conceal my embarrassment, then immersed myself in a gladness that filled heart, eye, and spirit.

40

I closed the bedroom door with a trembling hand. This wing of the flat was empty and silent. It was separated from the other, where my mother's room and the sitting room were located, by two small parlors that opened onto each other. Our room was square, with the bed located in the center. Directly to the right of the entrance there was a long seat covered with pink upholstery, and on the opposite wall were the dressing table and the clothes rack. Rabab went over to the other side of the room and sat down at the dressing table, whose mirrors formed a half-circle around her, thereby framing her with reflected images of herself. She began removing her crown of jasmine blossoms, while I stood in the middle of the room with my elbow resting on the bed's wooden frame. As I stood there I looked back and forth between her lissome back and her reflections, every one of which made claim to be prettier than all the rest. This room was my world, and with it I would be content. This girl was my share of the universe, and with her I would be content. She was my love, my happiness, and my hope, and from this day forth I would ask the world for nothing more.

My beloved finished removing her crown and began combing out her chestnut locks with the deliberateness of someone who wants to gain as much time as she possibly can. Sooner or later, however, the waiting period was bound to come to an end. And what was to be done then?

Lord! My heart was wakeful and eager, my knees were trembling, and I wondered timorously what the next step would be. I realized, despite my agitation, that we ought to change our clothes. However, I didn't know how this was supposed to happen when we were both in the same room with the door closed! She seemed to be waiting for me to do or say something. She'd finished arranging her hair, though she was pretending the opposite, and there was a look of uncertainty and embarrassment on her face. I knew some things, this was true. However, there were details that I'd missed, and I was at a loss for both what to do and the determination to do it. If only I'd asked my brother Medhat for information and advice; if only I had friends I could have consulted concerning such matters. Curses on the shyness that stood as a barrier between me and others, including even my own brother! Damn it! I thought. Why won't it leave me even now that we're alone together?

I'd had it with my muteness and inaction, and I was furious with myself. I *am* going to speak, I said to myself, even if it happens to be the weakest expression of faith.

So in a strange sounding voice that I hardly recognized I said, "How beautiful you are . . . ."

It was the first flirtatious word I'd ever uttered in my life. Aiming her gaze at my reflection in the mirror, she smiled, then looked down and folded her arms over her chest. It wouldn't do any longer to pretend she was still doing her hair, so she sat there with her arms crossed as though she were waiting. Feeling more awkward than ever, I bit my lip angrily. The matter of changing our clothes seemed like the biggest problem in the world. So were we going to remain in this painful state till morning? Why didn't I just go over to her and press her to my bosom until the problem had solved itself? But how was I supposed to take this momentous step? I could imagine it, and I could talk to myself about it. As for actually doing it, that was an impossibility. My heart was filled with anguish and rage, and I felt increasingly powerless and humiliated.

Determined at the very least to break out of my silence, I said, "Would you like to change your clothes, sweetheart?"

Figuring I'd arrived at the ideal solution, I took advantage of the opportunity and calmly began taking off my clothes, being careful not to let on how uncomfortable I was feeling. I placed my suit on the bed and picked up my pajamas, which were draped over the long seat. Then I stuffed myself inside them without budging from my place.

I waited for some time, then I asked her, "Are you finished, sweetheart?"

"Yes," she answered in a whisper.

I got up, and when I did so, I happened to catch a glimpse of myself in the mirror. I saw that I was still wearing my fez, so I took it off with a smile. Looking timidly over at her, I found her sitting where she had been before. Now, however, she was wrapped in a white silk robe and was sitting with her back to the dressing table. Going back to where I'd been standing before, I rested my elbow on the bed frame and stood there looking at her happily and amorously. Whenever she looked up at me, I looked down bashfully. We'd finished changing our clothes, but that wasn't all that had to be done. There seemed to be no end to the night's problems. My heart longed to embrace her. So what was holding me back?

It was nothing but a step I needed to take. And did a single step need to cause such suffering? My heart was thirsty and full of longing, but my shame was intense and perplexing, and my body was dead and immobile. Was I going to stay this way forever? Why not conceal my sense of lifelessness with conversation? But what would I say? Inner turmoil had tied my tongue, and every minute that passed left me weaker and more agitated. Then all of a sudden and without cause, my thoughts shifted to my mother's room. Has she gone to sleep? I wondered. Is she imagining what I'm doing now? Shame's fires blazed all the hotter, and I felt as though I was about to suffocate. For my part, I surrendered to despair and helplessness, wondering: Will we go on in this laughable situation till morning? Deep inside I longed to flee, and I almost wished none of this had ever been!

I was awakened from my gloomy reverie by my beloved's voice as she said, "It's hot in here."

She moved over to the window to open it. Finding the opportunity favorable, I came up behind her and helped her open the window the rest of the way.

This done, my beloved started to retreat. However, like someone crying for help I said, "Why don't we stand in the window for a little while?"

My beloved answered my cry and we stood side by side only an inch apart. The window overlooked the back of the building, and directly beneath it there was a church garden dotted with tall trees whose rustling sounded like whispers drifting upward in the silence of the night. There wafted over our faces a sultry breeze that I'd longed for the way a little boy longs to reach out and touch the moon. So here we were, separated by little more than a hair's breadth. I leaned toward her with deliberate slowness and caution, and our clothes touched. Then ever so gradually I began to feel something soft as our sides made contact. I let out an audible sigh that awakened my shyness anew and caused me to slow down somewhat. I was afraid she might resist me or move away from me, which would have caused me to feel defeated all over again and conclude that there was no hope. However, she stayed right where she was, leaning her elbow on the windowsill.

I brought my left hand back slightly, drawing it up behind her until it formed a half-circle around her waist. Then, slowly, cautiously and fearfully, I began narrowing the half-circle until it had come in contact with the folds in her silken robe. The feel of it caused a shudder to go to through my heart, and for a second time, I let out an audible sigh. Then, mustering all the courage I had in me, I encircled her waist with my arm. My beloved didn't move or resist me in any way, so I put thoughts of hesitation and defeat out of my mind. Pulling her toward me with my right arm, I took her into my arms and rested her forehead on my chest as I caressed the part in her hair with my lips.

Then, having gotten beyond my self-consciousness, I murmured, "I love you."

We remained this way for God knows how long. Then, still locked in our embrace, we stepped back and lay down on the bed without my letting her out of my arms. We rested our shoulders on two downy cushions, with my beloved—still wearing her robe—on my chest and in my arms. Strangely, I didn't intrude upon her with my eyes. Instead, I looked out the window and directed my gaze heavenward. My soul was filled with an aliveness I'd never known before. As for my body, it remained inert, cold, and unresponsive, as though my soul had soaked up the last drop of my energy. I was filled with a dazzling, spiritual intoxication that was joyous and sublime. And I stayed this way till the break of dawn without knowing how sleep had overcome me.

41

I awoke to find sunlight filling half the room beneath the open window. My glance fell on the mirror, and in a flash, memories of the previous night came back to me. I looked around the room and found it empty. Realizing that my beloved had left while I was still fast asleep, my heart welled up with affection and I sent her a greeting and a prayer. I told myself that the travails of engagement and nuptials had come to an end and that the future held nothing for me but unruffled tranquility. As I reviewed my memories of the previous day, my soul went roaming through a maze of intoxication and happiness. At the same time, I was aware that I hadn't even begun yet, and that I had yet to record a single word in the huge tome of married life. I got out of bed and looked at the clock to find that it was past ten in the morning. I was appalled at how late I'd slept, and immediately thought of my mother. I wondered what she would think of such an extended slumber, and I felt pained and embarrassed. What made the embarrassment even more painful was that nothing whatsoever had happened to justify such a late start to my day, and my happiness was tainted with a touch of distress. It was as if I were realizing for the first time that the night before hadn't been without its failures. Nevertheless, I resisted this treacherous feeling and, refusing to be alone with it, left the room. I was met in the parlor by the servant, Sabah, who had become part of our family. She congratulated me on 'the morning after' and informed me that the bride was waiting for me in the dining room. I went there and found her sitting at the table like a rose in full bloom. Delighted to see her, I came up to her, my face beaming, and kissed her on the cheek. We had our breakfast, which consisted of tea and milk, eggs, and cake and as we ate we engaged in ordinary chitchat: I asked her what time she'd woken up, and she told me she'd gotten up at eight o'clock, explaining that she always woke up early no matter how late she'd gone to bed. My mother came in and congratulated us together, then sat with us for a while. Then we moved back to our room and spent the day in sweet conversation without either of us feeling the least bit weary or bored. The forlornness I'd felt earlier took its leave of me, and as I entered into the joy of being with her, I told her the story of my love from beginning to end. We punctuated our conversation with happy kisses, and I asked her when she'd first felt my presence in her world. She said she'd first noticed me hovering around her and looking up at the balcony a year or so earlier, and that her mother had noticed it at around the same time. It was then that I'd become the talk of the household. Whenever the young servant girl caught a glimpse of me from the window as I approached from Manyal, she would say with a laugh, "Here comes Miss Rabab's groom!" whereupon she would get a stern rebuke. When I'd been slow to take a step, however, they'd become suspicious of me, and her mother had forbidden her to appear in the window or on the balcony at the times when I was at the tram stop.

"Didn't you feel anything toward me?" I asked her anxiously.

She smiled gently and opened her mouth to speak. However, she sealed her lips again without saying a word. I felt a voracious hunger to hear something that would bring me some solace, so I pressed her to speak.

Then in a voice that was barely audible she said, "I don't know. . . . I don't know when I began to love you."

With this there came over me a drugged feeling that I wished I could sleep on eternally. I took her face in my hands, drinking in the sight of her lips made fuller by the pressure of my palms. Then I placed my lips on hers and melted in a long kiss. I found my beloved captivating, her conversation sweet, her wit quick, and her intelligence astounding, so much so that my own conversation by comparison with hers sounded dull and insipid. She was so congenial and witty, I knew that her dignified bearing was simply a reflection of her good manners and modesty. For some reason I'd once imagined her to be a paragon of self-control— of aloofness, in fact. But in her kisses I experienced a warmth that would melt the heart, and in her eyes I glimpsed depth of feeling and refined sensitivity. She broke into a natural spontaneity more quickly than I had expected her to, a development that may have been encouraged by the exceeding shyness she saw in me.

When night fell and I closed the bedroom door behind us, I told myself with a sense of dread that had come upon me with the approaching darkness: Tonight it will happen, God willing. I'd had no previous experiences with women, and the only sexual life I'd known was the infernal habit from which I'd only recently escaped. However, I'd learned some things by way of hearsay at the ministry that, for all I knew, might or might not do me any good.

I saw my beloved standing in front of the mirror and combing her hair. Delighted by the sight of her tall, willowy frame, I came up to her and wrapped my arms around her. She turned around until I could feel her bosom touch my heart, and I drew her close in passionate affection.

This was love. I realized by instinct that I'd have to bring it down out of the clouds in order to do my duty by her. But how? She rested peacefully against my chest as though she were a sprite formed out of the fabric of pristine clouds, while I myself seemed like a pure, disembodied spirit. How was I to find my body? Suddenly my soul was permeated with feelings of agitation, tension, and fear, all of which were intensified by the previous night's failure. I hadn't thought of it as a failure until that morning, and during the day I'd come to the opposite conclusion, or nearly so. At that moment, however, the feeling returned with a hopeless certainty and resignation. Then, gripped by such a deadly shyness that my blood froze and my determination flagged, I was afflicted by a terrible fear of the bed. When I was in it, I could find no excuse for myself, although when I was away from it I could at least find a half-excuse of sorts.

These noxious thoughts went through my head while my beloved was still in my arms. I turned into a lifeless statue and the joy of all joys went the way of the wind. She sighed. She may have been annoyed by the fact that we'd been standing there for so long. Stung by her sigh, I couldn't bear my inaction any longer. So, picking her up in my arms, I carried my precious bundle to the bed, laid her down gently, then lay down beside her. Filled with longing, I covered her lips, her cheeks, and her neck with quick, copious kisses. Feeling tender and affectionate herself, she encircled my neck with her succulent arm and we lay there next to each other for a long time.

Feelings of love, despair, enjoyment, and fear were doing battle my heart as though I were in a blazing, trackless desert expanse with delirium tossing me to and fro among the phantoms of joy and the ghosts of fear. I was in a blissful dream, yet fear and hopelessness refused to let go of me. How was I to find deliverance when my body was dead and lifeless? My throat was parched with fear, and I stood bewildered in the face of my impotence and despair, wondering what to do. However, not for a moment did I think of retreating. After all, where was there to flee? On the contrary, despair moved me to take off her robe. My hand found its way to her belt clasp and undid it, and I could feel her bosom shudder beneath mine. I removed one side of the robe to reveal one of her breasts, and her lithe body appeared in a white silk gown that hardly concealed a thing. She made a move to bring the edge of the robe back over her chest, and I removed it again, causing it to reveal the translucent white gown. I gazed at the alluring sight of her body with eyes that agitation had nearly robbed of the ability to see. I was in a pitiful state, indeed. The torment of a dying person struggling desperately to cling to the life of his body couldn't possibly have been worse than my torment in those moments. Yet in spite of it all, I stubbornly persevered, drawing on my despair and torment for strength, useless though it might be. The timid person doesn't flee in the midst of the battle, since flight brings humiliation in the face of the enemy. It's true, of course, that he avoids the battle to begin with and gets as far away from a confrontation as he can. However, once he's on the battlefield and everyone's eyes are upon him, flight—no less than the battle itself—becomes more than he can bear.

I brought my beloved into a sitting position and removed the robe from her arms, leaving nothing but her translucent gown and her exposed body. She turned her head away from me and hid it in the pillow. Little did she know that I was consumed with despair, and that this entire scene was nothing but a farce. I felt more pained and ashamed than ever. Even so, I reached out again as though I were still aspiring to some unattainable hope. As I spread her out on the bed, she was trembling with despair and cold.

"I'm afraid," my beloved said in a whisper.

How outrageous! Who was she afraid of? Her whispered words stung me like a lead-spiked whip. Yet I didn't stop. Nothing could make me turn back—neither reluctance nor resistance—till I'd seen all I'd hoped to see. What had come over me? It wasn't just death I was suffering. It was something new, something frightening and disturbing. What had come over me? Lord! My beloved was beautiful and charming, yet ignorance and blind imagination were at work against me. I was blind and inexperienced, someone whose eyes had yet to see the light of life. I'd entertained all sorts of childish fantasies about it. Then when I saw the real thing, I failed to recognize it! It was a tragedy, though if it hadn't been for the death I was experiencing, it might not have been a tragedy at all. This cruel experience was teaching me that love creates beauty just as beauty creates love. Be that as it may, alongside the despair and shame I was already feeling, I was stricken by panic as well, and there was no more hope. I froze, my beloved's face buried in the pillow, placing herself at the mercy of her executioner. I froze, not knowing what to do or how to retreat, and in a certain terrible moment I nearly burst out laughing from sheer nervous tension. However, I got hold of myself. The very next moment I had the urge to cry, and if crying weren't considered shameful, I would have poured out my tormented soul in a river of tears.

Finding my inertia as wearisome as it was frightening, I took her in my arms and kissed her as feelings of pity and grief—for both of us— flowed from my lips. It was a lamentation uttered with kisses. As the minutes and seconds passed, they felt like the teeth of a saw cutting through my neck. Minutes passed, maybe hours. Then the situation became tedious and exhausting. Extricating herself from my embrace with a sprightly motion, she covered herself with her clothes. Sleep seemed like a laughable conclusion to the situation. But what was I to do? My beloved lay down to rest without our eyes meeting, and I don't know when slumber carried her away. As for me, I remained wakeful and weary, not knowing how I would face her in the morning. What demon had enticed me into marriage? Hadn't the former torment of longing been more bearable than this? How could my body have let me down? Wasn't it the same body that would consume fire when I was engaged in my infernal habit? How long would this despair go on? Meanwhile, my head was like a red-hot piece of iron, its thoughts like sparks flying in all directions.

42

My beloved was pure compassion and mercy. She greeted me the next morning with a bright smile, then went flitting gaily here and there. Consequently, I had no reason to doubt that she was a happy bride. If she'd seemed only to be pretending to be happy so that I wouldn't feel uncomfortable, I would have been unspeakably miserable. But she was acting out of an inborn simplicity that knew no such thing as affectation or pretense. I felt truly and sincerely that she loved me, and that hers was a big heart full of tenderness, compassion, and femininity. So I felt hopeful again. I told myself that we were still just starting out, and that countless joys awaited us once we'd taken this first, difficult step. We spent the day together, part of it talking and the other part looking at the drawings, games, and toys that she had skillfully prepared for her kindergarten class. In the evening we were visited by her family. We all gathered in the sitting room with my mother and talked for a long time, happily gobbling down chocolate and sweets. They tried to draw my mother into the conversation, but she, like me, wasn't a skilled conversationalist, and she came across as reserved and distant. I suspected she wasn't making a very good impression on them, and that Rabab shared their feelings. In fact, it wasn't long before I'd come to share the same impression, and I found myself feeling ambivalent toward her. On one hand I wanted her to be with me, which was a feeling I knew well and which came naturally to me. On the other hand, however, I felt painfully awkward having her living with me as a married man. In fact, the minute I thought of her my forehead would break out in a sweat. Once the social gathering had broken up and night fell, a sense of foreboding came over me. No sooner had our bedroom door closed behind us than the well of contentment in my heart dried up, and the hope that had sprung up in response to the day's happiness dwindled away to nothing. My sweetheart seemed to be suffering some of what I was suffering and to be feeling a distress that even her tact wasn't sufficient to conceal. I replayed the events of the previous night in my mind, and in less than a second my confidence had gone the way of the wind. I wished we could just go to sleep without making another attempt, since I was certain of failure even before I began. However, I had to do what I had to do. So I repeated the attempt down to the last detail, including kisses, hugs, and failure. Indeed: failure, failure, and more failure! My poor sweetheart. In the beginning she surrendered more or less fearfully, but by the end she wound up picking herself up, bashful and uncomfortable. We finished at a late hour the way we had the first time, then she went to sleep while I remained wakeful and brooding.

What's wrong with me? I wondered. I love her with everything in me! In fact, I adore her, and if she were to be absent from my home now, I would surely perish. Does the tragedy lie in the unexpected distress I felt from looking at her body? But that's ridiculous, since I'd already died before I looked, so what I saw has nothing to do with it. On the contrary, I was quickly getting used to a reality that I hadn't been aware of before, and childish delusions had nearly been defeated in the face of this true reality. Apart from this, nothing about me had changed. I was deeply affected by her embarrassment and discomfort as she put on her clothes, and I thought to myself: I swear I won't remove another article of her clothing until God changes me!

Meanwhile, our days passed in pristine love, and our spirits merged until they were a single spirit in two separate bodies. If it hadn't been for her deep love, her spontaneous exuberance, and the simplicity of her big heart, I would have died of sorrow.

They were extraordinary days, and it was a strange honeymoon. My beloved was the very essence of spirited feeling, perfect gentleness, and sincere affection. I would often steal searching, doubtful glances at her, and all I would see was serenity, gentle-heartedness, and contentment. It nearly persuaded me that she lacked nothing. Yet I can honestly say that those were the only moments when I experienced any sort of relief. At all other times, my life was a blazing inferno of which no one else knew. Happiness was limited to fleeting, scattered moments, like the occasional flashes of lucidity experienced by someone in the throes of death.

I was intensely aware of my need for someone to advise me, but my shyness stood as an impenetrable barrier between me and those from whom I might have sought counsel. Consequently, it was impossible for me to seek advice from anyone. The very thought of doing so would set a fire ablaze inside me and arouse an irresistible urge to flee. And as if that weren't enough, I didn't have any friends to begin with. My mother, who was the only friend I had in the world, was the last person I would have wanted to broach this particular subject with. Hence, I endured my affliction in a despairing, lonely silence.

The days were tolerable. In fact, they were happy thanks to my sweetheart, whose spirit would melt away anyone's worries. When night fell, however, a pall of gloom would descend upon us that nothing in the world could dispel. Both of us were feeling ill at ease, anguished, and afraid. After the failures of those first two nights, I didn't have the courage to try again. Instead, I contented myself with lying down beside her and holding her close to me as I waited—fearful, anxious, and restless—for the descent of mercy, when sleep would deliver me from my torment. Timidity continued to be a barrier between us. If we could have been physically united, the barrier would have been lifted little by little, but I wasn't able to confide in her about my concern. There were countless times when I wished I could get things off my chest by talking, but no sooner had I opened my mouth than I'd close it again, flustered and ashamed.

On one such occasion she asked me in a whisper, "Were you wanting to say something?"

In her question I could hear an invitation to talk, and my heart started beating like mad.

However, with an agitation that I managed to conceal only with difficulty, I said, "I always want to say I love you!"

This was true in and of itself. However, I really did want to say something else, and I sensed that she could read my unspoken thoughts. The burden of having uttered an untruth weighed on me miserably.

After a bitter struggle with my timidity I murmured, "What we've shared so far is nothing compared to what we have in store for us."

I thought I saw her blush, though it may just have been the effect of the nightlight's soft glow. She caressed my hair with her fingertips. Then she kissed me sweetly on the lips, drew her mouth up to my ear and asked, "Is there something bothering you?"

My body was ablaze with embarrassment and pain as I said earnestly, "Not at all."

I fell silent in spite of myself, my heart throbbing violently.

Then, wishing I could make myself invisible, I said, "It's just a matter of time."

This was how the days passed. And again I say: if it hadn't been for her deep love, her spontaneous exuberance, and the simplicity of her big heart, I would have died of sorrow.

One evening, three weeks after our wedding, I noticed her stealing uncertain glances at me, and she seemed to have something to say.

Wanting to encourage her to talk, I said, "You look as though there's something you'd like to say."

"Yes," she said with a nervous smile.

I went over to where she was sitting on the bench and sat down next to her.

"What's on your mind?" I asked, still hoping to bring her out of herself.

"My mother . . . ," she replied.

The word went off in my ear like a bomb. It was nothing but a single word, but it contained an entire book. And I, stupid as I was, understood what it meant. Perhaps the mother had been facing her with a certain well-known, natural question, and was hearing a single reply that had yet to change: "No . . . not yet!"

After a long silence my beloved said gently, "She never stops asking me, and I don't know why she's so impatient."

Mortified and furious at the same time, I said calmly, "These things are our business and no one else's. Isn't that right?"

"Of course," she said apologetically. "She just wants to make sure we're doing all right, that's all."

Grieved and distressed, I asked, "What did you say to her?"

"I didn't say anything at all," she replied hastily and a bit uneasily. "I just told her there was no reason to be in a hurry."

"And what did she say?"

She thought for some time as if to weigh her words. Then she said, "She told me that this type of situation isn't an easy one, especially for a shy young man who's lived a pure life, and if necessary, we could call on our cook, Sabah."

"Sabah!" I cried in consternation, my eyes wide with amazement.

Flustered, she nodded in the affirmative.

"And what could Sabah do?" I asked in astonishment.

She hesitated for a moment, then began explaining what had been lost on me in the beginning. I listened to her with rapt attention until I'd understood everything, and little by little I began coming out of my stupor. I have to confess that I was relieved at the mother's suggestion, since it would remove an obstacle from my path and relieve me of some responsibility, as well as exempt me from the mother's surveillance. After all, once it was done, I didn't think she would ask about anything again.

"And how will we tell Sabah?" I asked hesitantly.

"Sabah heard part of the conversation between my mother and me," she said simply.

Feeling both embarrassed and irritated, I cried, "How on earth could that be?"

"You don't have to worry about that," she said with a smile. "She's my mother, too, and we don't hide anything from her."

We exchanged a long, silent look.

Then I asked apprehensively, "Has anyone else learned of this?"

"No one at all," she said unequivocally.

I was relieved. However, still feeling the need for more assurance, I asked meaningfully, "I hope our 'secrets' won't leave this room!"

"Do you really have any doubt about that?" she asked with a reproachful look.

43

But that's not everything in marriage, I reminded myself. How could it be, when it was a 'duty' that Sabah was capable of performing? With laughable naiveté, I wondered what our married life could possibly lack. After all, was such a thing really necessary in this life? Strangely, I hesitated to give a definitive reply to the question. Aren't we happy? I wondered. We're living comfortably and contentedly, we love each other with all our hearts, and no one could possibly doubt our happiness. So why am I troubled by illusions? However, human beings are always prone to think about what they lack. In fact, they may be so preoccupied with what they are missing that they forget what they have. I was plagued by obsessive thoughts, and I wasn't at peace with my life.

Then one night as I lay on my back waiting for sleep to overtake me and as my beloved lay slumbering beside me, my thoughts took me to such faraway places that I forgot what was around me, or nearly so. There came over me a feeling of loneliness that was reinforced by the surrounding darkness. Then, ever so gradually, I felt an energy pulsating in my body, like the energy that used to be stirred up by darkness and loneliness. Beside myself with joy, I nearly shouted out loud. I turned to my slumbering beloved, wakening her with kisses until she opened her eyes with an irritation that soon turned to bewilderment. Several seconds passed before she came to. Then she put her arms around my neck and I drew her to me with passionate longing. However, no sooner had I done so than everything went back to the way it had been before. In less than a second, frigid death had stolen into my body, then taken it over entirely, and I reverted to a state of wordless confusion and humiliation. We exchanged a strange look in the night night's soft glow, and judging from the look on her face, she hadn't understood a thing.

"Were you dreaming?" she asked.

What a fitting word she'd chosen, however arbitrary the choice. The incident shook me so violently, it put an end forever to the faint hopes I'd occasionally entertained. I experienced similar moments of solitude in the darkness of the night when my beloved was sound asleep and the strange pulsations would come back to me, but I didn't have the courage to wake her up again. Instead, I found myself descending anew into the abyss from which marriage had extricated me just a month earlier. And without understanding how, I became enslaved once again to the infernal habit that no husband before me had ever known. The confusion and pain I felt were indescribable. How could this happen to me when I worshipped the very ground she walked on? How could it happen, when a single glance at her face was more precious to me than the world and all its consolations? She was my happiness, my world, my very life!

One day I noticed that she seemed to want to talk about something that was on her mind. My heart began fluttering with anxiety and fear. However, I couldn't ignore what I saw, and I preferred to meet the danger head-on rather than add something new to the litany of secret worries and obsessive thoughts that were already plaguing me.

"What's on your mind, sweetheart?"

Looking anguished and hesitant, she made no reply.

More worried than ever, I said fearfully, "Tell me what it is, and don't hide anything from me."

Then with a frustrated sigh she said, "My mother."

What she'd said struck terror in my heart. What was wrong with this woman, who refused to live and let live? How I detested her at that moment.

However, feigning nonchalance, I said, "What about her, Rabab?"

With her eyes glued to her feet she said softly, "She keeps asking me if there's something 'on the way.'"

Amazingly, I caught on right away to what she meant by the figure of speech. I understood by instinct, or perhaps by virtue of an unspoken fear.

Even so, I asked, "What do you mean, Rabab?"

Pointing to her stomach she whispered, "She means: is there anything new here!"

Unnerved, I looked down, grieved and not knowing what to say. What was the woman really asking about? Perhaps she wanted to know about other things indirectly. Be that as it may, I felt unspeakably bitter toward her. I stole a glance over at Rabab and found her looking somber and pensive. Was she really upset about her mother's question, or did she have some other motive for telling me about it? Had she come to share her mother's concern and apprehension? And why would she hide behind her mother? Guile didn't befit someone with her beauty and purity of heart! Besides, there was no need for her to beat around the bush. And thus it was that fear prevented me from appreciating the position that my poor girl found herself in. I was embarrassed to the point of exhaustion. However, I focused my attention on a single aim, namely, determining how much Madame Nazli knew of our secrets.

"What did you say to her?" I inquired.

"I told her the truth," she said simply.

"The truth!" I cried fearfully, my heart convulsing sharply.

"What's wrong?" she asked with a bewildered stare.

"Did you really tell her the truth?!" I shouted.

"Yes," she stammered quickly. "I told her there wasn't anything new!"

And with that, I heaved a sigh of relief! She'd been referring to a 'truth' other than the one I'd had in mind. Yet I was still bothered.

"Rabab," I said fervently, "is that all she said? Please don't hide anything from me. You know how much you mean to me!"

I could see the innocence in her eyes as she said uneasily, "What are you wondering about, Kamil? I didn't tell her a thing more than what I've told you. She asked me about the matter, and I had no choice but to answer her honestly. As you know, it's something it wouldn't do any good to lie about. Do you think I was wrong? Or did you want me to pretend to be pregnant?"

Somewhat relieved, I said, "Of course not, sweetheart. You did the right thing by being honest."

To myself, though, I was thinking: I'll never know a moment's rest as long as that woman is near me. O Lord! I'm keeping my worries all to myself, without a single friend or advisor to my name. I've had it with her mother, my mother, and myself! Then the old question came back to me: Is the thing we lack really necessary for married life? Does my beloved experience the same sorts of animal desires that drove me to take up my iniquitous habit? Is it conceivable that my pristine, chaste beloved would feel that same sort of untamed lust? The possibility was too abhorrent to imagine!

At last my vacation came to an end and I went back to the warehousing section at the ministry, where the employees gave me a warm welcome back. I didn't have a single friend among them, but the nature of the occasion—namely, a newlywed husband's return from his honeymoon— caused them to forget their usual reserve, and they approached me, some of them with congratulations and others with jokes, all of which I received with discomfort and embarrassment. They talked a lot, and one of them warned me against overdoing it. They got so involved in their conversation, in fact, that they forgot all about me. They got on the subject of the nature of man and nature of the woman and started citing examples, incidents, and anecdotes. My heart burdened and my soul in agony, I listened to them covertly while pretending to examine the typewriter. How I wished one of them would cite a case like mine!

However, 'a case like mine' hadn't even occurred to any of them. I listened till I thought my head would burst. Rabab was a woman. So, was what was true of other women—if the things I'd heard from the other employees were accurate—true of her also? Might she be getting bored with me? On the other hand, she seemed content. Never once had I seen her face but that it was aglow with happiness. Never once had she looked at me with anything but love and devotion, and surely her face wouldn't lie. On the contrary, it was like an open book that couldn't possibly conceal deceit or wrongdoing. They were lying! They were animals, and they saw other people as animals like themselves. However, I wasn't fully reassured, and I wasn't going to be reassured no matter how I tried to convince myself that things were all right. After all, the seed of doubt had been planted now.

When I was alone with my beloved that day, I looked pensively at her for a long time without saying a word.

Laughing, she said, "Do you miss your old habit of looking at me without talking?"

A pleasant gentle breeze wafted over my heart as I thought back to the old days when my heart was aflame, hope was alive, and the possibility of an ordeal like the one I was going through hadn't so much as occurred to me. I drank in the memory with relish.

"Rabab," I said apprehensively, "are you happy?"

She looked at me in surprise and said earnestly, "Very happy."

Then, looking down diffidently I asked, "Do you love me?"

She'd been sitting a handspan away from me, and when she heard my question, she moved over toward me till we were touching, looked up at me with a blush and murmured, "Yes, I do!"

I put my arm around her waist and kissed her lips and her cheeks. Then I took her lovely, petite hand in mine and began kissing her fingertips one at a time with tenderness and ardor. By what I had said, I'd actually been trying to prepare the way to talk about what I'd been keeping to myself with such grievous consequences. But when I was about to speak, I lost my nerve, and my tongue too. I wanted to tell her what was bothering me and confess to her that the problem I was facing in relation to her was a strange, passing thing that I didn't understand. I wanted to tell her that I hadn't been this way, and in fact, still wasn't this way when I found myself alone, and I wanted to ask her for counsel and help. These were the kinds of things I'd wanted to say. However, my determination gave out on me and I retreated in helplessness, conceding defeat as usual. Then I started justifying my retreat to myself, saying: It might offend her or make her angry for me to reveal such secrets. In fact, it might ruin her happiness forever!

When we went to bed that night, I was tempted to try again, but I hesitated. In fact, I hesitated for so long that fear got the better of me and I gave up on the idea. As much as I loved her, I'd begun to fear her body. As I pondered my life in the silence and darkness of the night, it seemed strange and disjointed, and the thought left me in such anguish that the only outlet I could find was tears. So I had a long cry.

44

Then it occurred to me to consult a doctor. The thought came unexpectedly. In fact, it may have been mere coincidence. I hadn't considered consulting a doctor before due to my exceeding shyness on one hand, and on the other, my belief that a doctor wouldn't be able to treat a condition like mine. However, one day as I was on my way to the ministry, my eye fell upon a large sign fixed to a balcony on Qasr al-Aini Street. The words "Dr. Amin Rida, Specialist in Reproductive Disorders, University of Dublin" were written on it in large script. I hadn't seen the sign before, and suddenly I had the urge to consult a physician. Even so, I didn't succumb to the idea without hesitation. The thought aroused my shame and fear, which nearly convinced me to change my mind. But this time, my longing for deliverance was more powerful than my shame, and I made up my mind to go that evening.

When I arrived at the clinic, the doctor was busy examining a patient, so I sat down to wait. The waiting room was empty, which was a tremendous relief to me, though it caused me to think less highly of the doctor. I wasn't kept waiting long, and a few minutes later I was invited into the examination room, which was impressive and pleasing to the eye: fully equipped, and fitted out with instruments so awesome that my confidence in the doctor was restored. He was sitting directly to the right of the entrance at a large desk covered with books and notebooks. A young man who couldn't have been more than thirty years old, he was tall and slender with kinky hair, a dark complexion, delicate but distinct features, and intense eyes that gleamed from behind an elegant pair of spectacles. One noticeable thing about him was a bushy, coal-black mustache that covered his mouth and lent him a dignified appearance that caused him to look more mature than his years. I greeted him, and he returned my greeting rather tersely. As he did so, he shot me a questioning glance that struck me as condescending and arrogant. He seemed to possess a self-confidence that bordered on conceit, and I didn't like him. Overall, his appearance was a disappointment to me, since I'd expected to find a distinguished-looking elderly man with a friendly smile on his face, like a certain doctor my mother had once taken me to many years earlier. Consequently, I felt offended, and wished I hadn't led myself into this trap.

"Have a seat," he said calmly.

I complied with his request, eyeing him apprehensively. He began looking at me as though he were waiting for me to speak first. However, my thoughts were scattered and my throat was dry, so I sat there without saying a word.

"Yes?" he said inquiringly.

I mustered the strength to speak, but all I said was, "I've come for an examination."

"What exactly are you suffering from?" he asked, sounding a bit puzzled.

It was only after a prolonged agony that I managed to say, "I'm a married man. . . ."

Then I stopped. Or, rather, my tongue was tied. However, I found my silence burdensome, and since the doctor's intense eyes were urging me to speak, I confessed everything. At first the words came out confused and faltering. Then, encouraged by the earnest, staid expression on his face, I started pouring out my story without a break. I felt I'd cast a heavy burden off my shoulders, and as though henceforth, he

253

was the one responsible for my recovery from the malady that had been afflicting me.

"How long have you been married?" he asked me.

"About a month and a half," I replied.

"And when did you start suffering this condition?"

"From the first night," I said bitterly.

"Did you suffer this same condition before you married?"

"I hadn't had any previous experiences with women."

Then he asked me about 'the other.' I hesitated momentarily, then answered him honestly. He asked me about some details, and again, I gave him a frank reply. Nor did I conceal from him the frightening excess to which I'd gone in my secret habit.

"Have you engaged in your habit since marrying?"

I was impressed with him for asking this particular question, which I saw as evidence of a special perceptiveness.

"Yes, I have," I said.

"So," he said thoughtfully, "it's as if your response only changes when you're with your wife."

"Yes," I said, feeling bewildered and sorrowful.

After a long silence, he said, "Now I'm going to ask you some explicit questions, and I ask you to answer them honestly. Do you love your wife?"

"Very much."

"Does she have any sort of perversion, or natural frigidity?"

"Not at all."

"Did you grow up together?"

"She's not a relative of mine."

After this he asked me questions that I found quite shocking. However, none of them applied to me, and I answered him with complete honesty. Then he got up and gave me a thorough, careful examination that I endured with a trembling heart and with a battle raging in my soul between hope and despair.

We returned to our seats and he began recording his impressions and conclusions in a notebook. Then he sat up straight and said to me,

"You're physically sound. It's true, of course, that you've harmed yourself through your pernicious habit, which has left effects that call for a special kind of cleansing. However, the problem you're suffering from, as I see it, has nothing to do with this. Your impotence has no biological basis, and you may be going through a psychological crisis. Don't you have psychiatric clinics in your country?"

I couldn't make any sense of this last question. I was also amazed by his use of the phrase 'your country,' as though he were a foreigner.

"You would know more than I do about such matters, Doctor!"

"The fact is," he said with a smile, "that I haven't been back home for very long, and I only opened this clinic of mine a few days ago."

Now I understood why I'd found his clinic empty, and why I hadn't seen his sign before. However, I also realized that the trouble I'd put myself through had led nowhere, and I went back to feeling hopeless and despondent.

Then he went on, saying, "You've got nothing wrong with you. You're fully capable of having marital relations, and you'll do so one of these days, so don't give in to despair. This is something that happens frequently to newly wed young men, but it isn't long before they're back to normal, though the problem may last longer with some than with others. Rest assured that your day will come. Meanwhile, I encourage you to come to me for cleansing to get rid of the slight prostrate congestion you're suffering from."

I listened to him with rapt attention, and with hope and despair still competing fiercely for the upper hand. When would my day come? And would it really come? The doctor had finished saying and doing all that he could say or do. However, I made no move to get up. Instead, I clung to my seat, my eyes fixed on him like someone pleading for help.

Then I asked, "What did you mean by 'psychiatric clinics'?"

"Ah," he said. "They're a new type of clinic which I don't think is available in our part of the world. However, don't worry about what I said. I don't think you're in need of one."

"You said I might be suffering from a psychological crisis. What did that mean?"

255

"I told you not to worry about what I'd said. I was overstating the case. At any rate, I'm not a psychiatrist, so I shouldn't go into areas with you that might do more harm than good. Your healing lies within your own power, so don't despair or lose confidence in yourself. Overcome your fear and anxiety, then expect recovery with full assurance."

My last question to him was, "Is your opinion conclusive?"

"Yes," he said confidently.

I left the clinic better than I'd been when I went in, and I went home feeling hopeful. I said to myself: Doctors don't lie or make mistakes. And with that I was transported with joy. I returned home on foot, and on the way I passed the building where my wife's family lived—the building of reminiscences—and my imagination carried me far away. Then, all of a sudden, my enthusiasm waned and I was gripped with anxiety, and before long I'd reverted to a state of sullenness and gloom. However, I kept repeating out loud to myself the things the doctor had told me, searching wherever I could for the confidence I lacked.

45

In spite of my perpetual anxiety, I cherished the hope of recovery. And as we carried on with our platonic married life, I was spurred on by this expectation. When I felt particularly anxious, I would steal a glance over at her, wondering to myself whether she was really as happy as she seemed, and whether she still loved me. As for her, she did truly appear to be happy and content, loving and devoted. By this time she'd stopped mentioning her mother, though I didn't know whether the woman had stopped asking her questions, or whether my beloved was keeping from me the conversations that would take place between them. But God, how I loved her! Our shared life together hadn't lost its magic for me. On the contrary, it had found a place in the deepest parts of my being. I would go into raptures over her as she sat next to me on the long seat or lay beside me in bed no less than I did in the days when she would appear on the balcony or in the window. And it was a miserable thing indeed that ill fortune had tainted those early days of our marriage, filled as they were with the most wonderful opportunities for happiness and bliss.

And as though ill fortune weren't content to afflict me through myself, it had come to afflict me through my mother as well.

Despite her courtesy, my mother was no good at hiding her feelings. If her tongue didn't give her away, her eyes did, and if her eyes didn't give her away, her feelings made themselves known by the peculiar, passive way in which she was conducting herself. She'd become withdrawn, making her bedroom into a prison that she rarely left, and she seemed to have devoted herself entirely to prayer and worship. Nor was this prolonged estrangement lost on Rabab. As any other woman would have done, she—despite her gentleness and mild-mannered nature—would respond to my mother with irritation and anger. She never tired of saying to me, "Your mother hates me!" My mother, unwilling to change her behavior, would justify herself by saying she wasn't good at mixing and social niceties anymore. Yet if I went to sit with her she would receive me graciously and with a smile, and speak to me with meekness and resignation. So it wasn't long before I realized that there was something amiss, and that a thick barrier had gone up between us. I could see that I was dealing with a different person than the mother I'd known throughout my youth. Whenever I mentioned to her that my wife was upset by her aloofness, she would say to me testily, "Your wife doesn't like me, and that's all there is to it."

As for me, I practiced being patient and forbearing even though pain was tearing me apart and my spirit was weighed down with sorrow.

Once my mother went to spend a couple of days at my sister Radiya's house. Then, seemingly happy there, she stayed a third day and was about to stay a fourth. These were the first days we'd spent apart, and her absence weighed heavily on my heart. In fact, I felt an unbearable forlornness with her not in the house. Hence, I went to my sister's house to bring her back, and she didn't resist my overtures.

While we were on our way back I told her affectionately, "I couldn't bear to let you stay away from home."

Her lips parted in a limpid smile.

She was generally moved by a kind word with the innocence of a little child.

However, she said to me, "It seems to me that my presence in your house is meaningless. In fact, it seems to bother the two of you."

Angered by her words, I said indignantly, "God forgive you for making such a false accusation! You've changed for no reason, Mama, and as a result, your perception of things has changed. All I can say is, God forgive you."

Looking at me strangely, she said with a calm certainty, "Your wife doesn't like me. Consequently, she doesn't want me in the house. I would have thought that whatever your wife wants, you should want, too."

I felt as though she was being deliberately unkind to me, and if it hadn't been for my sincere desire to make peace, I would have lost my temper. Suppressing my anger, I said gloomily, "My wife doesn't dislike you. On the contrary, she feels that you dislike her because of the cold, grumpy way you act toward her and your unwillingness to spend time with her. Shame on you for saying things that make my life miserable!"

Looking disconcerted, she didn't say a word. Lord, how she'd changed! Couldn't she grant me that bright smile of hers rather than this anemic one? Would she never go back to opening her heart to me in the confident, assured way she used to do? And I wondered: Is the only way to get her to pardon me and go back to being her old self for me to confide in her about my own sufferings so that she'll know that, in reality, I haven't married and I'm the most miserable man alive?

Then one day I came home from the ministry to find my wife in tears. Alarmed, I approached her feeling worried and pained. Sabah was present at the time, and she told me that she'd been working in the kitchen when my mother came in and hurled some scathing criticism at her. She said that my wife had intervened to put things right again, but that my mother had spoken to her sharply, and that she'd left the room in tears.

The minute I heard what had happened, I headed straight for my mother's room in a rage. But to my dismay, I found that she, too, had been crying herself red in the face. The minute she saw the frown on my face, she cried in distress, "So, did she send you to scold me?"

Looking heavenward, I heaved a deep sigh and said, "Lord, take me! Deliver me from the earth and everyone on it!"

"No, let Him take *me!*" she shouted back. "I'm nothing but a useless old woman. Wouldn't it have been better for your wife to put off her complaining until after you'd had a chance to change your clothes and have a bite to eat? But no! She wouldn't think of doing anything but follow her own stubborn, tyrannical whims!"

Offended and furious now, I said, "She's shedding bitter tears."

She shouted at me as though she'd lost her nerves, "She called me every name in the book! Then she met you at the door with those crocodile tears of hers to turn you against me, and she's succeeded!"

You'll never get at the truth by listening to women! I'd worn myself out reasoning and arguing, and it had gotten me nowhere. On the contrary, I was helpless to make peace between the two of them. For a long time our lives were miserable, and a spirit of discord reigned in the house. Eventually I threw my hands up in despair, leaving it to the passing of the days to accomplish what I'd failed to do myself.

Some time after this I began to feel an emptiness in my married life, and I was certain my wife shared the same feeling. It was no longer just the night hours that weighed on our nerves. Rather, the long hours we spent alone together during the day were something else we wouldn't be able to endure forever. Consequently, I suggested that we kill time with various sorts of entertainment until school was back in session and she had other things to keep her busy. Pleased with my suggestion, she invited me to visit her numerous relatives, so we began going from house to house, and they would come to visit us as well. Then I suggested that we go to the cinema twice a week, and she agreed. I don't know whether I was really looking for entertainment, or whether I was just running away from my empty life. In any case, I found a respite in going to the cinema even though, by nature, I preferred spending time alone. However, it wasn't long before I'd grown weary of the visits, where I would lose myself and fall prey to my usual shyness, awkwardness, and inability to express myself. Consequently, I began staying back from them, leaving my wife to go by herself.

I could have persuaded her to stop going on visits as I had done. However, I didn't want to deprive her of ways of entertaining herself and filling up her free time. Deep down, I may have started to fear that she'd find our time alone burdensome the way I'd begun to. I wanted with all my heart to make her comfortable and happy, and I wouldn't have hesitated for a moment to spend everything I had to please her. Rabab had become everything, and I was no longer anything to speak of.

However, my mother seemed not to approve of this new life of ours.

One day she said to me, "It isn't right for you to allow your wife to spend so much time away from home."

Annoyed by her observation, I replied curtly, "Have you forgotten that my wife is a working woman?"

"Even so . . . ," she retorted in that critical tone of hers.

Concerned that an argument might lead to undesirable consequences, I said imploringly, "Mama, can't you just live and let live?"

Irritated now, she said, "If you came to my defense the way you come to hers, she wouldn't have despised me and called me names!"

I made no reply, hoping she'd drop the subject. However, she went on, saying, "She goes out roaming for no reason. What would you say if she were a mother?"

Bellowing like a wild animal, I broke in, "Be quiet! And don't say another word!"

She gaped at me in alarm without saying anything, then looked down. However, rage and pain had robbed me of my senses, and I showed her no mercy.

It happened that several days later, my mother fell ill and took to her bed. The doctor we'd called told us that it was her heart, and he advised her always to follow his instructions in order to avoid further episodes in the future.

She stayed in bed for a long time despite the doctor's assurances that her condition wasn't serious. However, it seemed to me that she was letting the illness get the better of her and that her spirit was about to collapse. I felt responsible for her illness, and so I endured the bitterness of remorse and a troubled conscience in grieved silence. As if to atone

261

for my guilt, I assumed full responsibility for her care and medication. Nor did Rabab fail to do her duty. My mother had truly hurt me, but she'd done so with good intentions. As for me, I had hurt her deliberately under the influence of a frightening rage. Those were grim, dark days for me. I would sit looking at her pale, gaunt face with a broken heart, with her hand in mine and my tongue uttering continuous prayers of supplication. She was weary, and her fires were dying out. At the same time, though, I could see a look of contentment and joy in her eyes. It was as though, thanks to my sympathy and love, she'd forgotten all her sufferings.

46

utumn rolled around with its pleasant weather and its wispy clouds, and the schools embarked on a new year. My wife and I would go out together in the morning and take the same tram, and memories would wash over my heart in a blend of ecstasy and agony.

One time I said to her, "It was during days like this that I'd come rushing to the tram stop, dying just to catch a glimpse of your face."

She smiled gently and said, "And I was dying to see yours!"

Ah, my beloved! Never in my life had I seen anyone so loving, content, and happy. She was cheerful and attentive without affectation or hypocrisy. Had she suffered in the beginning, then overcome her sufferings thanks to her loving, pure-hearted disposition? How could I possibly know what was going on deep inside her, or the thoughts she was thinking about me and her life? She seemed happy, caring, and sincere. After all, what reason would there be for her to pretend constantly to be happy if she was really miserable or didn't love me? Nor did I have any reason to doubt her maturity as a woman or the depth of her feelings. She was the farthest thing from being frivolous and capricious. On the contrary, her heart was filled with vitality, fervor, and empathy. So, I thought, maybe she's living her life inspired by the same hope that I cling to with such patience and endurance. However, the fact of the matter was that I was so preoccupied with my own worries, I had little time to concern myself with those of other people. This may have been due, first and foremost, to my innate self-centeredness. My ignorance also had a part to play in it. I may well have viewed myself as the primary, if not sole, victim of this tragedy.

In the early days of that autumn we were invited by Gabr Bey and Madame Nazli to a lunch banquet that they were hosting for family members and relatives in honor of Rabab's brother Muhammad, who had recovered from a serious illness.

My wife went to the banquet, while my mother stayed home, saying she had to follow the new diet the doctor had prescribed for her. I went, feeling awkward and uncomfortable as usual, since for me a lunch banquet was a fate worse than illness, and because, like other gatherings of its type, it brought back memories of the orator's podium at the Faculty of Law. I made certain that we went early so that we could arrive before all the other guests, since this way, I wouldn't be subjected to people's stares when I walked into the reception room. My plan worked; when we arrived, no one was there but the family, which was my family as well. I loved them all, though I'd come to be deathly afraid of Madame Nazli. Then the guests began to arrive: Rabab's three paternal uncles and her four maternal uncles came with their wives and children. Her two maternal aunts also came, one of them with her husband and the other, a widow, with her eldest daughter.

Madame Nazli excused herself to receive a new guest, to whom I heard her say, "Why are you late, Amin?" The newcomer apologized to her in a low voice that sounded familiar to me, so I looked over toward the door with interest. As the new guest came into the room, I recognized him instantly. Before me stood the doctor I'd visited two months earlier and to whom I'd confided the secret of my misery! At first all I could do was stare at him, terrified, though I quickly got hold of myself. However, although I was capable of concealing what was going on inside me, there was nothing I could do to keep my heart from racing and nearly pounding its way out of my chest. Gripped with fright and deadly shyness, my heart was weighed down by an anguish so heavy, it was as though I'd fallen into a bottomless pit.

Then before I knew it, Madame Nazli was introducing him to me, saying, "This is a relative of mine whom I haven't had the pleasure of introducing to you before. He just recently returned from Europe, and he rarely honors us with a visit. This is my nephew, Dr. Amin Rida."

We shook hands as custom dictates and as we did so, our eyes met for a brief moment. However, I discerned nothing in his eyes but an expression of welcome, and there was nothing to indicate that he remembered me. Instead, he maintained his pompous, dispassionate bearing. When he'd finished shaking hands with seated family members, he sat down beside Gabr Bey and the two of them began to talk while I lost myself in frightened, distracted thoughts. Does he remember me? I wondered. Maybe, like doctors who are accustomed to encountering as many faces as there are minutes in the day, he's forgotten me. On the other hand, he's a new doctor, with only a few patients. Yet despite this fact, he didn't appear to remember me in the least. Or, I wondered: Perhaps he does recognize me but is mercifully pretending not to. If only I could find a way to confirm this point! Supposing he does recognize me, might he possibly divulge my secret to his relative, Madame Nazli?

It seemed a far-fetched possibility. Nonetheless, I was about as far as one could get from peace of mind. I was already drowning in a fathomless sea of obsessive thoughts and fears. Did I really need any more?

We were invited to the table, so I left my thoughts behind, though their effects lingered the way the smell of smoke clings to someone coming out of a fire. Once we'd sat down, Madame Nazli turned and said with a smile, "I know you're shy, Kamil, but beware, since banquets have no mercy on the shy!"

Some of them commented on what she'd said, which caused me to feel resentful toward her and even more distressed than before. However, it wasn't long before they'd all become too engrossed in the delectable food to pay any attention to me. I hardly felt the discomfort that usually assails me in such circles, so distracted was I by matters of greater moment. After all, the only cure for discomfort is more discomfort. Then we went back to the reception room and coffee was served. I took the cup and brought it to my lips, and as I did so, my thoughts were suddenly transported to the old pub on Alfi Bey Street, and in my mind's eye I saw a glass of liquor. How had the memory come back to me, and what had occasioned it? I was truly amazed, yet I also felt an extraordinary relief, like the delight you feel when you see a long-lost friend. Liquor . . . intoxication . . . bliss . . . . Ah, how badly I needed an escape! It was a strange, unexpected thought. But it was powerful, nay, irresistible. Cautiously and fearfully, I turned my attention back to my immediate surroundings. I glanced over in the direction of the doctor and found him engrossed in conversation, saying what he had to say with confidence, eloquence, and disdain while many of those present were jumping into the discussion with interest and delight. The conversation came around to the subject of life in Britain, and the doctor said that since his studies had taken up most of his time, he'd only rarely enjoyed his life there as a tourist. Nevertheless, he'd been able to observe first-hand the firm foundations on which the structure of political life there rested, people's high standard of living, and the wide-ranging freedom they enjoyed in all spheres.

"So," Gabr Bey said to him, "you seem to have continued to be interested there in the same things that interested you here before you went abroad."

Laughing, one of the guests chimed in, "That's right, Gabr Bey. Remind him of the days of the Faculty of Medicine and the nationalist revolution!"

Another said, "Who would have thought that you'd end up in enemy territory, or that you'd come back with such an admiration for the enemy's ways!"

"Well," he replied with a smile, "enmity isn't incompatible with admiration."

Then Gabr Bey asked him, "Aren't you still a radical Wafdist? You were thrown in prison once for the sake of the Wafd Party!"

Pursing his lips in disgust, the young man rejoined, "Now I see all Egyptians living in a huge prison. The fact is, sir, that the only news we used to hate to hear when we were in England was news from Egypt."

Madame Nazli said with a smile, "You love to take all sorts of burdens on yourself, as though you were responsible for the world and everyone in it. Focus your attention on your clinic, your life, and especially the matter of getting married. Haven't you noticed that you're thirty years old now? You're over the hill!"

To this one of Rabab's two maternal aunts added, "Don't worry! You may be hearing good news before the year is out."

The conversation turned to the daughter of a certain prominent physician. Rabab, who was sitting beside me, said to me in a whisper that the girl they were speaking about was a legendary beauty and the heiress to a huge fortune. She told me that the girl had been her class-mate for a period of time.

One of Rabab's maternal uncles seemed to be drawn to discussions of politics. The minute the discussion of marriage ended, he turned to the doctor and said, "There's no reason to be pessimistic. Everything will be reformed in the end, however long it takes. We're about to have new elections, and a favorable wind may be blowing."

The doctor's eyes took on an added intensity as he said testily, "It's better for this country to be ruled by a corrupt government. After all, a righteous government can't do anything to speak of under currently prevailing conditions. So let the corrupt government throw its weight around however it pleases, since this way it hastens the end—the inevitable end!"

"You're still a cynic and a discontent!" said Gabr Bey with a laugh. "Don't you see anything in Egypt that deserves your admiration and appreciation?"

"Well, yes," replied the doctor with a smile as he scanned his audi-ence with his sparkling eyes, "Umm Kulthoum."

And everyone roared with laughter. I'd begun listening to him with a mixture of interest and astonishment. However, I could hardly make any sense out of what he was saying. I was amazed at people who preoccupied themselves with such matters. Didn't they have worries in their lives to distract them from such affairs? Based on his conversation he'd struck me as a learned, perceptive man and a revolutionary with a conceited, pretentious air. Hence, it came as a huge surprise to me to hear him mention Umm Kulthoum as the one thing in the country that deserved his admiration. And I wondered: Is it really possible for a serious, stern, caustic person like this crazy doctor to love singing too? Since I myself liked singing, I was pleased to discover this shared predisposition, especially after having racked my brain to find the slightest commonality between us.

The doctor was the first to leave, and everyone present rose to shake his hand. I too shook his hand, all the while searching his eyes with fear and trepidation. However, I failed to see anything in his haughty glances that would give me cause for suspicion. We left the gathering at around five o'clock, and as we walked home, my sweetheart commented endlessly on the banquet and the guests, but I wasn't able to lend her my full attention. I'd succumbed to the profuse, tumultuous flow of my thoughts. How would I cope with the ill fortune that had crossed my path in the form of this mad physician? And how had fate led me to confess to him the secret that I dared not let even the walls hear?

47

After escorting Rabab to the door of our building, I made my way back to the tram stop, explaining my proposed absence on the basis of a few nonexistent errands I had to run. I took the tram to Ataba, and from there I made my way to Alfi Bey Street. My heart was pounding in fear and dread the way it had been the first time my feet carried me there, and in my mind's eye I could see the glass, its mouth open wide with seductive allure. I'd forgotten about it. In fact, it hadn't even crossed my mind since I'd won my heart's desire. It had only come to mind again that day when what I saw in a coffee cup had stirred something deep inside me. My mother + my wife + Dr. Amin Rida = liquor: this was the equation I'd arrived at.

When I was just a step away from my old pub, I hesitated. Feeling suddenly worried and gloomy, I wondered to myself: Wouldn't this be infidelity to my wife? However, I reprimanded myself for this peculiar logic and made my way inside. Then suddenly I imagined seeing my father, and my mind was assailed with images of him from the past. I reviewed them calmly and without any feeling of hatred or gleeful malice. Then I sat down at the table as I muttered, "May God have mercy on him and forgive him."

The waiter rushed over and hailed me, saying, "Where have you been all this time?"

Gratified by the way he'd greeted me, I said with a smile, "In the world!"

Then I showed him my wedding ring and he said, "Congratulations! Congratulations! Have you had a child?"

Feeling resentful and pained, I shook my head in the negative. Then I ordered a glass of cognac and drank it leisurely until I could feel its effects creeping into my heart and head. My lips turned up in a smile that made sport of all my troubles, and I said to myself: Welcome, welcome! I left the pub at around seven, having been careful not to overdo it. But no sooner had I made it as far as Imad al-Din Street than I remembered the pub in the vegetable market. By this time I was in a state of mind that made light of obstacles, and I asked myself almost reproachfully: Just because you're living comfortably now, does that mean you're going to forget the pub that took you in when you were poor? And with that, I hailed a taxi and got in, and it took me posthaste to the pub that served as the favorite haunt of bankrupt government employees and carriage drivers. As I'd expected I would, I found the place in an uproarious state, complete with singing and revelry. The elderly employee known for his vocal talents was belting out the lines, "We'll know all tomorrow!" while everyone intoned, "And then we'll see!"

When he saw me coming, he stopped singing and shouted, "Quiet, guys!"

My old buddies recognized me, and we met with warm handshakes. No sooner had I settled into my seat than the old man asked me in a singsong voice, "Where have you been, handsome?"

I laughed out loud and said, "In the world."

One of his chums said, "Let's curse the world that forces friends to forget the ones they love!"

So I happily cursed the world with them. Then one of them happened to see the wedding band on my finger.

"You really *have* entered a world, buddy!" he exclaimed.

The announcement of the news had an all-encompassing effect.

The amateur singer asked me, "So, how do you find this world?"

I was alarmed to see the conversation turning to this perilous topic. However, I had no choice but to reply, "It's nice! Aren't you married, sir?"

The man smiled, revealing the few teeth he had left and said, "Once a woman gets beyond her youth, she's not a woman anymore."

Affirming what he'd said, another added, "That's right. Woman has the shortest lifespan of all living creatures, even if she lives to a ripe old age!"

And another chimed in, "My wife picks a fight with me for every evening I spend here. So I told her, 'I'm willing to quit going to the pub on one condition: that you quit this world!'"

The fact that they were all disgruntled with their lives brought me a solace I hadn't known before, and I was amazed at all the strange things that bring drunkards together in brotherly fellowship. Then I noticed the absence of a certain baker who'd become famous among us for his addiction and his taciturn ways. When I asked where he was, the elderly vocalist replied, "Liquor won't do it for him anymore. So every evening he goes to the grocer and drinks pure alcohol."

Then they started singing again, picking up where they'd left off, and I started drinking the way I had in the old days. And how I could drink! I was weak and cowardly in the face of everything, and I had no confidence in either my mind or my body. As for my stomach, it could hold an entire pub! I left the place at ten o'clock, sent off with the most heartfelt farewells. I went wandering from street to street, feeling so rapturous and invincible I was sure I could take on the whole world. Then my beloved's phantom floated by. Seeing her in my drunken mind's eye, I thought: I've kept her waiting! She's gone to sleep by now! The thought of her intoxicated me even more, my heart fluttered amorously, and longing beckoned. My wandering eyes went in search of a taxi, and once I'd spotted one, I went over to it without hesitation. I asked the driver to move as fast as he could, and he virtually flew me to my destination. I got out in front of our building and rushed up the stairs, then went into the flat and headed quickly to our room. I turned on the light and my eyes fell on my beloved, who lay sleeping peacefully.

Her head stirred when the light came on and she murmured, "Who is it?" then resumed her slumber. With trembling hands, I hurriedly undressed. Breathing hard and fast from astonishment, delight, and apprehension, I rushed over to the bed and slipped under the covers. I took her in my arms and placed my lips on hers until she opened her eyes. Then I smothered her with joyous, passionate, voracious kisses until she woke up and began returning my affection. What was happening between us was like a dream so blissful, so incredible, that even slumber yields it only grudgingly. However, it was also a short dream that lasted all of a couple of seconds. I awakened from its enchantment feeling peaceful and confident, and several times drunker with happiness than I was from the liquor. I lay down blissfully and closed my eyes, surrendering to the sweetest thoughts and dreams. This time, however, my dreams weren't made of the stuff of mere imagination. Rather, they were made from the stuff of reality itself, deriving their content from my very own life. After all, the best life is the one lived by someone whose happy dreams are an echo of the reality he actually experiences. Receiving this new happiness with humble gratitude, I was certain that my worries were over forever. The following morning I looked over at my beloved with confidence and joy, and at last I felt truly that I was a husband and a man. The same feelings of happiness and pride stayed with me the rest of the day. When evening came I went back to Alfi Bey Street, then I came flying home to my beloved on the wings of intoxication. I drank again from the brimming glass with the same enjoyment and at the same speed. Then I lay down, serene and self-assured. It wasn't possible, of course, for someone like me to forget the mortal distress I'd had to endure in the past. On the contrary, true happiness inspires compassion even for torment's memories.

48

Some weeks—possibly no more than two months—then passed in serenity and bliss. When I remember those days, I'm afflicted with pain and sorrow. It isn't a longing for a happiness that no longer exists. Rather, it's a feeling of grief over the hugest deception I've ever been subjected to in my life. In other words, there was nothing to be happy about at all, and if I did enjoy comfort and happiness for a time, it was only because I was ignorant, gullible, and blind. There's nothing wrong with a blind man enjoying an illusory happiness so long as he goes on being blind. However, if his sight is restored and he sees that his happiness was nothing but a mirage, what will he reap from the memories of his happiness but an even greater unhappiness and never-ending sorrow? This was precisely my situation, but I only became aware of it with a painful slowness commensurate with my ignorance and stupidity.

I'd noticed that, what with her work at school and visits to her relatives, Rabab was spending all day and part of the night away from home. I'd gone with her in the beginning despite my reclusive nature, but when it became a hardship for me, I withdrew and stopped accompanying her on more than the occasional visit. My mother went back to making her embittered, sorrowful comments on the situation, while I came tirelessly to my wife's defense even though, somewhere deep inside me, I agreed with the criticisms. In the past I'd encouraged my wife to make such visits to help her get her mind off what I felt was lacking in our married life. Now, though, there was no reason that I could see to go to such excess in this regard.

Hence, after gathering my courage, I said to her one day, "It seems, sweetheart, that you're boycotting our house. Wouldn't it be possible for you to cut down on the number of visits you make?"

Looking at me suspiciously, she asked with a sharpness I wasn't accustomed to, "So, does she still busy herself criticizing me?"

I realized that she was referring to my mother, and it pained me to see that she harbored such a negative attitude toward her.

"My mother doesn't interfere in what doesn't concern her," I replied soothingly. "This is my request and no one else's. The fact is, I can't bear our house when you're not in it."

"Let's go out together, then," she said, having recovered her composure. "Why don't you like to be with people?"

"That's just the way I am," I said gently.

I don't know what changed her after what I'd said. However, she said testily, "Well, this is the only way life is bearable for me."

Ah, my love! I thought to myself. Your gentle-heartedness wouldn't allow you to speak this way! What's happened?

However, that wasn't all there was to it. After all, my heart would sometimes see things that my eyes missed. I had to rend the curtain of blindness and meet the truth face-to-face, bitter though it might be. It seemed to me that Rabab wasn't as happy with my recovery as I was. It was a bizarre reality, and one that had me completely baffled. But how long would I go on deluding myself? She seemed to be afraid for night to come and want to avoid it. As soon as we found ourselves alone together, she would be gripped by torment that I could see in her limpid eyes. And particularly of late, she'd begun making all manner of excuses, from tiredness to feeling ill to being desperately sleepy. And when she did yield to me, she would do so in a way that made it seem like a joyless capitulation. Then she'd wrest her body away from mine as though she were offended and angry. For all these reasons, she was no longer the smiling, cheerful, serene girl I'd once known her to be. Her laugh was tainted with affectation, her cheerfulness had grown tepid, and her affection had turned to flattery. Far be it from me to say that she openly declared any bitterness or resentment or that she behaved discourteously. After all, my sweetheart was above such things. However, I could sense her anxiety with my heart, and I picked up instinctively on her ambivalence. God knows, the whole world wouldn't have amounted to a hill of beans as far as I was concerned if my beloved was in pain. But what was bothering her? I missed her, but couldn't find her. And I had to find her lest I die of sorrow.

My misery reached its limit. Her seeming aversion to me had affected me deeply, making its way into the inner recesses of my being. It provoked a recurrence of my old malady, and the magical recovery I'd experienced went the way of the wind. Not even liquor did the trick anymore. I was so grief-stricken, I came close to losing my mind. Was impotence to be my lot again? Was I to be doomed once more to that deadly despair?

Once I said to her despondently, "What's wrong, Rabab? You're not the sweetheart I've always known."

She made no reply. Instead, she just lowered her eyes with a look of consternation and uncertainty on her face.

Imploringly I said, "My heart doesn't lie to me. So please, tell me what's changed you."

"Nothing," she whispered with a somber look in her eyes.

"But there *is* something!" I cried. "In fact, there's more than one thing. I'm your husband, Rabab, and I'm all yours. So don't hide anything from me. Oh, Rabab, how I grieve the happy days we once knew!"

She sighed, and a look of pain and embarrassment came over her face. Then she murmured tremulously, "So do I."

Stunned, distressed, and utterly confused, I asked her, "How could that be, Rabab? I don't understand a thing. Shouldn't our life be happier than this?"

275

The look on her face indicated that she was as confused as I was, a fact that stunned and baffled me even more. I wanted her to reveal to me what was causing her distress and, in so doing, to relieve me of my own. I waited fretfully until I began to suspect things that struck terror in my heart and, if true, would plunge me into humiliation and despair.

When I could bear to wait no longer, I said, "Why don't you tell me honestly what you're thinking?"

She wanted to reveal what was weighing on her delicate heart, but she either didn't know how, or didn't have the courage.

As for me, fear and despondency tightened their grip on me until my anguish knew no bounds.

"Rabab," I said. "You're not comfortable with the new development in our lives, are you?"

She looked at me strangely, then lowered her glance and began nervously chewing her fingernails. The cat was out of the bag now. However, her silence had started to disturb me, and with a feeling that bordered on exasperation I asked, "Isn't that so?"

She looked at me as though she were begging me to have pity on her.

Then, in a voice that was barely audible she said, "Shall we go back to the way we were before? It was a nice life."

I looked down in humiliation and dejection as though I'd been slapped in the face. This wish of hers could have given me a convenient excuse by which to conceal the impotence I'd begun suffering anew. Even so, my only response to it was to feel utterly mortified.

As though she saw the pained look on my face, she said gently, "I don't mean to upset you. It's just that I miss the life we had before. It was a pure, happy life . . . ."

As if to finish her statement for her, I said, ". . . and there was nothing in it to disturb your peace of mind?"

She blinked her eyes, and in them I could see a look of sympathy.

"We were happy, weren't we?" she said gently. "We lacked nothing at all."

I don't know why, but her gentleness caused me pain.

Then I remembered some of the things I'd heard from my fellow employees at the warehousing section and I said, "But that's the only thing that will make a woman happy!"

Blushing, she assured me hastily, "No! No! You're wrong about that!"

I looked at her in bewilderment. Is she really telling me the truth? I wondered. But what reason would she have to lie? I was nothing but a gullible, ignorant fool, and you won't find an easier prey for words of assurance than gullible, ignorant fools. Hence, I was moved profoundly by what she said.

Again I thought: Should I disbelieve my beloved and believe the harebrains at the ministry? Didn't this statement of hers express a belief that I myself had held before I was persuaded otherwise by my coworkers' bawdy remarks? Add to this the fact that now that she'd spoken this way, and now that I was impotent again, I couldn't have relations with her anymore.

So all things considered, I pretended to be relieved.

Feigning a smile, I said with resignation, "There's nothing I want more than your happiness, Rabab."

Her worries dispelled, a look of relief flashed in her eyes. Then she moved up close to me until we were touching and kissed me.

Thus we went back to the way we'd been before, and I went back to being a chaste husband with an ugly habit. I would say to myself: It isn't my fault that we've ended up this way. I'm an able-bodied man, and if it weren't for her disposition, I wouldn't have suffered this relapse. On the contrary, I'm enduring this strange life for her sake! It was a solace I'd badly needed. But did I really believe myself?

Whatever the answer, the memory of our era of blessedness didn't leave me for a single moment. How had it passed with such astonishing rapidity? And how could my beloved have been so troubled that she would end up breaking her silence with this sort of manifest grievance? Didn't this mean that I was a wretched soul with no way out of my wretchedness? I was sorely tempted to flee and reclaim my freedom, and I would think back nostalgically to the days when I'd go wandering aimlessly in the streets.

Had everything gone back to point zero?

Love continued to bring us together in embraces and sympathy, and my beloved went back to being her smiling, cheerful self as she divided her days between her school and the houses of her family and relatives. It sufficed me to see her happy and content. At the same time, her disposition may have undergone a slight change, a change that became apparent in recurrent episodes of gloom, as well as in a quickness to lose her temper over the slightest thing my mother would say.

Was I happy?

As far as I could tell, my beloved was happy, so it was only natural that I should count myself happy too. I hadn't stopped suffering from obsessive thoughts. But then, when had my life been free of obsessive thoughts? Life's current flowed inexorably along, its waves tossing me to and fro, with my beloved's happiness bringing me joy, and my mother's severity bringing me equal misery. I would spend tedious hours at the ministry followed occasionally by dreamy hours at the pub. As for my conscience, on account of which I'd long suffered a feeling of guilt, I regularly drowned out its wails and laments with mirthful laughter and carousing. Hence, whenever its pangs beset me, I would say to myself in a loud voice: I'm happy, and everything is fine.

Another winter passed, followed by spring and summer, until it was time to greet the autumn and the new school year together with the precious memories they ushered in.

49

Then something happened to me that seemed trivial, but that nearly turned my life upside down. Strangely, it came to light as a result of a coincidence, and it seems only right for me to wonder: Would my life have taken a different direction if it hadn't been for that coincidence? Then again, what is a coincidence? Doesn't life seem at times to be an endless chain of coincidences? What, other than coincidence, had placed Rabab in my path? Would it have been possible for me to marry her if my father had died a single month later than he did? What would have happened to me if my father had insisted on taking me back the way he did Radiya and Medhat? In the same vein I wonder: Isn't it possible that my life would have gone on just the way it had been till the day I died if the time I spent with my mother on that unforgettable day hadn't lasted a few extra minutes?

It was an afternoon in late autumn. I was planning to spend my usual evening out, and I'd just bidden Rabab farewell. As I left our room, I encountered my mother in the living room and discovered that she wasn't feeling well. Consequently, I went with her to her room and we sat there talking for quite a long time. Then I excused myself and left. As I was on my way out, I happened to glance in the direction of our bedroom. The door was open as it had been before, and I saw Rabab sitting on the edge of the bed and reading a letter. I realized immediately that the postman must have brought it when I was sitting with my mother, since otherwise, I would have known about it when it arrived. I assumed it was a letter to me from my brother, since Rabab didn't receive letters from anyone, so I went back to the room to inquire. As I approached the door, Rabab was so engrossed in reading that she didn't notice me until I said to her, "Is that a letter for me?"

She looked up at me in astonishment and her hand folded up the letter in a rapid, robot-like motion.

"Did you forget something?" she asked, obviously uneasy.

Feeling an anxiety I didn't quite understand, I said, "I was in my mother's room, and as I was leaving her I saw you reading this letter, and I thought it was for me."

She got up from where she'd been sitting and backed toward the dressing table. She was clearly trying to keep her emotions under control. However, her eyes betrayed the profound, unexpected effect my sudden appearance had had on her.

Letting forth a terse, dry laugh that did nothing to conceal her distress, she said, "It isn't a letter. It's just some comments I wrote down relating to my work at school."

A fear came over me that numbed my joints. She may have been telling the truth. However, her distress was catching, and I too had begun to feel a strange sort of fear, as though some unnamed, ominous presence was gathering on my already cloudy horizon. What reason would she have to lie? Yet I was certain that I'd seen a letter in her hand! I feared acting too suspicious lest she be in the right and I find myself in an embarrassing position that I could well do without.

Even so, I couldn't help but say, "But I saw a letter in your hand."

My statement came out sounding bad to me, and I felt I hadn't chosen my words well, since they expressed obvious suspicion.

I looked at her apprehensively, waiting for her to show me the paper irritably as she shot me a look of disdain and reproach. However, she was struggling with other sorts of feelings.

As if she were overwhelmed with some unnamed emotion, she turned her back to me, saying, "I told you it was comments having to do with my schoolwork."

Then suddenly I saw her tear it up, walk over to the window and throw it out. The move she made came so unexpectedly, I froze in place as if I'd been paralyzed. She turned to face me with a show of nonchalance. Furious and desperate, I felt as though a huge wall had collapsed on top of my life and buried it beneath its rubble. My eyes were being opened—after the delusions of blindness—to ugly realities. After all, what but ugly realities would provoke such distress and such clever deceit?

Mad with rage, I screamed, "You're lying! You said it was a paper with comments relating to your schoolwork, but it wasn't anything of the sort. It was a letter! I saw it myself! And you tore it up to hide something shameful from me!"

The blood drained out of her face, leaving it deathly pale. However, she didn't appear willing to give up without a desperate defense.

"You're wrong," she mumbled, "and you're not being fair. It wasn't a letter!"

By now I was seething with rage, and pain and despair were pounding on my head like a hammer.

"Why did you tear it up, then?" I cried. "Why did you panic? Talk to me! I've got to know the truth! I'm going down to the street to pick up the pieces."

I rushed distraughtly over to the window and looked down into the street, where I saw the narrow blind alley that separated the back of our building from the church garden. The minute I looked out, I despaired, since it was obvious that the wind had carried the bits of paper over into the churchyard. The world looked black to me, and it seemed as though she had emerged from a world of demons dancing in a stream of fire. How was I going to extract the truth from her lips? I turned around and found her standing where she'd been before, with all the life drained out of her face and a look of terror and consternation in her eyes. My heart went cold and I shot her a long, hard look.

281

"It was a letter," I insisted angrily, "and I won't back down until you've confessed everything to me."

She stepped back with a groan and leaned on the wardrobe mirror.

Then in a plaintive voice she said, "I beg you not to think ill of me. There's nothing at all for you to be angry or suspicious about. Please, don't look at me that way!"

However, I went on looking at her sternly and cruelly, my soul yearning to know the truth. It was either deliverance, or death. Lord! I thought. I'm having a nightmare! Could I ever have conceived of taking such a stance toward her in anything but a nightmare?

Then she said breathlessly, "Don't look at me that way! I really did make a mistake, but it's your fault that I made it! You took me by surprise, and I got flustered. Then I fell into a needless lie."

Lord, how I needed to be delivered. How badly I longed for a drop of rain to wet my parched being.

"It was a letter," I said in consternation.

"Yes, it was!" she rejoined hurriedly. "It had seemed trivial to me until you got suspicious over it. You got an angry look on your face, thinking that this trivial thing was something serious, so I tried to get out of the situation by lying. And then what happened, happened."

More confused than ever now, I asked her, "If it was a letter, then who sent it?"

"I don't know."

Sighing in exasperation, I said, "What sorts of riddles are these?"

Getting over her fright little by little and heartened by the fact that my anger had abated, she said hopefully, "Let me tell you the story of this ill-fated letter in a nutshell. I received it at school this morning, and I was shocked, since I'm not used to getting letters from anybody. When I opened it I found that it was unsigned and that all it was was shameless nonsense. So it had been written by some vulgar person! I was really angry at first, but after that I didn't let it bother me. I decided to keep it so that I could show it to you, since I thought I'd let it be a surprise that would give you a good laugh. But after you came home I changed my mind, since I was afraid it would cause you needless offense. So I hid it from you until I thought you'd left the house, then I got it out of my purse and reread it. I'd been intending to tear it up, but you took me by surprise when I was reading it. I realized the delicate position I was in, and it wasn't possible anymore for me to admit the truth. So, as I told you before, I fell into a lie, but I'm being punished for it in a way I don't deserve."

I listened to her with my undivided attention. However, when she came to the end of her story, I stood motionless and ambivalent. I feared the potential consequences of the madness that had overtaken me, yet it wasn't easy simply to believe her and let it go. I was in the grip of a deadly uncertainty. I prayed for God to deliver me from it, and to grant me the insight I needed to penetrate to the depths of this lovely soul that seemed to have been made to torment me.

Worn out with thinking and indecision, I said, half to myself, "Who sent it?"

As if the question had pained her, she looked down, her brow furrowed, and said, "I told you it was anonymous."

"That's ridiculous!" I exclaimed.

With a pained, miserable look on her face, she stamped her foot on the floor and said, "Are you accusing me of lying, Kamil, after I've told you the truth? I can't take this!"

Pained by her distress, I said, "I mean, what good would it do the person to send you the letter if he didn't give any indication of his identity? Had he sent you a letter previous to this one?"

"This is the first letter I've received."

"And what did it say?"

"Silly things," she said wearily as she looked down again.

I thought back suddenly to the sight of her hands as they tore up the letter, and I felt a pang of suspicion that caused my body to tremble with fright.

"Why did you tear it up?" I shouted. "Why did you tear it up?"

She let out a sigh of near despair, then remained silent for some time.

Finally she said in calm resignation, "I received this miserable letter at school. I don't think you can possibly doubt this, since it would have been madness for him to send it to the house. And now, ask yourself this question: Why would I have kept the letter and brought it home if it contained something suspicious? Why didn't I tear it up at school after reading it there?"

Silenced by the cogency of her argument, I think I regretted my wild shouting.

As for Rabab, she continued, "If I were guilty, you wouldn't find me in this bad position, and you wouldn't know a thing about it. I'll never forgive you for thinking ill of me."

Stung by her words and painfully embarrassed, I lowered my glance lest she see the signs of defeat in my eyes. Yet, pained though I was, I hadn't forgotten the mysteries I wanted to resolve.

"What you're saying is plausible," I said softly, "but maybe the person who wrote the letter didn't sign it because he thought it would be easy for you to guess who he is—somebody who stops you on the street, for example."

My gentle tone of voice did nothing to mitigate the effect of my words. In fact, it may even have exacerbated it.

"It's my habit when I walk down the street to look straight ahead and not pay any attention to anybody!" she said resentfully.

I knew well enough the truth of her words, having experienced it first-hand. However, in my mind's eye I could see the two men who had shared my admiration for her in the past.

So I asked, "Might it not be your former neighbor, the one who asked for your hand? I mean Muhammad Gawdat."

She replied without hesitation, "He's a dignified man who would never lower himself to such vulgar manners. Besides, I found out from my family around a month ago that he's about to get married."

After some thought, I said uncertainly, "During the same period when I used to hover around you, there was a heavy man that would regularly devour you with his eyes. Isn't it possible that he wrote it?"

She knit her brow in an attempt to recall the person I was talking about. Then she shook her head, saying, "I don't know anything about him."

I tried to remind her of who he was, but she seemed not even to have been aware of his existence.

So, feeling angry and desperate, I said, "I want to know who he is so that I can put him in his place."

In a tired-sounding voice she said, "Who cares who it was! If I hadn't been so flustered that I tore it up, we'd be sitting here now reading it and laughing about it! So why don't you just forget about it? It's caused us enough grief as it is!"

I bit my lip and said nothing, still feeling angered and defeated.

Then she continued, "It's a trivial matter. In fact, it's too trivial for us to be getting so concerned about it."

Heaving a sigh, I said mechanically, "If only you hadn't torn it up!"

"Are you still suspicious of me?" she asked me sharply, her eyes flashing with anger.

"No," I replied hurriedly, "but I won't find any peace until I can teach him a lesson!"

Irritably she replied, "But we don't know who he is, so what can we do?"

I was angered by what she'd said, but I avoided expressing how I felt lest I make her angry too. Apparently exhausted from standing, she moved over to the chair by the dressing table and sat down. At the same moment I felt a pain in my back, so I went over and sat on the edge of the bed. She was innocent and telling the truth, and the matter really was trivial. If only I could erase the memory of her tearing up that letter! Maybe the culprit was just some curious bystander who watched her coming and going. If only I didn't fall prey so easily to jealousy. I knew myself well, and I knew that I could feel jealous of an illusion, that is, of nothing. So where could I find a far-away island on which no man had ever set foot?

Then suddenly my imagination took me to my mother's room, and a chill went through me as I imagined her saying to me, "Didn't I tell you so?"

I exhaled forcefully like someone trying to drive away a bad dream. I glanced over at Rabab and found her staring into my face in dismay.

285

Then a new thought occurred to me that I didn't hesitate to express.

"Rabab," I said, "why do you go on working for the government? Why do you endure such hardship unnecessarily? Why aren't you content to stay at home like other wives?"

After looking at me long and hard, she said calmly, "Don't you trust me?"

"God forbid that I shouldn't trust you!" I said hurriedly, "But I . . . ."

Interrupting me, she said, "If you don't trust me, it's better for me to leave your house!"

"Rabab!"

Ignoring my anguish, she said, "But if you do still trust me, I'll stay at my job."

"As you wish," I said with resignation.

Then in the same tone she said, "I don't want to hear another word on this subject."

And so it was. I left the house and went wandering about aimlessly till I was totally exhausted, then I went home again. We met as though nothing had happened between us. We had supper together, then went to our room and exchanged a meaningful look.

Then, in spite of ourselves, we burst out laughing. We went to bed and lay down, and I gave her a good-night kiss. For some strange reason, I was tempted to make another attempt at what we had agreed to avoid. Even stranger is the fact that I didn't have an ounce of confidence, yet I still almost tried, and would have done so if fear hadn't brought me back to my senses. It occurred to me to ask her what had made her sentence herself to deprivation. My lips parted and I voiced the question in my heart, yet it froze on the tip of my tongue. And fear, again, was what stopped me.

50

When I opened my eyes in the early morning, I recalled the events of the previous day and pondered them in amazement. It seemed to me now that the issue hadn't called for so much suffering and pain. And I said to myself: If she'd torn up the letter at school, I never would have known about it, and the fact that she didn't do that is testimony to her truthfulness. Then I recalled the image of her as she tore up the letter and threw it out the window, and it was as though she'd been tearing my heart to shreds and scattering them to the wind. Before I got out of bed, a violent shudder went through my body and I shook my head angrily, as though to shake off the illusions that had accumulated there. When we'd finished our breakfast and were sitting on the long seat sipping our tea, I looked over at her furtively and found her beloved face to be serene, smiling, and radiant with beauty and peace. Seeing her this way, I was stricken with remorse for the way I'd acted toward her, and I said to myself: Truly, Satan is an accursed tempter! The next morning a thought came to me like lightning: Isn't it possible, I wondered, that she received the letter at home and that she hadn't had the chance to tear it up elsewhere? But I soon rejected the idea. After all, it was ridiculous, as she had said herself, to think that anybody could be so foolish as to send a love letter to the husband's home. Curses on illusions! My beloved was worthy of all trust, and trust is everything. If it weren't for trust, there's no telling what evil people might perpetrate.

We went out together and got on the tram. Many people may have been looking at us enviously, but could they imagine how we actually lived together? Indeed, what odd worlds are contained within people's souls. And the oddest of them all was the case of Rabab. How could she spurn marital relations with such peculiar resolve? How I longed to know her thoughts! As I thought about these things, I felt the need for a counselor to relate things to and listen to. Never before had I felt so lonely, isolated, or vulnerable. It was natural, of course, for me to think of my sole counselor in life, namely, my mother. Yet the minute she came to mind, I was gripped by shame and anger. After all, it would have been easier to announce my worries to the entire world than confide them to my mother!

Could I get to the bottom of the mystery by myself? Was it possible that God had made her a chaste creature for whom life could only be sweet if she was celibate? It was a plausible hypothesis, which was supported by the data. Nor did I regret this actuality, since if it hadn't been for this very fact, I would have been in an awkward position indeed. It was also a fact that my contact with her, even at the happiest of times, had never been without a vague anxiety and fear. It was during the time when she was distancing herself from me that my impotence had recurred. Consequently, I refused to see myself as anything but the victim of my beloved's eccentricity, the ransom for her happiness. When I'd reached this point in my thinking—by which time I'd almost arrived at the ministry— my mind went into a jumble and I felt an overwhelming anxiety that I couldn't explain. There seemed to be every reason for complete peace of mind, yet I was enveloped by an agonizing confusion, and I entered the ministry in a daze. Who was the scoundrel who had written that letter? It was quite reasonable to assume that he wasn't the dignified Muhammad Gawdat. So who might it have been? Mightn't it have been the other young man, the fat one with the disdainful look? It wasn't unlikely. He was within my reach. In fact, I knew the spot where he stood waiting every morning. Had she really been unaware of him, or had she just been pretending not to notice him? At the same time, I hoped fervently that he wasn't the one, since I hadn't forgotten for a single moment that he could fell me with a single blow. I thought to myself bitterly: If she'd just kept the letter, I could have done anything. But what did I mean by 'anything'? I didn't know exactly. Be that as it may, I found myself obsessing about the matter again after it appeared to have been resolved. By God, I thought, she only tore it up to keep me from reading it. O Lord, was I descending into the infernal abyss again? Let her beware of going too far!

On the other hand, I thought, anyone who would allow himself to doubt Rabab doesn't deserve to be part of the human race. Might it not be best for me to ask her over the phone whether she's received any more letters? I had an overwhelming urge to do so, but I was prevented by fear. In fact, an inner voice told me to run away. But who would I be running away from? And where would I go? I must be either crazy or just childish, I thought. In reality, we're a happy married couple, but my mind is perverse. Ah, if only I could delete yesterday from the record! If only the memory of her tearing up that letter could be erased from my imagination! And here's a new thought: If she read the letter at school, then why did she reread it in our room? Did it give her pleasure to reread it, or was she confirming a rendezvous? My forehead was about to explode from the intensity of my thoughts. When I left the ministry that day, the pleasant outdoor air ministered to me with a spirit of its own. I breathed in deeply and felt a refreshment that restored my tranquility. Then I started telling myself over and over: What a fool I am! When I arrived home, Rabab greeted me with a bright smile. My features relaxed and I asked her with a laugh, "Is there anything new?"

"You mean any new letters?"

"Yes," I replied, still laughing.

"No," she said, smiling, "the mail's stopped coming."

I left the house that afternoon without any particular destination in mind, and no sooner had I settled into my place on the tram than a

289

lovely idea came to me, namely, to visit Sayyida Zaynab. For many years her tomb had been my refuge and sanctuary. I had no hesitations about acting on the desire, and it suddenly filled my being. When I crossed the mosque's threshold, a breeze of blissful relief came wafting over me, and my head was filled with memories dear to my heart. In my mind's eye I saw myself walking to the sacred tomb with my hand in my mother's. I remembered the day when she'd brought me to repent of the sin that had now become almost second nature to me. The memory left a sense of such shame and remorse that I felt an urge to turn around and flee, but I kept on walking. I walked around the tomb reciting the Fatiha, drawing courage from my sense of lowliness and from the status I'd enjoyed since childhood with the saintly figure to whom it belonged. I placed my hand on the door and murmured beseechingly, "O Umm Hashim, you of all people know the goodness of my heart. You of all people know that never in my life have I harbored ill will toward anyone. So cause my reward to be in keeping with the things I've done. This is my prayer, Good Lady." Then I retreated into a corner and sat cross-legged on the floor. My nostrils were penetrated by a sweet aroma that may have been some perfume being sprayed by a magzub, while the sounds of the supplications being made by those circumambulating the shrine filled its corners with melodic echoes. A sheikh passed near me chanting verses from the Holy Qur'an in a hushed voice, and I remembered how I'd fallen away from the religion's obligatory rites to the point where the only thing I did regularly anymore was to fast during Ramadan. I thought to myself: If I returned to the right guidance found in the prescribed prayers, might not my heart find serenity and assurance, and might I not experience relief from the burden of anxiety and fear? Despite the pain it had endured, my heart had continued to find refuge in the prophets and the guidance they brought, and to drink deeply from a wellspring of cool, pure waters. I was flooded with a tranquility so profound, I wanted to soak up all I could of the wholesome, untainted serenity that I was experiencing in those moments. In that peace-induced rapture, my sufferings appeared to me as nothing but a fine thread in the fabric of destiny's invincible sway over all that is, and I was drawn into a state of contentment and surrender. A cloudlessness of the spirit set my soul in an upward spiral until I reached a pinnacle of bliss beyond anything I'd ever hoped for. It was as though my heart were a branch in paradise, swaying aloft as the dove of peace sat cooing upon it. I remained in this euphoric state for I don't know how long until all of a sudden, my imagination was intruded upon by the image of a panic-stricken Rabab tearing up the letter. Thus was I awakened, cruelly and forcefully, from my blissful reverie like someone jolted out of his slumber by a violent earthquake. I sighed out of a wounded heart, then rose to my feet, recited the Fatiha one more time and left the mosque. As I was coming out the door, I happened to see a geomancer. I have faith in such people just the way my mother did. I waited until a group of inquirers who'd gathered around him had gone their ways, then I came up to him timidly and asked him to read my fortune. The man began making hollows in the sand with his thumb and moving his seashells back and forth between them. Clad in a white garment, he was pallid and thin as a mummy, and he had lost all his teeth except for his upper incisors.

"You think and worry a lot," he said.

He's right, I said to myself, and proceeded to listen intently.

"And you have a cunning enemy."

At that, my heart started to pound! Wouldn't that be the person who'd written the letter?

The man went on, saying, "He's planning a cunning deceit, but God will bring his artful plot down on his own head."

Didn't this mean that Rabab was innocent?

"And you'll receive a piece of paper that will bring you long-lasting satisfaction."

"Do you mean a letter?"

"Possibly. What I see before me is a piece of paper."

What did this mean? Things were getting more and more mysterious.

"Will it come from the enemy?"

"No! No! It will come from some other party, and it will cause your worries to be dispelled."

291

"From what other party?"

"Blessing will come to you whence you know not."

Feeling bewildered, I wished he would explain more.

However, he said, "If new difficulties arise, this amulet will overcome them, God willing."

As he spoke, he gave me a tiny paper envelope with a thin string tied around it.

"Put it over your heart," he said, "and trust in God."

As I was on my way home, I remembered the pain I'd been having since the previous afternoon, and I could see clearly that a year's happiness wouldn't offset even a single day's misery. I couldn't settle down to anything, and I just grew more uncertain and confused. The tranquility that would hover over me at times was nothing but a summer cloud, and I knew I wouldn't be at peace until I'd confronted the truth face to face. I hadn't wanted my soul to be polluted with suspicion toward this one with the comely, pristine face. However, the seed of doubt had been sown, and it was bound to keep growing and bearing its infernal thorns. Driven by despair, I'd clung with all my might to the hope of finding serenity, but it had fallen to pieces in my hand. I couldn't bear to go on living my life being tossed back and forth between moments of illusory peace and long hours of agony. Hence, I had no choice but to try to see beyond the veils. I knew that it might mean my own destruction, but there are times when life requires that we run after our own destruction as though it were our most cherished desire.

I love you, sweetheart, I thought. But perhaps fate has cast this love into my heart in order, through this very love, to destroy me. And what power do I have to resist its decree?

I think I now realized why, even in my most untainted moments of happiness, I'd never been free of a certain sense of angst. Had my heart been catching glimpses of what fate had in store for me beyond the curtain of the unknown? At the same time, I didn't want to go to excess in my pessimism, since I knew that what was concealed from me might be other than what I'd expected, and that I might find the peace and assurance I longed for in what was yet unseen.

What was I to do, then? The right thing to do, I decided, was to ask for a vacation from the ministry, then devote myself entirely to surveillance from a vantage point no one else would know about. Would it be a trivial or easy thing for me to spy on Rabab? On the contrary, it would be agony for me! But nothing can compare to the agony of suspicion.

51

I set to work with an ache in my heart that only God knew. We went out together as was our custom every morning and got on the tram together. Then I got off at the ministry stop, hailed a taxi, and instructed the driver to take me to Abbasiya. I got to her place of work before she did in order to set myself up in a spot that would be well suited for surveillance. The kindergarten was located on Kamal Street, which branches off the main road to the left. Once one turned onto Kamal Street, one passed two houses, and the school was the third building on the right. As I stood at the tram stop scrutinizing my surroundings, I saw a side street that branched off the main road in the opposite direction to Kamal Street. At the intersection between this street and the main road there was a small coffee shop. If I sat there, I thought, I'd have a good view of the school from a distance and be able to watch my wife as she came and went. So I made my way to the coffee shop, whose entrance opened onto the side street, and chose a seat next to the entrance from which I could see what I wanted to see. At the same time, I'd be able to disappear from view if need be by moving my chair back a bit. It only took one glance to see how lowly the place was. Its tables were old and its chairs were faded and decrepit, while its patrons were all Nubians. However, none of this bothered me. On the contrary, I found it reassuring. I sat down, not taking my eyes off Kamal Street for a moment. Whenever a tram came by from the city, I snapped to attention. I wasn't kept waiting long, since I soon saw my wife crossing the street, looking right and left to avoid the vehicles that filled the roadway. After reaching the sidewalk on Kamal Street, she walked along in her pin-striped, lead-gray coat with her tall, svelte frame, her charming, refined gait, and her usual modesty and endearing poise. And as she turned to go into the school, the gatekeeper rose respectfully.

I was pained and ashamed to be in the position I was in, and my feverish, cynical heart was softened with sympathy and affection as I thought back on how I'd been dazzled by this same regal beauty the first time I saw her. O God, I prayed, If my beloved is an angel, then consume me with Your vengeance, and if she's a demon, then consume us all. And consume the world along with us, since in such an eventuality, there wouldn't be anything on earth worthy of Your mercy. Lifting my eyes heavenward, I murmured, "O Lord! If You've willed to allow the poison of treachery to penetrate the depths of this beauty, then forgive me my madness!"

I examined the street before me, wondering in dread: In a few hours, will I be seeing someone standing and waiting somewhere along this street? Will I see the two of them exchanging a signal or a smile, or see one of them following the other? And if this thunderbolt were to strike my head, what on earth would I do? I imagined the catastrophe as though it had actually taken place, and my body trembled with rage and terror. I kept imagining it until it had taken on flesh before my very eyes. Then again I asked myself what I would do. There's nothing easier than heroism, victory, and displays of strength in one's daydreams. Even so, my imagination didn't provide me with even a glimpse of any of them. It may have felt up against a wall, since the danger that threatened it wasn't far enough away to be enjoyed as a mere dream. On the contrary, it was near enough actually to materialize. Consequently, it stifled dreams, and the hideous situation presented itself before me as though it were actually happening. I visualized it with a timorous heart and a soul on the verge of collapse. The enemy appeared to me as a real person on a street teeming with passersby, but my imagination didn't enable me to stand up to him openly, announce my scandal to the world, or embroil myself in a battle I was certain to lose. Imagine a betrayed husband lying flat on his back after being punched in the nose by his betrayer! Damn me! How I loathed my weakness at that moment! I felt the rage of someone who'd like to level a mountain, and I sighed the sigh of someone who's too weak to lift so much as a pebble. Yet I had no choice but to act. After all, could I see Rabab with the one who'd penned the letter and then just stand there with my hands tied? Impossible! Rather, let me assail my rival, come what may. Either that, or content myself with witnessing the crime, then wait till she comes home and say to her with calm disdain, "I saw everything with my own eyes. Now back with you to your parents' house!" Why on earth had I done this crazy thing? Why had I gotten married? People like me shouldn't marry.

Just then there was an outburst of uproarious laughter in the coffee shop that extricated me from my daydreams, and I came to my senses weary as a sick man. I glanced over at the black faces engrossed in never-ending chitchat with their strange, excited voices, then I looked in front of me to find that my cup of coffee was still untouched. I brought it to my lips and took a few cold sips, then looked back at the street until my eyes came to rest on the entrance to the kindergarten. Rabab would be peacefully engaged in her work right now. And who knows? I thought. Maybe all this terror will lead to nothing, in which case I might think back with chagrin on this situation some day. Would those limpid, innocent eyes lie? Could that unsullied heart ever be guilty of treachery? The minutes dragged by in relentless thought until I was roused from my reverie by the clattering sound of a window being opened. I turned instinctively to look across the street, and what should I find but a woman looking out a window on the second floor of a large building. She may have been surprised to find a gentleman like me sitting in the Nubians' coffee shop, since she was looking my direction with interest. There was a boldness in her gaze that caused me to look away bashfully. And although I didn't look at her for more than a few moments, I nevertheless came away with a vivid image of her homely face and her well-endowed bosom. A feeling of anxiety came over me, since the window directly overlooked the place where I was sitting. I looked up warily to find her smoking a cigarette and looking at something in front of her on the windowsill. Emboldened by the fact that she'd looked away from me, I took a long look at her. She looked to be over forty, though I was no good generally at guessing people's ages, and despite her stylishness and the makeup she was wearing, she was uglier than she was pretty. She had a round, thickish face and protruding eyes with heavy eyelids, a short, flat nose, full lips, rounded, puffy cheeks, and shiny, kinky hair. A short while later she disappeared from the window and my anxiety abated. However, the door leading onto a balcony next to the window then opened wide, and out she came dragging a chair. She stood for a while resting her elbow on the edge of the balcony, allowing me to see her short, stout body. Then she sat down on the chair and crossed one leg over the other. The balcony was closer to the main street than the window was, which made it possible for me to see whoever was standing or sitting on it without needing to turn my head. I began stealing glances at her plump, dark legs and her bright red slippers. Her presence delivered me from the hellish torrent of thoughts going through my head, albeit in a way that gripped me with an unexpected disquiet. She began exhaling smoke through her thick lips and looking around her. Whenever her glance came my way, she examined me with such consummate daring that I could feel my face flush with embarrassment. Awkward and uncomfortable, I wondered: When is she going to disappear? I was flustered by her insistent staring into my face, which had another, peculiar effect on me as well. It was an effect not without an element of guarded satisfaction and a sexual tension the reason for which I couldn't discern. Whenever I looked in her direction, she would turn her head toward me and cast me a shameless, penetrating look. It was as though she could see with her ears, or as though she was endowed with a sixth sense that made her aware of glances being directed at her from any and all directions.

Consequently, I began to feel wary and apprehensive. Careful not to look in her direction anymore, I began to wonder how long this disquiet and tension would stay with me.

Then suddenly her voice—which was full and melodic—rang out as though she were addressing someone in the street. "I'm coming, Mama!" she said, whereupon she got up and went inside. I couldn't help but smile to myself in a combination of surprise and disapproval. I was taken aback to hear her say, "Mama," since she was clearly beyond the days of her youth. And I was amazed that, for no particular reason, she would answer her mother's call in a voice that could be heard all the way down the street. She could simply have gone to her without saying a word, or addressed her mother after going into the room where she was. Consequently, she struck me as being not only brazen, but a bit eccentric, someone who's fond of appearances and attracting attention while disregarding the most patent laws of common sense. Glad to have her gone and to be free from her intrusive gaze, I returned to myself, and to the street I was keeping watch over until the day was over. The time crept by tediously, and I started to get bored. Wouldn't it be better for me to wander here and there until it was nearly time for the kindergarten to let out? But what was to guarantee that things wouldn't happen during my absence? So then, I thought, let me remain hostage to this seat of mine till the inevitable happens. I stayed where I was, patiently enduring the ordeal minute by minute. Then I heard a noise coming from the balcony. I looked up and saw the woman move her chair to a sunny spot on the balcony, then sit down again. She happened to glance over at the coffee shop, and when her eyes fell on me, a look of curiosity and incredulity appeared on her face, as though she were wondering what would have led me to go on sitting in such a wretched coffee shop all this time. In her usual unabashed way, she made a point of letting me see how astonished she was. All that was left now was for her to ask me what was keeping me in my seat. She lit a cigarette, then began smoking with relish and amusing herself by looking over at me from time to time. Determined to focus my attention on the purpose for which I'd come, I looked at the street. However, my feelings were occupied elsewhere. I no longer had the will to resist the temptation to look up. I felt terribly shy and awkward since, given the narrowness of the street, I felt as though this woman and I were in a single room together. At the same time, I derived a certain satisfaction from finding myself the object of a woman's attention for the first time in my life. By this time I was fully aware of the sexual tension that was being aroused by the woman's uncomely face and chubby legs. And although her audacity bothered me, it nevertheless brought me a vague satisfaction. Perhaps it was a feeling of admiration that didn't want to make itself known. And I wondered in astonishment: If all women were as bold as this one, would I have spent my past lonely and companionless? Without knowing why, I felt led to draw a comparison between this delightful audacity and the lovely decorum that characterized my beloved wife. However, I soon rejected the unseemly parallel, and was filled with anger and disgust.

The woman sat on the porch for an hour, then went back inside and closed the door. I heaved a sigh of relief and muttered, "May she never come back." From then on I waited alone, and the time passed with exhausting tedium. I started amusing myself by watching the six or seven Nubians who were the only customers left in the place. Three of them kept up their chatter, while the others sat motionless in their seats like bronze statues. When I looked at the main street, I would count the men and women passing by and note the trams coming and going. Whenever I heard the rumbling of a tram coming from afar I would try to guess whether it was No. 3 or No. 22 and whether it had an open car or a closed one, then I'd count up the number of times I'd been right and the number of times I'd been wrong. When it was time for the kindergarten to let out, I snapped to attention again, and my anxiety and trepidation intensified. My eyes went wandering over the street until they came to rest on the school door. My heart pounded like mad when I saw a group of schoolteachers leaving the kindergarten. They were followed by Rabab, accompanied by one of her colleagues. She made her way toward Abbasiya Street as the two of them talked and laughed. They parted on the main street, at which point the other girl went left and my wife went to the tram stop. When she was standing in such a way that she had her face toward the side street, I pulled my chair inside the coffee shop sufficiently to disappear from view. As I carefully scrutinized the sidewalk, my heart was pounding so hard, it nearly jumped out of my chest, since something told me that within moments I'd be receiving the death blow. There was a smattering of men and women waiting for the tram. However, my wife kept to the far end of the waiting area, standing modestly as was her wont and looking neither to one side nor to the other, apart from an occasional glance behind her shoulder in the direction her tram would be coming from. I saw nothing that looked the least suspicious. I didn't take my eyes off her for a moment until the tram came and she got on, at which point I got up hurriedly, hailed a taxi, got in, and asked the driver to follow the tram from a distance. I sat next to the left window, my eyes glued to the ladies' compartment, until we'd reached Ataba. My wife got off the tram and crossed the square to the stop for tram No. 15, which goes through Roda. Meanwhile, I had the taxi go around and let me off near the Mouski section. Seeing her standing in the midst of a crowd, I began looking frantically at the circle of people immediately surrounding her. The tram arrived, she got on, and it took her away. I followed it stop after stop until it had reached the stop for our building, then I saw her get out and cross the street to go home. The taxi took me on to the next stop, at which point I got out and walked home. On my way there I felt a mixture of relief and shame, and I wondered uncertainly: Is my girl really innocent, or will I discover things tomorrow that I didn't discover today?

When I reached our flat, both my mother and Rabab were fretting over my delay, and I explained to them that my work would require me to stay late at the ministry every day for at least a week. In the late afternoon, Rabab began getting dressed to go out. She told me she was going to visit her mother and, as she usually did when she went out, she invited me to come along. I'd wondered to myself how I'd be able to keep an eye on her in the evening. It wouldn't be as easy as it had been in the morning, since the houses she visited most often were in nearby neighborhoods and she would usually go from one to another on foot. Consequently, I knew that if I followed her, I'd run the risk of exposing myself. However, if I accompanied her personally, I'd ensure that the evening passed without incident, as it were, since I wouldn't have given her a chance to do anything wrong. This way, if there had, in fact, been any wrongdoing, she would be obliged to commit it during the first half of the day, in which case she would fall into my trap unawares. Consequently, I accepted her invitation gladly.

Laughing, I said, "I'll go with you to avoid the boredom that kills me when you're not around."

Pleased that I'd accepted her invitation, she said hopefully, "I wish you'd always come with me, since there's nothing I'd love more than for us to go and come together."

52

The next morning we went out together as usual, and I repeated what I'd done the day before. I took a taxi to the Nubians' coffee shop and took up my position at its entrance. Rabab arrived at the same time she had the day before and went to the kindergarten. Then, as I was tracking her with my eyes, I happened to think: If she had the perceptivity of that strange woman—whom I hadn't thought about from the time I'd left Abbasiya by taxi the day before until this thought leapt into my mind—and if she happened to look in my direction and saw me sitting here, she'd turn on her heels, march over to me in disbelief, and ask me what had brought me to this coffee shop. Envisioning the situation with terror in my heart, I shrank into my seat, smarting with shame and remorse. However, my wife turned into the schoolyard peacefully and unsuspectingly, oblivious to the eyes that were keeping their wary, suspicious vigil over her. When she disappeared through the door, my tension and fear left me, and I dreaded the prospect of the second day-long wait I'd have to endure. I cast a weary, sweeping glance around me, taking in the side street where the coffee shop was located, what I could see of Abbasiya Street, and the coffee shop itself with its dark-skinned clientele. These were the places where I'd been condemned to remain like a mad prisoner, wandering aimlessly through a maze of dark thoughts and hellish, fugitive apparitions.

As I watched my wife going to the school I remembered the strange woman, so I looked up toward the building across from the coffee shop, but found both the window and the balcony closed. I wondered how I could bear to wait the entire day without some sort of entertainment to help kill the time. It was a dubious question, one that concealed a desire to see her that I didn't like to admit. Yet what reason did I have to deny such a desire? Wasn't it a desire simply to amuse myself and kill time? It was true, of course, that the woman had stirred up something erotic in me. But there was nothing new in that, since I'd always responded erotically to the ugliest, filthiest of women. Marriage had done nothing to change me or heal me of my condition. On the contrary, it was after marriage that I'd gone back to all my old habits. I looked back at the window again as though I were enduring two long waits.

I decided to try to understand myself better. I wasn't just looking for amusement. No, I really wanted to see her again. I wanted her to devour me with her eyes the way she'd done the day before, so that I could experience that deep sense of satisfaction and pride and salvage some of my lost confidence.

No sooner had I lost myself in thought than I heard the clattering of the window. I looked up and saw it being opened wide. The woman appeared in the window and our eyes met. She hadn't been expecting to see me, of course, and a look of evident astonishment appeared in her eyes. She stood there looking at me for a minute or so, then moved away from the window and disappeared from view. With a happiness that ill-befit the miserable nature of the mission I'd come there to carry out, I shifted my gaze over to the balcony, waiting for it to open. And so it was: a hand pushed open the leaves of the door leading out to the balcony and they collided violently with the wall on either side, whereupon the woman came out, pulling a chair along with her short, solid body. She looked rather like a barrel in the pink dress she was wearing, though it was tailored in a crude sort of way. She placed the chair in the far corner of the balcony, sat down on it facing the coffee shop, and spread her arms out on the balcony's wooden railing. We were face to face, there were no shops on the side street, and hardly anyone ever came down it. As for the coffee shop regulars, they were so engrossed in their chatter, they saw nothing outside. My table was situated so close to the entrance that it was more or less isolated from the others, and I imagined the two of us as being alone in a sense. A moment later, though, I felt flustered and embarrassed. I didn't know how I could remain at the mercy of her brazen stares, and I wished my unspoken desire hadn't been fulfilled. I began looking at the distant street part of the time, and part of the time over my shoulder at the inside of the coffee shop. Yet either way, I could feel the weight of her heavy eyes on my face.

I wanted her presence, of that there was no doubt. At the same time, though, I couldn't bear it. Every time I stole a glance in her direction, I would find her scrutinizing my face calmly, thoroughly, and without the slightest embarrassment or hesitation. This sent me into raptures, while at the same time it left me unbearably flustered and embarrassed. Her eyes would spend a long time looking, but they didn't just look. Rather, they spoke with the most eloquent of tongues. Whenever our eyes met, I would imagine her speaking to me, then lower my gaze as though I were running away from her. Once when I looked her way I found her lighting a cigarette. She put out the match with a couple of shakes of her hand, then threw it in my direction, and if it hadn't been blown off course by the wind, it would have reached its target. She took a deep breath, her eyes smiling. Meanwhile, my heart started pounding wildly and I swallowed with difficulty.

What did this woman want? And how could she be so audacious as to ogle me in this brazen, intense fashion? Indeed, how could she engage in this silent pursuit of me when she had no previous acquaintance with me, and had only seen me twice in her life—once today and once the day before? I became muddled and agitated. In fact, I'd become so preoccupied with the balcony that I only cast the most fleeting, perfunctory glances at the entrance to the kindergarten, and when I did so, I hardly saw a thing. Noticing that I'd looked her way, she crossed

304

her legs, thereby drawing my eye forcibly to a large swathe of her thighs, whose meeting and intertwinement caused alluring dark folds to appear. Feeling something akin to the rush brought on by a shot of booze, my throat went dry and my emotions overcame my shyness to the point where it melted as snow melts under the sun's fiery rays. I stared at her without shame or hesitation. Then what should she do but get up and leave the balcony, leaving me in an unbearable tumult! I said to myself irritably: What sort of abyss is opening up under my feet? Gradually, however, I regained my composure, and I felt the sting of remorse and shame. Casting the balcony an angry look, I muttered as I had the day before, "May she never come back!" Waiting might be tedious, but it was better than this evil that had begun to threaten me. I had no doubt that she was coming back, and I could have left the coffee shop forever and gone in search of some new location from which to carry on with my surveillance and waiting. However, I persuaded myself that this out-of-the-way coffee shop was the ideal location for my task.

The woman's absence was a brief one, and before long she was back with a smile in her eyes. I was furious, not because she'd come back, but because of the pleasure I felt on account of it, and I thought to myself: She's shameless, and I've never seen an uglier, more uncouth woman in my life! Even so, I went back to stealing glances at her, hoping she'd make herself at home and cross her legs again. I also went back to enjoying the way she aroused me with her looks and attention. Transported by her interest in me, I was ravenous for more. Was her attention anything but a response to my good looks and my slender build? In childish conceit I said to myself: Maybe she's impressed with my green eyes, my fair complexion, and my towering height. Then all of a sudden there stole into my consciousness a voice that whispered to me sarcastically: And since when have your good looks done you any good? As the voice spoke I thought about my marital unhappiness, and it was as though a huge piece of ice had fallen on the flames of my enthusiasm. Suddenly I felt suffocated, my euphoria dwindled away, and instead I felt miserable and disillusioned. I put the balcony out of my mind and my thoughts went rushing toward the kindergarten. I wanted the truth to be revealed to me, however ugly or harsh it happened to be, so that I could settle the matter once and for all. And I hoped—if such a thing was bound to happen—to see the person who'd penned the letter meeting with Rabab and speaking to her today rather than tomorrow or the day after that. In fact, at that moment there was something else in my mind that's hard to put into words. It was as though I hoped my suspicions would be confirmed. I'm not mistaken about this. This was the fact. Yet how can I explain it? Had my doubts and suspicions become such a burden to me that I wanted to be delivered from them even at this exorbitant price? Had I become so distressed over the strange inadequacy that had turned my marital life into a farce that I hoped to use my wife's crime as an excuse to flee my life? Or was my overworked conscience looking for punishment and atonement? However, it was only a passing feeling, and just a moment later not a trace of it remained. Instead, a feeling of melancholy and resentment came over me. The woman left the balcony in response to a summons from inside the house and didn't reappear. I waited for a long time, tossed to and fro by frightening thoughts and visions until another day of waiting had drawn to a close. As I had the day before, I saw Rabab coming toward the tram stop. There were no new developments, and we came home— she on the tram and I in the taxi. That evening she suggested that we go to the Cinema Royale together. I agreed to the idea without hesitation, and out we went.

53

On the morning of the third day, the taxi took me to the same destination. On the way I remembered the strange woman, and in my mind's eye I could see her with her homely face and her fleshy, squat body. However, I wasn't remembering her for the first time that morning. The thought of her had come to me while I was at home grooming myself in front of the mirror, a fact that had moved me to take extra care in combing my hair and putting on my necktie. As I did so I felt ashamed, guilty, and anxious. However, I cast the blame for my predicament on Rabab, whose bad behavior was what had driven me to this ridiculous spying operation.

Could I really say I hoped she wouldn't appear on the balcony? Could I bear the day's long wait without her presence and her delightful effrontery? I took my regular seat in the coffee shop and was approached by the waiter, who was clad in a faded robe, worn-out sandals, and a skullcap that was cocked toward the back of his head in such a way as to reveal a stiff tuft of hair. He greeted me in a way that may have been reserved for regular customers, and I ordered coffee that I proceeded to sip with loathing and disgust. Meanwhile, I wondered to myself resentfully what on earth could come of this loathsome espionage. Wouldn't it better for me to desist from what I'd taken upon myself based on an unfair verdict and unfounded suspicion? After all, my wife had now spent two entire days under my watchful eye. Had I seen anything that would give me cause to distrust her? Had I observed any sort of annoyance or discontentment? Wasn't she, as I'd always known her to be, the embodiment of serenity, warmth, and happiness? Such thoughts brought with them a sense of assurance and relief. More time passed, and before long I was weary and bored. I looked at my watch, thinking: Shall I inquire of it about the time that's passed, or ask it when the window is going to open? At any rate, the window did open and the woman appeared with her usual coarseness and gaudy adornment. When she saw me her eyes bulged out in disbelief and she raised her penciled eyebrows as if to say: You're still there? She looked down to conceal a smile, and my heart fluttered with joy. Then I began feeling ashamed of myself again, so I began telling my conscience that I wasn't looking to do anything wrong, and that someone in my circumstances had the right to feel happy if he received attention from a woman. Indeed, I was innocent, I reminded myself. I'd come to this coffee shop with a purpose that had nothing to do with this woman, and in a few more days I'd be abandoning the entire neighborhood forever, never to bring her to mind again. As for the woman, she disappeared from the window, opened the balcony, came out with her chair and sat down in the corner facing me, her eyes smiling like those of someone who needs no further introduction. By now I'd become more able to endure the situation. However, I still pretended to be looking at the main street while looking furtively now and then at her compact, sturdy legs through the iron bars of the balcony. I hadn't gotten over my awkwardness. In fact, it may even have increased in response to the way her eyes twinkled whenever they met mine. What an audacious woman! She could do whatever she pleased without fear. As for me, I had no choice but to avert my gaze. And I wondered: Has it occurred to her that I'm married? And that I only came to this coffee shop in order to catch my wife red-handed in the act of betraying me? Would she go on being interested in me if she knew all this? The questions I'd posed to myself left me feeling pained and humiliated. I began wondering to myself: Who is she? Is she married, or a widow? What does she want? Then I happened to lean my left elbow on the table and rest my chin on the back of my hand. And what should she do but lean her left elbow on the edge of the balcony and rest her chin on her hand with a playful look on her face. I was so embarrassed by her teasing, I couldn't see a thing for a moment, and my heart started pounding so hard, it was ringing in my ears. She was flirting with me openly now. I felt as though 'manliness' required that I overcome my inertia, but I didn't make a single move. In fact I was so flustered, I was in a pitiful state. I removed my left arm from the table and folded my arms over my chest, and in no time she had withdrawn her arm from the edge of the balcony and folded her arms over her chest, her grin broader than ever. I smiled in spite of myself as I looked down, feeling indescribably self-conscious. However, smiling released some of my pent-up anxiety, and I relaxed a bit. I was even able to experience again some of the happiness I had been. I was acutely aware of the age difference between us, and it felt good. I wished I could go back to being twenty years old or younger. Lord! I was falling for her hook, line, and sinker! But I didn't care about anything anymore. Just then I glanced down toward Kamal Street, and at the corner, I happened to see the outline of a woman turning left. However, she disappeared from view because the coffee shop wall had come between us. Thinking I'd seen a lead-gray coat like Rabab's, my heart started beating so wildly, it nearly came out of my chest. What would have caused her to leave the school at this time? What would have made her turn left when she would need to turn right to go to the tram stop, assuming she had some legitimate reason to come home? I jumped to my feet and went racing down to the main street, throwing caution to the wind. I looked in the direction the lady with the lead-gray coat had gone, only to find a fifty-year-old woman rushing down the sidewalk. I sighed deeply and, as I did whenever I escaped from a predicament, murmured, "I seek refuge in God from the accursed Satan!" Then I went back to where I'd been sitting in a state of near exhaustion. Never in my life will I forget the panic I went into that day. And if this was the state I was in when nothing had happened, what state would I have been in if my fears had been realized? I looked up at the balcony and saw the woman staring, bewildered, into my face. Her eyes seemed to be asking what had come over me. As for me, I broke into a smile. I'd been so upset that I forgot my shyness, and I smiled. So now we weren't hiding our smiles anymore. Nor were we hiding the silent conversation between us, which expressed itself sometimes with the eyes and other times with the eyebrows. Nor was the infernal sensation I was experiencing a secret to me any longer. If what I was feeling had been love, I would have been gripped with fear and anticipated the consequences. However, it seemed perfectly clear to me, so I didn't lose my confidence. I sat there for over an hour receiving this flirtation silently, bashfully, and with an amazing erotic satisfaction. Then the woman got up and stretched, and as she did so, her robe parted to reveal a succulent, swelling bosom that threatened to make her translucent pink blouse burst at the seams. She cast me a friendly parting glance, then winked before disappearing behind the door. She'd left me in a blazing inferno whose flames consumed the remaining hours of my wait. When her workday was over, Rabab left the school and headed as usual for the tram stop, then we came home, each of us in our own way. That evening we didn't go out, since Radiya and her husband came to visit us and we had an enjoyable family gathering.

54

As we were waiting for the tram together on the fourth day, Rabab said to me, "I'll be late coming home today, since I'm going to visit a colleague of mine who's been absent from the school for the past two days."

I shot her a suspicious look which, if she'd seen it, would have led to no good. Then I quickly looked down, holding my feelings in check.

"Where does she live?" I asked nonchalantly.

"In Heliopolis."

"And when will you be back?"

"The time the visit takes plus the time I need to get back. . . . I'll be back by seven at the latest."

So, she'd begun trying to avoid my oppressive company! I stole a furtive glance at her, and she looked dazzling to me. But the next moment I was gripped by a sudden impulse to fall on her with an ax and split her in two. When the tram arrived and we got on, I was in a bad way indeed. I got off the tram at the ministry stop and hailed a taxi, which delivered me posthaste to the Nubians' coffee shop. I greeted the closed window with a long look, then returned to my thoughts. That visit to Heliopolis. I wasn't going to let her go alone. I was determined to follow her somehow, but would my effort succeed? Supposing I trailed her to Heliopolis, then saw her going into a house or a building. How could I possibly know what lay within its four walls? She might really be visiting a colleague of hers, or she might be in a lover's arms. Trembling violently, I bit down till I could hear my teeth grating against each other. However, I was determined not to go back on my resolve. I *would* follow her, and perhaps I'd see the two of them together in the street. In fact, I might find it easier than I'd imagined to catch her in the act. This is so horrible! I thought. At the same time, though, it was the most likely thing to bring me relief. After all, if catastrophe was bound to strike, it would be more merciful for it to happen quickly. Overwhelmed by anxiety and apprehension, I was certain I wouldn't be able to endure the day. I looked over at the closed window and fixed my gaze on it in something like a cry for help. I felt as though I were being crushed by a violent force, and I longed for an outlet for some of the fierce emotions that raged deep inside me. I ached to get things off my chest, even if the process brought guilt and ignominy in its wake. At ten o'clock the window opened and the homely face greeted me with a bright smile. My attention shifted to her, delivering me from myself. I fixed my gaze on her with a boldness I'd never known myself to have. My features relaxed in spite of myself, and I reciprocated her greeting. She disappeared from the window, and my eyes preceded her to the balcony. However, the wait lasted longer than usual. Then she appeared in the window again, and what should I find but that she'd put on a coat and gotten ready to go out. A thought flashed through my mind like lightning: Was she going to invite me to go somewhere with her? A wave of pleasure, indecision, and fear came over me. How badly I needed the invitation! But did I dare leave Rabab on this crucial day? It was a day worth an entire lifetime! My very fate was bound to Heliopolis. Still, how was I going to resist the woman's invitation if it came? She finished making herself up, then stood there looking at me, beaming and relaxed. Then she looked at something in front of her. My eyes followed her, and what should I find but that her fingers were folding up a small piece of paper, then refolding it from both ends. She looked up and down the street, then threw it, and it landed near my feet. I picked it up hurriedly and unfolded it. Redolent with an intoxicating perfume, it contained these words: "Wait for me at seven sharp this evening at the bridge at the end of the tram line." I was relieved to find that she'd unwittingly given me some lead time. But would I be able to keep the appointment if I agreed to it? Wasn't there something in Heliopolis that would keep me from it? I didn't have time to think, as she was peering at me questioningly and waiting for my response. Hence, I had no choice but to nod my head in agreement. Smilingly at me sweetly, she bade me adieu with a nod of her head, then closed the window. I understood that she must be going out on a visit or some such thing. Thus it was that, propelled forward by that weakness in me that doesn't know how to say no, I'd committed myself to the proposed rendezvous even though I didn't know where I'd be at the agreed upon time. And thus it was, also, that I'd fallen into the very transgression I was accusing my wife of! Was I likely to be glad that I'd taken this daring step, or would I live to regret it? Would the day end with love, or in tragedy? How I loathed life at that moment! I merged with a stream of consciousness that was a kaleidoscope of conflicting emotions: from joy to fear, from hope to despair, and from eagerness to apathy. At last, though, it was topped off with a wave of longing for adventure as a way to escape from the burden of worry that had brought me to my knees and nearly run me into the ground. After reading the paper countless times, I folded it up and slipped it in my pocket.

I waited alone until the kindergarten let out and I spotted Rabab approaching from a distance. This was the moment I'd been waiting for for the last four days—the most miserable days of my life. I would follow her, of that there was no doubt, and leave the rendezvous to circumstances alone. I expected her to turn left in the direction of the tram stop that leads to Heliopolis. However, she veered right instead, in the direction of the tram stop where she waited every day. I realized immediately that she'd made up the story about the sick colleague so as to create an excuse for her absence, and my chest went into such turmoil I could hardly breathe. Had the time come for me to be rid of this torment?

As she stood there on the sidewalk, I shot her a fiery look, marveling at the phony decorum that served as a veneer for such unspeakable wickedness and depravity! Then came the time for the chase, which I hoped would bear fruit this time. She got on the tram and I hailed a taxi. As I rode along, I kept my eyes glued to the car she was in. Where would she get off? Where would she commit her dastardly deed? It was nearly unbearable for me to imagine her in such questionable situations. If the actual reality proved my suspicions correct, revealing to me its ugly, grotesque face, nothing would satisfy my thirst for revenge but to crush her skull with the stones of this huge city! What would have caused her to fall into such iniquity, she who was too chaste for legitimate marital relations? Or did she only want such things by crooked means? I was torn by indecision and tormented by bitterness and rage. At the same time, though, I held out the hope of being delivered from this torment once and for all, and from this bitter life so filled with disappointment and doubt. In just a few minutes everything would be over, and there would be no more reason for me to ask myself whether she was innocent or guilty. There would be no more obsessive thoughts driving me to endure the horrors of surveillance and espionage. The house would be empty of all but the old, familiar faces and the humble, quiet life I'd once known. It was true, of course, that I wished I could crush the head that had crushed my heart. However, I valued my life too much to let it be lost for the sake of an iniquitous woman. My rage was intense and formidable, but my love for safety was stronger and deeper. Wasn't it strange that my thoughts should be revolving around fear and safety even at that terrifying moment? We approached Ataba, and again I wondered where she would get off. I saw her go to the stop on the square as she did every day. I got out of the taxi for fear of losing her in the crowded square. Then I saw her cross the square and head for the other stop where she usually waited. I circled the square and stopped at the section wall. It galled me to see her standing there in her usual decorous fashion, calm and collected, as though I weren't burning up over her. Having ruled out the possibility of her meeting someone in such a crowd, I began looking out for the tram she was about to

314

catch. Trams came and went in succession with their various numbers until at last the Roda tram arrived, whereupon she rushed up to it and took her place in the ladies' compartment. I was stupefied. Was it going to happen in our very own neighborhood? I rushed over to another taxi and we followed the tram. My heart began pounding more and more wildly with every stop we passed. Then we came onto Qasr al-Aini Street. We passed one stop, then a second, then a third, then a fourth until we reached the stop that led to our house. To my dismay, I saw her get off the tram. Looking out the back window of the taxi, I saw her cross the street and walk into our building. I rested my head on the back of the seat and closed my eyes, exhausted and bewildered. What was behind all this? Had I lost my mind? Would there be no end to this torture? In any case, I went home myself, and when I arrived, she'd just finished getting undressed and putting on her robe.

"I thought you'd gone to visit your colleague!" I said to her in astonishment.

She broke into a smile and said, "She wasn't that sick after all, and she came back to work today before anyone could go to the trouble of visiting her."

And I wondered: Will all my suspicions lead to nothing but a handful of wind? I only asked God for one thing, namely, to be able to live with her in peace and assurance.

As I was changing my clothes she said to me, "My aunt called and invited me to visit her this evening, and she asked me to invite you on her behalf."

"God willing," I replied unthinkingly.

The minute I opened my mouth I realized I'd spoken hastily, since I remembered the appointment at the Abbasiya Bridge. But did I really want to go? I was far from the window and the balcony and their influence now, so was I still thinking about this woman seriously? What sort of demon was beguiling me? My heart belonged to my beloved and to no one else. So why was the strange woman's siren song so overwhelming and irresistible? The longer I thought about it, the more I surrendered to the fiendish summons until the only thing left to prevent me from going was the promise I'd made to myself to accompany my wife that evening. But, would she have invited me to visit her aunt with her if she harbored any ill intentions? I thought about it again with considerable effort, since there's nothing more taxing for me than to have to choose between two different things.

However, after considerable hesitation, I said, "I'm sorry, I just remembered—I have an important engagement!"

In what seemed like genuine distress, she said, "Do you mean you won't be able to go with me?"

Feeling as though my foot were slipping into a bottomless pit, I said, "Please convey my regrets to your aunt."

55

I reached the Abbasiya Bridge a few minutes before the scheduled time. The weather was pleasant and it was quite dark, so I waited under a gas lamp. I'd come in a state of angst and tension that reminded me of the state I'd been in on the day the carriage took me to the pub on Alfi Bey Street for the first time. And all this for the sake of a woman with neither beauty nor grace. In fact, I would have been embarrassed to be seen with her in public. When it was nearly time for her to arrive, I was ridden by the same fear that I'd felt over and over during the wait that had begun that afternoon. What if the tragedy repeated itself? There was still time to flee. But I didn't budge. This woman was my only chance to reclaim my lost confidence. Besides, I was possessed by a spirit of adventure the likes of which I'd never seen in myself. "Give it a try!" it said to me. "You won't lose anything. Or, at least, you won't lose anything new." I was roused from my thoughts by a medium-sized car that pulled up in front of me next to the sidewalk. The car window opened and through it I saw the face of the strange woman, who was seated behind the steering wheel. She smiled at me and invited me to go around and get in on the other side. Muddled, I did as she said, and in less than a second, I was sitting next to her. I pulled the door closed and remaining sitting right up against it, so self-conscious that I was hardly aware of what was around me. I could feel her eyes on my left cheek, but I kept looking straight ahead until she burst out laughing.

Then, in a voice that sounded delicate by comparison with the coarseness of her face and body, she said provocatively, "There's no need to be shy anymore."

She took off, handling the car with deftness and ease, and said, "Let's go to Pyramids Road."

She was driving so fast I was petrified, and whenever she was forced to slow down by other cars or a traffic light, I breathed a sigh of relief. Yet strangely, she stopped speeding like a maniac when she'd left the busy streets behind. After catching my breath, I looked furtively over at her and got a close-up view of one side of her homely face and her compact bosom. At the same time, I recalled an image of her plump bronze legs. Then I remembered that she was just an inch away from my leg, and my body went into an uproar. I was amazed to find her calm and serene as though she were accompanying her husband or her brother, not a strange man about to die of awkwardness and self-consciousness.

Her eyes still on the road, she asked me, "What shall I call you?"

"Kamil Ru'ba," I replied briefly.

I contented myself with this rather than adding the title 'bey,' which often drew a laugh.

"Nice name," she murmured.

I felt as though I ought to ask her for her name, too. I'd chosen a suitable phrase to use and was gathering my courage to utter it when she said simply, "You can call me Inayat."

"Nice name," I muttered shyly, though all she heard was a whisper.

Then suddenly she turned toward me and said with a smile, "Strange that you're so shy! Don't you know that shyness is out of style? Even virgins have given it up without regret. So why are you holding on to it?"

I laughed nervously and made no reply.

"But enough of this," she went on. "Medicine is only effective when it's given at the right time. Now tell me, for heaven's sake, what led you to mix with the Nubians in that filthy coffee shop?"

318

Wondering what to say, I thought for a while until I hit on a fib that would get me out of my fix.

I said, "One day I was coming back from a long trip, and it was the only place I could find to rest."

"That's about the first day. But what about the second and third days?"

A fitting answer came to me off the top of my head. So, overcoming my shyness, I said softly, "You were the reason for the second and third days."

She looked at me with a laugh and said shrewdly, "Are you telling me the truth, or are you just trying to evade the question by flirting?"

"No, I'm telling the truth," I said.

Looking back at the road coquettishly, she said, "So then, why do you keep sitting up against the door as though you don't want to touch me?"

Feeling muddled, I didn't know what to do.

"But we're on the road," I said apologetically.

She burst out laughing, then said, "We're in the car, not on the road! Besides, even the road wouldn't keep people like us from sitting up next to each other if we wanted to. Don't make phony excuses. Now tell me, how old are you?"

"I'm twenty-eight."

"For shame! And how many women have you been with?"

I made no reply, feeling I wasn't up to her and her questions. Then, as though she were surprised at my silence, she said reproachfully, "Do you mean to say you've never been with a woman before? Am I the first woman in your life? My Lord! Haven't those green eyes of yours snagged anybody yet? If not, then I got to you just when you were about to drown, and may God reward me richly for my good deed! My Lord, who could believe this? How do you live, and what are you doing with your life?"

Again I made no reply, as her words had pained me without her realizing it. However, she may have seen the look of discomfort on my face, since she let up on me and asked me no more questions for some time. Then she asked me about my work, and I replied that I was a government employee. I added that I was on a short vacation, after which silence reigned once again. Meanwhile, she shifted slightly in my direction until her shoulder was gently touching mine. The contact sent life coursing through my cowering heart, whose pulse raced to the beat of my fear and shyness.

When I went on clinging to the door and not making a move, she stifled a laugh and said pithily, "A step from me and a step from you. Now are you still scared?"

Her invitation met with a willing soul and a fearful heart. Resisting the fear with everything in me, I slid over ever so cautiously until my side—from the lower leg to the top of the shoulder—came in contact with tender flesh that was redolent with a sweet, captivating perfume. I paused for a moment to take in the luscious feel of it, my whole body trembling. Then she turned toward me, and I felt her breath on my cheek.

"Are you still scared?" she whispered in my ear.

Not at all. I'd been intoxicated by passion. Still breathing on my cheek, she leaned her head toward me until my mouth dove into her swelling lips, whereupon she quickly shifted her head away from me and looked back at the road ahead of her. I placed my left arm around her thick waist and began covering the side of her neck with kisses.

"Easy does it!" she murmured with a laugh as she veered off to the side of the road.

Then she stopped the car, saying, "Let's rest for a while here. It's a safe place."

Looking out, I saw that she'd chosen a spot halfway between two streetlights. It was pitch dark and the area on either side of the car was vacant. Aside from the cars whizzing by us at lightning speed, we were surrounded by a deep silence.

"Isn't it dangerous?" I asked her in a whisper.

Wrapping her right arm around my neck, she said, "It's safer than your house."

She then turned until her right shoulder was touching the back of the seat and folded her right leg under her left thigh. We were now face to face, and the neck opening in her dress receded to reveal her swelling bosom. I leaned forward and rested my head on her chest, filled with amazement and tenderness, and I was intoxicated by the fragrance of a human body more delectable than the sweetest perfume. I rested there peacefully for I don't know how long as her hand played with the hair on my head. Then I lifted my face toward hers and devoured her lips, and she devoured mine. It was as though we were eating and swallowing each other alive. Fear was gone now, since there was nothing left to justify it, and I was filled with life, with madness, and with boundless confidence. I don't know where the confidence came from, but this woman was fully in charge of the situation, and in her I found the guide that I'd lacked all my life. She restored to me both confidence and peace of mind because she relieved me of all responsibility and took me slowly and gently. At that moment, more than ever before in my life, I realized that the laying of any responsibility on me was liable to cause me to lose myself, and that I could only find this fragile self of mine when I was in strong, steady hands. The world melted away in a wild, magical intoxication, and I emerged drunk on the wine of victory and profound satisfaction. Deep inside, I felt a desire for this woman equaled only by my desire for life itself. In fact, she herself was life, dignity, manhood, confidence, and happiness. My lips parted in a smile of victory and joy and I cast her a look of gratitude the depth of which she couldn't possibly have fathomed. In her presence I was wallowing in the dirt. But it was good, loving dirt that yielded confidence and happiness. I realized the mistakes I'd made in the past and I remembered my beloved wife with a sense of grief and despair that nearly shattered my dreamlike bliss. Yet I had no hesitation about holding her responsible for all my misery. That's how it seemed to me. At the same time, my heart pined for her even at that moment and in that place

As for the woman, she tapped my nose with her fingertip and said, "Happy?"

"Very," I replied from the heart.

She took my left hand in both of hers and murmured, "What a wonderful child you are."

"A child in his third decade!" I said with an embarrassed laugh.

Then a look of seriousness and concern flashed in her eyes, and I noticed her running her fingers over my wedding band. With a stunned look on her face, she cried, "Are you married? That never even crossed my mind!"

Fear came over me, and I looked at her without saying a word.

Then she laughed out loud and said, "How is it that that never even occurred to me? But how can I believe this? My Lord, why did you run after me? Isn't your wife to your liking? How dissolute can you get?"

Discomfited and befuddled, I looked down and didn't say a word.

"Don't you love your wife?" she asked in a tone of concern.

I was vexed by the question, and I hesitated for a moment, not knowing what to say. However, the delicacy of the situation forced me to say in a voice that was barely audible, "She's a nice lady."

She broke in, saying, "I'm asking you whether you love her!"

Sensing that lying becomes a virtue when in the presence of women, I said with an indignation that I concealed with a smile, "No."

Her features relaxed.

Then again she asked with concern, "How long have you been married?"

"Nearly two years," I said, saddened by the mention of marriage.

"Didn't you love her before?"

"No."

"They married you to her without your having known her previously?"

"Yes."

"What an unforgivable sin!" she cried angrily. "And she, doesn't she love you?"

And for the first time I replied truthfully, "She doesn't love love."

Her eyes widened with incredulity, and she opened her mouth so wide that I saw a couple of gold teeth that I hadn't seen before.

"Ahhhh," she said. "Now I get it. There are women like that. And why wouldn't there be? Not all women are complete."

We exchanged a long, wordless look accompanied by a smile.

Then I asked her with a laugh, "And you. Aren't you married?"

Without taking her eyes off me she replied, "I'm just a widow. My husband was a prominent rear admiral by the name of Ali Pasha Salam. When we married, he was old and I was young. Then a few years later he died. So I came back to live with my mother. And only God knows who I'll be living with tomorrow!"

She smiled at me and began to whistle. Then she picked up her purse, took out a powder puff and proceeded to dust her face and her neck with it. After arranging her disheveled locks of hair, she cast a glance at her face in the car's side mirror.

"When does your vacation end?" she asked.

"In a few days."

"We'll meet often," she said calmly. "Every day, if possible. The car will do until we can find a more suitable place."

She sat up straight again behind the steering wheel. However, I took hold of her wrist, then put my arm around her neck. She let out a brief chuckle and held me to her rounded bosom as she said, "Who do you think you are, smarty pants, making me spruce myself up all over again?"

56

I got back home at exactly 10:00 p.m. I didn't ask myself whether I'd erred, since what I'd recovered by way of confidence and happiness went beyond questions of right and wrong. My mother had gone to sleep, and Rabab was sitting in bed reading a magazine. The minute I saw her lovely face, a joyous light glowed in my spirit, and I felt as though I were being transported from one world to another. I had a sudden pang of revulsion at what I'd done with myself, but it didn't get the better of me, since it was driven out of my consciousness again by the thick veil that stood between me and my wife. She received me with a smile, conveying her aunt's greetings and her reproach for my not having come with her. Then she told me that my supper was waiting on the dining room table, so I went in and devoured it like the hungry, tired person that I was. I came back to our room wondering what my wife would do if she knew of my transgression.

She told me she'd been invited to give private lessons to a first-grader who was the daughter of a prominent judge, and she asked me what I thought. Although I didn't see any reason for suspicion, I wasn't enthusiastic about the proposal, and I said, "You tire yourself out enough all day long!"

"You're right," she said casually.

Pleased by her quickness to agree with me, I thought to myself: I'll never find the slightest reason to doubt her! I lay down beside her, whereupon she shoved the magazine aside, turned out the light and lay down peacefully. I had every reason to go right to sleep. Instead, however, I experienced a strange sort of wakefulness. My thoughts went flying away to Inayat, and to the car on Pyramids Road. I'd been unfaithful. How astounding! Who would have thought that an impotent husband would take a lover! At that moment I wished my wife could know of this astounding fact. However, the moment was a fleeting one, and it wasn't long before my heart had shrunk in fear and shame. I'd gone trailing my wife, suspecting that she'd been unfaithful to me, and I ended up being unfaithful myself beyond the slightest shadow of a doubt. In her, I'd seen no evidence of anything but integrity and modesty. How was it that with her, my portion had been impotence and failure, whereas in the arms of the homely, crude woman, I'd been blessed with the wildest bliss? I was unspeakably confused, and my soul longed for a ray of light.

What made my confusion even worse was that I felt deeply that I couldn't do without either of them. In fact, I couldn't find any way to compare them in such a way as to see which was superior to the other. One of them was my spirit, and the other was my body, and my torment was that of someone who isn't able to reconcile his body with his spirit. What would the world be worth without that lovely, pristine, nay, perfect face? But then again, what pleasure and sense of manhood would I have left if I lost the other woman? I became so engrossed in thought that there was no way to sleep. First Rabab would appear to me, and then Inayat. Then suddenly the vision in my mind's eye turned for no apparent reason into my mother, who took her place in the string of successive images. My confusion finally reached the point where I was enveloped in a cloud of sadness and gloom. Nevertheless, the feelings one experiences by night rarely survive the light of day. By night they merge into the stream of a mysterious melody in a fog-enveloped, ethereal atmosphere. But once the day breaks, nothing

325

remains of them but faint echoes that do nothing to prevent us from searching out our paths in life.

The morning of the fifth day arrived, and I took off as usual for Abbasiya. But was I really going there to trail Rabab, or was I going in obedience to that irresistible summons? My wife's behavior left no room for doubt: what she was on the outside, she was on the inside. Hence, she must have told the truth in what she said about the ill-fated letter, and if there was a traitor, it was I.

I went to the Nubians' coffee shop, which was the perfect symbol for my new love. I waited until the window opened, and we greeted one another with an amiable smile. She disappeared for a moment, then reappeared, ready to go out, gesturing to me to wait for her at the previous day's rendezvous spot. I hadn't expected us to meet in the morning. However, I called the waiter without hesitation, paid the tab, and headed straightaway for the bridge, which wasn't far away. On my way there, it seemed to me that I'd realized a fact of life, namely, that there isn't a single movement among men but that there's a woman behind it. Women are to men's lives what gravity is to the stars and other heavenly bodies. Hence, there isn't a man alive but that there's a woman in his imagination, be she present or absent, attainable or unattainable, loving or hateful, faithful or unfaithful. Now I understood in a new way the meaning of the saying, "Love is life, and life is love." In fact, it hit me so forcefully, it was as though I were thinking about it for the first time. It wasn't that there was life, after which there was love. Rather, there was love, therefore there was life. And at that moment I swore that never as long as I lived would I turn away from love!

The car arrived, and I took my place in it as I had the day before.

Laughing, the woman asked, "What brought you at this hour? Hadn't we agreed to meet this evening?"

"You, you're the reason," I said with a smile.

Smiling back at me happily, she said, "We've got to stick ourselves together with glue so that we'll never be separated."

As the motor revved in preparation for the car's departure, I said imploringly, "It's daytime, so please avoid the busy streets."

"Are you afraid someone might see you?"

"Yes," I said in an embarrassed tone.

"Ah! I forgot you were married! Pardon me, Mr. Husband, but we're going to Heliopolis!"

And the car took off at its usual break-neck speed.

On the way she asked me, "What did you do with your wife yesterday?"

I furrowed my brow involuntarily and made no reply.

"Do you hate to mention her that much?"

Then, disregarding my silence and discomfort, she asked, "Don't you sleep in the same bed?"

I tried to force a laugh, but I couldn't, and I felt a resentment that ruined my tranquil mood.

"How I'd love to see her!" she said with a raucous laugh.

Wanting to cheer me up in her own way, she caressed my lips with her finger and, like a mother speaking playfully to her little boy, said, "My little chickadee!"

The car pulled up in front of a tea shop. We sat there chatting happily away about whatever came to mind, and she told me she'd chosen the seamstress's house as the place for our lovers' trysts. As we left the place at noon, she wanted to pay the bill, but I wouldn't let her, and we parted after reaffirming the evening's meeting time. We met repeatedly, and when the vacation ended two days later, we continued our meetings in the evenings. The experience of success convinced me that love is health and well-being. My habit of spending the evenings out was a secret to no one, and although Rabab preferred, as she said, for me to spend my evenings with her on her endless visits, she didn't press me about it. Hence, we each lived our lives in the way we pleased. This was no secret to my mother, either. Once she said to me, "I've noticed, son, that you haven't been yourself lately. I've been afraid that if I said anything you'd be angry. In any case, if you enjoy spending the evenings out, spend the evenings out. All men are like that!"

57

I spent a month or more in a state of unmitigated bliss. Peace took the place of suspicion and doubt, and my relationship with Rabab was restored to one of goodwill and pure affection. At the same time, I surrendered myself to Inayat in tumultuous passion and triumphant joy. She was a woman of means, and not once did we go to our beloved nest in the seamstress's house but that she presented her with a gift of a riyal, and sometimes half a pound. As for me, my sense of dignity required that I, too, be generous toward her, albeit within my more limited means. Without realizing it, she made it possible for me to resume drinking on a regular basis, since the seamstress would keep bottles of whisky and soda in constant supply for us. In fact, she nearly got me into the habit of smoking. In addition, she had certain virtues, and what virtues they were! She was possessed of perfect femininity and vitality, as a result of which she was a source of pleasure to lovers despite her middle age and her lovable homeliness. At the same time, however, she possessed such virtues alongside an alarming degree of wantonness and audacity. For her, loving a man was everything, and for its sake she deemed anything and everything permissible. She may not have been truly the type that devotes herself unstintingly to her man. Rather, she may simply have been a woman driven by anxiety and despair. In other words, she may have been driven by an awareness of the fact that the brightness of her youth was fading, as a result of which she couldn't bear to let a day go by without a taste of love. The most peculiar thing about my passion for her was that the things about her that enchanted me were the very things that might normally be looked upon as shortcomings—her maturity, her home-liness, and her audacity. She filled me with boundless confidence, and when I was with her, I worried about nothing. If it hadn't been for the angst that would come over me as a result of the frightening divorce I experienced between body and spirit, I would have enjoyed life in unruffled tran-quility. Yet even with such perturbation, it was a happy life.

Then one afternoon, right after I'd finished lunch, I went in to spend some time with my mother over a cup of coffee as was my custom every day. As soon as I walked into the room, I noticed her limpid eyes searching my face anxiously as though there were something on her mind. Looking intently into her face, which looked drawn and languid, I realized immediately that she wanted to say something.

I felt worried, but I said with a smile, "What is it, Mama? Tell me what's on your mind."

A look of hesitancy flashed in her eyes for a few moments.

Then she said, "Yesterday I heard some things that shocked me. Could you tell me more about what's going on between Rabab and her mother?"

This was the last thing I'd expected to hear. My eyes clouded over with dark memories and my fluttering heart wondered: Has the woman gone back to her nagging? Rabab had told me nothing about her mother's visit to her the day before, contenting herself with conveying her mother's greetings to me.

In a calm voice—or, at least, in a voice that I made appear to be calm—I replied, "Everything's just fine between them."

Shaking her head skeptically, my mother said, "There may be things you're missing. I wasn't able to receive Madame Nazli yesterday because I hadn't been feeling well, so when Sabah came to tell me she'd arrived, I pretended to be asleep. The visit went on for quite a long time. At one point, I slipped out of the room to go to the bathroom. On my way back, I came past the sitting room door. When I did, I was shocked to hear the woman say, 'This is intolerable!' Then Rabab came back at her angrily, saying, 'Don't meddle in my affairs!' As for me, all I could do was come back to my room."

My forehead burning with humiliation, I felt furious and unspeakably bitter toward my meddlesome mother-in-law.

Intruding on my thoughts, my mother asked, "Don't you know anything about it?"

"Their disagreements are none of our business," I said firmly.

When I returned later to our room, I found Rabab reclining on the long seat. When she saw me, she drew her legs toward the back of the seat to make room for me, and I sat down broodingly. How could she have kept such a thing from me? Was she afraid of upsetting me?

As if she hadn't noticed my altered state of mind, she began talking about how it was Friday and suggested that we go to the cinema together.

I let her finish what she had to say. Then I asked, "How's your mother?" to which she replied that her mother was fine.

Then I looked her straight in the eye and asked her, "Did yesterday's visit go well?"

"What do you mean?" she asked with a disconcerted look in her eyes.

"Rabab," I said gloomily, "Don't hide anything from me. Has your mother started harping on that old theme again?"

Her face clouded over and she made no reply.

"What would you know about it?" she retorted sharply.

"I want to know everything!"

So I told her what my mother had told me.

After listening to me attentively, she exploded, "Your mother! Your mother! Always your mother!"

Feeling the same sting that I always did whenever I was reminded of their mutual dislike, I said, "There's no reason to get angry. She heard what she did by chance, and she passed it on to me with good intentions as far as I can see. I beg you, don't get angry. Just tell me: Has your mother gone back to that old subject?"

Drawing her legs out from behind me and planting them on the floor, she looked down gloomily and angrily.

"The thing I hadn't wanted to upset you with was that she suggested that I go to a doctor to see why I haven't gotten pregnant. I rejected her suggestion, of course, and we got into an argument!"

We carried on with the odious conversation for quite some time until she asked me not to say anything more, and to lie down and get some rest after my day at work. Complying with her wishes, I went and lay down on the bed, grieved and melancholy. It took me quite some time to doze off, and I don't know how long I slept. However, I woke to the sound of something that caused slumber to flee from my eyes. I opened my eyes feeling disturbed, and my ears were bombarded by a ruckus coming from the living room. As I listened attentively, it soon became apparent that Rabab and my mother were exchanging the harshest of words in a noisy shouting match. Alarmed, I jumped out of bed, then rushed into the living room.

I found Rabab with sparks flying from her eyes as she screamed, "This sort of spying doesn't become a respectable lady!"

When my mother saw me, she lowered her eyes as she said, "This impertinence is more than I can take!"

"Rabab!" I cried.

However, she avoided me and stormed back into our room in a rage. As for my mother, she turned around and proceeded to her room with heavy steps. As I came toward her in a pained silence, I saw her take hold of the doorknob, then stand there without turning it as though she'd changed her mind about going in. Then she placed her hand on her forehead and seemed to gradually slump over. I rushed over to her, and no sooner had I touched her than she fell into my arms. Terrified, I called to her, but she didn't respond, her head and arms drooping lifelessly. I summoned Sabah with a shout and she came running, then together we carried her to the bed and lay her down. I brought a bottle of cologne and sprinkled some of it on her face and neck, then used it to massage her limbs. Hysterical by now, I began calling to her over and over in a hoarse, trembling voice. She remained unconscious for several minutes that dragged by like hours. Then she opened her eyelids to reveal lusterless eyes.

"Mama!" I cried with a gulp.

She focused her gaze on me, then pointed to her heart without uttering a word. I left the flat and took off for the grocery on the first floor of our building, where I called her doctor and asked him to come. Then I went back up to the flat and sat beside her feeling terrified and grieved. I didn't take my eyes off her for a moment, and eventually her lackluster gaze drew out the tears that had been trapped inside me. I felt like the most miserable person on earth, and my soul was filled with bitterness and despair.

Then the doctor came and examined her. He said she'd had a heart attack and would require extended bed rest and intensive care, and as he normally did, he prescribed some medicine.

I told him she'd fainted after an argument with the servant.

In reply he said, "The argument was a secondary cause, but the underlying condition has been there for a long time."

That night was a dismal one. Rabab, feeling responsible for what had happened, disappeared into our room and cried her heart out. As for me, all I could do was try to console her.

Patting her on the shoulder, I said, "You've cried enough now. This was God's will, and may He cause everything to work out for the best."

58

It wasn't long before the house was filled with visitors. Rabab's family and a group of her relatives came to see us, as did my sister Radiya and her family. Rabab also came to see the patient, kissing her hand and tearfully asking her forgiveness. I even hoped that, through this incident, we could start a new life free of rancor and hearts in conflict.

Then, taking advantage of a few moments when no strangers were in the room, Radiya said to me, "I'd like to ask your permission to take Mama home with me until she gets her strength back."

"That's impossible!" I said, alarmed at the suggestion.

Smiling at me sympathetically, she went on, saying, "Don't you see that she needs constant care? Who will care for her here? You're busy with your work and so is your wife, and Sabah is responsible for taking care of the house. So who will you assign the job of taking care of our mother?"

However, her suggestion remained totally unacceptable to me, and I resisted all her compelling arguments.

With an insistence that came from the depths of my heart, I said, "She won't have to stay in bed for long, God willing. According to the doctor, she'll only need someone to be constantly at her side for the first week, and I'll be sure to find a servant who can devote herself full-time to caring for her."

Radiya tried valiantly to persuade me of her suggestion, but to no avail, and the discussion ended with her deciding to stay in our house until I was able to find a servant. On the third day after my mother's heart attack, my brother Medhat—whom I'd informed of her illness by special delivery letter—arrived with his wife. During the first days after her attack, she was very ill indeed. She didn't move a muscle and she would hardly utter a word. When she opened her weary eyes, they were languid and dull. She would look around at us in silent resignation, and I felt as though my heart was breaking. We didn't leave her side, and if she revived slightly, she would look back and forth among us with a smile on her parched lips, or spread out her hands and look heavenward, murmuring a prayer of supplication in a low, feeble voice. However, she didn't remain in this near-comatose state for long, and by the end of the first week she'd begun to improve slightly. She realized clearly that all her children were gathered around her, and it gladdened her as though she were seeing them all together for the first time in her life. One day when we'd congregated around her bed, she sat there happily and looked at us for a long time without saying a word. Then, her face glowing with joy, she said in a feeble whisper, "How happy I am with you all! Praise and thanks be to God!"

Her eyes glistening with tenderness and emotion, she continued, "If illness brings us together this way, then I hope it never ends."

Despite her illness, then, she seemed happy, and her happiness found its way into our hearts as well. Our family, which God had caused to be scattered in its earlier years, had been united. We were all under one roof now, eating and drinking together, and our hearts beat as one. What wondrous days those were! Our very beings breathed out sympathy, tenderness, and joy. However, the togetherness was short-lived. It wasn't long before my mother's health improved and the danger passed, although the doctor insisted that she not get out of bed for a month at the very least. Medhat bade us farewell and took his family back to Fayoum, promising to visit from time to time. Radiya also went back to her own house once I'd succeeded in finding a servant for my mother, with the agreement that she would visit our mother every day. And thus it was that the gathering broke up, we went our separate ways, and everything went back to the way it had been before. Hardly two weeks had passed before my mother began recovering her vitality and alertness and was able to sit up in bed with a pillow folded behind her back. It thrilled me no end to see Rabab fulfill her obligations toward her mother-in-law, and never will I forget the bitter pain and distress she suffered during the first days of my mother's crisis.

Now that our peace of mind had been restored and all my mother needed was rest, albeit of an extended nature, we resumed our usual ways of life. Rabab went back to entertaining herself with evening visits to her relatives, and I took off again to my old haunt. I had asked my mother for permission to go out several hours a day for rest and recreation, and she'd given her enthusiastic consent, telling me how it pained her to see me having to stay by her side like a prisoner. And I left the house thinking: If I were the sick one, would she ask my permission to leave the room for rest and recreation? Life's logic seemed harsh to me. But what was to be done about it?

I went flying back to Inayat. She would telephone me at the ministry every morning, so she knew why I hadn't been able to see her. We went back to meeting the way we had before in our lovers' nest, where we would get drunk and make love. It was a strange life. However, what I fear the most is that my memory may have failed me, if even in relation to a few of the details. Was I really happy? My heart was divided between my mother, my wife, and Inayat, between memories of the past, a sublime, ethereal love, and another love that was torrid and down-to-earth. I felt that I'd found refuge from life's storms in a tranquil harbor. Even so, the old anxiety began knocking cautiously and hesitantly at my door again, as if shyness prevented it from storming in for no apparent reason. It's true, of course, that I was proceeding on my way, but I would pause and hesitate every now and then as though I were wondering if there was something I'd forgotten. I'd think to myself: Should I keep on going full steam ahead, or would it be better for me to stop and take a look at what's around me? However, I would conclude that there was no reason for hesitation and continue merrily on my way.

Then one day I noticed that Rabab wasn't her usual cheery, energetic self. When I asked her what was wrong, she told me she'd had a tiring day at work and that she thought she might be coming down with the flu. I stayed home that evening, and the following morning, not long after she woke up, she vomited unexpectedly, then lay down exhausted. I suggested that I call her a doctor, but she rejected the idea, saying it was just a minor cold and that she could treat it without a doctor's help. Her mother came to visit her and stayed the entire day in her room. However, on the third day Rabab insisted on going back to work, telling me she felt well again. And in fact, she went to the kindergarten despite my having advised her to stay home for a day or two longer. When she came home from work that afternoon, she was worse than she had been in the morning. Even so, she insisted that she was perfectly healthy. In fact, she got dressed and left the house the following two days as well. When she came home from the kindergarten on the second day at her regularly scheduled time, I was at the seamstress's house. But when I got home at half past eleven, I didn't find her in our room. Sabah, who appeared to have been awaiting my arrival, came rushing up to me and said, "Miss Rabab will be spending the night at her mother's house, and they sent the servant to inform us of it."

Bewildered and upset by the news, I asked Sabah, "Why is she going to do that?"

In a fearful tone of voice, the servant replied, "She's fine, sir. I visited her and saw her myself. But she has a bit of a fever, and the Madame wasn't willing to expose her to the night air, so she thought it best for her to spend the night at her house until the fever goes down."

I left the room straightaway in exasperation, saying, "I warned her that this might happen, and I told her again and again not to leave the house!"

I was met in the living room by my mother's servant, Nafisa, who told me that my mother wanted me to come see her. When I went to her room, she expressed her regret over Rabab's illness and instructed me to tell Rabab that she was praying for her. I thanked her and left the house, furious and worried.

59

Everyone was asleep and the house was completely dark except for a light that emanated from the mother's room. I went directly there and found Rabab lying in bed and her mother sitting in a bed opposite hers on the other side of the room. Rabab greeted me with a smile, while the mother slipped out of the bed she'd been sitting in and came toward me, saying, "That's what we figured! We said, 'He'll be upset and come the minute he finds out.' However, it's just a touch of the flu."

I went over to Rabab's bed and took her hand.

"Didn't I to advise you not to go out?" I asked reproachfully. "What's wrong? Why didn't you come home?"

In reply, she pointed to her mother with a smile and said, "I wanted to, but Mama wouldn't let me."

"Her condition isn't anything to worry about," affirmed Madame Nazli hastily. "However, it could be very dangerous to be exposed to the outside air."

"I'll call the doctor right away," I said decisively.

"We already did that," said the mother. "In fact, it was the doctor himself who advised her not to go out. It's nothing serious at all, though, and she'll be back home within a week or ten days at the most."

Feeling at a loss, I sat down on a plush sofa between the two beds. However, the mother's seeming composure gradually made me feel calmer myself.

The mother then went on, saying, "Influenza is nothing serious in and of itself. However, we have to be careful that she doesn't have a relapse."

As I listened absently to the mother, I looked over at my beloved with both my eyes and my spirit. Rabab looked over at me with a wan smile. There was a look of exhaustion in her eyes, and a veil had descended over her usual sweet, sunny look. Silence reigned for some time. Then suddenly I remembered Gabr Bey and asked about him. The mother replied that he was on an inspection tour and would be back at the end of the week. When the clock struck eleven thirty, I excused myself, kissed my wife on the forehead, and left the house.

The next morning, I left the house twenty minutes earlier than the usual time. Sabah had requested my permission to visit Rabab, so we turned household affairs over to Nafisa and I went right away to Gabr Bey's house. When I met Muhammad and Rouhiya on the stairs, I greeted them and asked them about Rabab, and the little sister replied that she was fine. Once inside the flat, I went to the room, where I found Rabab in bed and her mother sitting on the couch. She returned my greeting with a gentle smile, but her eyes were so dull, she seemed not to have slept a wink the night before. Seeing her this way, I felt fretful and dejected. However, rather than letting on how I was feeling, I lied, saying, "I see that you're better!"

With a resignation that made my heart ache, she replied, "Thanks be to God."

I sat near her on the edge of the sofa and gazed steadily into her face. She'd wrapped her head in a brown handkerchief that framed her face, which looked gaunt and pale, and her eyes were solemn and lackluster. A pall of gloom descended over my spirit, the world looked dismal to me, and her face looked ashen and unattractive.

Noticing my dejection, Madame Nazli said in astonishment, "Is this the first time you've seen somebody with a cold? You pamper her too much, Kamil!"

It consoled me somewhat to see that the person who was making light of her condition was her mother herself, since if my wife had been suffering from something truly worrisome, her mother would have been beside herself. I leaned slightly toward the bed and placed my hand on her cheek, which was hot.

However, she smiled at me and said, "If I'm not doing well, it's because of some insomnia that came over me last night. If I can manage to sleep even a couple of hours, I'll get my energy back."

"Try to sleep no matter what it takes," I said imploringly.

I gazed into her eyes for a long time. She looked at me for a minute, then quietly looked down again. I had to go, so I got up, promising to visit again after coming back from the ministry. Then I left.

I arrived at the ministry at ten past eight and set to work. However, the work wasn't sufficient to make me forget myself. I went back to thinking about Rabab. I pictured the grave look in her eyes and felt a forlornness I couldn't explain. I tried valiantly to lose myself in the task at hand, but it did no good. I was defeated by my own thoughts, which have always had a tendency to create fear out of nothing. Feeling more worried than ever, I thought to myself: Here's Rabab unable to come home and looking gaunt and frail, so how can I be at peace? And how can I leave her? Faintheartedness in the face of the most minor misfortune was nothing new to me. After all, there were countless times when I'd been unable to sleep on account of some minor indisposition afflicting my mother. So, I thought, maybe this fear I'm feeling is an effect of that chronic faintheartedness of mine. But oh, what a terrible, heavy gloom had come over me! My heart shrank in fear and pain as though it were holding back a cry for help that was trying to make itself heard. Why torture myself by forcing myself to endure such a wait for no reason? And with that, I folded up my papers and requested permission to leave, explaining that my wife was ill. I left the ministry at nine-thirty and got to the house a few minutes before ten. The closer

I got to the house the more forlorn I felt, and I entered the building in near dread. I rang the doorbell, and before long it opened. But to my astonishment, the person who opened the door for me was Dr. Amin Rida. The doors to the small parlor onto which the front door opened were closed, and he was the only person there. I hadn't seen him since the day of the luncheon that had been hosted in this same house. What on earth would have brought him here at such an early hour? And why would he be staying alone in this closed room?

I extended my hand, saying, "Peace be upon you!"

"And upon you be peace," he replied as he extended his hand in turn.

I seemed to notice him looking at me strangely through his spectacles as he said, "Won't you come in?"

Then he turned away from me, saying, "I'll wait for you in the reception room."

Then he headed for the reception room, opened the door, and went in. As for me, I went to the large parlor, opened the door and went in, then proceeded to Madame Nazli's room. However, I'd hardly taken two steps when my ears were bombarded by an eerie sound that I don't know how to describe. Was it a prolonged sigh? A muffled scream? Whatever it was, it was clearly coming from beyond the closed door to Rabab's room. I went rushing toward the door, turned the knob, and went in, my heart aflutter with dismay. I looked over at the bed and saw Rabab lying there. She was covered up to the neck and her hand-kerchief was wrapped around her face from the top of her heard to below her chin. Her eyes were closed and her face looked haggard and sallow, with a frightening whiteness to it. The handkerchief-bound face brought back vague memories that I didn't have time to clarify. However, it awakened an unspoken terror deep within me. The next moment I became aware of the fact that Madame Nazli was sitting on the edge of the sofa sobbing piteously with her head buried in the bed pillow. As for Sabah, who hadn't seen me come in, she stood at the foot of the bed weeping and wailing.

Lord! Had Rabab really died?

60

I cried like a madman, "Tell me what's happened!!"

Turning toward me, Sabah shouted hysterically, "Sir! Sir!"

The woman looked up in obvious terror and gaped into my face with eyes red from weeping. For a moment she froze and neither spoke nor wept as though my arrival was, to her, a fate worse than death. Then she gasped and burst into tears. I looked back and forth between the two women in a daze, then my eyes came to rest on the handkerchief-bound face. How was I to submit to the verdict of this terrifying reality? My shattered heart made me want to throw myself on my wife and to blubber and scream till I died. But I didn't move a muscle. A strange force caused me to stay frozen in place and filled me with a ruthless madness. I was overtaken by a wild rage that was willing to defy the power of death itself and the tyranny of Fate. I refused to believe my eyes, and it was impossible to convince me. What did this mean?

Gesticulating wildly in the mother's face, I asked her in a voice that I was hearing for the first time, "How? How?"

She spread her arms in despair, too choked up to speak. However, Sabah came toward me, terrified and delirious, and in a muffled scream, said, "The miserable operation! God damn the operation!"

341

Turning toward the servant in bewilderment, I shouted, "Operation? What operation?"

It was then that I knew something suspicious was afoot. I looked around the room until my eyes fell on a table in one corner. On the table I saw some medical instruments arranged together with some containers and cotton. I came up to the table and examined it with eyes that could hardly focus. When had they brought all this? When had the decision to do it been agreed on? How had this happened? Then I looked at my mother-in-law and found her eyeing the servant with a strange, cruel look. Now I was more alarmed and confused than ever, and my heart turned hard, unforgiving, and frantic.

"What operation is Sabah talking about?" I asked in a terrible voice.

The woman looked at me in bewilderment and alarm. Then, in a low voice choked with tears she said, "My daughter's condition suddenly got worse, so I called the doctor, and he advised that an operation be performed right away."

Having been transformed into a new, formidable person quite unlike the one the world had known thirty years earlier, I asked her, "In which part of the body?"

She said, "The doctor said it was the peritoneum."

I was hearing the word for the first time. However, I passed over the matter and asked in the same fearsome voice, "And was the operation performed?"

"Yes," she said, weeping, "and it ended with what you see before you!"

Stamping the floor with my foot in a rage, I screamed, "But I was here two hours ago and there was nothing wrong with her! Didn't you assure me that her condition was nothing to worry about?"

In a voice choked with tears, she said, "Her pain got suddenly worse! What could I do? What could I do?"

"And who might be the doctor who murdered her?"

Looking at me brokenly through her tears, she mumbled, "He did everything he could. But God's decree intervened!"

"Who might he be?"

342

She fell silent for a moment as though she were taking a breath, then she said, "Dr. Amin Rida."

A violent tremor went through my body as I repeated over and over, "Amin Rida!"

Then I cried in fury and contempt, "Dr. Amin Rida? He's just a beginner! Besides, his specialty is reproductive disorders!"

Flustered, she said he'd been the nearest doctor, that she thought doctors understood all sorts of disorders whatever their specialties happened to be, that there hadn't been time to hesitate, and so on. Trembling with rage, I waited until she was finished.

Then I let forth a frigid laugh and cried, "An obstetrician who performs an operation on the peritoneum! It's no wonder you killed her!"

I did an about-face, walked quickly to the door and thundered, "Doctor!"

I repeated the summons until he came from the other end of the house, his face white as a sheet. He entered the room with a meekness that ill befit his usual pompous bearing. Feeling a hatred and bitterness toward him that would have filled the earth itself, I said to him, "The Madame tells me that you performed the operation that killed my wife. Now, would you care to tell me what prompted you to take it upon yourself to perform a dangerous surgical operation when surgery isn't your specialization?"

With a distressed expression on his face, he shot Madame Nazli a strange look that brought to mind the way she had looked at Sabah, and I nearly exploded with rage. I'd begun to get a vague feeling that they were hiding something critical from me.

"Answer me!" I screamed at him savagely.

He turned to me with a furrowed brow, then remained silent for a moment as though he were consulting his lost dignity.

Then he said in a low voice, "She needed an urgent operation."

Clapping my hands together, I said, "So why didn't you call me to come? Why didn't you call for a surgeon?"

"There wasn't time!" said the mother nervously.

"But there was time to kill her!" I screeched.

343

The woman stared into my face as though she'd lost her mind, then she began to repeat, "Kill her . . . kill her . . . kill her!"

Then she lost her senses and exploded suddenly, slapping her cheeks uncontrollably. Wanting to come between the woman's hands and cheeks, Sabah came up and tried to stop her. However, she struck the servant in the face with such force that she reeled backward in terror. Then she stopped slapping herself, turned toward us and screamed in our faces—the doctor's and mine—in a voice that sounded like a roar, "You're the ones who killed her! Get out of my face!"

The doctor then slipped out the door and I remained alone, eyeing her with a cruel stare that had no regard for her outburst. "You're the ones who killed her!" The woman was talking nonsense, and I would have no mercy on her. I wouldn't rest until I'd done something that would send people reeling. I was faced with a crime. And unless it was merely a crime of ignorance and stupidity, he would pay for it dearly. The meek submission of an entire lifetime had now given birth in me to a devastating eruption, a fiery rage, and impending wickedness. I forgot the corpse and my grief and demons appeared before my eyes. To hell with the criminals!

Filled to saturation with the woman's obnoxious wailing and Sabah's incessant sobbing, I suddenly turned away from them and left the room without looking back. Then I rushed outside as though I were fleeing for my life.

61

The whole world looked bright red to me, and I was filled with a hellish determination, the likes of which I'd never seen in myself before, to commit any sort of wickedness as a way of releasing what I felt inside. I doubted that I'd be able to achieve any sort of result that would actually quench my thirst for revenge. Even so, I didn't hesitate for a single moment. I hailed a taxi and instructed it to take me to the public prosecutor's office. Entering the place without any particular plan or explicit accusation in mind, I found myself in the midst of a stifling crowd and my ears were bombarded with a din like the roar of the sea. I stood there uncertainly for a few moments until I caught sight of a policeman. I came up to him and asked him to tell me where the district attorney's office was.

"On the second floor," he replied gruffly.

I went up the stairs and found my way to the room with the help of an employee. After receiving permission to go in, I saw before me a desk behind which there sat a short, slender young man who was poring over some papers in front of him. He looked up when I came in, eyed me with a penetrating glance and said, "What do you need?"

Shocked by this simple question, my mind went blank, and I stood there in a daze as though I didn't know exactly why I'd come.

With a questioning look on his face, the young man repeated his query, saying, "What do you need?"

I had to speak no matter what it took. So, letting my tongue lead the way, I said, "My wife . . . has died." I nearly said, "has been murdered," but fear held me back.

Furrowing his brow in bewilderment, he said, "What does the public prosecutor have to do with that? And who are you?"

I took a deep breath and found my fear gradually leaving me. I introduced myself, then said, "Here is my story, Your Honor: This morning I left my wife at her mother's house, since she was feeling ill. Two hours after leaving the house, I went back and found her dead. They told me she'd suddenly begun to feel much worse and that they'd called a doctor who is a relative of her mother's. This doctor was of the opinion that her condition required immediate surgery, so he performed the operation, and she died."

I gulped, then stood there looking at the man for a long time. Seeing that he wasn't satisfied with what he'd heard, I went on, saying, "The fact is that this doctor is a specialist in reproductive disorders. So, is it permissible for him to perform a surgical operation? And if the operation performed has led to the patient's death, is he not to be held responsible for it, and shouldn't he be brought to justice?"

The man was silent for a moment, then he asked me, "Was she taken to a hospital?"

"No. The operation was performed in the house where she now lies dead."

"Who was it that called the doctor?"

"My mother-in-law."

"And how is it that she called on an obstetrician with no connection to your wife's illness?"

"I asked her the same question, and she told me that he was the nearest doctor. She also said she thought that regardless of what a doctor's specialization happens to be, he'll be familiar with all kinds of illness."

"Is he the one who advised that the operation be done?"

"Yes."

"And is he the one who performed it?"

"Yes! I asked him how he could have performed a surgical operation even though he isn't a surgeon, and he told me that my wife's condition called for immediate surgical intervention."

The man thought for some time, then asked me, "Are you leveling a particular accusation at this doctor?"

Not understanding what he meant, I looked at him uncertainly without saying a word.

So he asked me, "Do you have reason to accuse him of premeditated murder?"

My heart aflutter, I shook my head in the negative.

Then he asked, "Do you suspect that an error occurred during the operation, and that this led to her death?"

"That's very possible, Your Honor," I said. "And it wouldn't have been simply an error. Rather, it would have been the error of a man who has no experience as a surgeon. Hence, there's no doubt as to his responsibility in the matter."

He thought again, then asked, "I can't make a judgment until the medical examiner has examined the body and clarified the causes of death."

His words filled me with fear and gloom, since I couldn't bear the thought of the doctor's tampering with my beloved's body.

In a pained voice, I asked, "Couldn't you call the doctor to interrogate him first?"

Disregarding my objection, he picked up the receiver and dialed a number. Then I heard him speaking to the medical examiner. He asked me for the house address, then asked the doctor to go there to examine the body and write a report on the cause of death.

After hanging up, he turned to me and said, "If it's determined that there's criminal liability, I'll come to conduct the interrogation."

After completing the official procedures, I left the public prosecutor's office. By this time my impulsiveness had left me, and I was aware of the seriousness of what I had done. This was no joke: It involved a prosecutor, a medical examiner, police, scandal, and gossip. The investigation might lead nowhere, in which case we'd be left with nothing but the scandal and the gossip. And how would I face people after that? How would I face her family, my family, and everyone else? Wasn't it enough that my wife had suffered such a miserable fate without my subjecting her to forensic examination and making her the talk of the town? Oh, my smoldering heart! As I went back to the house, my soul was weighed down with worry and endless thinking. As I came within sight of the building, I paused, with a voice inside me urging me to turn on my heels and run. However, there was no escaping what I had to do. I had no choice but to drink the bitter potion to the dregs.

I rang the bell, then went in, despondent and resigned.

62

All the doors were closed with the exception of the door to the reception room, which was ajar. The house was devoid of the commotion that usually engulfs households when one of their members has died. Consequently, I was filled with an astonishment that drowned out my inner turmoil. It was past eleven in the morning. How was it that they still hadn't rushed the heartbreaking news to the houses of family and relatives? I was revisited by feelings of rancor and suspicion.

I looked at the young servant who had opened the door for me, her eyes red from weeping, and asked her, "Hasn't anyone come to the house?"

She shook her head in the negative in silence and grief. Then I pointed to the reception room's half-open door and asked her, "Is there anyone in there?"

"Dr. Amin," she murmured.

My body trembled with rage and hatred. The servant went over to the door to the large parlor, pushed the door open and went in, after which she proceeded to the room where Rabab lay at the other end of the house. As for me, I stayed alone in the small parlor, not knowing what to do. I was terrified at the thought of what I'd done, while the atmosphere around me aroused feelings of anger and hatred. Then I heard footsteps coming from inside. A moment later Madame Nazli, clad in black, emerged through the door to the large parlor.

Shooting me a frigid look, she asked me irritably, "And where have *you* been, sir?"

Her appearance and her question aroused my fears, as well as the feeling of shame that had ridden me since the moment I left the public prosecutor's office. Even so, I couldn't bear any longer to keep the terrible secret to myself, and I had the urge to confess, to meet the danger head-on.

So I said calmly, "I went to the public prosecutor and asked for an investigation to be done."

Her eyes grew large as saucers and her mouth dropped open.

Then, gaping at me as though she couldn't believe her ears, she muttered in astonishment, "The public prosecutor!"

With a terrible coolness, and in a voice loud enough to make myself heard by those in the reception room, I said, "Yes. I went to the public prosecutor's office, and the medical examiner will be here soon."

Before long the doctor emerged from the guestroom. He stood not far away, looking ashen and somber.

Then the woman, dumbfounded, asked, "And what are you accusing us of?"

Enjoying my ire and desire for revenge, I said fiercely, "There isn't any accusation. However, I'm certain that the death resulted from a serious mistake, a mistake that comes as no surprise from someone who has no experience as a surgeon, and who takes it upon himself to toy with people's lives!"

A tense, painful silence ensued, in the course of which people looked at each other, then looked away.

Then the woman gasped nervously and exclaimed, "How could you find it so easy to turn your wife's body over to the public prosecutor!"

Pierced to the quick, I nearly collapsed. However, I concealed my pain with a feigned rage and shouted, "It's easier for me than to see her die in vain!"

The doctor opened his mouth to say something. However, just at that moment the doorbell rang so loudly, we all nearly jumped out of our skins.

I went to the door and opened it. I was greeted by a policeman, who asked me, "Is this where we can find the late wife of Mr. Kamil Ru'ba, an employee at the Ministry of War?"

I answered in the affirmative. Then the man stepped aside, saying, "His Honor, the medical examiner."

There then entered a medium-sized man carrying a doctor's satchel, who was followed inside by the policeman. Happening to meet Dr. Amin on his way in, the medical examiner asked him, "Are you the husband who informed the public prosecutor?"

"No, I'm the husband, sir," I said as I closed the door. "This is the doctor who performed the operation."

Perplexed, the doctor looked back and forth between us with a faint smile on his lips.

Then he asked Dr. Amin, "What operation was it?"

"It was an operation on the peritoneum," he replied softly.

"And what was the cause of death?"

"The peritoneum was punctured due to an accident beyond my control."

Addressing the medical examiner, I said in an agitated tone, "Ask him, Your Honor, what made him perform surgery when he isn't a surgeon!"

The man hesitated for a few moments, then said in a loud voice, "I've come to perform another task. Where is the body, please?"

Madame Nazli was still standing near the door to the large parlor, scanning our faces with her tear-reddened eyes in a dazed silence. However, when she heard the doctor asking where the body was, she let out a moan and cried without thinking, "This will never happen!"

The doctor cast her a quick glance, then said to her gently, "Please bear your misfortune with patience, Madame."

Shooting me a fiery look, she said to the doctor imploringly, "The deceased is the daughter of a prominent government employee, Gabr Bey Sayyid, chief inspector for the coastal area. Perhaps you know him, sir. I beg you to have mercy on the weakness of a woman like me, and wait until his return. I've wired him to inform him of the tragedy."

The doctor replied kindly, "The body has to be examined without delay so as to allow the burial to take place at the proper time. Don't worry, Madame. Everything will be over in a matter of minutes."

She then flung herself helplessly onto a chair and broke into bitter sobs. Meanwhile, I preceded the doctor to Rabab's room. When I reached the door I could hear Sabah sobbing inside. I pushed the door open and called to her without having the courage to look in the direction of the bed. The servant answered my summons and I prodded her aside to make room for the doctor, who entered the room without hesitation. Then I closed the door behind him. She asked me about the man I'd brought, but I scolded her impatiently and nudged her out of the parlor. Then I began pacing up and down, my soul in a turmoil that enveloped my every nerve. A deadly melancholy descended upon me as I imagined my beloved wife's body in the hands of this strange doctor, who would uncover her and handle her without feeling or compassion.

I let forth an agonized groan, and I felt a sharp pain that seemed to be tearing my heart to shreds. I spent some moments in a stupor, imagining myself the victim of a demonic nightmare. I looked around me as though I were searching for an escape hatch. But had I forgotten the pallid, handkerchief-bound face as death's fearsome specter crouched upon her brow? Lord! Little by little I was returning to myself, leaving behind the world of madness that had taken hold of me for the real world of loss and grief. The horrific reality took shape before me in a kind of solemn stillness, as though I were comprehending for the first time that Rabab had really died. She was no longer among the living, and my life would be devoid of her forever. She would never come back to my house as her mother had said she would. Never again would I accompany her to the tram stop in the morning, and never again would I greet her in the afternoon after her return from school as she fought off fatigue with a sweet smile. Tender youth had come to an end, and a flaming love had been snuffed out. Hopes and more hopes had withered and dried up. Where was that happy history that had begun at the tram stop, woven its memories out of the ethereal stuff of love, taken me roaming through the valleys of bliss, then created me anew? Where was that enchanting history? Had it really come to an end in a moment through the error of some foolish doctor? And what fault of mine was it?

Death is a dreadful tragedy. Yet it isn't convincing. Hadn't I been talking to her just a few hours earlier? Hadn't she been like a succulent rose just a day or two before? So how could I believe that she and the first person to have died millions of years before were now one and the same? Besides, she was still alive in my soul. I could see her with my own eyes, and hear her, and touch her, and smell her! She still filled my heart and soul. So was there no way to correct a simple mistake?

Just then there was a movement—I didn't know whether it was coming from the outer parlor or from the chamber of sorrows. Be that as it may, it brought me back to my senses, and I began thinking about the doctor and what he was doing. It also brought me back to my turmoil, my anxiety, and my fears. What would I do if the doctor found nothing of significance? How would I face people later? How I hoped for God to punish the murderer! Even so, I remained in a state of such turmoil that I lost touch with myself and my reason. Time dragged on until I imagined that I'd grown old and decrepit and was dying. Then the door to the room opened and the doctor emerged with a blank expression that told me nothing. He advanced a few steps until he was in the middle of the parlor. I stood before him with my mouth open and my gaze fixed on him.

Running his fingers over his brow, he said plainly, "I've finished writing my report. I'll submit it right away to the public prosecutor, and I believe it calls for an immediate investigation."

63

I should have felt relieved and vindicated. But instead, my strength suddenly gave out on me and I collapsed onto the nearest chair, then sprawled my legs out and nearly fell asleep. The only thing that happened during the waiting period that followed the doctor's departure was that Madame Nazli and Sabah went rushing to the deceased's room and proceeded to weep and wail at the top of their lungs. I glanced over at the small parlor, where I saw Dr. Amin Rida pacing the floor with slow, heavy steps while the policeman sat on a chair at the reception room door.

At twelve-thirty the doorbell rang. The policeman got up and opened the door, and the district attorney came in followed by a clerk and another policeman. My heart pounding with fright at the sight of the government officials, I rose to my feet and walked up to the man, then raised my hand in greeting. He asked about the deceased's room, then proceeded there right away followed by the clerk. Not having the courage to follow them there, I waited outside, and a few minutes later they were back. The man glanced around him, then went to the reception room with me close on his heels. He sat down on a sofa, while the clerk sat down on a nearby chair and spread his papers out on a table. After asking me my name, age, and job, he asked me to relate whatever information I had about what had happened. I complied with his request and the clerk recorded every word I said. Then he called for Dr. Amin Rida, who came in looking stony-faced and pallid. He allowed him to sit down in front of him, then addressed himself to me, saying, "You're free to stay if you'd like."

There was something in his tone of voice that sounded more like a command than an invitation. In any case, I was dying to be there for the interrogation. So, filled with dread and anticipation, I sat down on a chair next to the sofa the interrogator was sitting on. The man began by asking him general questions, such as his name, his age, and his occupation.

Then he said to him, "Can you tell me how you first became involved in this situation?"

Without hesitation, Dr. Amin said, "I was called upon to visit the patient at around nine this morning, and I found her in a great deal of pain. When I examined her, I found that the peritoneum was inflamed and needed immediate surgery. So I decided to perform the operation in order to save the patient's life. I gave her mother my opinion and she agreed to allow me to proceed, so I performed the operation right away. However, it happened that the membrane was punctured in such a way that my efforts to save her were in vain, and she died."

"Had you treated the patient at any previous time?"

"No."

"Not even in connection with this final illness?"

"No. However, I learned that she'd been ill in bed for one night and that they thought she had a cold."

"Has this family been in the habit of calling on you when one of its members falls ill?"

"This has never happened before. However, I've only been practicing medicine for a little over a year, and I don't recall anyone in the family having fallen ill during this period of time."

"Do you think that if any of them had fallen ill, they would have called on you?"

"The fact is that they did call on me the first time they were faced with this situation."

"Don't they know what your specialization is?"

"Yes, they do. However, the seriousness of the patient's condition caused the mother to seek out my help due to the fact that my clinic is nearby, and because I'm her relative."

"I don't see anything in these circumstances that might influence one's choice of physician. Besides, how could you yourself agree to treat a pathological condition that you knew to be outside your area of expertise? In such circumstances, don't doctors generally recommend that the appropriate doctor be called upon?"

"I thought it most fitting to answer the call right away. Consequently, I went with the idea that it was a case of fainting, a severe stomachache, or something of that nature, and which wouldn't be difficult for any doctor to treat. I believe this is what the people who called on me were thinking as well."

"However, you found the situation to be more serious than you had expected. So what did you do?"

At this point the doctor refrained from answering. Instead, he lowered his head in embarrassment, as if he were pondering the matter.

"Why didn't you recommend that a surgeon be called?" asked the interrogator.

"The operation needed to be performed without delay."

"Had you done any surgeries prior to this?"

"In medical school, of course."

"I mean, since then."

"No."

"I can hardly imagine your having undertaken to perform this dangerous operation!"

In a slightly altered, irritable tone of voice, Dr. Amin said, "I told you that the patient's condition was critical, and that it required that the operation be performed without delay!"

"And how did you obtain the necessary medical instruments? Were they in your clinic?"

For the first time, the doctor hesitated before replying.

Then he said, "No."

"How did you get them, then?"

"From a colleague of mine."

"A surgeon?"

"Yes."

"And why didn't you bring the colleague himself?"

"He was scheduled to do other work at the same time."

"Who might this doctor be?"

He hesitated again. Then his pallid face flushed and in a low voice he said, "The fact is, I brought them from the hospital, from the Fuad I Hospital."

"Aside from the question of whether this behavior was sound from an administrative point of view, wouldn't it have been more appropriate for you—since you must have realized that you'd have to spend some time getting the instruments in an illegitimate manner—wouldn't it have been more appropriate for you to call a surgeon, especially in view of the fact that calling him wouldn't have taken any more time than it would take to bring the instruments?"

He thought for some time. Then, obviously unsettled, he said, "I was so upset over the patient's condition, I didn't think about that."

"It would be more logical to say that precisely because you were upset over her condition, you should have thought about it. Supposing what you say is true, why didn't you take the patient to the hospital, where there are plenty of specialists?"

"Her mother wouldn't agree to have her taken to the hospital."

"Wouldn't this have been less dangerous than placing her in the hands of someone with no experience? However, we'll leave this issue aside for now. . . ."

The interrogator spread out a piece of paper before him and scanned its contents.

Then he sat up straight and said, "What do you think of this? I'm reviewing the medical examiner's report, which asserts that an inflammation of the peritoneum doesn't call for the kind of haste you're talking about. In other words, it's different from situations such as certain cases of appendicitis, for example. What do you say about that?"

The doctor fell into a deep silence, while the gleam in his eyes revealed his disquiet and the intensity of his thoughts.

The interrogator went on, saying, "The report also says that this operation takes several hours to prepare for, during which time the patient is generally given an enema. Were you not aware of these basic principles relating to the art of surgery?"

"I learned that the patient had been given an enema yesterday evening, and that she hadn't eaten anything since that time."

"Was she given the enema in preparation for the operation?"

"No. It was given to her based on the fact that she was thought to have a cold. As for the idea of the operation, it didn't come up until after I arrived this morning."

At this point I began paying even closer attention, and I was amazed that no one had mentioned to me that my wife had been given an enema. I remembered how she'd been kept in this house despite the fact that she could have come home, if even in a taxi, and an ominous sense of uncertainty and confusion came over me.

Then the interrogator said, "What I have here is an operation that was performed with maniacal speed for no known technical reason, by a doctor who isn't a surgeon and who could, no doubt, have called on a surgeon with the proper qualifications. What is the meaning of this?"

The interrogator cast the doctor a cold, penetrating look. I looked back and forth between the two men with a sense of growing anxiety and a strange sort of fear, and I was in such turmoil that I tensed up all over.

Then I heard the interrogator say, "I'm wondering why it was deemed necessary for you in particular to perform this operation, and at this particular time?"

He remained silent for some time, then continued, "And what was the cause of death?"

"A puncture in the peritoneum."

"The medical examiner states otherwise," rejoined the interrogator coldly.

"What might the cause be, then?" asked an indignant Dr. Amin Rida.

"That's a question you'd best answer for me yourself!"

In the same tense, nervous tone of voice, the doctor said, "I don't understand what you mean."

"I'll clarify the matter for you, then. The medical examiner states that the peritoneum was, in fact, punctured, but that there was no pathology or inflammation to be seen in it. In fact, he states that it required no treatment of any kind, much less surgery."

"But I performed the operation myself!"

"You performed no operation whatsoever with the exception of puncturing the peritoneum."

His voice trembling, the doctor said furiously, "Do you mean to say that I punctured the peritoneum for no reason? What's the meaning of this?"

"You punctured the peritoneum and killed her!"

"In the course of performing the operation."

"I assure you, you did not perform an operation on the peritoneum."

"Are you accusing me of pretending to perform the operation in order to kill her?" shouted the doctor in a rage. "Are you accusing me of murder, sir?"

"Yes, I am," replied the interrogator. "And before long you'll come around to my point of view. You'll see for yourself, without any need for my advice, that nothing will be of any use to you but complete honesty and candor."

The doctor's face turned pale and gloomier than ever, and he appeared to be in a miserable state of defeat. Casting a final glance at the medical examiner's report, the interrogator continued, "Why did you make this deadly puncture in the peritoneum?"

In a morose, almost despairing tone the doctor replied, "I answered this question before!"

"You'd be well advised not to act stupid, since you're undoubtedly an intelligent young man. You punctured the peritoneum in order to create an apparent, 'legitimate' cause for a death you believed to be inevitable."

The doctor lowered his head in silence like someone who's confessing and giving up the fight.

Then the interrogator went on, saying, "You were, in fact, performing an operation on another part of the body. Then a perforation occurred by accident in this other part and, given your lack of experience as a surgeon, you thought that this perforation was bound to lead to the patient's death. So what did you do? If the true cause of death were known, the illegal operation you were performing would come to light. And it was at this point that your disturbed mind led you to resort to a maniacal ruse, namely, to puncture the peritoneum so that it would be thought that *this* was the cause of death. Now you claim falsely that you were performing an operation on the peritoneum, and in this way you conceal the crime of having performed the illegal operation. If you had caused a patient to die by accident, this wouldn't be considered a crime according to the law. However, contrary to what you may have thought, the patient didn't die from the first perforation. Rather, you killed her when you made a hole in the peritoneum."

Trembling violently, the doctor shouted at the interrogator like a madman, "No! No!! She'd already died when I punctured the peritoneum!"

With a faint smile on his lips, the interrogator looked triumphantly at the doctor. As for the latter, he closed his mouth in dismay. Enraged and desperate, he looked up twice at the interrogator, and as he did so, he reminded me of someone who's been knocked prostrate by a blow from the enemy. However, my mind was in a state of such heated turmoil that I paid him no attention. An illegal operation? The operation on the peritoneum had been nothing but a ruse to cover up a crime? Either I was crazy, or these two men were crazy! She'd already died before he punctured the peritoneum? Lord! I was nearly beside myself, and I almost started raving like a lunatic despite the presence of this daunting interrogator.

However, he broke the oppressive silence, saying calmly, "So we agree. And I think the time has come for you to confess that you in particular, out of all the doctors in Egypt, were chosen to perform an abortion!"

And he didn't stop there. He went on talking. He may have mentioned, among other things, anesthesia and its effect, or something of that sort. And the other may have said a few words as well. However, I was no longer aware of a thing being said. My mind stopped at the word 'abortion' and refused to go a step further. I fell on the word and it split me in two, then ripped me to shreds. It rang in my head till I was oblivious to everything. The three men disappeared from before me, the room disappeared, and I saw nothing but a terrifying, red and black void where terrifying specters of memories and thoughts danced. An abortion. So Rabab had been pregnant! The letter. This young doctor. Satan could undoubtedly have woven the tale of a horrific crime out of these disconnected facts, mocking both the suspicion that had, at one time, driven me to spying, and the peace of mind in which I'd mistakenly taken refuge at another. The interrogator was doing his utmost to expose a medical crime, but along the thorny path leading there he was going to stumble upon a crime far more heinous and inhuman. Hadn't my heart perceived the catastrophe from the beginning? Might the doctor be the person who had written the letter? Or had they called on him due to the fact that he was a relative and could thus help them keep things quiet? The mother must have known everything . . . everything about my married life, and about her daughter's slip-up. Perhaps she'd wanted to wipe out evidence of the scandal through the operation, only to have death ruin her plans. Ah, Rabab! We deserve every tribulation we're afflicted with in this world, since we give ourselves over to it heart and soul when, in reality, it deserves nothing but loathing.

I was roused from my thoughts by the voice of the interrogator as he called out to me, "Hey there . . . wake up!"

I looked up at him, trembling, and little by little I recovered my awareness of my surroundings.

The man said, "I'm asking you: Hadn't your wife spoken to you about not wanting to be pregnant? Hadn't she told you of her desire to have an abortion?"

I cast a quick glance at Dr. Amin, thinking to myself: He knows the entire secret from beginning to end. In fact, he may know far more than I know myself. It pained me to lie and expose myself to another insult.

"No," I muttered.

"Did you think she was happy to be pregnant?"

In a listless, doleful tone I said, "It's only now that I'm finding out that she was pregnant."

The interrogator raised his eyebrows so high that they appeared above his spectacles, and I fixed my gaze on his eyes as he ruminated.

Then he asked me, "How do you explain the fact that she was hiding the matter from you?"

His question shook me to the depths of my being. All I had to say was one word, and my secret would become the butt of everyone's jokes. Feelings of rage and the desire for revenge tempted me sorely to reveal what I'd striven so mightily to keep hidden so that I could likewise expose the secret that had been kept hidden by my depraved wife and avenge myself on the criminal. I wanted to say that there was nothing in the past year or more of our married life that could have led to pregnancy so that the interrogator could put his callous hand on the wanton trespasser. I was sorely, sorely tempted to do so, and the words were almost on the tip of my tongue. However, I didn't say a thing. Instead, I was stricken with a total paralysis that I couldn't explain. Could shyness influence me even in a situation like this? Was my desire to conceal my impotence so great that it overrode my longing for revenge? I wasn't able to utter the decisive word, and with every second that passed I grew more helpless and resigned to defeat.

"I don't know," I muttered breathlessly.

And before I knew it, Dr. Amin had jumped to his feet and taken two steps back, folding his arms over his chest in pompous defiance.

Then in a confident, supercilious voice he said to the interrogator, "You're asking him something he knows nothing about. She was a wife in name only, and I'm responsible for everything from beginning to end!"

64

I left the house without seeing any of those who lived there. After all, it wasn't my house any longer, nor were its residents my family. As I stood at the door to the building, my gaze shifted over to the tram stop, the tram stop of memories. I looked back and forth between it and the balcony, then closed my eyes to see the procession of memories marching past in the twinkling of an eye. It was a true picture of life, one that brought together its joys and its tragedies. Then I took off down the street without any destination in mind as though I were running away as fast as I could. My heart had turned into a firebrand from which sparks of rage, misery, and hatred were flying in all directions. I figured that this world, so preoccupied with its own concerns, would forget its sorrows the next day and drown itself in talk about my scandal. At the same time, I still hadn't gotten over my shock, and I kept wondering what on earth had prompted that crook of a doctor to confess the terrible truth. I'd been so defeated by cowardice that I'd concealed the truth, and in so doing I'd given him a chance to flee if he had wanted to take it. But instead, he'd jumped to his feet in a rage and, in that self-important, arrogant way of his, he'd let the truth come out through his own two lips: "Don't ask him something he knows nothing about. She was a wife in name only . . ." My God! Why hadn't I beaten him to a pulp? Why hadn't I hurled myself at him and dug my fingernails into his heart? It was a memory that would sting me like a flaming whip till the day I died. But what had made him fling himself into perdition?

Had his despair of being acquitted of one of the two charges led him to confess to the other? Was he so dismayed at the fate to which love had doomed his lover that he was moved in a moment of despair to share with her in her dreadful fate? Was it an uprising of the conscience, of the heart, or both? How could I possibly become privy to the secrets of that disdainful heart? At the same time, I became increasingly bewildered and wondered to myself: How could he have permitted himself to send her to the grave shrouded in disgrace? Wouldn't it have been more fitting for him to seize the opportunity at hand to save himself and protect the honor of the woman he had loved, and who had loved him? Do you suppose he now regretted what he had said, or was he still holding his head high in arrogance and conceit? It was a puzzle to me then, and it always will be. My heart was so bloated with bitterness and rage that the fate that had been meted out to them—her in the grave, and him in prison—was a source of relief and joy to me.

By this time my feet had carried me to Ismailiya Square. Finding no place better to flee to than the Qasr al-Nil gardens, I headed toward the bridge. I thought: If only I could disappear from Cairo for a whole year. It hadn't even occurred to me to attend the funeral of this woman who'd been my wife. After all, I wouldn't be able to face any of the people who knew of the tragedy. But had I really even married? It had been nothing but a long, drawn-out farce or, more properly speaking, a tragedy. My family were sure to be shocked when they learned that my wife had died and been buried without any of them being invited to the funeral. However, their shock would be quick to dissipate once they knew the truth, and it wouldn't be long before they were too distracted telling jokes about it to think of anything else. Anybody who got hold of this story would be the life of the party. My heart shrank, and I felt a coldness flowing through my limbs. How badly I wanted to flee, just as I always had in such situations. Where could I find a distant land in which no one had ever set foot? And how could I cut off every tie that bound me to my odious past? If only I could be born again in a new world in which I wasn't haunted by a single memory from this one! Indeed, I wouldn't be able to carry on with my life as long as I was being followed about by my past like a heavy shadow.

I spent the rest of the day wandering down streets or sitting like a vagrant in public parks. I felt no heat, no cold, no thirst. Then at last the sun announced its imminent departure and evening shadows spread over the treetops. I went back the way I'd come with heavy steps, and by the time I reached Ismailiya Square, darkness had fallen over the universe. I was gripped with uncertainty, not knowing where to go. Then suddenly, an image of the pub flashed into my mind. I heaved a deep sigh and my taut, frayed nerves uttered a sigh of relief as though I'd suddenly caught a glimpse of happiness after a long, oppressive ordeal. The very next moment, a taxi was taking me to Alfi Bey Street, but my relief was short-lived and soon replaced by anxiety, dejection, and indecision. Wondering whether I shouldn't be heading somewhere else, I got out of the taxi in front of the pub, but didn't go in. Instead I began walking slowly down the sidewalk with a heavy head and heart. Overcome by despair, however, I let it lead me back to the pub. After finding myself an isolated corner, I drank one glass, then another, and kept on drinking. My head was hardly responding to the liquor, but I suddenly felt ravenous, so I ate with an astounding, voracious appetite. And no sooner had I finished eating than I was overcome with a fatigue that enveloped my stomach, my head, and my entire body. It was as though the effort I'd expended in the course of the excruciating day, catching me in an unguarded moment, had come marching over me with its hordes and crushed me beneath their weight. I got up unsteadily, left the pub, and got into a nearby taxi that took me in the direction of Qasr al-Aini. Overwhelmed with fatigue, a numbness spread through my body, and a sudden feeling of apathy came over me. I looked with a mocking eye upon my tragedy, and for a moment it seemed as though it were someone else's misfortune rather than my own, or as though it had been removed from my personal life and taken its place in the procession of shared human heartbreaks. The taxi continued down the road until we were within sight of the building through which the world had put me to the test. I looked toward it with open eyes and with a timorous, racing heart. I saw light emanating from the balcony and the windows, and in front of the building I could see two tall poles from which two large lights were suspended. So, it was all over. . . .

65

As I was going up the stairs to our flat, I remembered my mother and I was seized by a violent fear. At the same time I was gripped by a terrible rage as though it were Satan himself. What had made me so angry? I wondered what on earth I might say to her. Lord! What had brought me home in the first place? Did I really think I'd be able to spend the night in Rabab's room and on her bed? Nonetheless, I continued up the stairs as though it were my ineluctable fate. As I entered the flat, my chest was tight and gloom was written all over my face. I could hear my mother's voice as she asked anxiously, "Who is it?"

I froze in place, furious and bitter.

"It's me," I replied gruffly.

In a tearful voice she cried, "Kamil! Come here, son!"

My heart pounded violently, and I knew for a certainty that she'd heard about Rabab's fate. I went to her room and found her sitting in bed.

Sobbing, she reached out to me with her hands, and in a tear-choked voice, she said, "If only I could have died in her place. She should have remained alive for you!"

I stood in the middle of the room, ignoring her outstretched hands.

"How did you hear the news?" I asked her in a stiff, harsh voice.

"How could you have forgotten to tell me yourself, son?" she cried in the same muffled voice. "From this I can see how grieved you are. My heart is breaking for you. If only I could have been the ransom for both of you. After all, I'm just a sick old woman. But this was God's decree."

Her emotion didn't make a dent on my hardened soul, and I made no reply.

Then, as if I hadn't heard what she said I asked again, "How did you hear the news?"

"I'd been waiting anxiously for you to come home today, and when it got to be evening and you still weren't back, I got scared. So I told the servant how to get to the building where her family lives and sent her there. Then she brought me the horrible news."

Looking at her suspiciously, I asked in a low voice, "Do you know how she died?"

"No, son!" she replied, crying again. "I'm still completely in the dark about it. I feel so sorry about the poor girl. How could she have suffered such an untimely death?"

Upon hearing her response, I felt a relief that soon grew tepid and lost its effect. Why deceive myself with false comfort when I knew that there was no power in the world that would be able to keep my scandal a secret? Her weeping annoyed me, since to me there was no questioning the fact that it was a phony show of grief of the sort that women sometimes put on.

So I said rudely, "She died the way people do every day and every night. The way my grandfather and my father died, and the way all of us will die."

In my anger, I stressed the word "all."

Then I asked her wearily, "Why are you crying?"

Looking at me dolefully through her tears, she murmured, "I wish I'd died in her place."

Too agitated to contain myself any longer, I said testily, "That's a lie! No one would ever be willing to die in someone else's place! Would you have said that if she were still alive?"

She gaped at me in alarm, then looked down in pained silence.

No one said anything for a long time.

Then she broke the silence, murmuring, "May God send His peace into your heart."

"I don't need prayers," I said harshly, "and I hate hypocrisy. I'll never forget that you hated her even before you'd laid eyes on her!"

Looking up at me with a pained look on her face, she said, "Kamil! Have mercy on your mother! God knows I'm not being dishonest with you. You'll hardly find a household anywhere that doesn't witness the kinds of disagreements we used to have."

However, I showed her no mercy. At the same time, I don't know what sort of force moved me to remind her of the unfortunate past as though I were really grieving over Rabab. I was so hard on her, you would have thought she was the cause of the catastrophe that had befallen me. And what made me even more bitter and angry was my sense that through her show of grief, she was concealing a malicious glee.

Hence, I added furiously, "The fact is that you're beside yourself with joy! I know you as well as I know myself, so don't try to deceive me. You're hiding your joy with these crocodile tears of yours!"

"Kamil!" she groaned. "Don't be cruel to your mother! Don't say that! God knows I didn't hate her! And whatever grieves you, grieves me!"

I let forth a cold laugh like the cracking of a whip in the air, and said, "And in case you're not happy enough yet, let me tell you that she didn't just die. She was killed!"

She gaped at me in terror and, perhaps fearing that I'd gone mad, murmured, "God have mercy."

Then I shouted with the nonchalance of a madman, "She was killed when the doctor was performing an abortion on her."

"An abortion!" she cried, striking her chest with her hand. "Was she pregnant? Lord, I didn't know that!"

"Neither did I! She hid it from me because I wasn't the child's father."

"Kamil!" she cried in distress. "Have mercy on yourself, and on me! You don't know what you're saying!"

369

"I know more than you'd expect me to. I found out in one day more than what someone like me would normally find out in a generation. As I told you, she'd hidden the matter from me. Then she went to the child's father to perform an abortion on her, but he made a mistake and killed her."

"Have mercy, O Most Merciful of the merciful!"

"Is He still the Most Merciful of the merciful? Farewell, since I won't be worshipping Him from now on. As for you, you may be saying to yourself with a strange sort of satisfaction, 'The sinful woman has gotten some of what she deserved. I had a feeling something like this might be happening from the very beginning. But you didn't listen to me!'"

My mother heaved a miserable sigh. Then in a voice that sounded more like a moan she said, "What you're saying grieves me no end. You're killing me without mercy."

In reply, I screamed at her like a lunatic, "Revel in your malicious glee all you like! But don't you dare imagine that we'll live together. The past is over, with its good and its bad, and I'll never go back to it as long as I live. I'll be alone from now on. I won't live with you under one roof. I'll ask the ministry to transfer me somewhere far, far away, and I'll live there for the rest of my life."

With tears glistening in her eyes and pain tying her tongue, she sat there looking at me in terror and speechless indignation.

Then, as if what I'd said already weren't enough, I seethed, "Go to my sister or my brother, and from now on, consider me dead."

Then I turned my back to her and left the room as her sobs rang in my ears.

66

It never once occurred to me to go to my room. In fact, that was the farthest thing from my mind. I even avoided looking at it. Instead I went to the sitting room and flung myself on the sofa, exhausted and depressed. The night passed slowly and heavily, and the only sleep I got was in the form of intermittent naps permeated with nightmares. Then a faint light began filtering in through the shutters, heralding the break of day. Heaving a sigh of relief, I stretched wearily, then got up and left the room with the urge to flee and disappear from sight. I came up gingerly to the outer door and placed my hand on the doorknob. However, once there I froze in hesitation and moved no further. Instead I retreated quietly toward my mother's room. Ever so carefully I pushed on the half-open door and stuck my head in. I could hear the servant's rhythmic snores, and on the bed lay my mother in a deep stillness.

Hardly able to make out anything but the upper half of her face, I cast her a quick glance, then retreated and headed again for the outer door. As I closed the door noiselessly behind me, I heard—or at least I thought I heard—a voice calling me. I thought she'd awakened despite the care I'd taken not to disturb her, and she seemed to be calling to me. I paused, my hand on the banister, and my heart softened toward her. But I was in a state of such despair that I wasn't handling things well, so I shrugged my shoulders indifferently and went down the stairs. It was still early morning and the street was abandoned, or nearly so, and a cool, damp breeze wafted over my face. I stood there for a while hesitantly, not knowing where to go, then I headed for the gas station where the taxi stop was and caught a taxi to Ismailiya Square. On the way I cast a glance at the other building. Enveloped in silence, its windows were closed, and the two lights hanging from the pole outside had been turned off. I arrived at the square, then went to a milk vendor's and sat at a table at the far end of the place. After having a simple breakfast, I was suddenly overcome with fatigue. I spread out my legs, and an overwhelming drowsiness advanced like an army over my entire body. No longer able to hold my head up, I surrendered to its dominion and before I knew it, I'd fallen fast asleep. When I woke up again, I found myself leaning over the table with my head resting on my forearm. I lifted my head and looked around me feeling disoriented and embarrassed.

I left the place without daring to look at the other people sitting there, and when I looked at the clock in the square, I found to my astonishment that it was past two in the afternoon! I'd slept for eons, absent from my gloomy world, and how delectable it would have been to sleep forever! I headed in the direction of the Qasr al-Nil gardens, painfully aware of how unkempt and shabby I looked. As I walked briskly along, I asked myself what I was going to do with my life. However, in keeping with my usual tendency to avoid dealing head-on with serious problems, a voice inside me suggested that I postpone that decision till later.

Then I found myself thinking about Rabab. I felt a rage toward her that refused to leave me, as though it were some sort of permanent handicap. How I wished she could be resurrected, if only for a minute, so that I could spit in her face! Will I ever forget that I rejoiced over her death with the spiteful satisfaction of someone filled with bitterness and rage? That's the way I am, and there's no point in hiding the fact. At the same time, I was sufficiently calm by that time that I could think about things rationally. The strange thing is that despite my extreme self-centeredness, I never begrudge an opponent a fair hearing. This isn't because I'm so fond of fairness, but I've grown accustomed to making excuses for my opponents as a way of concealing the fact that I'm too weak to get even with them. And this is why I made excuses for Rabab in her tragedy. I said to myself: I was wrong to believe her claim that she didn't enjoy making love. Rather, it was my inadequacy that cast her into the arms of temptation. At the same time, how could I have doubted that she'd loved me sincerely? Memories went wafting over my imagination as fragrant breezes go wafting over a blazing fire, memories of shared glances, the unforgettable encounter on the tram, the way she resisted her first suitor in preference for me, and the enchantment that was the most joyous gift of ephemeral happiness I've ever received. It had been a sincere love, but it had been exposed to an icy wind that pulled it up by the roots and deprived it of the water of life. So hadn't I been an accessory to her murder? At that moment, I called upon God to hasten Judgment Day and, in His mercy, to deliver human beings from life's ordeals. My love for Rabab had been a God-given bliss. However, it had passed away, leaving hatred and rage in its wake. But had it really passed away? Suppose that, by some miracle, what had happened to me had been nothing but a bad dream. Wouldn't my love have been brought back even more powerful than it had been before? Of course it would have. So, then, it was still there under the wreckage of hatred and loathing. A limb that's been severed never grows back. Hence, it no longer has any real existence. Similarly, a love that returns must never have really gone away. But, I thought, What's the use of all this agonizing rumination? And with that I furrowed my brow as if to frighten away the memories that were assailing me.

I made up my mind to flee from my memories, even if it meant facing up to the critical problem that I'd been running away from just a short while earlier, namely, the problem of what I was going to do with my life. I mustn't leave things to chance, I said to myself. I'd find a way to get rid of Rabab's furniture, then move to a new neighborhood. But did I really want to move somewhere far away? How badly I wanted to flee, but I was too weak to leave Cairo. This was how I felt; it was a certainty for me. And would I really abandon my mother? Would I be capable of abandoning her? For a long time the desire to leave her had come to me in the form of vague dreams. But could I actually do it? It was a critical step, one that I was well-advised not to take without serious thought and consideration. Why had I been so cruel to her? What was I avenging myself on her for? I knew for a certainty that the mere thought of her could well send me flying back into her arms, weeping and repentant. What an odious love it was, a love from whose grip I didn't know how to free myself.

I went back to the square a little after three in the afternoon, and I found myself remembering Alfi Bey Street with my usual enthusiasm. Not far from the tram stop I glimpsed a colleague of mine from the ministry, but I ignored him. However, he happened to see me as well. Coming up to me with a solemn, concerned look on his face, he extended his hand and said, "I'm so sorry to hear of your loss, Mr. Kamil."

A tremor went through my body and I wondered anxiously: How did he hear about it? And what does he know about it?

"Thank you," I mumbled.

The man squeezed my hand and said, "Excuse me. I'm going to get a bite to eat, then come back to attend the funeral."

My Lord! I thought the funeral had been held that morning or even the day before, and that my predicament had passed. However, I was still expected to attend, and they'd placed the obituary in the newspapers! What sort of predicament still lay in wait for me?

In a low voice I asked him, "Did you read the obituary in *al-Ahram*?"

"No," he said, looking bewildered. "I don't think it appeared in *al-Ahram*. Otherwise we would have found out about it at the ministry. I read about it in *al-Balagh*."

He slipped the newspaper out from under his arm, opened it up and pointed to a column, saying, "Here's the obituary."

Discomfited and embarrassed, I took the newspaper and scanned the following lines: "Daughter of the late Colonel Abdulla Bey Hasan passes away. She is survived by her son, Medhat Bey Ru'ba Laz, a

374

prominent member of the Fayoum community, her son Kamil Effendi Ru'ba Laz, employee at the Ministry of War, and her daughter, the wife of Sabir Effendi Amin."

I gaped into my friend's face like a lunatic. Then I reread the obituary, my entire body trembling.

"That's impossible!" I shouted. "This is a lie!!"

I went running like mad toward a nearby taxi, threw myself inside it and told the driver to get me to my destination as fast as he could. It was a lie, a story somebody had made up! I'd find out what had really happened, and then I'd know how to punish whoever it was that had played this ridiculous joke on me! The taxi went speeding along, my neck craning toward the road. Then there appeared a large tent that had been set up in front of our house. When I saw it, my chest heaved and my limbs began to tremble. The taxi stopped and I got out, hardly able to see what was in front of me. I wasn't grieved or pained. I was crazy. I saw my uncle sitting at the entrance to the tent. Then I saw my brother Medhat coming toward me. I rushed up to him in a frenzy and grabbed his necktie.

"How could you keep the news from me?" I screamed in his face.

Freeing himself with difficulty from my grip, my brother cast me a worried, disturbed look. Then my uncle came up to us and said, "Where have you been, Kamil? We looked all over for you, and couldn't find you."

I looked back and forth between the two men. Then I looked strangely at the tent and muttered, "Is this real?"

"Get hold of yourself and be a man," my uncle replied.

In a fearful whisper I asked my brother, "Did she really die?"

"I received a telegram at nine o'clock this morning," he replied glumly. "This is God's decree. Where have you been? I was scared to death we might to have go out for the funeral procession without you."

"And what's all the hurry?" I shouted angrily. "Why didn't you put off the funeral till tomorrow?"

"The doctor said that the death had occurred at midnight last night, so we decided to have the funeral today."

My feverish body shuddered and I muttered in dismay, "Midnight last night? But I saw her sleeping in bed this morning!"

A look of sadness flashed in Medhat's eyes.

"She wasn't asleep," he said mournfully. "It was her heart, Kamil."

My limbs quaking, I conjured an image of the despondency I'd seen in her face, and I strained my memory to recall what I'd seen. And I asked myself: Was it really the face of a dead person?

Feeling I was about to collapse, I said in a feeble voice, "I want to look at her one last time."

Placing his hand on my shoulder, my brother said, "Wait a little while till you've pulled yourself together. Besides, the room is full of women now."

However, I shoved him out of my way and went rushing pell-mell into the building, then took the stairs in leaps with my brother close on my heels. As I went into the flat, my ears were filled with the sounds of weeping. To my dismay I found myself surrounded by women on all sides. My eyes stopped focusing and I was overcome with fatigue and awkwardness. However, just then my brother caught up with me, grabbed my arm and led me toward the bedroom, saying, "Don't resist. You need to be alone for a while."

He sat me down on the long seat and closed the door. Then he sat down on the edge of the bed in front of me and said sadly, "Be rational, Kamil. We mustn't be overcome by grief like women. Wasn't she my mother, too? But we're men."

My mind began swinging like a pendulum in a frenzied kind of concentration between two things: the ill-fated argument I'd had with my mother the day before, and my seeing her that same morning. Then suddenly a memory flashed through my mind and I cried, "The doctor lied! She didn't die at midnight! I heard her calling me as I was leaving the flat this morning!"

With a look of incredulity on his face, he asked, "And did you answer her call? Did you speak with her?"

Heaving a miserable sigh, I said, "No, I didn't, because I was angry with her! I was so rude and cruel to her!"

Then we both fell into a grieved silence. My head was about to explode with pain and fever.

Then, as though I were talking to myself, I said, "I killed her, there's no doubt about it. Lord! How could I have allowed myself to say what I said to her?"

My brother looked at me despondently.

Then he said to me in a menacing tone, "Don't you dare give in to thoughts like that!"

My head spinning like mad, I said stubbornly, "I was only saying the truth. I killed her. Don't you understand? If you want to verify the truth of what I've said, just call the public prosecutor and the medical examiner."

Groaning, Medhat said uneasily, "You must be delirious. Otherwise, get hold of yourself, because if you don't, I won't let you march in the funeral procession."

I let forth a cold laugh and said, "Our family is afflicted with the 'parent-killing syndrome'! Our father tried to kill our grandfather and he failed. Then I tried to kill our mother, and I succeeded. And thus you can see that I was more successful than my father."

With a worried look on his face, the young man got up. Then, looking me hard in the face, he said, "What do you intend to do with yourself? The funeral is just an hour away."

"What?" I said in amazement. "You're going to let the funeral proceed without conducting an investigation first? What a merciful brother you are! However, duty comes before brotherhood. Call the public prosecutor. I'll tell you where the office is, since I found out myself yesterday. Tell the district attorney that you're calling on him to interrogate the person who called on him yesterday to investigate his wife's murder."

Looking like someone who's just remembered something distressing, my brother cried, "How awful! Why didn't you send me a telegram, Kamil! The servant told me about it today, and I could hardly believe it!"

In near delirium I said, "Believe it, brother. If you don't get yourself used to believing tragedies like this, you'll leave the world the same way you came in: gullible and ignorant. I killed my wife, too. But I had an accomplice, namely, her lover."

Clapping his hands, Medhat cried, "There's no way you're going to leave the room when you're in this condition!"

Shaking my head angrily, I rose to my feet and said, "Let's go."

But no sooner had I finished speaking than I fainted.

67

I know nothing about the long hours I spent in a complete coma. However, there were other times in which I would grope about in a darkness that lay somewhere between consciousness and unconsciousness. It was a strange, shadowy world interspersed with dreams. I would get the feeling I was alive, yet so weak and helpless, I was more like the living dead. I don't know how many times I struggled, miserably and desperately, to move a part of my body, only to be so exhausted by the effort that I would surrender to the stifling pressure and vague fear that never seemed to leave me. At other times I would have the illusion that I wasn't far from regaining consciousness. I would almost be able to make out familiar voices and see faces I knew well, and I would cry out to them to hurry and save me. I often called out to my mother, and I would be infuriated and bewildered at her failure to respond to me. Strange dreams would go through my feverish head. I would see myself riding on my mother's shoulder as she carried me back and forth the way she used to do when I was a little boy, and at other times I would see myself grabbing hold of my brother Medhat's collar in a noisy, violent struggle as he shouted at me, "Don't kill me!" I imagined that I'd had many other dreams too, but that they'd been swallowed up by the darkness.

My unconsciousness went on for such a long time, I thought it would never end. But then I opened my eyes and returned to the light of the world. Heaving a deep sigh, my glance fell on a mirror that reflected my image. Feeling someone at my head, I looked in that direction and saw my sister Radiya sitting on the bed with her hand on my head. Our eyes met and her features brightened while a look of pity flashed in her eyes.

"Kamil," she murmured tenderly.

I tried to smile, and as I did so she let forth a fervent sigh, saying softly, "I bear witness that there is no god but God."

She uttered the testimony of faith in a voice that bespoke the fear and torment that had now left her. She didn't take her hand off my head, but the next moment, however, I felt something under her palm.

In a feeble voice that sounded to my ears like a muffled shriek I asked, "What's this thing on my head?"

Someone else's voice then came to me, saying, "A bag of ice, sir."

Turning in the direction from which the voice had come, I saw my brother Medhat sitting on the long seat. It was at that moment that I realized where I was, and I was assailed by the memories from which I'd fled through this heavy coma. Life peered at me with its ashen face once again. I looked over at the alarm clock, whose hands indicated that it was a bit after ten, ten in the morning judging by the sunlight coming into the room. So, then, I'd spent the dismal night in a deep sleep!

Looking at my brother brokenly, I asked, "Is the funeral over?"

He looked back at me for a long time, then said tersely, "Of course."

After another long silence he continued, "Perhaps you don't realize that you were gone for three whole days."

I peered at him in disbelief. Then I closed my eyes in consternation and murmured woefully, "So, I was destined to escort neither my mother nor my wife to her final resting place."

I looked over at my sister, whose eyes were filled with tears, and I was enveloped by an eerie melancholy that caused life to look like death. At that terrible moment, life looked utterly alien and empty to me, and I felt a terrifying void. The house was empty, my life was empty, the entire world was empty. When my mother was alive, I'd had a steady source of serenity, and deep in my heart I knew that no matter how miserable the world became, I had a room to go to that always glowed with smiles and affection. But now, I was like a boat that had been cut loose from its moorings in a stormy, raging sea. Even my sister, who was caring for me with such tender affection in my illness, was bound to tell me tomorrow or the next day that she needed to return to her house and her children, and I would be left alone. Lord, was I— the pampered child—made for this kind of life?

I cast my sister a long look of gratitude and affection. I gazed into her face with a longing of which she wasn't aware, drawn to those aspects of it that resembled my mother's. My chest heaved, overflowing with affection and profound grief. I cast an uncertain look at my surroundings, and found Rabab's furniture staring at me in a weird sort of way.

Feeling anxious and dejected, I said, "I'll never be happy staying in this house. I'll live with you, Sister.

"That's what I'd decided myself," came her earnest reply. "You're most welcome."

Then I whispered sorrowfully in her ear, "Take me to her room so that I can look at it."

Her eyes clouded over and filled with tears as she murmured, "You can't get out of bed now. Besides, there's nothing left in it."

· I pictured the empty room: four walls, a ceiling, and a floor. How like my own life!

I sighed dejectedly and murmured, "I'm so miserable."

To which Radiya replied imploringly, "Why not put off grieving until after you've gotten well?"

I was bedridden for about a month. Radiya stayed with me for a week, after which she had to return home. However, she visited me every afternoon, and she wouldn't leave me until sleep had closed my eyes. Medhat also went back to Fayoum, but he would spend the weekends with me.

By the time I entered the recovery phase, the fever had left me nothing but skin and bones. The only life I had left was in my imagination, whose vitality flourished, and which became so vigorous and active that it nearly became an obsession. There wasn't a waking hour when I wasn't plagued by feelings of loneliness and fear. Consequently, life seemed too arduous and terrifying to endure, and my ears were filled with that old voice which—whenever I found myself faced with afflictions—would urge me to turn tail and run away. But where would I run to? If only I could be remade as a new person, sound in body and spirit, who didn't have fear and alienation nesting in the corners of his soul. Then I could cast myself into the midst of life's hustle and bustle without embarrassment or feelings of aversion. I would love people and they would love me, I would help people and they would help me. I'd find pleasure in their company and they'd find pleasure in mine, and I'd become an active, useful member of their grand, collective organism.

But where was I to find such happiness? And on what basis could I hold out such false hopes? I hadn't been made for any of this. Rather, I'd been made for Sufism. It was strange to find this word inadvertently coming to mind. Yet it wasn't long before I'd taken hold of it, albeit with astonishment and uncertainty. Sufism? I wasn't even sure exactly what it was. However, I did know that it involved solitude, abstention, and contemplation. And how badly I needed those things. Strange . . . hadn't I complained of too much solitude throughout the time I'd been bedridden? The fact of the matter, however, is that I hadn't been complaining about the kind of solitude I'd been accustomed to throughout my life. Rather, the kind of solitude I was suffering from most recently was the forlorn sort of loneliness that had been left by the loss of my mother. As for the solitude I'd been familiar with before, I craved it badly. First of all, though, I would have to cleanse my body both inside and out, then devote my heart to heaven. For in reality, I'd been created a Sufi, but life's desires and attachments had led me astray. I imagined myself in an extraordinary state of purity, my body being bathed in fragrant water and my spirit being lifted up, transparent and serene, with my sights set on nothing but heaven, and no thought springing up in my soul but the thought of God. These were the nightingales of paradise singing their sweet melodies in my ears, and this was the stillness of peace coming to rest in my heart. My imagination had been active in the past, but it had often been traitorous. It would lift me up to that plane only to abandon me without warning, and I would find myself plummeting from the heights, then returning once more to my old anxiety and chronic fear.

One morning during the final phase of my recovery, the elderly servant came and said to me, "A lady is here who would like to see you, and I've let her into the reception room."

Looking up at her in astonishment, I asked, "Don't you know her?"

She replied with a shake of the head, "I've never seen her before, sir."

A certain apparition flashed through my mind, causing my feeble heart to tremble until it was pounding so hard that I became short of breath. Lord, might it really be her? Had she found the courage to storm the house? And hadn't she taken thought for the consequences?

Looking at the servant hesitantly, I murmured, "Invite her into my room."

I scrutinized myself in the mirror, then picked up a comb and hurriedly ran it through my hair. Feeling terribly self-conscious, I looked toward the door, wondering: Will my suspicion be confirmed? How could she have vanished from my memory all this time, as though she lived only in the healthy blood that had dried up? Then I heard footsteps approaching, and the visitor's face looked in at me with a smile of longing and compassion.

When I saw her, I exclaimed in what sounded like a cry for help, my voice betraying the emotion that had welled up in my heart, "You!"

Glossary

djinn: Invisible beings, either harmful or helpful, that influence the lives of human beings.

Eid al-Adha: 'The Holiday of Sacrifice,' Eid al-Adha is the holiday on which Muslims celebrate the time when God had commanded Abraham to sacrifice his son Ishmael and found him willing to obey His command. God ransomed the boy with a ram that appeared miraculously in a nearby bush.

Eid al-Fitr: Literally, 'the Holiday of Fast-breaking,' Eid al-Fitr is the three-day holiday that follows the Muslim fasting month of Ramadan.

Fatiha: The Fatiha is the opening sura (chapter) of the Qur'an.

fuul: A dish made of cooked fava beans seasoned with salt and cumin.

al-gadeed: A children's game of chance.

magzub: Literally, 'drawn, captivated, charmed,' a magzub is a Muslim mystic who has been so fully taken up into the presence of the divine that he appears as a madman; he is in the world but not of it.

Munira al-Mahdiya: Born Zakiya Hassan Mansur (1885–1965), Munira al-Mahdiya rose to fame for her musical and theatrical abilities and enjoyed an illustrious singing career that spanned three decades. She founded a coffee shop in the Azbakiya area of Cairo called Nuzhat al-Nufus, which became a meeting place for politicians and men of letters from Egypt, Sudan, and the Levant, who would also meet to discuss their ideas in her home.

Sayyida Zaynab's shrine: This shrine, housed within a mosque, is devoted to the memory of Sayyida Zaynab, patron saint of Cairo, who was the granddaughter of the Prophet Muhammad (the daughter of Ali ibn Abi Talib and Fatima, the Prophet's daughter).

"*. . . that's Lazughli's grandson*": Lazughli Pasha was the minister of finance under Muhammad Ali in the late eighteenth century. His real name was Muhammad Laz; the affix *ughli*, which means 'pasha,' was then added as a title of respect. There is a square in Cairo named Lazughli Square, in the center of which stands a statue of Lazughli Pasha.

Throne Verse: Qur'an 2:255, the recitation of which is believed by Muslims to bring protection and peace of mind.

Umm Hashim: 'Umm Hashim' is an epithet of Sayyida Zaynab.

Umm Kulthum: Born Umm Kulthum Ebrahim Elbeltagi in 1904 in Egypt, Umm Kulthum was a renowned singer, songwriter, and actress widely known for her exceptional voice and the sustained, powerful emotional connection she would make with her audiences. Her phenomenal vocal strength and the length of her songs may be seen in the fact that, at the height of her career, her concerts would consist of the performance of two or three songs over a period of three to six hours. Umm Kulthum died in Cairo in 1975, and three decades after her death, she is recognized as one of the Arab world's most distinguished vocal artists.

Modern Arabic Literature
from the American University in Cairo Press

Ibrahim Abdel Meguid *Birds of Amber* • *Distant Train*
No One Sleeps in Alexandria • *The Other Place*
Yahya Taher Abdullah *The Collar and the Bracelet*
The Mountain of Green Tea
Leila Abouzeid *The Last Chapter*
Hamdi Abu Golayyel *Thieves in Retirement*
Yusuf Abu Rayya *Wedding Night*
Ahmed Alaidy *Being Abbas el Abd*
Idris Ali *Dongola* • *Poor*
Radwa Ashour *Granada*
Ibrahim Aslan *The Heron* • *Nile Sparrows*
Alaa Al Aswany *Chicago* • *Friendly Fire* • *The Yacoubian Building*
Fadhil al-Azzawi *Cell Block Five* • *The Last of the Angels*
Liana Badr *The Eye of the Mirror*
Hala El Badry *A Certain Woman* • *Muntaha*
Salwa Bakr *The Golden Chariot* • *The Man from Bashmour*
The Wiles of Men
Halim Barakat *The Crane*
Hoda Barakat *Disciples of Passion* • *The Tiller of Waters*
Mourid Barghouti *I Saw Ramallah*
Mohammed Berrada *Like a Summer Never to Be Repeated*
Mohamed El-Bisatie *Clamor of the Lake*
Houses Behind the Trees • *Hunger*
A Last Glass of Tea • *Over the Bridge*
Mahmoud Darwish *The Butterfly's Burden*
Tarek Eltayeb *Cities without Palms*
Mansoura Ez Eldin *Maryam's Maze*
Ibrahim Farghali *The Smiles of the Saints*
Hamdy el-Gazzar *Black Magic*
Tawfiq al-Hakim *The Essential Tawfiq al-Hakim*
Abdelilah Hamdouchi *The Final Bet*
Fathy Ghanem *The Man Who Lost His Shadow*
Randa Ghazy *Dreaming of Palestine*
Gamal al-Ghitani *Pyramid Texts* • *The Zafarani Files* • *Zayni Barakat*
Yahya Hakki *The Lamp of Umm Hashim*
Bensalem Himmich *The Polymath* • *The Theocrat*
Taha Hussein *The Days* • *A Man of Letters* • *The Sufferers*
Sonallah Ibrahim *Cairo: From Edge to Edge* • *The Committee* • *Zaat*
Yusuf Idris *City of Love and Ashes* • *The Essential Yusuf Idris*
Denys Johnson-Davies *The AUC Press Book of Modern Arabic Literature*
In a Fertile Desert: Modern Writing from the United Arab Emirates
Under the Naked Sky: Short Stories from the Arab World